PRIVATE LIVES

Geoff Palmer

PODSNAP PUBLISHING
WELLINGTON, NEW ZEALAND

Podsnap Publishing Ltd., 17 Moir Street, Mt Victoria,
Wellington 6011, New Zealand.

Published by Podsnap Publishing Ltd., 2017

ISBN: 978-0-473-40029-3

Acknowledgments

Once again, my heartfelt thanks to my beta readers who have helped make this a better book. To ...

Hannah Burrowes
Jenny Dobson
Kate Mahoney
Gavin McCleave
Sue O'Connell
&
Margaret Robinson

Thank you!

1

Bitch!

Jane Child smiled sweetly at Melody Bloody Harper, sipped her coffee and ground her teeth. She was going to kill Matt. Slowly.

Melody saw her expression. 'Different, isn't it? I love it. We have a little man in Ethiopia who blends it just for us. Get it flown in specially.'

'Mmm.' Jane took another sip.

Before she strangled Matt though, she'd beat Melody Bloody Harper to death, possibly with the filter-on-a-handle thing from her very expensive coffee machine. Jane knew it was a very expensive coffee machine because Melody Bloody Harper had told her so – twice. 'An absolute snip at seven thousand. I mean, can you believe it? A Super-Galattico for seven thousand pounds?'

No, Jane couldn't believe it. She wouldn't pay that for a car.

The machine, a miniature cathedral of chrome-plated pipes and black lacquered steel, sat on a bench in a corner of what Melody Bloody Harper called the Tasting Room. On one side, the Tasting Room looked like a standard office kitchen, but on the other it resembled a mad scientist's laboratory with racks of beakers and test tubes, a vacuum oven, an exceedingly accurate digital scale, and stoppered glass bottles that held variously coloured substances with unpronounceable names. And, of course, the Super-Galattico and the special plumbing that occupied much of the wall space beside it.

Jane knew all about the plumbing too. How incoming water passed through the two large filters, on to the UV cleansing unit below, then into the chilled holding tank of the Super-Galattico. She knew about the size, cost and capacity of the filters, the temperature of the holding tank and the wavelength of the light output by the UV unit ('Two to four hundred nanometres, obviously.') The only things she didn't know were the name and inside leg measurement of the "little man" who came in twice a week and cleaned it all out.

'I mean, London tap is just so *blah*, right?' Melody said. 'You must have noticed. Really, I don't know how people drink it. Gerrard calls it toilet flush because that's all its good for. That or washing the car.'

Jane doubted Melody Bloody Harper have ever washed a car in her life. Or, for that matter, flushed a toilet. She probably had a little man come in and do that for her too.

Melody had then spent five very long minutes preparing two very small cups of coffee. Grinding the beans, tamping down the exact measure in the filter-on-a-handle thing, locking it in the machine, checking and adjusting various nozzles and gauges, then inspecting and rejecting four potential china cups before finding two that met her exacting standards. Finally, she opened the steam tap. The Super-Galattico sighed like an exhausted lover and oily black drips accumulated in the cups.

'It's sort of nutty and bitter, don't you think?'

'Mmm,' Jane said again.

The phrase might have summed the pair of them up.

No, that wasn't true. She'd never felt bitter towards Melody Bloody Harper. It wasn't her fault she'd been born with a silver spoon in her mouth – and, quite possibly, one up her bum too – but she might have been a little more tactful about the fact.

Or a lot.

They'd become what Melody called "grand pals" and Jane called "acquaintances" at university half a lifetime ago. Other students avoided Melody, partly because they couldn't compete with the latest fashions, the sports car, or the Dom Perignon she'd bring to parties, and partly – actually, mostly – for her braying laugh and crass insensitivity. Still, beneath that veneer, Jane had sensed something human, vulnerable even, and made an effort.

She'd glimpsed flashes of a more melodious Melody from the outset. In quiet times, in one-on-ones, away from other eyes, she could actually be a decent person. Generous, serious, with a hint of real warmth. But the least distraction, the slightest interruption, and the shutters would slam down leaving Melody Bloody Harper behind. Loud and brash, like a character in a farce.

It might have been her East End/North London upbringing. Her parents had separated when she was eight. Her real father, the one she called Dagenham Daddy, was a secondhand car dealer *par excellence* who owned yards and dealerships throughout the southeast. Her stepfather, Islington Papa, was something big in local government – Jane had never determined what – and both indulged her shamelessly, competing for her affection with toys and trinkets in lieu of their precious time.

Jane's initial persistence was just bearing fruit when two things happened simultaneously. She realised the guy she was seeing was secretly besotted with her friend and only stuck around in the hopes of getting closer to Melody, and Gerrard Vine turned up in an ageing Aston Martin and tattered Dussault jeans. He was like an upmarket James Dean – though with less chin – and even affected a rebel-without-a-cause insouciance, though some comedian quickly renamed him the Rebel Without a Clue.

Three-R Gerrard – another nickname – had been sent down from Cambridge for unspecified offences. An angry aunt – there were no other close relatives – insisted he finish his education at Leicester where, since she lived nearby, she could keep an eye on him. Gerrard was one-hundred percent of what Melody was ninety-five percent of the time, so it was a match made in heaven. Or possibly hell. The warm, generous creature Jane had been coaxing from its burrow was squashed flat. The steel shutters came down with a clang of finality – followed by a braying laugh.

Jane had distanced herself after that. It hadn't been difficult. Three-R Gerrard moved in different circles and Melody moved off with him. Besides, that had all been fifteen years ago. There'd been no reason to make a connection when Matt waved the file at her that morning.

'Got much on at the moment?'

She glared back. Those amber eyes. That conversational question. The oh-so-innocent expression. He knew damn well she hadn't. Apart from a client's missing cat.

When the first call to their new business landline came in, they'd tossed a coin to see who'd answer it. Jane won. And lost.

Matt hadn't exactly teased her about it, or her lack of progress, but there had been hints. A collection of Sherlock Holmes mysteries on her desk a couple of days ago. Francis McDermid's *Forensics* today. He'd scribbled TCOTMM on the whiteboard beside her name, explaining it stood for The Case of the Missing Moggy ...

'No, why?' Jane said carefully.

'That call I took on Monday.' He meant the second call. The interesting one. 'Some crowd called Harper and Vine. I'm supposed to pop in and see them at two, get some background, but I forgot about my checkup.' He patted his left side. Two months earlier he'd had keyhole surgery for a ruptured spleen after Jane's former boss had tried to run him over.

'Can't you reschedule?'

'Doesn't look good, does it? Our first proper ... I mean, our second client? But if you're busy.' He reached for the phone.

'What's it about again?' She pretended she'd forgotten.

'Counterfeiting and industrial espionage. Something sneaky in the world of coffee importers.'

Industrial espionage, damn him. And there she was, stuck looking for Tibbles McVicar!

He picked up the file and read out the notes he'd made: Harper and Vine, established seven years ago, importers of exclusive coffees for some of London's more exclusive restaurants and clubs, had discovered copies of their products at less salubrious establishments. Someone was ruining their very good name.

'What do you need?' Jane asked.

'Details. Background. Who, what, when, where. Plus an impression of the client. Who we're dealing with, etcetera.'

She could probably fit that in between a second round of pasting up Missing Cat flyers.

'Two o'clock?'

He handed her the file. 'In *Cat*ford.'

Did she imagine that subtle emphasis?

He looked at her, guileless, then added, 'That's four miles south of the Isle of Dogs.'

She flung the file back at him. That crack alone was just cause for slow strangulation.

'Fancy you ending up working for a private investigator,' Melody Harper said, sipping from her dainty cup.

I *am* a bloody PI, Jane thought, but it was a bit late to point that out now. She'd made the mistake of saying Mr Healy would be working on their case and that she was just there to get some background information.

'Weren't you keen on the arts? I always imagined you directing plays or managing symphony orchestras or something.'

'What about you, Mel? I thought you might go into your father's car business.'

Melody gave her an indulgent laugh. She didn't like to be reminded of those particular roots.

'So what's this is all about, Mel?' Jane took a notebook from her shoulder bag. 'You import coffee, right?'

'There's a *little* more to it than that.'

Jane raised an eyebrow.

'We're coffee-preneurs. We import exclusive coffees; special blends for special clients. From all over the world. Africa, Indonesia, Panama. Most of it goes to the clubs. The Carlton, the

Chester, the Chesapeake in Knightsbridge. Do you know it?'
Melody returned the raised eyebrow with a faint smile that
suggested of course Jane didn't.

Definitely provocation to assault and battery with that filter-
on-a-handle thing, Jane thought, but instead of acting on the
impulse, she wrote "Imports coffee" in her notebook in letters large
enough for Melody to read upside down.

'The thing is, someone's been pirating our brands using
inferior materials and passing them off as ours. What's more,
they've been selling them on to other places. Places like cafes and
middling hotels.' She curled her lip. 'We were alerted to the
problem by Reginald Trivet of the Chesapeake, or rather, Gerrard
was. He's a member, you know. The Chesapeake take almost all
our Kopi Luwak, but it seems there'd been rumours, and Mr Trivet,
being the man he is, investigated. He discovered a grotty little
place in Soho that claims to have genuine H&V KL – only they
didn't acquire it through us.'

'Sorry,' Jane said, trying to keep up, 'Reginald Trivet is ...?'

'Executive Director of the Chesapeake, of course.'

'Of course. And KL – Kopi Luwak – that's civet cat coffee,
isn't it?'

Melody nodded.

Jane had read about Kopi Luwak. The coffee berries were
eaten by civets whose innards digested the fruit and fermented the
beans before excreting them. Their droppings were collected, the
beans liberated, and the result was one of the world's most
expensive coffees.

She wrote "Shit coffee" in her notebook.

'So it's fake?'

'Certainly. Even if it is KL, it's not *proper* KL. Not *our* KL.'

'Sorry, can you explain that?'

'There are two types of Kopi Luwak: natural and farmed. The
farmed stuff has a variety of ethical issues: animal cruelty, tiny
cages, battery farming, force-feeding – that sort of thing – but the

main consideration from our perspective is selection.'

'Selection?'

'Proper KL requires selection *and* digestion. In the wild, civets get to choose which coffee berries to eat, so naturally they go for the choicest, plumpest and juiciest – which also contain the best beans. A caged civet gets no choice. It has to eat whatever it's given.'

'And you can taste the difference in the … end product?'

'It takes a refined palette, of course, but one can tell.'

Jane amended her previous entry to read, "*Real* shit coffee".

'So this place in Soho—?'

'It's KL, all right, but not *our* KL. Despite what the beastly little man does with the packet.'

'What does he do with it?'

'Flashes it around the table like he's presenting a bottle of fine wine, apparently. All totally unnecessary to a connoisseur. You'd never find Trivet's staff pulling a stunt like that. The flavour speaks for itself.'

Jane scribbled down the hotel's name, added "Untrivetable behaviour", then said, 'But you've not actually seen him do this? The beastly little man, I mean.'

'I beg your pardon?'

'You said *apparently*. That suggests your information is secondhand.'

Those Sherlock Holmes stories were paying off.

Melody made a face. 'Gerrard paid them a visit. Incognito. I wouldn't be seen dead in the place.'

'And confirmed it's counterfeit?'

'Without a doubt. It's damaging our good name, flooding the market and ruining all the work Gerrard and I have put in over the last seven years. Do you know there's been talk of ...' Melody glanced left and right and dropped her voice even though the room was empty, '... a Royal Appointment? One of the princes – I'm not at liberty to say which, so don't even *think* of pressing me – is a huge fan of H&V. Won't start his day without it. You can imagine the damage this would do if it got out. Harper and Vine selling second rate coffee? To cafes?'

'It's a compliment in a way though, isn't it? To have a brand worth counterfeiting. How much are we talking anyway?'

'Per cup? Retail?'

When Melody told her, Jane almost choked on her last sip of the little Ethiopian man's blend.

'So Gerrard checked them out,' she continued, making more notes. 'Have you done anything else? Complained to the police or the fair trading people?'

'God, no. You've no idea what this business is like, Jane. It's a bitchfest. We deal with top-end international suppliers who are very protective of their brands. Any hint of irregularities and they'd drop us like a hot potato. There are plenty of wannabes out there ready to swoop on our contracts.

'That's why I called your firm. I want someone to look into it from outside the business. I don't have time to go chasing all over London, and what's more, I can't be *seen* to be chasing all over London. If our rivals suspect anything, they'll put the boot in. So I told Gerrard I'd get someone in. I had a squiz at the internet and your little man came up. Healy. Looks rather dishy, I must say.'

'It's an old photograph,' Jane said. 'He's getting on a bit now.'

'In a George Clooney sort of way, I bet. Good breeding. I can usually tell these things. Why couldn't he make it, by the way?'

'Medical appointment,' Jane said. 'Vasectomy.'

Melody made a face.

'Well, after six kids, someone has to call a halt, right?'

'Yes, quite.' She set down her cup and straightened it prissily. 'Now Jane, this is all strictly on the QT, yes?'

'Of course. Why do you ask?'

'It's just that ... we don't want any record that *we* came to *you*. It would be much, *much* better if, say, your little man came to us with information he'd picked up from another investigation. Then we could act all shocked and surprised. I told you what a bitchfest this business is, plus there's that Royal Appointment I didn't mention earlier.' She winked unconvincingly. 'They don't hand them out willy-nilly, you know, and not without background checks. If they learn we've been chatting to a private investigator because we think someone's counterfeiting our stuff, well, you can kiss that goodbye.'

'What about this Reginald Trivet?'

'A gentleman. The soul of discretion. He knows how these things work.'

Jane studied her notes a moment. 'If you don't want any records, how are we supposed to invoice you?

'I'll pay you cash.'

'We charge a retainer for cases like this. A minimum of seven days at ...' she glanced at the Super-Galattico and its filter-on-a-handle, thought of the price of a cup of Kopi Luwak and added a hundred to their daily rate. 'Plus expenses, of course.'

Melody blinked but didn't throw her out, which was just the reaction she'd been hoping for. Contract negotiations were always tricky. A 'Yes, yes' and the wave of a hand would have meant she'd pitched too low. A gasp followed by a request to think about it would've meant too high. But blinking and gulping put them at the top end of the client's expectations. The sort of figure they could stretch to at a pinch.

'I only have some cash on me. I can give you a personal cheque for the balance if that's all right?'

'Well, since I know you.' Jane smiled.

As she wrote, Melody said, 'Your Mr Healy better be good.'

'We both are.'

'We?'

'If you'd scrolled down further you'd have seen Matt and I are business partners.' And proper partners too, she thought smugly but kept that to herself.

'You? Little Jane Child from Leicester? A private detective? I thought—'

'That I was his secretary?'

'You dress like one.' A moment's awkward silence then Melody added, 'Sorry, I didn't mean—'

'I'm glad you were fooled,' Jane said, tucking the cheque and wad of cash into her purse. 'We often work in disguise.'

Melody gave her a thin smile. 'Well, is there anything else?'

'One thing.' Jane pointed to the Super-Galattico. 'What's the name of those filter-on-a-handle things? The ones you pack the coffee in then clamp into the machine?'

Melody glanced at it, bemused. 'It's just a filter. Why?'

Jane shrugged. 'Just curious.'

2

'What the hell ...?' Matt said as Jane up-ended her purse over his desk, covering it in a slew of bank notes.

'I knocked off a building society on the way back,' she said, studying his features. 'You do look a bit George Clooney-ish, you know.'

'Eh?'

'How did the checkup go?'

'Oh, fine. All clear. What is this, Jane?'

'A seven-day retainer from Harper and Vine.'

'In cash?'

'Not quite. Here's the balance.' She took out Melody's cheque.

'There's more than a week's retainer here,' he said, leafing through the notes.

'I upped our rate because she's a bitch. You should have told me it was Melody Bloody Harper and the loathsome Three-R Gerrard.'

'You know them?'

'I did once, back in university days.'

Matt shrugged. 'Well, all the details are in the file.'

'So I see,' she said, looking at it properly for the first time.

He gestured at the pile of cash. 'But well done, you! A bonus already, and only our second case.'

'Don't get too excited. Some of that's already spent.'

'What on?'

'I need a new outfit. Then you're taking me out for coffee.'

Jane had never been a shopper, partly because her old job had taken up so much of her time, and partly because of her upbringing. She and two older brothers had been raised by a hard-working mum who'd sacrificed her life and health for her children. That they'd all done so well was a credit to her – Elsie Child would have been proud – and part of the reason for that was the family's overriding ethos of making-do. Jane had made do with a bike her brothers scrounged from the tip and patched up while all her friends had new ones. She made do with hand-me-downs and cast-offs while everyone else went shopping. Learned ancient crafts like dyeing, darning and invisible mending to refurbish things and keep them going instead of discarding them at the first signs of wear.

Her innate thrift, even when she started "earning big" at the head office of one of the country's largest banks, had stood her in good stead. Not many thirty-five-year-olds owned their own townhouse in London's SE1. There was an element of luck in her purchase – she bought shortly before the whole South London property market went berserk – but there was no luck in the way she paid off her mortgage. While friends and colleagues bought expensive cars, designer furniture and went on overseas holidays, Jane continued to make do.

Being a banker, she knew the magic of compound interest. Paying fortnightly instead of monthly, upping her repayments as her salary rose, and paying off lump sums whenever she'd saved a bit had knocked more than a decade off her mortgage, leaving her in the happy position of being able to walk away and try her hand at a brand new career.

One of her former colleagues, wearing a thousand-pound business suit with a two-hundred-pound pen in one pocket and a seven-hundred-pound cellphone in the other, told her how lucky she was. 'God, I wish I could afford to do that.'

Instead of heading for Oxford Street or one of the local

fashion chain stores, her first port of call was a charity shop on New Kent Road. Melody was right, she did look like a secretary. Or another faceless rush-hour Tube traveller heading off to a partitioned cubicle in a steel and glass City tower. It was time to chip herself out of the corporate mindset and shake off the culture of business suits and career clothing, of taupes and greys and beige and blue.

She settled on a subtly patterned wrap skirt, a short smart leather jacket that fitted like a glove, a pair of bright red straight-legged pants, a sleeveless tie-neck blouse in blush pink, and a white three-quarter sleeve blouse with a plunging neckline, all for the price of a single day's surcharge on the Harper and Vine account. She even talked the charity shop into putting one of her Missing Cat flyers in their window.

She decided to splash out on some new smalls at a little boutique up the road – something sexy to surprise Matt – and emerged to find herself splashing out for real. The joys of an English summer, she thought as she raced for the shelter of the nearest bus stop.

The schools were out and it was packed with fellow rain refugees, all glowering at the unexpected downpour. A bus approached, its wipers working furiously. Through them, she could see it was already crowded. The group around her surged forward, anxious for any free spots. Jane backed away as it hissed to a halt, tucked one carrier bag inside the other, folded down the top and stepped out into the storm.

The rainwashed pavement was empty save for a few scuttling creatures that raced past, their heads bowed, muttering crossly as they stomped through puddles. Traffic slowed to a crawl and motorists switched on their headlights. Jane walked on, oblivious, enjoying the warm rain on her face and the delicious feel of creeping dampness as it found its way past her hair and collar and sent tiny trickles down her spine. She shuddered and laughed and turned her face to meet the downpour.

Her feet were sloshing in her shoes by the time she reached her townhouse. She set her bag down and felt about her soggy pockets for the key. What was wrong with people? It was only a little rain. Clothes were supposed to protect us. In the end, we spent all our time protecting them. Besides, it was only a stupid old business suit.

She smiled at the brass plaque on the door:

Registered office of
Bluebelle Investigations

It had only been a few weeks, but she already sensed that leaving the corporate world behind had been the best thing she'd ever done. No, second best. The best had been finding Matt.

She brushed raindrops from her cheeks and shook her head from side to side, releasing a shower of spray as the cat for whom the company was named glared up at her from the step.

'Hello, Bluebelle.'

Bluebelle, scrunched in a corner, sheltered by an overhang of porch, arched her back and straightened at the sight of Jane.

'You don't need to sit out here, you know. You do have a cat door now.'

Matt had spent most of Saturday installing it, insisting that it go through the wall beside the door, not the door itself, an undertaking that involved a large number of power tools borrowed from his plumber friend. Jane had watched the excavation with growing dismay, both at the noise and the mess, but held her tongue. Anyone would think he was digging a new tunnel for the Underground. In the end, she'd gone to visit her friend Sally – a long-term survivor of the handyman instinct – and returned to find a clean, tidy townhouse with a new addition by the front door. He'd made a beautiful job of it. It fitted neat and square and flush, looking like it had been built right in there with the house. He'd even lined the little tunnel through the brickwork.

And Bluebelle refused to use it. She still planted herself beside the front door each night and meowed to go out, then waited outside on the mat to be let back in again. They'd both spent time on their hands and knees, holding the little plastic flap for her, and she would eventually go through it, but she seemed to think that, like the larger door beside it, it too required a human to hold it open.

'Look.' Jane knelt and demonstrated its operation once again.

Bluebelle looked and sniffed, then rubbed her face against Jane's.

'Not me, you idiot. Over here.'

Bluebelle set her front paws on Jane's damp legs, stretched up and rubbed around her face, purring.

'Oh honestly! You are an old smoocher.'

The door opened and Matt stood looking down at them, hands on his hips. 'Bluebelle! What have you got there now? How many times have I told you about dragging in half-dead vermin?'

Bluebelle didn't pause to answer but darted through his legs, heading for her food bowl.

Matt reached down and helped Jane up. 'I know there's a shortcut through that car wash, but I sometimes wonder if it's worth it.'

Jane grinned and dripped. 'What was that bit about half-dead vermin?'

'Confidential client information, I'm afraid. Can't be revealed to— *Gah!*'

Jane lunged at him, catching him in a squishy embrace. He staggered backwards.

'Mind the ribs!'

The same ex-boss who'd tried to run him over had also broken five of his ribs in the process.

'Sod your ribs.' She planted a rain-damp kiss on his mouth.

'You're sopping, woman! Besides, we're still in business hours. Remember the Child-Healy Agreement?'

'Sod the CHA.' She caught him by the hand and dragged him out. The rain had eased after the initial downpour, but now, perfectly on cue, it surged again. Fat droplets patterned the shoulders of his shirt. Already damp from her embrace, he was soon just as wet. And seemed to care just as much. He took her in his arms and kissed her.

'Did you buy a new outfit then?'

'Mm-hmm.'

'Going to show me?'

'Later.'

'Let me help you out of the old one.' He found the hem of her skirt, tugged it up and backed her up against the high front wall.

'Matt! What about the neighbours?'

He paused and considered. 'They can join in later if they want.'

Jane giggled. He drew her close and kissed her again.

Bluebelle returned to the doorstep, licked one paw and regarded them curiously, half lost in the grey fog of the downpour. What was wrong with the silly creatures? What were they still doing out there? The front door was open now.

3

The Philadelphia Hotel was a discreet place in the theatre district across from Soho Square. Jane and Matt walked the short distance from the Tube station, the afterglow of their afternoon reflected in the early evening sky. The storm had passed and the air was mild, giving way to a long summer evening.

A doorman in green livery welcomed them and they crossed a small, richly carpeted lobby to the cafe-restaurant on the far side. *Le Chat Noir* consisted of two distinct areas. The glassed-in porch – flagstones, potted palms, a dozen tables with gingham tablecloths – was for coffee and light meals, while the restaurant beyond, with its starched white tablecloths, wooden chairs the size of thrones and mood lighting (provided your mood was melancholy), was for more serious fare.

Matt glanced at the sign above the entrance and the framed prints around the walls, amongst them Steinlen's famous poster advertising a tour by the original *Chat Noir's* cabaret troupe.

'I know what you're thinking, but this is your case, not mine,' Jane said as the maitre d' approached, greeting them with a smart bow.

'Madame. Monsieur. Good evening. Welcome to the *Le Chat Noir*. May I show you to table?'

Jane nodded. Beyond him, she could see that half the cafe tables were occupied by smartly dressed couples in late middle-age. Matt noticed too. 'You know all the hotspots,' he whispered as the maitre d' led them to a table in the corner.

'We're on our way to a show,' she told the tuxedoed figure in her best Melody Bloody Harper voice. 'Friends said we must pop in and try your coffee.'

He bowed again, more deeply this time, and gestured to a waitress for some menus, presenting them with one each.

'You have a full range of Harper and Vine,' Jane said admiringly.

'Madame is familiar with their coffee?'

'Oh yes,' she gave him an indulgent smile. 'I think we'll try the Kopi Luwak.'

She arched a brow at Matt, who nodded his assent.

'A splendid choice, madame.' He snapped the menus away from them. 'And for the serving, may I recommend our little treasure?'

'Your little treasure?'

'A *Belge Royale*, an antique coffee syphon, made around 1850. Still in perfect working order.'

'Sounds intriguing.'

'It yields a delightful *au naturel* result.'

'Perfect. Let's try that.'

After another bow, he marched away, as straight-backed as any of the guards outside St James's Palace.

Matt leaned across the table. 'I don't know what you ordered, but I did see it was forty quid a cup. Plus a tenner surcharge for the antique coffee pot.'

'It's a business expense. Make sure you get a receipt.'

'Oh, so I'm paying?'

'I told you, it's your case.'

Further discussion was stifled by the return of the maitre d' pushing a wooden tea trolley draped in white linen. On it sat the *Belge Royale*, a curious device in brass and glass that looked like a model built to illustrate some large-scale industrial process. Set on a marble slab, the apparatus was balanced like an old-fashioned set of scales. One side held an oversized wine glass with a lid, while the other contained a brass tank – also lidded – with a tiny tap in its base. The two lids were connected by a curved brass pipe, and the tank pivoted above an alcohol burner.

The maitre d' took a carafe of water from the lower shelf of the trolley, lifted the lid of the brass tank and filled it. As he did so, the weight of the water caused the tank to drop, settling directly over the burner.

'The Kopi Luwak,' he said, producing a small foil sachet embossed with a gold H&V. He presented it to them as though presenting a fine wine, turning it over so they could inspect the expiration date on the back.

Jane nodded her acceptance. He produced a pair of scissors, snipped off one corner, and poured the beans into a hand-cranked coffee grinder at the other end of the tea trolley. After a dozen turns, he drew a small drawer from the base of the machine and presented it to them again like a magician demonstrating every stage of a trick. The grounds were dark and had an aroma reminiscent of freshly turned earth.

Raising the lid from the *Belge Royale's* glass container, he tipped in the coffee, forming a little pyramid at the bottom. Then he lowered the connecting tube which ended in a flared head containing the filter, setting it squarely over the grounds before setting the lid back in place.

He stepped back, drew a box of matches from his pocket, and lit the burner beneath the brass tank.

As the water began to boil, steam found the only exit – the curved copper tube leading to the glass container – and condensed inside it, running down to cascade over the coffee grounds and slowly fill the glass. The declining weight caused the water tank to lift from the flame, tripping a small lever as it did so.

'How clever,' Jane said.

The maitre d' raised a finger. The trick wasn't over yet.

Nothing happened for around thirty seconds, then there was a faint creak from the brass tank. It cooled quickly away from the flame, creating a vacuum that drew the contents of the glass vessel back through the filter, up the syphon tube and down into the brass tank again. The tripped lever allowed the tank to sink back all the way, and as its weight increased, it dropped steadily, past its original resting point, until its base finally smothered the burner. A faint clunk and the sputtering of the flame announced the completion of the process.

'*Et viola!*' the maitre d' said, placing a bone china cup beneath the tap at the bottom of the tank and releasing a thin stream of silken liquid.

He presented the first cup to Jane, the second to Matt, bowed, then made his retreat.

Jane felt like applauding. 'What a performance!'

'And we get to keep that, right?' Matt gestured at the syphon. 'I mean, at forty quid a cup ...'

Jane closed her eyes and sipped her coffee, trying to put thoughts of its origin to one side. It had a rich, earthy consistency and an intense aroma. Dark chocolate perhaps, with a hint of caramel.

She sipped again. It was good, but she wondered how much of that feeling had been tempered by her own expectations, its presentation and the price.

'Well, what do you think?'

'I'm not very good at this stuff.'

'What stuff?'

'Fine wines, fancy coffee, posh nosh. I sometimes think I'm nasally illiterate.'

Jane laughed. 'Nasally illiterate?'

He held up his cup and took a draught. 'I mean, I get it. It smells different and tastes pretty good, but I can't tell you what, why or how. I can't say "Ah, cinnamon with a hint of macadamia nuts" or whatever. And I don't get any sort of taste sensation that would send me queuing for another cup. It's pleasant, different, but at the end of the day it's just another coffee.'

She looked at him, considering.

'Sorry. My peasant stock, right?'

'Not at all. I was just thinking the same thing.'

'Really?'

'Sally and I did a wine tasting course once. One evening a week for six weeks. Six different Chardonnays one week, six different Merlots the next. It was fun comparing different vineyards and different vintages because you don't normally open half a dozen bottles at once and try a sip of each.

'The last session was champagne. The chap who took it – a master of wine from one of the better hotels – brought along everything from a five-pound bottle of Aussie *méthode champenoise* through to a sixty-pound bottle of French champagne. We did it blind, him included. All the bottles were all in brown paper bags and we marked our tasting cards and rated each one.

'I preferred number three. So did the instructor. I remember him holding up the bag and saying, "Ah, number three. The fineness of the bubbles, the subtle complexity, that gentle aftertaste. It can only be ..." then he whipped off the bag and his voice went up an octave, "... the *Australian?*"

'He made some excuse about how good they were getting, but I wasn't convinced. If a master of wine can't tell cheap plonk from French champagne, what hope have I got?

'Since then I've just ignored those people who prattle on about it at restaurants and parties. I doubt any of them could've told the difference either.'

'And all these years I thought it was just me!' Matt grinned. 'Now, mind telling me what this is all about?'

'What do you know about coffee and where it comes from?'

'I know that coffee beans are actually seeds from the berries of the coffee plant, of which there are more than a hundred varieties.'

'Did you look that up?'

'Background research.'

Jane swirled her cup. 'What about Kopi Luwak? Ever heard of it before and how it's ... processed?'

He shook his head, so she told him – all about civet cats eating the berries and excreting the beans.

'So I'm drinking something an animal poohed out – and paying forty quid a cup for the privilege?'

'Poo seems to be a common theme with us, doesn't it?'

'What do you mean?'

'One of the first things you ever told me about yourself was how a pigeon once crapped on your sandwiches in Trafalgar Square.'

'You're right.' He grinned. 'Here's to poo.'

She clinked his cup.

'And it's not even the real McCoy according to Melody Bloody Harper.'

'But the sachet ...?'

'Counterfeit, apparently. H&V don't sell to such lowly establishments as this.'

'So it's fake poo coffee?'

'It might be genuine KL, just not H&V's. It's like the difference between free range and battery hens. The stuff they import comes from wild civet poo gathered from the forest. This stuff is from animals in cages.'

'And there's a difference? How can you tell?'

'It's all in the taste, apparently.'

'Like the difference between free range and battery eggs?'

The maitre d' reappeared to see if everything was to their satisfaction.

'Is this a new venture?' Matt asked. 'The coffee, I mean? I was here a few months ago and don't recall seeing it before.'

'You're quite correct, sir. Chef Maurice and I only launched our little *entreprise'* – he pronounced the word in the French fashion – 'in early May.'

'When were you last here?' Jane said once he'd gone.

'Never.'

'Then how did you know about—?'

Matt tapped the side of his nose. 'I may not be able to tell Kopi Luwak from Nescafé, but I do know a thing or two about the detecting business.'

Jane frowned.

'Don't tell me you missed it? My protege!'

'Come on, spit it out.'

'The menu. The tiny type at the bottom. It had the name of the graphic designer, their web address and the date: June this year.'

'So it really is a new *entreprise*.'

Matt nodded thoughtfully. 'And all apparently based on counterfeit Harper and Vine.'

4

Jamie Burton didn't even see the car door open. He was on his home stretch and looking to break his all-time record. The phone clamped to the handlebars of his bike was running an app that showed – amongst a multitude of other data – his time, distance and maximum speed. The figure currently read 53.7 mph, but on an easy downhill run like this with no traffic – it was just after dawn – a dry road and good light, he should be able to hit the mystical 60 miles an hour. It had eluded him in the past. He'd once managed 59.4 with a slight head wind, but today there wasn't even that.

He notched the derailleur up a gear and pounded harder on the pedals.

The driver of the parked car, a big man, watched his approach in the wing mirror. The mirror had a sticker on it: "CAUTION: Objects may be closer than they appear" but he allowed for that when he threw the door open.

His timing was perfect. The bicycle hit it half a second later and stopped dead. But its rider didn't.

'Oops, that was careless,' the big man's companion said as the rider somersaulted through the air. 'We better check on him, yeah?'

The big man was already out, kicking the mangled bike aside.

Jamie Burton landed heavily on one shoulder and tumbled along the road, coming to rest in the oncoming lane thirty feet from the bike's impact point. Against all expectations, including his own, he was still conscious and still breathing when he came to a halt.

And despite the early hour and empty street, help was

immediately at hand.

He lay on his back, head to one side, his vision jarred and blurry. All he could really focus on were a pair of large brown army boots directly in front of his nose. Beyond them, two faces peered down at him; one white, one black.

'Fucker's still breathing,' the darker face said.

Two huge hands appeared and cupped Jamie's head. He wanted to tell them they shouldn't move him, should just call an ambulance, but before he could begin to form the words, the hands gripped tightly and wrenched his head in a direction it was never meant to go.

* * *

Across town, Matt shuffled off the Tube at Leicester Square wearing his dad's old army greatcoat, tatty jeans and a pair of scuffed boots. He hadn't shaved or brushed his hair and weaved slightly as he walked. It was still early, pre-commuter rush, and only a handful of people stepped off the train with him, all giving him a wide berth. He let them surge ahead to the escalator and followed at a distance.

The sky outside was a pearly contrast to the neon signs dotted around the square. In many ways, this was his favourite time of day. The city still seemed habitable and human, especially in places like this with its trees and bird song. The traffic was a distant hum and the crowds were still hours off.

He shuffled round the square, glancing into overflowing rubbish bins. An unnecessary action, but old habits died hard and it helped him get into character. Besides, London was one of the most surveilled cities in the world. It was reckoned there was one camera for every eleven people in Britain, and he knew from his time in the police that the Greater London Authority operated close to a thousand cameras in the City alone. You never knew who was watching, especially at this time of the day, and the quickest way to draw attention to yourself was to do something out of character.

He shuffled down a side street, then another, then a blind alley that led to the less glamorous backs of the buildings lining Soho Square. The rear of the Philadelphia Hotel had a fire exit on one side and a loading ramp leading to a rear door on the other. From the sounds and bustle visible through the steamy windows, it was clearly the kitchen. To the right of the ramp was a red-painted skip with an angled top and a heavy black plastic lid.

Matt checked left and right then raised the lid. The skip was half full. And smelly.

He took a breath, muttered, 'Home sweet home,' and clambered in.

* * *

Bluebelle Investigations occupied the back bedroom of Jane's South London townhouse, a room that had been used on a handful of occasions by visiting friends and relatives, but that had mostly served as a hideaway for abandoned projects. Till recently – in addition to the spare bed and dresser – it had been occupied by a dressmaking dummy of two year's vintage, (from an evening class she'd started with a rush and failed to finish), an electronic keyboard of four years vintage, (something she'd plunked away at for a few weeks while safely ensconced in headphones so that only she could hear her meagre efforts), and some home handywoman tools Sally and Paul had given her as a house-warming present when she first bought the place more than ten years earlier. She'd come to think of it as her hobby room, though her previous very full-time job had left her little time for hobbies.

Bluebelle Investigations certainly wasn't a hobby. They'd both given up their careers and put some of their savings into the business, but despite the clear out and a complete refit, the room still had a few of its old connotations.

The curtains perhaps, Jane thought as she entered. Too bright and stripy. They didn't really match the sober look of the rest of the room with its office desks and office chairs, credenza and conference table. The place was starting to feel like a proper workspace with notes pinned to the corkboard beside her desk, some of Matt's scribbles on the whiteboard, and a collection of tea-stained cups on the table in the corner.

Jane gathered them up and carried them across to the bathroom opposite where she rinsed them out.

The ultimate aim was a proper office somewhere in town, but they were just getting started and the hobby room would do for now. SE1 was a good, relatively central location, and it had the key advantage of being rent free. The only real costs had been the secondhand office furniture, a kettle, a small fridge, a couple of desktop computers and a printer. Jane's natural thrift combined with Matt's knack for bargaining had got that lot for a song, and the only thing they'd paid full price for was the installation of a business phone line. Matt insisted on that. They couldn't use her private number. It was important to keep work and home life separate. Besides, a landline suggested stability and commitment. 'There's a lot of cellphone cowboys in this game,' he told her, 'and when we can afford a proper office, it can come with us.'

The bed and dresser had been moved to the box room, along with her handywoman tools, and the rest of the clutter had gone to charity shops, perhaps destined to become someone else's failed hobbies.

She heard the door downstairs slam and Matt bounded up, meeting her on the landing as she returned with the cups.

'Morning Ms Child.' He gave her a peck on the cheek. His hair was damp and he smelled freshly showered, but there was an undertone of something less savoury.

'Oh god, it's this isn't it?,' he said, seeing her expression and holding up the bag he was carrying. 'I double-bagged it too.' He gave it a tentative test sniff. 'Oh yeah. I'll leave it out on the porch.'

'What is it?' she called as he bounded back down the stairs. 'And what did it die of?'

'My dad's old greatcoat. It got a bit mucky.' The front door banged again and he raced back up to meet her.

'Morning Ms Child.' He took her in his arms this time and kissed her on the mouth.

Jane laughed. 'We've already done that bit. Anyway, it's office hours, remember?'

'Spoilsport.' He released her. 'You making tea?'

She switched on the kettle. 'You're full of something. What have you been up to?'

'Did a spot of dumpster diving at the Philadelphia Hotel this morning. It's fascinating what people throw out.'

'Why there?'

'Number one: that packet from last night. I should have souvenired it. It's evidence of counterfeiting.'

'You didn't fancy going back for another cup?'

'And another eighty quid?'

'Fair point.'

'The kitchen's out the back, so I paid their bin a visit in what you call my Mad Matt disguise. It was pretty pongy. Turns out they're only on a weekly collection cycle, which happens to be today.'

'Weekly? Urgh! A restaurant? That doesn't sound very professional.'

'You'll see why.' He took several plastic evidence bags from the pocket of his jacket, unfolded them and handed them to her. 'Just don't ask about the rats.'

There were six bags in all. Each contained a crumpled or stained piece of paperwork. The corner of one page had been gnawed and shredded by tiny teeth. Jane didn't ask.

She spread them on the conference table and studied them as the kettle boiled. What they showed was a business struggling with rents and wages. A familiar enough story to a former banker.

Invoices stamped "A friendly reminder" or "Overdue". A torn bank statement showing a sizeable negative balance.

'I imagine that's only part of the story,' Matt said. 'Most stuff's online these days.'

'How does this help us?'

'It's circumstantial evidence, but it paints a picture of a struggling business that might be tempted to the dark side of counterfeit coffee.'

The last sleeve contained a crumpled Kopi Luwak sachet. 'Is this ours from last night?'

'I think so. It was near the top.'

Jane turned it over, studying both sides. 'It looks genuine enough, but I don't know what I'm comparing it to.'

'Me neither. I need to get hold of a proper one and look at them side by side.'

She made the tea and handed him a cup. 'Does that mean a visit to *Cat*ford?'

'*Purr*-fect chance to meet the clients, don't you think?'

'Remember to be discreet. Technically, they haven't employed us.'

He nodded. 'What about you? More Missing Moggy?'

'I don't know what else I can do about poor Tibbles McVicar,' Jane sighed. 'I'll give the animal shelters and SPCAs another ring-round, but he's been microchipped. If he turns up anywhere, they'll call the Tinchcombes direct.'

'You've done all you can, Jane. Sometimes these things happen.'

'I've been steeling myself to go round and tell there's nothing more I can do. They'll be so upset.'

'Tough call, but when you've done so I could do with some help on the H&V case.'

Jane bit her lip and nodded. A far more interesting case. But she was dreading her visit to the Tinchcombes.

5

Jane took Matt's greatcoat with her. There was a dry cleaners on the way to the Tinchcombes so she didn't have to take it far. Still, she kept it held away from herself as she walked and at arms length when she placed it on the counter.

The elderly man who ran the place had the sort of face that had seen everything and was surprised by nothing. He unbagged it without so much as a nose wrinkle, handed her a ticket and told her it would be ready Friday afternoon.

Jane pocketed the ticket and continued on.

As she passed the charity shop, she saw the Missing Cat flyer they'd happily put up the previous day had been taken down.

Already? And I spent a hundred quid in there!

The Tinchcombes lived in a semi-detached Georgian terrace at the bottom of a cul de sac in one of the older, leafier parts of the area. Like most of the houses in the street, part of its front fence had been cut away and part of the garden paved to make room for the couple's elderly Rover, which now sat sunning itself in the abbreviated driveway in front of the house. Jane never understood why people did that. It took a car park from the street, ruined the front garden, and its sole benefit was to move the car a few feet closer to the house. Did people really love their vehicles so much that they preferred to stare out at them from the lounge window, rather than look on plants and trees?

Patricia Tinchcombe opened the door, despite being wheelchair-bound. Until her accident two years before, she and her husband had been senior civil servants in the Ministry of Education. Afterwards, they'd both taken early retirement. They lived quietly and comfortably, had four children scattered to four corners of the globe, and – until recently – a cat named Tiberius Constantine McAlistair-Vicory, a pedigree British Shorthair, now missing for a week.

'Oh!' Patricia Tinchcombe said when she saw Jane. 'Gordy was about to ring you.'

'Is he back?'

The woman blinked up at her, unsmiling, wheeled back and summoned her husband from the kitchen.

'Ah!' Gordon Tinchcombe said. He was a stocky, barrel-chested man with a military bearing and an overbearing manner. He was retired and presumably at leisure, but he still wore a jacket and tie. Jane had never seen him in anything else, even when she'd called round and found him pruning the roses in what remained of their front garden.

'Ms Child. Good of you to call. I was going to give you ring this morning. Thank you for all your help, but we no longer require your services.'

'Is he back?' Jane repeated.

A look passed between the couple. 'I ... um ... If you'll just let us know what we owe you. An invoice, perhaps? We're more than happy to pay you for your time. And thank you again. Good morning.'

With that, Jane found the front door closed gently in her face.

She stared blankly at the black paint, brass knocker and carriage lamps either side. Had she just been fired? From her very first case? She stepped back and headed up the path.

She *had* been fired!

Wasn't that what she wanted? Hadn't she been steeling herself to tell them there was nothing more she could do?

Still, to be dismissed in such a manner ...

It was odd. In the past, they'd always been so friendly. Inviting her in, sharing a cup of tea, having a chat. Now it felt like she was the last person on earth that they wanted to see.

She returned the way she'd come, passing the charity shop where the young woman who'd served her yesterday was outside washing the windows. 'Oh hello,' she called, recognising Jane. 'Good news about the cat, eh?'

'The cat?'

'The owner called in when we opened up this morning. Said he didn't need the flyer any more. Even left a donation as a thank-you.'

'The owner? An older chap, very upright, jacket and tie?' Jane said.

'That's the one.'

'Did he actually say the cat was back?'

The young woman shrugged. 'Why else would he want the flyer taken down?'

Why indeed? Jane thought.

* * *

Matt took a cab from Catford Bridge station to the industrial park that housed Harper and Vine, a low-rise greenfield initiative overlooking the Ravensbourne river. It was, according to a gushing description on the Lewisham Borough Council's website, a council-sponsored, lottery-grant funded redevelopment of the area – although these days the preferred term was apparently "regeneration".

This particular regeneration had involved the demolition of a line of terraced houses and replacing them with a line of two-storey concrete cubes each slightly offset from the other to break up the monotony. Front gardens had been ploughed into a grassy band dotted with saplings, and it was hoped the park-like grounds and proximity to the river would attract high-tech startups. From what he could see as they drew up, half the units were empty and the high-tech startups had so far stayed away.

Harper and Vine occupied the cube at the end of the block.

Matt was early for his appointment so walked past the entrance and continued round the side to get a fuller idea of the building's layout. The northern wall was a blank slab of concrete with a couple of windows on the first level, giving them a view of a kink in the river and, through the trees, an overbridge on the A212. At the rear of the building, he found an access lane with a couple of cars parked in marked bays and a steel-shuttered door for deliveries and despatches. The column of a stainless steel extractor vent ran up to the roof and he caught sharp odour of roasting coffee.

A painted sign on the front door directed him to reception upstairs where he was greeted by a big-boned girl in a floral print dress. She was seated behind a tall desk emblazoned with the same gold H&V logo he'd seen on the Kopi Luwak packet. There were framed photographs on the wall behind her: smiling coffee pickers, bags of red berries and a cute furry animal peering out through green leaves.

'Mr Healy, is it?' she asked, giving him a toothy smile as he stepped from the stairwell. He guessed they didn't get many visitors. 'Ms Harper and Mr Vine are expecting you. This way, please.'

She led him to a wood panelled door and the plushly furnished, richly carpeted, wood panelled office beyond it.

'Mr Healy.' Melody Harper rose from behind her desk and greeted him with an outstretched hand.

'Ms Harper,' he replied. 'Sorry I couldn't make it yesterday.'

'Yes, Jane told me all about it. How is ...' she looked him up and down '... everything?'

'Fine, thanks. On the mend.'

She was a good-looking woman with shoulder-length ash blonde hair in a beachy wave, dark blue eyes and a trim but shapely figure.

'My partner, Gerrard Vine.' She gestured to the man standing at the window.

'Mr Vine.'

'That's Gerrard with three Rs,' Vine said.

'I'm Matt, with two Ts.' He shook a hand as limp as a wilted lettuce leaf and received a dour look for his remark.

Vine was a man of thirty-five going on fifty. He had a smooth round face, thinning hair slicked back from a high forehead, and a certain fleshiness about the cheeks and jowls suggesting the early onset of middle-age spread. Even the finely crafted suit couldn't quite disguise his incipient portliness.

Matt was no clothes horse. Marks & Spencer was about as upmarket as he ever got, but he *was* a professional and had made it his business to recognise the signs of status. Vine's navy suit was beautifully tailored, complimented by a shining ice-blue tie, and there was no mistaking the Vacheron Constantin watch on his wrist. The shoes also looked handmade.

'I take it Jane's brought up to date?' Melody gestured him to a seat.

'Completely.' Matt thought back to her scant notes now filed away with the H&V paperwork. She'd typed up a somewhat fuller summary, but her originals were hardly up to Crown Prosecution Service standards. He'd have to have a word with her about that.

'As I understand it,' he consulted his notebook, 'a Mr Trivet from the Chesapeake Club first alerted you to the counterfeits.'

'It wasn't an alert,' Gerrard said. He remained standing by the window, despite the extra seat in front of Melody's desk. 'It was an enquiry. What the devil were we doing selling to a third-rate establishment like the Philadelphia Hotel?'

'And you told him ...?'

'That we weren't.' He glanced at Melody.

'How did Trivet find out?'

'Other chaps at the club, I expect. Or through the grapevine. He's in the business. Keeps an ear to the ground.'

'But it was news to you?'

'Absolutely!'

'And you checked it out. Incognito.'

'Immediately.'

'What did you find?'

'The coffee? Disgusting. Factory-farmed rubbish.'

'You can tell the difference?'

'Of course!'

'Have you discovered anyone else selling it? I mean, anyone who shouldn't be?'

'That's your job, isn't it?'

'Partly,' Matt nodded. 'I just wondered if your Mr Trivet had heard of anyone else?'

'No. No.' Gerrard said. 'Just the Philadelphia so far, thank god.'

'So, you tried the coffee, found it lacking, then what did you do?'

'What do you mean?'

'You didn't alert them? Call them out on it?'

'I was tempted. Had to restrain myself.' Another glance at Melody. 'But I thought it better to play a long game. Keep my cards close to my chest. Find out where they'd got the stuff.'

'They have a full range of your coffees, don't they? All eight of them.'

'You've been there already?' Melody seemed surprised.

'The whole bloody lot,' Gerrard said. 'When I find out who's behind it ...' His voice trailed off.

'Have you done anything else since you discovered this?'

'What do you mean?'

'Increased security, for example. Eliminating suspects.' Matt gestured around at the premises.

'You don't think someone here might—?'

'Theft is easier than counterfeiting.'

'When Gerrard told me, I did a full stocktake,' Melody said. 'Nothing's missing.'

'What did that involve?'

'Everything. Beans, stock on hand, roasting and grinding tallies, stuff in transit. I tied it all back to what's on the computer. There's nothing missing.'

'How does your ordering and supply process normally work? Say this Trivet character at the Chesapeake wants a top-up?'

'We have a secure website,' Melody said. 'Customers log in and place orders, and we roast, package and deliver via courier.'

'So you don't hold much stock?'

'Roasted coffee has a limited shelf life so we try to keep it to a minimum.'

'Any deliveries gone missing lately?'

'None. Never.'

Matt made a note. 'How do customers find you? Do you have a rep?'

'Normally they approach us. When we were first getting started, Gerrard or I would make the initial approach, but that's unnecessary these days with our reputation.'

'Presumably you vet all applications?'

'Absolutely!' Gerrard said. 'No riff-raff, eh Mel?'

'Gerrard and I personally approve all applications,' she added. 'There's no way these people could have slipped in under the radar.'

'And none of your current clientele are likely to have on-sold some of their surplus?'

'That's strictly forbidden by the terms of our contract.'

Matt turned to Gerrard. 'I'm interested in the packaging.'

'The packaging?'

'I understand it was presented to you with something of a flourish. Did you notice any differences between the counterfeit and your own packets?'

'I ... didn't pay it much attention, but it looked real enough. That's no guarantee though, is it? You can copy anything these days. Picture on a mobile phone. Colour printer.'

'Quite,' Matt said thoughtfully. 'Do you have any samples I

could use for comparative purposes?'

'Empty or full?' Melody gave him a wry smile and left the room for a moment, returning with a selection of foil sachets, all but one of them open and empty. 'Here. A little bonus for you. Some Jacu Bird. Treat Jane.'

The sachets' designs were almost identical: H&V in a chevron at the top – embossed gold lettering against a black background. A white china cup sat in the bottom right-hand corner being filled by a rich dark stream of unseen origin. In between lay the brand and byline: "Jacu Bird Coffee," the full sachet said. "Premium Biodynamic Coffee from Camocim, Brazil."

'What is a Jacu bird?' Matt asked, turning the packet over.

'A type of pheasant.' Melody resumed her seat.

'That eats coffee berries?'

'They're very discerning.'

Not that discerning, he thought. Not if they can't actually digest the things.

There was a batch number and use-by date on the back.

'I take it you keep a record of the batch numbers?' he asked.

'Of course. I can email you the list if you like.'

'Speaking of lists, you gave Jane a list of staff yesterday. Six in total, I believe. I take it you did all the usual checks before you hired them?'

'Naturally.'

'No part-timers or temps?'

'No.'

'How many of your staff know about this problem?'

'The counterfeiting? None of them. It's just Gerrard and myself, and we'd like to keep it that way.'

'Of course. What about ex-employees? Someone with a grudge, perhaps?'

'There aren't any. We're a young company and our staff are loyal.'

'Anyone help you with the stocktake?'

'No, I did it myself last weekend.'

'Stock *and* packaging materials?'

'Everything, yes,' she said smoothly. 'Everything's accounted for. We run a tight ship.'

'So why us, Ms Harper? Why a private detective agency instead of the ACG or the police?'

'The police?' she snorted. 'I doubt they'd be interested. And as for the Anti-Counterfeiting Group, it would be take a number, wait months and we *might* get back to you. We want this cleared up as quickly and as quietly as possible. Did Jane not explain why?'

'The Royal Appointment? Yes. You can rely on us, and our discretion.'

'I certainly hope so.'

'Jane said you'd like us to alert you as if we'd come across evidence of the counterfeiting in a parallel enquiry.'

'Is that a problem?'

'Not at all. I was just wondering how you'd like the alert.'

'A report of some sort, detailing all you discovered.'

'And what if we find the perpetrators?'

Melody raised an ash blonde eyebrow. 'Is that likely?'

'Hard to say. Most product counterfeiting's done overseas, but someone's bringing the stuff in and distributing it.'

'Then ... that should go in your report too.'

'But we're to take no other action? The police? Customs and Excise?'

She shook her head. 'Gerrard and I will see to that. Along with our lawyers.'

Matt closed his notebook, thanked them for their time and wished them a good morning.

Gerrard Vine remained by the window, watching the private investigator walk away from the building. Melody moved in beside him.

'Well, what did you think?'

Vine sniffed. She could tell he was annoyed. 'He asked a lot of questions.'

'That's his job.'

'You didn't mention some of our full-timers might soon be part-timers.'

'Not relevant.'

'Then what is, Mel? What the hell is going on?'

'All in good time, darling.'

'You keep saying tha—'

She kissed him. He still looked cross so she kissed him again. 'Trust me, Gerrard. Please? I'll tell you when you need to know.'

He'd always been a lousy actor. Best to let him play along and play it straight, she thought.

6

Jane returned to the office, mulling unhappily over her summary dismissal by the Tinchcombes. They were the client and they got to call the shots, but it didn't feel right somehow. The mood was all wrong. If they'd got Tibbles McVicar back, they'd have been jubilant and would surely have introduced her. They knew she liked cats. She'd told them about Bluebelle. But the look Patricia Tinchcombe gave her husband had been troubled. There was no other word for it.

Perhaps something else had happened to him. A road accident, and he had to be put down. But they'd have told her, surely. There'd have been tears too. A cat loved so much that they called in a private detective when he went missing wouldn't have passed away unmourned.

Above all, Jane felt she'd failed them and him; that she hadn't done enough. But what more could she have done? She'd spoken personally to every householder in the street, including those over the back of the Tinchcombe's property, put Missing Cat flyers in every letterbox and shop window she could find, even slipped them in plastic sleeves and attached them to lampposts and bus stops. She'd made regular calls to animal shelters and the RSPCA, checked unattended sheds and outbuildings nearby, but turned up nothing. Not even a possible sighting.

Her first case too.

The firm's first case.

She guessed what Matt would say: write it up, invoice them and move on. And he was right. She'd done her best. She shouldn't take it personally. But just when she'd talked herself round, she got back to the office to find another reminder stretched out in a patch of sun on her desk.

'What are you doing there? This is a workplace, not a cat's home.'

Bluebelle stretched languidly by way of reply and ignored the reprimand.

Jane slumped at her desk, stroking the cat distractedly. The fact was, she *did* take it personally and *didn't* feel like moving on.

* * *

'Admit it Jane, you miss us terribly and are dying to come back,' Alistair Downley said, sitting back and crossing his arms. 'What do you think, Barry? Should we take her?'

'In an instant,' Barry Tonks said.

'Some negotiator you are! You're supposed to prevaricate and go, *Hmm, well, I don't know. This chap they got in to replace her is rather good.*'

'But he isn't.'

'Yes, but *she* doesn't know that. We could have got her back at half her old salary.'

Jane smiled. 'So what is he like?'

'Fair, fat and fucking boring – if you'll pardon my French.'

'He is rather dull,' Barry confirmed.

'Hear that? Even Barry thinks so.' Only Alistair could get away with a comment like that.

Barry smiled and cut another chunk off his panini.

They were sitting in Duke's coffee shop, not far from Bartley's bank, Jane's former employer. It seemed hard to believe she'd spent twelve years there – almost a third of her life – the last two sharing a ninth floor cubicle with these two reprobates. Chalk and cheese probably had more in common. Barry was middle-aged, reserved, quiet, a family man, while Alistair was younger than Jane, flamboyant, outspoken and openly gay. Yet they'd become firm friends – a friendship forged, in part, due to the antics of Jane's former boss.

'The thing about Roger Roger is that he *tells* you all the boring details.' Alistair slumped at the table like a deflating balloon. 'I don't *care* what sort of four-wheel drive he's thinking of buying, or how brilliant his daughter's school play is, or how he did at golf at the weekend, but he insists on giving you a blow by blow account of every fucking detail!'

'Roger Roger?'

'It's actually Roger Rogerson,' Barry said.

'Even the name's about as imaginative as a pothole.' Alistair rolled his eyes. 'Please come back to us, Jane. We used to have such laughs.'

For a moment, Jane felt tempted. But only for a moment. It was odd looking back, how the mind locked on the good times to the exclusion of almost everything else – the long hours, the ridiculous deadlines, the battles with management, and the sheer daily grind of it all.

'We can still have a laugh,' she said. 'We could make this a weekly get-together.'

'Splendid idea,' Barry said. 'And you can tell us what life is like on the outside.'

Alistair sighed. 'I suppose so. If we really can't tempt you back.' Jane shook her head. 'So what's it like being a private dick?'

'As opposed to being a very public one, you mean?' Barry asked, raising an eyebrow.

'Oh, bitch! Take that!' Alistair laughed and gave him a slap.

The tattooed waitress delivered their coffees, giving Jane a nod of recognition. Another pang. This had been her old stomping ground. Familiar faces, familiar routines. It was hard to break away sometimes.

'We really only started this week,' Jane told them, 'but we've already got a couple of cases.'

'Marital infidelity, I bet,' Alistair said to Barry. 'I've read the books. Zoom lenses through motel windows, couples *in flagrante* and all that sort of thing.'

'Not quite,' Jane said. 'One's a counterfeiting case and the other's a ... missing person.' She couldn't quite bring herself to say missing cat.

'Ooo, a missing person! Are you dragging the Thames? Looking for body parts in railway station lockers?'

'Just what sort of books do you read?' Jane laughed.

'Counterfeiting?' Barry said. 'Anything we should know about?'

'Not bank notes,' Jane assured him, 'but I can't really say any more at this stage.'

'Is that what these weekly get-togethers are going to be like?' Barry said. 'You're going to hint at all these exciting things you're doing but not give us any details?'

'I will when I can.'

Alistair harrumphed.

'Besides, it's not *that* exciting. There's a lot of legwork involved.'

'Legwork is my speciality.'

'Not *that* sort of legwork.'

Barry laughed and told Alistair, 'You'll just have to put up with Roger Roger in the meantime.'

'Oh god!'

'Tell you what,' Jane said, 'we haven't had a launch party for the new business yet. It's all been a bit hectic getting set up and sorted out, but once we crack our first case, we'll have a double celebration. How does that sound?'

'Did she just mention the P word?' Alistair said to Barry.

'I believe she did. And we'll finally get to meet this new chap of hers.'

'Oh yes, the famous paint pot.'

'Paint pot?'

'Matt Finish, isn't it?'

'Healy.' Jane laughed. 'And yes, you'll finally get to meet him. But he's strictly hands-off.' She raised a warning finger at Alistair. 'Or there *will* be body parts in railway station lockers.'

* * *

On her way home, Jane took a short diversion from Borough station, crossing to the red brick and Portland stone facade of St George the Martyr church. In the gardens beyond, away from the bustle and traffic, she slowed, reflecting once again on all she'd lost. Despite her certainty with Alistair and Barry, she still had doubts about giving up her career. Had she done the right thing? Wouldn't it have been more sensible to carry on working, at least for a few more months while Matt got the business established? He was the detective, after all.

That again. That's what it came down to. A sense of failure. Of not having done enough.

By the surviving wall of the old debtor's prison, with its crowding ghosts of many miserable years, she saw a black cat stalking a bird and stamped her foot. The bird flew off and the cat, equally startled, bounded away in the opposite direction.

She moved on, passing a large tabby reclining on a sunny square of lawn, its eyes closed but its ears angling as it tracked her steps. A white longhair watched from a living room window across the road while a ginger tom, almost hidden by a leafy bough, glared down at her as she passed beneath.

Cats, everywhere.

She paused at a corner shop, one of the many sites where she'd placed Tibbles McVicar's Missing Cat flyer. It was gone now, replaced by three others, with a fourth in the process of removal.

The doorbell pinged as she went in and the owner, a cheerful Indian man in a brightly patterned shirt, looked up, recognised her and smiled.

'A happy outcome?' she asked, nodding at the A4 page in his hands.

'Indeed, yes. It seems that Bartholomew Brick has found his way home at last,' he said, reading from the flyer.

The photograph showed a brick-coloured Oriental Longhair with a delightfully whiskery moustache and tufts at the side of his neck that made him look like a grouchy old man. The date showed he'd been missing a week.

'The one I brought in ...?'

'Mr Tinchcombe himself called this morning. A second happy outcome. Also gone one week. I am putting it down to my window. Place your poster here, and pussy will come home.' He smiled.

'Do you get many missing cats?'

'Hardly a one until two weeks' ago. Now this.' He gestured at the window. 'My wife says they are like buses; all come at once, or rather, go. Me, I am thinking that maybe it is summer. Time for holidays.'

'You think they're all sunning themselves down Margate or Southend?'

'No, no, these are executive pusscats. They will have their own clubs and hotels on the Continent. Margate is much too common.'

Jane laughed, bought a bottle of milk and a packet of fancy cat treats for Bluebelle, then paused outside looking at the other flyers. He was right, they were all executive pusscats. She took out her phone and took a picture of the line-up.

The Tinchcombe's cul de sac was nearby. Another short diversion, but she couldn't resist. Patricia Tinchcombe had told her of Tibbles McVicar's favourite spot; the sunny front window with its commanding view of the street. If he was back, perhaps she'd catch a glimpse him and be able to put her unsettled thoughts to rest.

The road was quiet, the elderly Rover still in its spot, and there, in the window overlooking the undemolished half of garden, sat a large silver-blue cat with golden eyes that regarded her inscrutably from four doors away. Tiberius Constantine McAlistair-Vicory was back.

Jane paused. There was something implacably dismissive in his unblinking eyes. 'Fat lot of use you were,' he seemed to be saying.

A fat lot of use, all right, Jane thought.

7

Henry Baxter was poised for a fall. He knew that because he was angled out from the top of a set of metal stairs that ran down from the shower block on the landing of E Wing. The angle was about forty-five degrees. A foot placed squarely behind his heels prevented him from stepping back, and he was only restrained from a nasty downward plunge by the hand that gripped his coveralls. The restraining hand wasn't too much comfort, however, as it was the same hand that had propelled him there in the first place.

'Hello Hen, fancy seeing you here,' the restraining hand's owner said. 'Had any more thoughts about our offer?'

'I can't.'

'Ten percent, that's all. Seems pretty reasonable to me.'

'I told you, it doesn't work like that.'

'Are you sure?' The hand shoved him forward then jerked him back. 'Are you saying we got it wrong? I hope not. That kind of talk could be dangerous.'

'It's all gone. There isn't any left. The Fraud Squad said as much.'

'That only proves they didn't look very hard. You're a clever man, Hen. After all, you got away with it for almost twenty years. So where is it? Swiss bank account? Some Caribbean trust fund? Must be a nice little nest egg by now. And all we want is ten percent of the principal, not the accrued interest. Seems pretty reasonable to me since you ripped it off from the likes of us in the first place. Ten percent, Hen.' The hand gave another jerk. 'That's less than VAT.'

'I told you. You got the last of it. My ex-wife took—'

'And I told you we don't believe those tales. Or that fancy claptrap your fancy lawyer spun the court. So think on. If you don't want your ex-wife to become very much more ex, I suggest you cooperate.'

The restraining hand drew him back, turned him round, brushed down his coverall and patted his shoulder.

'I hear you've got a transfer coming up. Nice little D-Cat like you, inoffensive, white collar crim, no danger to society. Make an ideal candidate for one of the open prisons.

'Think of it. Minimum security, minimal supervision. Some of the birds even get daytime jobs on The Out. But remember, open means it's open both ways. It means you're easier to get at too. You will remember that, won't you?'

Henry Baxter looked at his tormentor and said nothing.

'If you ever get there, of course.'

Baxter didn't understand what he meant. Then a hand shoved him in the chest and the next moment he was flying. For a second or two, at least.

* * *

Matt took a train from Catford Bridge to Charing Cross, going over his meeting with Melody Harper and Gerrard Vine while making notes in the small blue notebook he carried. Jane was right. There was nothing likeable about them. But there was no rule that said you had to love your clients.

They'd been thorough. He couldn't fault the way they'd checked out the rumoured counterfeiting or their swiftness in doing a stocktake to eliminate the possibility of theft by a member of staff. Only two things bothered him: the extent of the operation – there were eight counterfeit coffees on *Le Chat Noir's* menu, H&V's entire range – and the third-party nature of the report he was supposed to present at the end of his investigation. An unusual request, although perhaps not in the circumstances. He guessed it was meant for someone else. Not the ACG or the police, given Melody's evident disdain, but some coffee importers disciplinary body perhaps.

There was a Green Park bus at the kerb outside the station, but he decided to walk instead. It was a pleasant afternoon, there was no rush, and he should phone ahead anyway. Besides, it was – as the Americans would say – all on H&V's dime.

The Chesapeake Club had a discreet entrance off St James's Street. Matt followed a collection of business suits up the steps and waited in the foyer while one signed the others in. A door opened ahead of them and Matt caught sight of a high-ceilinged room lined with leather armchairs and a Turkish carpet. Its mullioned windows were hung with heavy brocades and the burgundy walls were dotted with gold-framed portraits. There was even a modest chandelier, on in the middle of the day.

The foyer was equally plush. Matt paced across the marble floor to read a brass plaque on one wall commemorating the achievements of a number of Field Marshalls and Brigadier Generals in their successful execution of the Malayan Emergency (1948-60). 'A war by any other name,' his dad had called it. Gus Healy had spent the last of his army years there, serving on the ground, going on patrol, losing mates to enemy and friendly fire while the men who commanded and directed operations did so well behind the lines, no doubt from the Malayan equivalent of institutions like this. Even the term "Emergency" had been a con, insisted upon by the British owners of the tin mines and rubber plantations. By not calling it a "war" they could claim their losses against insurance.

The suits moved on and Matt found himself addressed by an oversized traffic bollard dressed in green livery. The man's barrel chest and the cut of his long jacket contributed to the bollard impression, but he seemed just as immoveable.

He looked Matt up and down.

'Are you a member, sir?' His expression suggested he was certain that Matt wasn't.

'No, but I've—'

'It's members only, I'm afraid.'

He didn't look like he was afraid of anything.

'I have an appointment to see Reg Trivet.'

'Mr Trivet?' The bollard consulted a register. 'I don't have anything here.'

'Possibly because I only just made it.' Matt held up his phone.

'The office and deliveries entrance is—'

'Just get me Trivet, will you,' Matt said, loud enough for one of the business suits ahead of him to glance back.

The bollard gave him an implacable glare and picked up a phone. 'Who shall I say is—?'

'The man he was talking to five minutes ago.'

The bollard dialled.

Matt felt a little guilty for his belligerence. It wasn't the bollard's fault, but places like this burned him up. Money, exclusivity, privilege, the Old Boy network. There were real people out there in the real world, struggling to get by, while in places like this plans were made to gouge them deeper and cream off still more of the cream. The pension funds of hundreds – his dad's included – had vanished into the pockets of men who frequented places like this. After years of expensive investigations, judges and barristers – also members of clubs like the Chesapeake – had lightly chastised their fellows and made recommendations that were never implemented while those affected struggled to pay their bills and heat their homes in their declining years.

'This way, sir.' The bollard put the phone down and led him to a side passage off the foyer and through a miniature maze of corridors.

At least we're back to *sir*, Matt thought.

He stopped before a frosted glass door at the back of the building, tapped twice with a knuckle, held the door for Matt then closed it behind him.

Matt found himself in a small but ornately furnished office shaking hands with a very upright man whose grey suit matched the pallor of his skin.

'Reginald Trivet. I've spoken with Ms Harper of Harper and Vine and she assures me you have her full confidence.'

'She is paying the bills,' Matt said as Trivet gestured him to a seat.

'Where would you like to begin, Mr Healy?'

Matt took out his notebook. 'How did you first hear of H&V coffee?'

'From Mr Vine himself. He was a member of the club.'

'Was?'

'Still is, I should say. I believe he's currently reviewing his options.'

Matt's eyes narrowed. 'You mean he hasn't paid his dues?'

'An administrative mix-up, I'm sure. Our members are busy people, Mr Healy. They lead busy lives. It's only been a month or two.'

'But you still do business with his company?'

'We'd be foolish not to. It's a fine product.'

'I know what you're thinking: Old Boys Club and all that. But you couldn't be more wrong. I'm something of a coffee aficionado, and when I sampled Harper and Vine's offerings, I was most keen to stock them in the club. It was a bonus to discover they came from a fellow Chesapeakean.'

'How long ago was that?'

'Five or six years, I'd say. Shortly after the company's inception.'

'And you've had no problems with them?'

'None whatsoever. The quality is remarkable, and consistent, and their service is outstanding.'

'Where and when did you first hear about the counterfeits?'

'Ten days ago, here at the club. I was passing through our

dining room when I overheard a couple of members talking. One mentioned he'd had H&V in Soho. The other laughed, but the first was insistent. I ...' he coloured faintly, '... hovered. It's in the club's interest to protect the exclusivity of its brands, you understand. The Philadelphia Hotel was mentioned and I made a note to investigate it.'

'Did you?'

'Not directly. My wife paid them a visit the following day. If anything, her palette is better than mine. She tried their Finca Sanssouci and rated it perfectly acceptable.'

'Nothing counterfeit about it?'

'The term hadn't even come up at that stage. The fact that a middling establishment like the Philadelphia would stock one of London's most exclusive coffees seemed surprising. I telephoned Ms Harper for clarification, and she assured me they certainly shouldn't have it, that it was either stolen or counterfeit. She telephoned me back the following day to say it could only be the latter.'

'So this would be last Wednesday or Thursday?'

'Wednesday. As I said, their service is exemplary.'

'How difficult would it be to counterfeit a coffee?'

'Remarkably easy if you have a good nose and access to some of the less judicious suppliers. Take Jacu Bird, for example. The Jacu is fastidious, taking only selected berries while leaving more than half the bunch intact. Were someone to harvest them and blend them with those the birds' deposit, it would take an expert to tell them apart.'

'Someone such as you? Or your wife?'

Trivet nodded modestly.

'Are there any chemical tests they can do?'

'You mean, seek out the force that through the green fuse drives the flower?'

'I beg your pardon?'

An indulgent smile. 'No, I don't believe there are. Too many variables. Coffee's not a single-source, single-preparation product like, say, manuka honey.'

'Manuka honey?'

'From New Zealand. They only produce seventeen hundred tons a year, yet somehow eighteen hundred tons get sold in the UK alone. But that's a testable product with clearly identifiable constituents. Coffee's a much more subtle beast.'

'Like wine.'

'Precisely.'

'Have you heard of any other places stocking H&V? I mean, ones that shouldn't.' Trivet shook his head. 'And your own stocks are all accounted for?'

'Absolutely. A product of this nature requires strict management.'

'Any idea where the counterfeiters might be getting their supplies?'

'Whatever their source, it's good. One thing occurs to me though. It's a fiercely competitive business. It's not beyond the realms of possibility that one supplier might seek to discredit another.'

'You mean like industrial sabotage? But you said yourself the quality was good.'

'As one might expect with an initial shipment subject to the greatest scrutiny. After that, ratcheting down a brand's quality would effectively destroy it.'

Despite his grey suit and grey manners, Trivet clearly had a devious mind.

Matt made a note and took his leave. Trivet directed him to a rear exit, but Matt found his way back to the main entrance and gave the bollard a cheery wave as he departed.

8

'There's a list of all the cafes and hotels in central London on your desk,' Jane told Matt as he breezed in, 'and Melody sent through a list of their stockists. I take it your meeting went well?'

'What a pair!' He rolled his eyes. 'He's got a flea in his ear about something, and she's a bit hard-boiled, despite that candyfloss appearance. But hey, the money's good and there are perks.' He pulled a wad of coffee sachets from his pocket, sifted through the empty ones and handed her the sealed packet.

'Jacu Bird. A whole thirty-five grams worth. Wow.'

'Don't mock. You could probably secure a mortgage with that.'

'*Premium Biodynamic Coffee*. What's the biodynamic touch?'

'Organic farming for toffs.'

'And the Jacu bird?'

'More poop.'

'No, really? What is it with coffee snobs and animal excreta?'

'I've no idea, but I got that from the horse's mouth. Which has to be better than the bird's bottom.'

Jane turned the sachet over. 'It's old stock. The use-by date's expired.'

'The miserable cow! Melody gave me that and said, treat Jane. I'll definitely bill her for that stuff we had last night now.'

He passed her the empty sachets.

'Looks like you three had quite a party.'

'I didn't get offered so much as a glass of water.'

'Lucky you. Gerrard calls it toilet flush. Only good for washing one's car, apparently.'

'Here.' He took the Kopi Luwak sachet he'd retrieved from the hotel's skip and placed it beside the one Melody had given him. 'See if you can spot the difference.'

'Difference? Singular?'

'That was all I could find.'

Jane looked from one to the other. Two thirty-five gram packets. She turned them over and studied the backs. One was a little more crinkled, but apart from that, they were identical. She felt the foil packaging, held them up to the light, even sniffed the empty interiors.

'The only difference I can see is the use-by date and batch number stamped on the back.'

'Me too.'

'But isn't this one supposed to be a forgery? Look, the stamp line's even in the same place.' She checked with a ruler. 'The font and ink colour are the same too. The only difference is one's five digits, the other's six.'

'What about the branding?'

Jane turned the bags back over and looked at the scrolly gold lettering. 'They're both embossed. That's another part of the printing process, isn't it?'

He nodded. 'Most forgers wouldn't bother. Plus, see how the H&V looks sparkly? It's been stamped out of gold foil. You don't get that effect with regular inks.'

'So someone's gone to a lot of trouble to make exact copies of H&V's packaging, even down to using the same batch number stamp.'

'Almost too much trouble, wouldn't you say? At least for a few sachets of coffee.'

'So it could be a big operation.'

He nodded.

'Or someone could have stolen the bags.'

'Melody said she did a stocktake. Coffee and packaging. Nothing's missing.'

'What did she say when you showed her this?' Jane held up the forgery.

'She didn't say anything because I didn't show her.'

'It's a clue, isn't it?'

'There's one thing you have to remember about this game, Jane: trust no one, including the client.'

'You don't seriously think Melody Harper's counterfeiting her own coffee.'

'No, but there may be more to this than meets the eye. I paid her Mr Trivet a visit at that club he runs. Did you know Gerrard hasn't paid his subs this year?'

'He told you that?'

'Not in so many words.'

'Well, it's not going to be a problem, however much they are. The Vines are old money.'

'Something Trivet did mention was the possibility of industrial sabotage. Another importer deliberately trashing the name of a competitor. A possibility I hadn't thought of.'

'Is that likely?'

'It's a cut-throat business, apparently, and a rival would have the beans and machines to roast, grind and package the stuff. All they'd need is the bags. I'll call her back and get a list of competitors. See if they've pissed anyone off lately, or if someone else might be vying for that Royal Warrant.'

Matt took out his notebook and glanced through it. 'Trivet did say one odd thing. I asked him whether you could chemically analyse the coffee and he muttered something about green fuses driving flowers.'

Jane grinned.

'Go on, what have I missed?'

'Only an education.'

'You forget I'm just an East End boy at heart.'

'*The Force That Through the Green Fuse Drives the Flower* is a poem by Dylan Thomas. You do know Dylan Thomas, don't you?'

'Oh, him. Yeah.' Matt grinned back. 'Welsh fly-half, wasn't he?'

* * *

Suspecting a spinal injury, they took Henry Baxter to hospital on a scoop stretcher. It was a purely precautionary measure as he was still conscious and could move his hands and feet, but after a fall like that the prison authorities didn't want to take any chances. X-rays showed a broken collarbone and wrist, cracked ribs and dislocation of the fifth cervical vertebra. There was ligament damage to one knee and both elbows along with multiple cuts and some nasty contusions from the metal stair treads. By early evening he was returned to the infirmary at High Down prison and given a week's bed rest. Physiotherapy for his neck would begin the following day.

His dinner, a vegetable and bean salad pre-selected from a standard menu card earlier in the week, was approved by the nurse and served to him in bed. He consumed it hungrily, having missed lunch, and wished now he'd ordered something more substantial.

The Custodial Manager visited as he was finishing up, forcing him to refrain from running a finger round the plate to get at the last of the tasty dressing, and he watched regretfully as an infirmary assistant took it away.

'Well, Mr Baxter, you are a clumsy one,' CM Blumer said. 'Another little accident, eh? Looks like you'll miss another placement. I'm starting to suspect you don't really want to leave us.'

Baxter looked after his departed plate and said nothing.

'Care to tell me what happened?' Blumer crossed her arms. She was a big woman, almost sexless in her uniform, but not unkind.

'I tripped,' he glanced up briefly before dropping his eyes to the three silver stripes on her epaulettes.

'Again?'

He said nothing.

'Because if it's something more than an accident, I'd really like to know about it.'

'No, no, I just ...' A twinge from his neck made him stop and brace it with a supporting hand. 'I wasn't paying attention. I stumbled. I think I must have tripped myself up.'

'Tripped yourself up,' Blumer repeated.

'Yes,' he said, unwilling to trust his throbbing neck with a nod.

'You picked a hell of a place to do it, didn't you, top of a stairway?' She left a long pause. Baxter said nothing. 'But if you're certain about that, I'll put it in my report. I won't finish that report till tomorrow morning though, so if you recall anything in the interim, you will let me know, won't you?'

'Yes, Miss Blumer.'

'Which brings me to my next subject; your next of kin. She'll have to be informed.' She saw the look in his eyes. 'It's standard procedure. What would she think of us if she came for a visit at the weekend and found you in here?'

'I don't want to worry her, that's all.'

'You make the call yourself if you like. And we don't need to do it right away. Tomorrow morning, perhaps? When you've had time to settle in and think things through. Before I finish my report.'

'Yes, all right. Thank you, Miss Blumer.'

'Good night, Mr Baxter. I'll see you in the morning.'

* * *

Jane had an early evening self-defence class run by a formidable Scottish ex-policewoman named Fiona Burgess. It was a refresher in Jane's case – she and her friend Sally had done similar classes together almost ten years before – but she thought it prudent to brush up on her technique given her new career.

She liked Fiona immediately for her no-nonsense approach: 'Forget all that ju-jitsu crap and assuming the stance and balancing on yer toes. Real life's nae like that. If a bloke comes at you, run away and yell yer head off. If a bloke comes at you wi' a knife, run faster and yell louder. Only use the stuff I'm goin' ta tell yer aboot if yer canna run away.'

Her basic advice could be summed up in five words: go for the squishy bits. 'A kick in the goolies is remarkably distractin', and a poke in the eye'll dissuade him too. And use yer knuckle, not your finger. You don't want to break it. Or wreck your nails.'

They spent the rest of the lesson practising how to get out of a variety of unpleasant situations, then Jane headed for the showers, happy at her progress and what she'd retained all these years.

Sally and Paul lived one Tube stop on. Jane, due there for dinner, grabbed a bottle of wine en route and arrived earlier than planned to find the house still in a state of toddler turmoil.

'I did say it was nothing fancy,' Sally cautioned, settling her on the sofa and handing her a glass of wine.

Dylan came bounding in, fresh from his bath, wearing nothing but a smile and dragging a stuffed elephant by the ear. His father bounded in behind him, carrying a towel. 'Come here, you monster!' He wrestled the gurgling boy to the carpet and finished drying him.

Sally clinked glasses. 'How was the class?'

Jane told her about the Scottish ex-policewoman's advice.

'Watch out for those two,' Paul whispered to Dylan. 'They're after our squishy bits!'

The boy giggled.

Jane sipped her wine. 'How are you, Sal? How's it all going?'

Sally sighed and patted her belly. 'Ticking off the days. Twenty-two weeks down, only sixteen to go.'

'As bad as that?'

'No, not really, but I am starting to feel like a bouncy castle.'

'Bouncy castle? No, no, no,' Paul said. 'More like the Michelin Man's missus.'

'Thanks for the compliment.'

He puffed out his cheeks and seemed to inflate himself as he hovered over Dylan. The boy ran off squealing with Paul waddling after him.

'I can't believe I let him talk me into going through all this again,' Sally said in a lower tone. 'Not that I mind, not really, but men get off so easily. I had been hoping to get back to work this year.'

'You still can.'

'I am actually doing a little from home. Part-time telecommuting. But it's not the same as going into a proper office every day.'

'I know what you mean. I had lunch with some old colleagues today and realised I actually miss my old job. Or bits of it, at least.'

'The question is, would you go back?'

Jane made a face and shook her head.

'Sounds like you've made the right decision then.' Seeing her expression, Sally added, 'There's no perfect solution, you know. Anywhere. To anything.'

'No, I know.'

'How're things going with Matt? Still keeping to that ridiculous agreement of yours?'

'Yeah, mostly.'

Sally laughed. 'Your mouth went down at the corners when you said that, Jane Child. I won't ask for details, but I will say I admire your self-control. He's a hunk!'

Being in a relationship *and* becoming business partners had been a huge move, especially as neither Jane nor Matt had been in anything like a proper relationship for some time. The prospect of living band working together was exciting and a little daunting, and when they discussed it, they realised they both valued their independence too. So the Child-Healy Agreement was born. Matt would continue on in his dad's old place in Greenwich, with Jane in her Southwark townhouse four miles to the west. They'd keep a work-life balance by coming together as a couple only at weekends or for the odd meal or movie during the week, subject to prior arrangement. Like being in an office surrounded by other people. During business hours they had to be professional.

'There was one lapse,' Jane said. 'During that downpour yesterday.'

'Only one?'

'So far.'

Sally clinked her glass again.

'I'm just not sure if I'm cut out for this business,' Jane sighed. 'I used to be really good at my job, but I'm floundering around in this one.'

'It's going to take a while to find your feet. You've only been going a few weeks.'

'I got fired today. Our very first case too.'

'The Tibbles the cat one?'

'My services are *no longer required*. It looks like he came back on his own.'

'That's unusual. He's been gone a while, hasn't he?'

'A week exactly.'

'I thought he'd be roadkill by now.'

'Oh, don't. The point is, where's he been and why couldn't I find him? What did I miss? I spoke to all the neighbours, front and back. Checked all the sheds and lock-ups I could find. Put out flyers.'

'Hasn't been off on his hols, has he?'

'You're the second person to suggest that.' Jane thought back to the corner shop and the other Missing Cat flyers.

'He probably got himself shut in somewhere. Did he come home half-starved?'

'If he did, he doesn't look it. I saw him in their window this afternoon. He's a British Shorthair and their official body type is *cobby*.'

'Cobby?'

'I'd never heard the term before and had to look it up. It means thickset and stocky. Well, he didn't look any less cobby than in the photos the Tinchcombes showed me.'

'Who's cobby?' Paul asked, returning to the lounge with Dylan under his arm, dressed now in blue pyjamas. 'Are we still talking about Sal?'

'I'll cobby you, Paul Thompson. And you, Dylan Thompson,' Sally leapt to her feet.

'Look out, Dylan. Mind your squishy bits. The bouncy castle's after us!'

9

The Plover's Plumbing van was still parked outside Matt's place when he arrived home. Jake Plover was an old friend from his school days and only lived a dozen doors away, but he'd still driven down.

Matt's house, inherited from his father, sat at the end of a pleasant tree-lined street in Greenwich. Semi-detached with a high brick wall enclosing a long, narrow, overgrown backyard, the house was clean and tidy, but felt a little old-fashioned and in need of some TLC. The curtains and floor coverings were faded, the wallpaper mottled at the edges, and Jane had complained about the vicegrips on the tap in the laundry. Getting Jake in to fix that had only been a half-hour job. Modernising the upstairs bathroom was taking somewhat longer.

'You're like my fairy godmother,' Jake said as Matt walked out the back to find him in the garden, having a cigarette. 'I was just thinking how I needed help with that old cast iron bath upstairs, and *poof*, you appear.'

'Not so much of the *poof*, eh? Where's Tommy?' Matt said, referring to Jake's gangly apprentice.

'Week off. Hurt his back.'

'How'd he do that?'

'Old iron baths. Curse of this job.'

Jake took a final drag on his cigarette and flicked the butt into the garden.

'Oi! Mind my landscaping.'

'Your what?' Jake glanced at the wilderness, scratching his considerable belly through a hole in his T-shirt. 'Oh yeah, I forgot you was Capability fucking Brown.'

'What's got to be done with the bath?' Matt said.

'Needs moving out a bit so I can get to the pipework behind it.'

'So *you* can get to the pipework? Jesus, we'll have to move it into the front bedroom.'

'Fuck off, you skinny git. Cheryl likes me cuddly.' Jake patted his belly.

'I don't even want to go there,' Matt said. 'How long's this going to take?'

'Move it out, I'll do me biz, move it back. Half-hour, tops.'

'Right then, let's do it.' Matt slipped off his jacket.

Two hours later, he stood looking at his friend's lower half. The rest of Jake was bent over the back of the bath, his arms and head inside the large hole they'd been obliged to knock in the wall. His torch jiggled and there was the clank of tools accompanied by some choice swearing.

'Nearly there.' The words were muffled.

'You said half an hour, two hours ago.'

'Don't time fly when you're having fun.'

'That's just it, I'm not.'

'Well ... I'm almost ... There, that ought to do it.' He dragged himself out, straightened and brushed back his hair.

'Right, can we move this thing back now?'

'I wouldn't do that yet. You got to fix that hole first.'

'Oh, right.'

'No rush. Let me know when you're done and I'll pop back, finish up and turn your water on.'

'The water's off?'

'Course it is. I can't reconnect the taps till the bath's back in place, can I? You'll only get one flush of that,' he pointed to the toilet, 'so you better make it a good 'un, but I filled your kettle up downstairs and I see you've got a few ales in the fridge.' He gave Matt a consoling pat on the shoulder. 'Don't worry, mate, you can go for days without water, you know.'

* * *

One of his canaries was dead. Ernest Cricklewood – Bitz to the online community – stared at the screen, mildly shocked.

He'd set up a news alert on the name "James Lawrence Burton" along with its variants – "Jamie", "Jimmy" and "Jim" – never expecting to see any of them triggered. They formed part of an early-warning system that would alert him if anyone took an undue interest in certain of his historic activities, but he never expected them to be triggered like this.

He reread the three-paragraph item from a North London newspaper headlined CYCLIST DIES AT SCENE.

A hit-and-run. The police were seeking two men and looking for a blue or grey four-wheel drive, possibly with a damaged driver's door.

The police, Bitz scoffed. The police were idiots.

So Jamie Burton – Spree, to use his online handle – had suffered what his fellow gamers jokingly referred to as an NVD: a non-virtual death. Clearly, he wouldn't make the game tomorrow. That was a shame. He'd been a good scout and a clever fighter; a real asset to the team. Bitz couldn't mention his death though. That would indicate an RL connection. Even in the innocuous world of online gaming, he was careful to keep his real life separate from his virtual one.

It was good to know his early-warning system was still active though, that the triggers he'd set up months ago were still there, primed and ready to be sprung.

He pulled the tab on a fresh Red Bull and toasted the departed hacker. It had been one heck of a heist. Possibly the biggest ever. He wondered what Burton had done with the bitcoins he'd earned.

* * *

'Penny for 'em,' Paul said as they drew up outside her townhouse.

'They're not worth that much,' Jane replied. 'I'm just tired, I think. It's been a long day.'

'I heard what you said to Sal about having doubts about your new business venture. If you want my grandfatherly advice,' Paul was two years older than Sally and Jane, 'go on having doubts, but don't let them swamp you.

'I always try to imagine the worst case scenario. The business falls apart, you don't get any work, or you find you hate the work you do get. What the hell? You gave it a shot. With your experience, Bartley's or any of the other banks would snap you up in an instant if you change your mind.

'The important thing is you're giving it a go, following a dream. The rest of us poor wage-slaves envy you that. We might be stuck on the sidelines, but we're still cheering you on.'

She looked at him in the glow of the dashboard lights. 'You think I'm being a wimp?'

'Nah, I think you're being human.'

Buoyed by his words, she gave him a hug and a kiss goodnight and thanked him for the lift.

A shadow stirred on the front step as she waved him off.

'Oh Bluebelle, you do have a door of your own, you know.'

The cat snaked around her as Jane knelt to demonstrate its operation once again.

It had been a long day. Losing the Tibbles McVicar case, missing her old job, seeing old colleagues in old familiar places carry on without her. And Sally and Paul, so settled and comfortable with each other, their plans and future happiness all mapped out. Why didn't she have a life like that? Where had she gone wrong?

Except ... Paul's words came back to her. Not the words so much as the tone. Who was she to judge the lives of others?

She got to her feet cradling the cat and found her key.

'Sod that stupid cat door, eh puss? Who needs that when

you've got your very own chauffeur?' She kissed the top of Bluebelle's head and carried her inside.

10

Gerrard Vine had almost cleared a sixteen-by-sixteen grid of mines when Melody burst into his office, her face ashen. He switched back to the spreadsheet he was supposed to be working on before getting to his feet.

'What is it, poppet? What's happened? You're as white as a sheet.'

'Papa. He's had an accident.'

'Not another one.' Gerrard regretted the words almost as soon as he spoke them.

'It's serious, this time. He's in the infirmary.'

'Oh god.'

'Broken bones, sprains, bruises, cuts. A dislocated neck too.'

'But ... that's all ...?'

'He's in hospital, you arse!' She took a breath. 'But no, no head injuries. Nothing life-threatening.' She slumped into a chair beside his desk.

'Are you going out to see him? If you are, I can hold the fort.'

'He said not to bother. We're not to make a fuss. Just visit him at the weekend as normal. Pretend everything is bloody normal!'

Gerrard took the seat beside her and took one of her hands. She yielded it unwillingly. 'It's ... the same old thing, is it?'

'What do you think? He was due to be transferred next week.'

'What did he actually say?'

'That it was an accident. That he tripped and fell down a flight of stairs. What the hell else was he going to say? They probably monitor his calls. For all we know, it might be the bloody prison staff themselves.'

It was too late to say they should never have paid in the first place. They'd already had that argument, twice. The damage was done now, the precedent set. The only question now was, how much? And they wouldn't learn that till they saw Henry in person.

It had begun modestly enough as a sort of "new boys" fee that would ensure a few extra privileges and protection from some of the prison's rougher elements. Gerrard expressed his doubts. He'd been to a public school and knew how these things worked. Gangs of boys were gangs of boys, irrespective of their location. The moment you showed a sign of weakness or a hint of vulnerability was the moment they piled into you. He'd tried to tell Mel that but she was insistent. It was only a couple of thousand and High Down was only a holding prison for those on remand and those recently convicted. He wouldn't be there long. Besides, didn't they owe him something after all he'd done for them?

That was the argument that won through every time, the argument to which he had no reply.

The second demand was accompanied by an accident. A fall in the showers, a collision with a concrete step on the way down resulting in a couple of broken fingers and bruised and badly swollen face. It looked much worse than it felt, Henry assured them. That had cost them twenty thousand, a ten-fold escalation, and the biggest row they'd ever had.

Fortunately – or perhaps unfortunately – Gerrard's quarterly allowance had just come in. It would swallow most of it, but at least the money was there. With a few economies and a few deferrals, they could manage for a few months, Melody said.

'If we pay this, they'll never stop,' he told her. But she was deaf to his words. She'd always been blind to reason where Islington Papa was concerned.

They rowed.

She called him cheap and mean – the words bounced off – then she stabbed him with the line for which he had no defence: 'After all he's done for us!'

Now what, he wondered? Another twenty thousand? There was no way they could afford that. His next allowance was still three weeks away, and the spreadsheet he'd been working on said they'd barely scrape through. He could talk to his aunt. An advance, perhaps. But why would she listen to him now when she'd never done so in the past? Long-term of course it would all work out, but long-term could take another ten years. This needed something more decisive.

'A flight of stairs,' Melody sniffed. 'He tripped and fell down a flight of stairs. Easy, eh? The perfect *accident*. I'm sure it happens all the time.'

In one of those miracles of prescience, the plan came to him fully formed. Neat, complete, perfect. Decisive action at last!

'Listen ... I ... won't be able to make it tomorrow, Mel,' Gerrard told her. 'Banstead. The prison. A visit, I mean. I just had a call from Harvey Harry. He wants to see me.'

Melody looked at him. 'Harvey Harrison? About this place? He's a tit, Gerrard. He couldn't raise the wind to blow up a paper boat.'

'No, no, not him. A business contact of his. He wants me to pop over and meet with them.'

'When?'

'They'll only be there for the weekend. I thought I'd catch the afternoon train from St Pancras and come back Sunday afternoon.'

'To Paris?'

'It's worth a shot, isn't it?'

'You'd be better off buying a lottery ticket in my opinion. But then, when have you ever listened to me?'

Or you, me? he thought.

<h1 style="text-align:center">11</h1>

Matt called from home to say he'd head straight out and check on some the of the fancy cafes and hotels Jane had detailed the day before. In the meantime, would she mind doing the usual checks on H&V's staff?

The usual checks turned up nothing. They were all squeaky clean. None of them showed a hint of a criminal past or criminal associations. Just what you'd expect from an employer like Melody Harper who suspected that busking was a front for muggers and that the homeless retired each night to country estates.

Jane had a few other admin tasks to do, amongst them the Tinchcombe's invoice. She printed it out, enveloped and stamped it, then set it to one side, wondering if she should start an Unsolved section in the filing cabinet. No, that was a bit dramatic. And disheartening. Imagine if it grew larger than the Solved section. In the end, she just made sure the folder was properly indexed with the case number ("A0001") then slammed the grey drawer on it. As Matt said, best to put it behind her and move on.

She recalled the photo she'd taken of the Missing Cat flyers in the shop window the day before, printed it out and went to add it to the file for the sake of completeness. Or incompleteness. Then she paused, studying it.

Tibbles McVicar was a British Shorthair. Bartholomew Brick – the whiskery-looking grouch who'd turned up after a week's absence – was an Oriental Longhair. These three were also pedigrees; a Selkirk Rex, a tiger-striped Savannah, and a white Turkish Angora that looked like it had just had a close encounter with a washing machine.

'Executive pusscats,' she told Bluebelle, recalling Dev Patel's words. 'All pedigrees. What are the odds of that?'

What was the ratio of pedigrees to plain old moggies? Somewhere between one in a hundred and one in a thousand, she guessed.

'Not that there's anything wrong with plain old moggies,' she reassured Bluebelle.

But that meant the odds of striking five missing pedigrees in a row must be pretty long. You could even call it a pattern.

Matt had told her about patterns and how useful they were in crime solving. One of his first successes as a young PC had involved a series of burglaries in the same street, each one a fortnight apart. Number 83, number 101, number 109, then number 131. The frequency corresponded to the week after fortnightly benefit payments were paid, but the choice of houses seemed random – to everyone but Matt. When he staked out number 149 and caught the burglar in the act of breaking and entering, he was hailed as a hero – and something of a nerd. The house numbers were all prime numbers, two primes apart, and the perpetrator – as Matt had jokingly suggested – lived at number 71, a recent maths graduate finding it hard to reconcile his party lifestyle with the Jobseeker's Allowance.

Jane picked up the phone and dialled the number on the first flyer. The phone rang and rang. No answer and no answering machine. She tried the Selkirk's owner. A machine this time. She left a message. Not wanting to identify herself as a detective and not wanting to raise a worried owner's hopes, she pretended she was from the local paper looking to do a story on missing cats.

The third call was answered after a single ring.

'Oh good morning, I'm calling about your missing cat.'

'What is it now?' A cross voice. 'I've done all you asked. You said he'd be back by eleven and it's now ten-to-twelve. The money's here, waiting. Cash, just like you said.'

Jane thought quickly. 'Sorry, there's been a bit of a mix-up. What was your address again?'

'Twenty. Five. Ainsley. Road.' Each word was clearly enunciated.

Jane wedged the phone with her shoulder and brought up a local map on her computer. Ainsley Road was a twenty-minute walk away. Ten if she ran.

'As I told your man last night,' the woman continued.

'On the way now.' Jane threw down the phone and sprinted for the door.

She wasn't dressed for running – jeans, a short-sleeved blouse and sneakers – but there was no time to change. What they really needed, she thought, was a company car. Then she turned into the high street to find a knot of traffic in both directions. North and southbound lanes were stalled, bumper-to-bumper. A pensioner with a zimmer frame was making quicker progress.

Roadworks, a breakdown or an accident somewhere, she guessed. It didn't take much to cause gridlock. The southbound lane was making inching progress, but the northbound one was locked solid. Some drivers sat stony faced and fuming behind their windshields. Others read newspapers or consulted mobile phones. A handful stood outside their vehicles, smoking or leaning on partly open doors and exchanging banter with other strandees.

Jane picked up speed, grinning smugly as she headed up the gentle incline towards the turn-off. The real cost of car ownership was wasted time. Space too. Most vehicles had just one occupant. A single bus could have carried a mile's worth of drivers.

Ainsley Road lay at the bottom of a line of rectilinear terraces. It was a pleasant street of semi-detached houses and lush gardens. Number twenty-five had a high privet hedge and a recently painted metal gate that opened noiselessly on to a well-tended but overly busy garden. The front door was painted a green so dark it was almost black, giving the house a sombre look. The windows were heavily net curtained and the brass knocker gleamed.

Jane knocked.

The door was opened by a woman in early middle-age with prim, neatly curled grey hair, a monstrous bosom and a light grey cardigan done up over a cream blouse that was buttoned to the neck. Her dark grey skirt and matronly figure reminded Jane of an old-fashioned Ealing comedy headmistresses, and she would have been perfect for the role except for the tatty sheepskin slippers she was wearing and the large, slim, leopard-spotted cat she carried in her arms.

'Ah,' Jane said, recognising her quarry from the poster. 'George.'

The cat stared back at her, unblinking. It had wide grey-green eyes and overly large pointed ears.

'I beg your pardon?' the woman said in the tone of one displeased at being interrupted.

'George,' Jane pointed. She was out of breath. 'I see he's back.'

'Yes?' The reply was really a question.

'I called a few minutes ago.' Jane checked her watch. 'Twelve, to be exact.'

'Well, he was returned approximately two minutes after that.'

'Who by?'

The woman's eyes narrowed and she regarded Jane critically. 'Who are you? What is your interest in this matter?'

Jane reached into the pocket and produced a business card. It was slightly crumpled and slightly damp. The woman made no effort to take it, kept both hands on the cat, but arched her head and studied it.

'My name's Jane Child. I'm a private detective. I recognised George from his flyer in Patel's Superette. And you are?'

The woman wouldn't be drawn. Instead, she said, 'That flyer should have been removed. I sent the neighbour's boy to—'

'It probably has been by now. I photographed it yesterday. I called you because I'm interested in the process of George's ...

retrieval.'

The woman regarded her for a long moment then backed slightly and began to close the door. 'I'm sorry, I can't help you.'

'You mentioned money on the phone. You said "The money's here, waiting. Cash, just like you said."'

The door stopped closing, but the woman said nothing.

'Did you have to pay a reward for George's return?'

The woman's lips pursed.

'That's called extortion, you know.'

She said nothing.

'You're not the only one. There's been a spate of these,' Jane said, surprising herself, making it up as she went along.

'These what?'

'Catnappings, for want of a better word.'

'Don't be ridiculous,' the woman snapped and closed the door, leaving Jane staring at the sombre green paint.

She pushed her business card through the mail slot and called, 'In case you change your mind.' Something told her the woman still standing on the other side of the door. 'There are other people in your position, you know. Some of them can't afford to pay.'

Jane waited, but there was no reply. No response. She headed back to the gate.

George had been returned two minutes after her call, which meant that either his abductors were local and had returned him on foot, or she'd passed their vehicle in the snarl up on the high street.

Not local, surely. He was supposed to be returned by eleven. It was now almost twelve.

If they were late because of the traffic jam, they'd know the road was chock-a-block in both directions. It didn't seem likely they'd head straight back into the chaos. A better strategy would be to hole up in a nearby pub or eatery and wait for the traffic to clear. They'd just had a payout too, and it was lunchtime.

She took out her phone, brought up the maps app and zoomed out from her current location. There was a park, a pub and a group of shops three blocks to the east. As good a bet as any. She set off at a gentle jog, trying to work out what she was looking for.

Captured animals would be kept in cages, so that implied a van. A car would work, but animals – even caged ones – drew attention. You wouldn't want your abductee being spotted by passers-by if, say, you got caught in traffic. Besides, they were likely to be dealing with more than one animal at once, so a small van would be ideal.

What else?

She recalled the woman's words: "As I told your man last night."

So, a man in a van. It wasn't much to go on, but it was something.

12

Matt's morning was less productive. Using the cover story that he was a researcher for a web development company looking at producing an app for coffee connoisseurs, he visited every cafe and hotel coffee shop he could find.

'Say you're looking for your nearest shot of Jamaica Blue. Bring up our app and you'll find it, along with reader reviews and ratings,' he told countless proprietors and managers.

He soon had a fat collection of menus and notes, but none of them mentioned Harper and Vine.

Late morning. He stopped at a greasy spoon for an old-fashioned mug of tea. It arrived with a cheese scone the size of a small brick and just about as dry. He chewed and sipped and worked his phone, bringing up all he could find on the only Harper and Vine stockist he knew of so far.

Le Chat Noir was an independent operation, based in and subcontracted to the Philadelphia Hotel. Its holding company, JMJ Catering Limited, had been formed earlier in the year. Companies House listed its directors as Jon Patrick Smith, Maurice Todd and Jennifer Joan Smith. Matt sipped his tea, recalling the maitre d' saying how he and Chef Maurice had only started their little *entreprise* in May.

The nearest Tube station was across the road. He finished his tea, left half the scone, and returned to Leicester Square, heading for the rear entrance of the Philadelphia Hotel.

It was just after eleven-thirty. A well-ordered kitchen would be ticking along smoothly by now, finishing prep work and relaxing before the lunchtime rush. Good time for a quiet chat. But when he poked his head round the outside door, he got a sense of barely suppressed panic. The chef, a burly man with a balding head and ginger sideboards, was stirring pans and checking ovens with the air of someone trying to do ten things simultaneously. The maitre d' and a waitress were stooped over trays of canapes, arranging and garnishing them on china platters, moving with quick economy and furtive glances at the clock.

'I thought you booked a temp?'

'I did. Should've been here half an hour ago. I—'

'Here now,' Matt said, thinking on his feet.

'Where the hell have you been?' the chef bellowed. 'I'll be having words with your agency. Get him sorted, Tony. We've got sixty in for lunch and I want that lot sparkling.' He pointed to a stack of plates and glasses piled beside a pair of stainless steel dishwashers.

Tony – short, square and thickset with wisps of dark, pube-like hair visible under the bottom of his toque – jabbed a finger in Matt's chest. 'Get some fucking whites on and get cracking.'

It was a snap decision, and the undercover cop in Matt relished another role. It was a good opportunity to look around and perhaps even get some inside information.

He found a pair of white coveralls and an oversized white jacket on the rack out the back, and returned a minute later, adjusting a disposable hairnet.

The kitchen was divided into four distinct zones around a central cooking island: storage in one corner, preparation opposite, service by the Out door and cleaning by the In. The frosted face of a glass-fronted fridge sat beside a wardrobe-like walk-in freezer near the changing room, the bench beside it littered with thawed, frozen and fresh produce. To its right was a line of deep shelves. Smaller pans and trays hung on a hinged rack in front. Behind it sat a variety of stockpots, some almost large enough for pygmies to boil missionaries in. In the far corner, he saw a steel-shuttered cabinet fixed to the wall. Where everything else was open and accessible, this was closed and locked.

'Having a good gawp, tosser?' Tony shoved his way past.

'Just getting familiarised.'

'At least you know your name.' He laughed.

Matt took his place beside a three-compartment sink with a spray arm dangling over it. There were two lever-operated stainless steel hoods to his left. These, he guessed from the racks of plates and glasses stacked beneath them, were commercial dishwashers. Unfortunately, he'd never even operated a domestic one. Friends had them, Jane included, but Matt had never felt the need. Although he enjoyed cooking, he rarely did so for more than one or two, and washing up afterwards had never really seemed a chore.

The double doors in and out made soft *whump-whump* sounds as the waitress and maitre d' scuttled back and forth, carrying trays of food. A brief glimpse of the restaurant beyond showed the tables and chairs had been moved to one side leaving a large open space with a long buffet table in the middle. A podium had been erected at one end.

'Yeah, next fucking Tuesday'll do!' Tony bellowed as he shoved past again carrying a foil-covered tray.

Matt made a show of sorting baskets of cutlery while checking out the dishwashers. Given a little time to experiment he could certainly figure out their operation, but if anything, the pace in the kitchen had increased. He was expected to hit the ground running.

He stepped back with a sigh, then spied a laminated sign taped to the wall between the two raised hoods. Operating instructions. For temps like himself.

After that, it was all straightforward and he set to work, rinsing plates and loading racks. Soon, both machines were hissing and sloshing while he organised follow-up loads.

The air of quiet panic in the kitchen eased, the *whump-whump* of the In and Out doors lost its urgency, and he spotted the maitre d' pausing to adjust his bow tie in a stainless steel reflection.

'You want the posh stuff, Jon?' Chef Maurice called.

'Publishers? I doubt it. You know what a tight arsed lot they are. But you never know.' Jon Smith, the maitre d', replied.

Maurice Todd unlocked the cabinet and threw up the shuttered door revealing a packed line-up of foil sachets. Even at wholesale prices, a quick glance told Matt he was looking at a couple of thousand pounds worth of coffee.

'We've got to start shifting some of this stuff,' the chef said.

'I'm pushing it as hard as I can. I told you, we need to advertise.'

'You know we can't afford that. Another year, maybe. Once we're established.' He waited till the waitress came and went then added quietly, 'Can't you have a word with your mate?'

'You think I haven't tried? Won't return my calls. Anyway, it was friend-of-a-friend stuff. It's not on sale-or-return.'

From his tone and the cautious glance at the Out door, Matt guessed that the waitress was the other third of JMJ Catering; Jennifer Joan Smith; wife of Jon. He also guessed she didn't know the source or the true cost of the coffee.

She breezed in and out again. The two men fell silent.

Matt set a rack of cups and saucers down and began loading them on to shelves beside the cabinet. 'Is that H&V?' he said, wanting to keep them on-topic, 'Good stuff, that.'

'What d'you know about it?'

'I do a bit of temping at the Chesapeake. The boss there is always going on about it.'

The two men exchanged glances.

'Oh yeah?'

'Pricey stuff, I hear.'

'Do much temping at the Chesapeake, do you?' Smith said.

'A bit.'

'Regular gig?'

Matt nodded and continued stacking cups.

'I hear Reg Trivet's a picky bugger. Not many get a callback.'

He glanced at the chef and gave him a make-yourself-scarce tilt of the head. 'What's he like to work with?'

'Like you say, a picky bugger. Bit of a poker-up-the-bum type, if you know what I mean, but he knows his stuff.'

'He does.' Smith nodded, considering his words. He extended a hand. 'Jon Smith, Co-owner of this place.'

Matt wiped his hand on his whites and shook it. 'Jake Plover,' he said, adopting the first name that came into his head.

Smith's eyes narrowed as he studied Matt's face. 'Have we met before?'

'Don't think so. But I get around.'

Smith nodded. 'Sounds like it. So, how's temping going for you, Jake?'

Matt gave a dismissive grunt.

'Hard to get a foothold, isn't it? That first big break. At least you're in demand. No chance at the Chesapeake then?'

'I don't think I speak right for that lot,' he said, subtly emphasising his East End accent.

'Permanent temping can be a tough life.' Smith let the words settle. 'We might need someone here in a month or two. We're always on the lookout for blokes with a bit of nous, a bit of initiative.'

'Yeah?' Matt raised an eyebrow.

Smith dropped his voice. 'Willing to go that extra mile.'

'I'd go an extra two, Mr Smith.'

A corner of Smith's mouth went up. 'I believe you would, Mr Plover.' He drew a breath, glanced about conspiratorially then continued. 'We've got a bit of dilemma. That H&V up there came through a third party, not direct from the suppliers. You get my drift?' Matt nodded. 'Problem is, it's not shifting as quick as I'd hoped. Some of it's getting a bit close-dated. The sort of punter that's into that gear is pretty picky, so once the use-by's gone it's bin liner.

'Now if you could think of some way I could swap older stock for newer, you'd find me very grateful. It wouldn't be like stealing or anything, just swapsies, one sachet for another. I reckon somewhere like the Chesapeake would go through that lot in a week or two.' He gestured at the cupboard.

'Easily,' Matt said.

'Be a shame to waste good gear like that, wouldn't it?'

'A terrible shame. Especially if it was preventable.'

'Even by a temp like yourself?'

'Like I told you, Mr Smith, I'm known there. Trusted. And I know my way about.'

'Let me give you my card, Jake Plover.' Smith produced one from his jacket. 'If you give me a call next time you get a call, perhaps we can come to some arrangement. A few quid cash in hand. And long-term, well, you scratch my back and all that.'

Matt grinned and pocketed the card. 'I'll see if I can come up with a solution to your problem, Mr Smith.'

'You do that.' Smith gave him a wink, adjusted his bow tie again and pushed out into the restaurant.

'What was that about, tosser?' Tony jabbed him in the back with his stubby fingers. 'Sucking up to the bosses, were you? This is my gig, prick, and you better remember that.'

Matt raised one of the dishwasher hoods, releasing a cloud of steam in the man's face.

'You fucking—'

The waitress reappeared. 'Vol-au-vents, Tony?'

'On the way, Jen.'

He slammed a tea trolley into Matt's leg. 'Clean that too. *By hand!*' He followed her out.

Matt looked down and recognised the antique coffee syphon.

He set the steaming rack aside to air dry and opened the second dishwasher. The steam obscured the side door briefly. Through it, he saw an uncertain figure enter and glance around. The maitre d', sous chef and waitress were out in the restaurant. The chef was at a whiteboard at the far end of the kitchen, writing up menus and list of ingredients.

'Excuse me, is this—?' the uncertain figure said.

'You're late,' Matt whispered.

'The agency said twelve.'

'It's all right, I've been covering for you. But chef'll have your balls if he sees you. Get changed double-quick and get busy here.'

The newcomer was about Matt's height and build. In whites and a hairnet he'd make a passable double. By the time Matt had put away the contents of the second rack, the young man was in position, rinsing and stacking like a pro.

'Right,' he told him, heading for the locker room. 'I'm off.'

'What do I do with that?' The young man pointed to the coffee syphon.

'Bung it in the dishwasher. That's what Tony said.'

* * *

The futility of Jane's quest struck her as she neared the collection of shops and slowed to a walking pace. She was looking for a man in a van, possibly two, with no idea of his (or their) ages or appearance, or that of the van, or that it actually *was* a van, or even that it come this way. The whole idea, at first full of possibilities, suddenly seemed ridiculous.

A takeaway bar by the corner crowded with workers in high-vis coveralls and jackets, presumably part of the roadworks gang causing the congestion on the high street. At least she could identify potential catnappers amongst that lot; anyone *not* wearing bright orange or yellow was a suspect.

Since she was here, she decided to make the best of a bad idea and took out her phone. It would look odd photographing parked vehicles so she switched it to video, held it loosely in one dangling hand, and strolled along the street with the lens facing out. There were plenty of vehicles in the angled parks outside the shops, more in a bay around the back. She wandered both, steadying the camera on any suspect vehicles, then shut it off and pressed on to the pub further up.

* * *

Bernard Carpinter rolled his eyes at Francis Cricklewood as a beery man, clutching a half-consumed pint, rubbed his forehead saying, 'Hold on, hold on, it'll come to me ... BBC, yeah? That one with the butler and his posh mate ... Got it! *Crick and Carp*, right?'

'Yes, indeed.' Francis Cricklewood gave him a patronising smile.

'My boy used to love that programme. Course he's growed up now. "Benson, I believe my bum's on fire",' he added with a roar and a splutter of beer froth, repeating one of the show's catchphrases. 'I've still got it on DVD somewhere. You should do another series, you know. You were really good.'

'Alas, that choice isn't ours.'

'Well you tell them White City wankers that Dennis down The Rose & Crown wants another series, all right?'

'We shall indeed, Dennis. Thank you for your input.'

Dennis gave them a beery thumbs-up and lurched away.

'Fucking peasants,' Bernard Carpinter addressed the comment to his haddock and chips. 'That was twelve years ago! It's like we'd never done anything else. One piss-pot comedy series and that's all anyone remembers.'

Cricklewood picked at his hotpot. His friend was right to feel aggrieved. The one thing worse than never making it at all was fleeting fame. Despite the years of West End Shakespeare, the touring companies, the character and extra work in countless films and television series, they were still regarded as the acting equivalent of Chumbawamba or Splodgenessabounds; one-hit wonders forever tarred with the brush of a bad comedy.

'It's up to us to change that. And it will change once they

discover what we've been working on.'

'We've got to write the damn thing first.'

'No, first we have to buy ourselves some writing time. Concentrated time, not half an hour between flipping burgers, pulling pints and racing down the Garrick to deliver a couple of lines in someone else's play.'

'And how does spending half the fucking morning stuck in fucking traffic help that little venture?'

'It's a business, Bernard. We're building a business. This is just the groundwork. Once the foundation's established, we'll have a nice steady income. And don't tell me you're not already enjoying the perks.' Cricklewood gestured to the bottle of Chablis standing between them.

Carpinter sat back and sampled the wine. 'I s'pose so. Oh Christ, not another one?' He shielded his face with his free hand.

Cricklewood turned to the window. 'It's all right, she's not interested in us. She's taking pictures of the view. And rather a nice view it is, I must say.'

Carpinter looked back. 'Personally, I prefer a fuller figure.'

'The fuller figures I prefer are those on one's bank statements.'

'Now *there* is a fucking toast, Francis! I'll drink to that.' With a laugh, they clinked glasses and drained them.

13

The red light was blinking on the answerphone when Jane got back to the office. She'd meant to forward calls to her mobile before she left and cursed her oversight. They weren't exactly inundated with work and couldn't afford to miss calls.

The voice was vaguely familiar, the number too. She called it back right away.

'Lowella Foote speaking.'

'Jane Child, Bluebelle Investigations returning your call. I believe we met a short while ago at your front door.'

'Ah. Yes. I should like to apologise for my reception, Ms Child. Your visit was unexpected.'

'I understand. You and George had only just been reunited.'

'Yes ...' Her voice trailed off.

Was that it? She'd just called to apologise?

'He's a fine looking animal,' Jane said, sensing a way through her reticence. 'Wonderful markings.'

'Did you know savannahs are part serval?'

'You mean the African wild cat? That explains the ears then. Like a miniature radar installation.' Lowella Foote laughed. 'He's magnificent.'

'He's also very dear to me, Ms Child. Which means things are a little more ... complicated than they may seem.'

'How so?'

'Perhaps I should begin from the beginning?'

'Please do.' Jane picked up a pen and began making notes.

'George went missing a week ago. He has a cat door at the back and comes and goes as he pleases. There's a cemetery at the bottom of my garden – part of St Noakes church – but he doesn't wander far. He has a basket in the lounge and food dishes in the conservatory. He loves the long summer evenings and was still out when I went to bed last Thursday. There's nothing unusual in that. He usually jumps on my bed in the mornings to tell me his food dish has mysteriously emptied itself overnight.'

Jane smiled.

'But he didn't do so last Friday. In fact there was no sign of him, and his food hadn't been touched. I went out looking immediately. He's very distinctive and well known in the neighbourhood. Savannahs are very friendly, you know. More like dogs than cats, but no one had seen him. I made all the usual enquiries and even employed one of my neighbour's sons to make up flyers and put them in shop windows. But I received no response at all until Tuesday night.

'By then, of course, I was frantic with worry, half-convinced I'd never see him again. The telephone call came just after seven pm. A man's voice. Three words only: "We've got George." Then he hung up.

'I tried dialling 1471, but the caller's ID was blocked.

'The second call came about the same time the following night. The same voice, but a longer message: "If you want George back, gather a hundred pounds together and I'll call again tomorrow."

'At first I suspected an opportunist, someone attempting to cash in after seeing one of the flyers. After all, it had almost been a week by then. Still, I withdrew some money from my savings account the following day, and when I got home the mail had arrived. Amongst it was an envelope containing George's collar. Nothing else. No return address. Just the collar.

'The third call came just after seven, like the others. The same man asked if I'd received any mail. I said I had, and he said that if I didn't do exactly what he told me, I'd be getting more mail; George's head in a box.' Her voice wavered. She regained control.

'I was to tell no one about the calls or their demands. If I did, I'd never see George alive again.

'He said I'd receive a call tomorrow morning – meaning today – between the hours of seven and twelve. They were watching my house and the street, and if they spotted anything out of the ordinary I'd never hear from them again. "Except via the postman."

'They called around ten-thirty saying they'd be here by eleven, but they were late. I was at my wit's end, thinking they'd seen something untoward in the street and been frightened off, although I'd done exactly as instructed. Then you called. I thought you were one of them. A few of minutes after that, George was returned.'

'How?' Jane asked.

'A man turned up carrying a toolbox. A gas man. I don't have gas, Ms Child. He asked if I had anything for him. I asked if this concerned George and he said, "Is that its name?" I said I wanted to see him before I handed over the money. He said, "You'll either see him in two minutes or in two day's time. Depends how quick the mail is round here."

'So I gave him the envelope. He stood there and checked it, then opened the front of his toolbox. Only it wasn't a toolbox. It was a cat carrier disguised as one. He simply tipped George, closed it and walked away.'

There was a short silence as Jane caught up her notes. 'Was George all right?'

'Yes, he seemed fine. He'd obviously been cared for and wasn't even hungry. He was a little wary and disoriented at first. It took me a minute or so to coax him inside. Shortly after I did so, you arrived.

'To be perfectly honest, I was a little wary and disoriented too. I wasn't expecting visitors. I even wondered if you'd been sent as some sort of test.'

'A test?'

'Then you gave me your card. But I *couldn't* talk to you. They said they were watching the house.'

'But you had George back by then.'

'There's something else. When he tipped George out, just before he walked away, he said, "Keep your mouth shut. We've got our eye on you. We'll be in touch."'

Jane scribbled down the words. 'What do you think he meant by that?'

'It was a threat, clearly. What they've done once ...' Lowella Foote couldn't continue with the thought and changed the subject. 'They said last night they were watching my house. They could be neighbours. Someone in the street.'

Jane thought about the traffic jam and the late delivery. 'When he left, did you see or hear anything in the road?'

'The privet obscures my view. Besides, I was more concerned about getting George inside.'

'Of course.'

Failure to notice the presence of a vehicle didn't rule one out.

'You must have got a good look at the man who dropped him off, this so-called gas man. Can you describe him?'

'Completely unremarkable. Average height, stocky build, one of those American peaked cap things pulled down low. Blue overalls with London Gas on the breast pocket and an ID card on a lanyard round his neck. He had a dark beard and sunglasses so I couldn't really see his face, but it wasn't the man I'd spoken to on the telephone.'

'How do you know that?'

'He didn't know he was called George, for a start. Each call had mentioned him by name, but this man said, "Is that its name?"'

'It wasn't just that, it was his voice. I'm good with voices, Ms Child. Tones, nuances, accents, speech patterns. I spent my entire working life listening to them. I used to be a translator with EU.

'This voice was deeper, a little rougher round the edges; more befitting a gas man. The voice on the phone had an equally

common accent, but there was something in his choice of words
that suggested it was an assumed accent. I was told to "gather a
hundred pounds together" for example, not "get". He asked if I'd
received any mail, not *got* any mail. Slight incongruities, but I had
the impression he was *down-marketing* himself, as they say.'

'But not the delivery man?'

'No. Or perhaps he was just better at it.'

Scribbling furiously, Jane said, 'Thanks for the information.
You've been a huge help, but I need to see how this ties in with
another missing cat I've been working on.' Tibbles McVicar!
'Would be all right if I called you again?'

'Certainly, yes. But no visits, please. Just in case ...'

'Of course. In case they're watching.'

14

A crocodile of schoolchildren wove along the school playground over the back, laughing and calling to each other, two teachers in attendance. Jane watched them from her office window, seeing but not seeing, her heart still racing from Lowella Foote's phone call.

File A0001 was still on her desk. She'd filed it away once the drew it out again. Really, she should reopen the case. Except they didn't have a case. Or, at least, a client.

The cries of the children faded as she turned back to her notebook, found a blank page and started to write.

There were two problems with kidnappings, two areas where the perpetrators were exposed and vulnerable. The first was the initial grab, the second was collecting the payoff. As far as cats were concerned, they were probably using humane traps. Driving out late at night, placing them around the target properties – it had to be a van – and returning at dawn for the collection. Five cats in the immediate area, a hundred quid a pop; not bad for a night's work.

This wasn't a random cat grab. They knew where they were going and who to target, which meant they had a list; a database of some sort. Breeders, cat fanciers, show clubs, perhaps even the RSPCA.

The collection was more interesting. The gas man get-up was clearly a disguise. A baseball cap, sunglasses and stick-on beard would obscure anyone's features, and what could be more natural than a tradesman wandering a residential street carrying a toolbox? Tipping him out at his owner's feet was a smart move too. Both animal and owner would be surprised and disoriented, with the latter too busy trying to coax the loved pet inside to pay much attention to where its abductor went.

But what about that warning? "Keep your mouth shut. We've got our eye on you. We'll be in touch."

Clearly a threat. But also a promise of things to come. *We'll be in touch.* Why? What about? What more could there be? If they were going to catnap George again, they wouldn't give a warning.

She heard a key in the lock and Matt's footfalls on the stairs. Jane closed her notepad and slipped the file in a drawer, looking up a little guiltily as he breezed in carrying a handful of paper bags.

'Have you eaten?' he asked, tossing a handful of paper bags on to the conference table and switching on the kettle. 'Then I've got a treat for you. White bread sarnies, filled rolls, cream cakes and sticky buns. All proper healthy stuff, not like that fruit muck you usually eat.'

'A healthy *and* a balanced diet.'

'Not quite. Missing two major food groups: chips and beer.'

'But you'll make up for that tonight, right?'

He nodded and handed her a ham and cheese roll.

As they ate, he regaled her with his story of posing as a kitchen hand at the Philadelphia Hotel. 'It was a bit of a risk, but I learned more as a bogus temp than I would ever have done as a private detective.'

'So Smith got the coffee from a friend of a friend,' Jane said. 'A female friend, perhaps? One unknown to his wife?'

'Unknown, but who no longer returns his calls, which suggests some sort of falling out. I also had the distinct impression he knows Reg Trivet from the Chesapeake.'

'Would that be so surprising? They're basically in the same business.'

'I doubt Trivet would agree with you, but that may be why he sent his wife to check on their H&V rather than going himself.

'I also realised there's an inconsistency in Melody's story. She said she did a weekend stocktake to confirm it wasn't theft, but

Trivet said she called him back the day after he reported his wife's findings, which means she must have done it on a Tuesday night.'

'Maybe she did a quick check to see if anything was missing and a full check when she got the chance.'

'Seems reasonable.' He finished his sandwich.

'So what's your next move?'

'I thought I might use that dodgy kitchen hand disguise to get hold of some of the actual counterfeits. Swap it for some of the real McCoy. A coffee aficionado like Trivet might be able to identify the source of the beans.'

'Do you think *Le Chat Noir* know they're selling counterfeits?'

'I didn't get a sense of that, no.'

'What if they found out?'

'You mean put some pressure on?'

'It might encourage Smith to give up his friend's friend.'

'A two-pronged approach? I like it.' He studied one of the cream buns. 'It'll also make him keener to swap some stock. But you'll have to do that. I'm known there now.'

'I'll go this afternoon.' She'd been looking for an excuse to slip out. 'After this gourmet health-fest of yours, of course.'

Matt's mobile rang. 'Avery, what the fuck do you want?' he said by way of answering it.

Jane returned to her desk, took out her own phone and transferred the videos she'd shot near Lowella Foote's house on to her computer. The more she thought about it, the more certain she was the catnappers had used a van. She'd go through the footage later – in her own time.

Matt finished his call. 'That was Avery.'

'No, really? I'd never have guessed.'

'He's heading for Islington. Going to be out there most of the afternoon. There's a couple of posh cafes up there I need to check and I've got a printer mate nearby I want to speak to about those coffee bags, so we'll catch up and go straight on from there.'

"Straight on" meant to a meeting with former colleagues. It was a long-standing arrangement; a monthly get-together of old police mates now scattered across various services and various divisions. It was good to keep in touch, he told her, especially in his new line of work.

'You are OK about it, aren't you?'

'Absolutely. Mondays to Fridays are our own time unless something's mutually arranged. It's in the CHA.'

'You can come along if you like.'

'God no! A bunch of old coppers reliving past victories? No thanks.'

'I'll make it up to you tomorrow.'

'I doubt you'll be conscious tomorrow. Especially if you and Avery are meeting up beforehand.'

He grinned and started typing up his notes from the morning. She got to her feet, gathered up her things and gave him a peck on the cheek. 'Right, I'll go and have a chat with *Le Chat*. See you tomorrow.'

'If you give me ten, I'll come with you.'

'I've ... got a spot of shopping to do first.'

'Shopping?' He waved her away. 'God no! I'll stick with old coppers any day.'

Jane smiled. She was hoping he'd say that.

* * *

It was only a short diversion to the Tinchcombe's cul de sac and Tibbles McVicar's golden eyes followed her all the way down. Jane smiled back at him. He was cobby all right. A real teddy bear of a cat. Rounded, chubby cheeked with a lovely silver-blue coat. He only looked away when his master slipped out the front door carrying step stool. Gordon Tinchcombe set it beneath one of the two carriage lamps beside the door.

'Hello,' Jane called from the street.

Tinchcombe turned, saw who it was and said, 'Ah.'

'Problem?' She nodded at the lamp.

'Bulb,' he said, although it looked a bit more than that. There were slivers of broken glass on the path. 'Can I help you, Ms Child?'

'I was just passing. I thought I'd check on Tibbles.' She gestured at the window. 'See if everything was all right.'

'Yes, yes, perfectly fine, as you can see.'

He picked up a shallow cardboard box. Jane saw a brush and pan nearby.

Jane ventured up the path and said quietly, 'Did you have to pay a reward for his return?'

'What?' Tinchcombe coloured. 'I ... I ...'

'A hundred pounds, wasn't it? He wasn't lost, he'd been stolen. Catnapped and held to ransom.'

Tinchcombe said nothing, but he gripped the corner of the box hard enough to crush the cardboard.

'You've been told to keep quiet, haven't you? Did they say they'd be in touch?'

'I ... don't know what you're talking about.' He gripped the box tighter, his hand shaking slightly. 'Go away, Ms Child. Don't bother us again. Please?' There was an element of pleading in his voice and his eyes flicked past her to the empty street. He looked like a frightened man.

Jane said nothing more and walked away. Instead of cutting straight across, she followed the path around the bulb of the cul de sac, acutely aware of her surroundings. The parked cars, the high houses, the quiet gardens. What had he been looking at? Were they still out there, watching?

She took out her mobile phone, the twenty-first-century equivalent to lingering over a cigarette, and took stock of the street while pretending to send a text. There was no one else about, nothing out of the ordinary. A number of vehicles were parked in the road and up driveways, but no vans except for a couple of truck-like four-wheel drives, all unoccupied.

She thought of Lowella Foote's words – *they might be neighbours* – and guessed this was part of their routine. The suggestion that Big Brother was watching would unsettle their victims.

But enough of her hobby project. She put away her phone and headed for the station. She had real work to do.

* * *

'I don't believe this fucking traffic,' Bernard Carpinter said. 'It's only three o'clock!'

'This is the cost of lingering too long over luncheon,' Francis Cricklewood informed him.

'To say nothing of stopping for a spot of target practice.'

'I took out that light fitting with a single shot. After half a bottle of Chablis too. Not bad, eh?'

'Not bad at all.'

Francis gestured at the choked street. 'This is the dreaded school run. Mummies from all over are converging to rescue their offspring from the foul clutches of our foul education system.'

'Little shits. They should bike or walk like we used to. Or her.'

'Ah, the lovely from the pub. Perhaps we should offer her a lift.'

'Why would she bother? She's moving faster than we are. Fucking traffic.'

15

Jane found the lane leading to the rear of the Philadelphia Hotel and recognised Chef Maurice from Matt's description and the stitching on his whites. He was taking a break, leaning against the side of a large red skip and blowing lazy smoke streams from his cigarette. He was a big man, but not intimidating and had a casual, somewhat negligent air. His smooth pale skin made him look younger than he was and only the lines beneath his eyes hinted his true age, which Jane guessed to be about fifty.

'Mr Todd?'

He eyed her casually. 'Who's asking?'

'My name's Jane Child. I'm actually after your business partner, Mr Smith.'

'Afternoon off. Be back around five. What's it about?'

Five o'clock was hours away. Jane made a snap decision. 'I was hoping he could help me find a coffee wholesaler.'

'A coffee wholesaler?'

'In particular, a supplier of Harper and Vine.'

His eyes narrowed. 'Who did you say you were?'

'I'm a private detective.' She handed him her card. 'An *understanding* private detective.'

He studied the card, then her, taking another puff of his cigarette. 'What's that supposed to mean?'

'It means I understand your situation. A new business. An impulse purchase. A locker full of expensive coffee sachets nearing their expiry date. Am I right?'

He stared at her but said nothing.

'Did you know it's counterfeit?'

'*What?*'

'As fake as a false nose.'

'How do you—?'

'It's my job, Mr Todd. But more important to you and your business are the aspects that *aren't* my job. It isn't my job to go running off to the authorities about this. Or alert coffee aficionados. Or even mention it to Harper and Vine themselves. You get my drift?'

Todd said nothing.

'All I want is the name of your supplier.'

'Look, I don't know.' He scratched the back of his head. 'Jon organised it all. I do the kitchens. Back of house stuff. He wanted to steam straight in with the upmarket coffee, get moneyed types in from the get go. I told him that's something you build up to as you go along. Word of mouth. Unless you're got some serious brass to start with. But oh no, that's what Millicent Trivet was planning, and if it was good enough for her ...'

'Millicent Trivet? Any relation to Reg Trivet from the Chesapeake?'

'His missus. Know him, do you?'

'Only by reputation.'

'Look, we subcontracted for the cafe, but we weren't the only ones interested. Apparently, Mrs T just wanted the front bit of the restaurant for a high-class coffee shop. Wasn't interested in the rest. Hotel management wanted the whole package. We put in a bid and got it, but when Jon heard about what she'd proposed, he wanted to give it a crack. All this and heaven too, you know? I told him you need the background and the contacts for that sort of stuff, and it all went quiet for a couple of months. Then this ...' he glanced around and dropped his voice '... Lydia turns up who's got certain contacts.'

'Lydia? She got a surname?'

'I don't know any more than that. Never met her. But she had a pal in the coffee trade who cut Jon a deal. I presume that's who you're after.' He took one last drag, dropped the butt and exhaled a stream of smoke as he stomped it out. 'Look, he had a bit of fling, she ditched him and now we're stuck with a load of overpriced coffee. Counterfeit, from what you're telling me. Jesus!'

'I take it your *other* business partner doesn't know about this Lydia?'

'Jen? Are you joking? She'd have his balls on a silver platter. I'm stuck playing piggy in the middle, covering his arse for all this shit, pretending it's *my* supplier.' He shook his head.

Jane gestured at her card, 'Tell him I called and that I'm looking forward to hearing from him. If I don't, I might lose track of where my job actually begins and ends, and we wouldn't want that, would we?'

* * *

Gerrard Vine drew two hundred pounds from an ATM on St Pancras station and wondered if this was what it felt like to be poor. As he stood in line for a ticket to Paris, he studied the transaction slip with its negative balance and felt a sense of rightness flood through him. The poor were poor because of their own indolence, everyone knew that. If they got off their lazy arses, they too could live like kings, but acceptance of one's lot was an easy trap to slip into. He'd been guilty of it himself. *Mea culpa*, he thought. It was time to correct that.

At the window, he bought a return trip to Paris, paying for it with his company credit card. His train was due to leave at 4.30. He stuffed the useless tickets into a pocket and carried on down the concourse of shops, coffee bars and bureaux de change known as The Arcade to the domestic rail ticket office at the far end. En route, he found a bathroom and slipped into a vacant stall.

He took a crumpled Burberry from his holdall and put it on, along with an equally crumpled fedora, folding the soft felt brim down to shield his face. Back in the bathroom proper, he washed his hands while checking his look in the mirror. When he stepped back out on to the concourse, he assumed the casual pace and swagger of an American tourist while beneath the hat's wide brim, his eyes darted left and right. But no one gave him a second glance.

Another ticket window, another queue. When he reached the grille, shielded by the brim of his hat, he made sure to ask for a ticket to Lye-cester.

'You mean Leicester, mate?'

And Mel thought he couldn't act!

He paid cash and checked his watch. The next train left from Platform Two on the upper level in forty minutes. Plenty of time for an errand and a phone call.

His phone! Christ, he'd forgotten about his phone. They could trace you by that. Idiot! He'd meant to leave it at the office, but picking the damn thing up was as automatic as picking up one's keys. It was still switched on too. If there were ever any questions, if anyone ever checked, they'd be able to follow his progress.

He could just switch it off. But that would seem suspicious in itself. A dead battery ... What, he couldn't locate a charger in the whole of Paris over the course of a whole weekend. No, no, no. No one would believe that.

Oh, Christ! What to do? What to do?

For one panicked moment he thought of abandoning his plan. Then he saw a bunch of youths at the corner table of a takeaway bar. Grimy sorts. Ne'er do wells. Out on the make, most like. He recognised the type from *Crimewatch* and sensed they recognised his type too: gullible tourist.

He bought a Coke and took it to a table nearby, emptying his pockets before sitting down. Newspaper turned to the crossword, pen, phone. He checked the screen then pushed it to one side, taking up the pen, turning slightly and focusing on one across.

He read the clue a dozen times but the words wouldn't go in. His senses were turned outwards, his heart racing. In the end, he ignored the clues and started filling in the blanks with whatever came to mind. His hand moved without conscious thought, then he looked back at what he'd written: MURDER MOST ROTTEN.

The words startled him and he stared down, pen poised, transfixed by them as one of the youths brushed past on the way to the counter. He connected MOST and ROTTEN with SATURN which seemed to take the edge off it, and when he looked up he saw with relief that his phone was gone.

* * *

With twenty minutes still in hand, Gerrard headed out into the bustle of Euston Road. A five-minute walk took him to the outlet of a nationwide sporting goods chain where he bought a spool of fishing line. Back on the street, he bought a five-pound phone card from a corner shop, found a phone box and punched in the number he'd committed to memory.

After an interminable series of rings, it was finally answered. 'Yah?'

'Harvey? Gerrard.'

'Oh, hi Ger.'

'I just wanted to check it's all OK for the weekend.'

'That? Oh yah, yah, sure. What time am I not meeting you?'

'The seven forty-five from St Pancras. And I'm heading back on the four o'clock on Sunday.'

'Right. Let me ... fucking pen. Hold on.' There were rummaging noises followed by some low-level cursing. 'All right, got that.'

'And if anyone asks, we dined at your club tonight, and tomorrow at that little bistro you took me to last time.'

'She's not likely to, is she?'

'No, but just in case.'

'You can rely on me, old man.'

'I owe you one, Harv.'

'You do indeed, and I shan't let you forget it!' He laughed. 'All I can say is, this new bird must be pretty special if you're flicking off old Mel for a weekend tumble.'

Gerrard smiled at his friend's choice of words. 'Yes, she is. Very special.'

16

One of the possibilities on Matt's list was an exclusive wine bar, coffee shop and delicatessen off Holloway Road, but after getting regretful shakes of the head on mention of Harper and Vine, and blank looks of incomprehension from the manager of a private dining club nearby, he decided to visit Brian Laing instead.

Laing was foreman at a large printing company that occupied a converted warehouse near Emirates Stadium. The connection was tenuous. He'd been an apprentice, learning his trade from Matt's father and taking over his role when Gus Healy retired after more than forty years with the same firm. He'd kept in touch with his old mentor and was one of the many mourners after Gus's sudden death at the age of 76. Matt had promised to keep in touch, but somehow ...

He headed for the despatch dock at the side of the building, avoiding the office with its reception desk, glossy brochures and slick sales staff, preferring to find his own way through what he considered familiar territory. He'd grown up with the smells of fresh stock and ink, the thrum of machinery and the orderliness of printing plants.

'Help you, mate?' a middle-aged man in blue overalls asked before directing Matt to a half-glassed cubicle on the far wall.

'Bloody hell, Matt Healy!' Laing sprang to his feet and reached out a hand. 'Come in, come in.'

Matt closed the door, turning the hum of machinery into a low murmur and took a seat in front of a well-ordered desk. Laing had lost none of the awkward, angular features Matt had known since he was a teenager. He still had the lantern jaw with its five o'clock shadow, still had the long sideboards – the rich black hair now touched with tufts of grey – and the big teeth, wide mouth and horsey laugh.

Laing made tea and they spent ten minutes catching up on the minutiae of each others' lives and reminiscing about old times, old friends and Matt's dad. Finally, Matt produced the Kopi Luwak sachet and asked for Brian's professional opinion.

'Metallised film stand-up pouch. They're pretty standard these days. It looks like foil, but that base material's actually plastic. Polyethylene terephthalate; PET for short. The same stuff they make drink bottles out of, just stretched very thin and run through a vapour deposition machine.'

'A what?'

'They heat aluminium till it evaporates and condenses on the cold polymer. Clever stuff. There could be up to seven different layers there before we even ink it.'

'Where's it made?'

'Europe, mostly. Comes in five thousand metre rolls, but you can get smaller quantities.'

'Who around town would have it?'

'Pretty much anyone doing packaging. It's widely available. Not like your dad's day, printing on aluminium foil.'

Matt nodded, a little disappointed. 'Anything else you can tell me about it?'

'It's good material, a quality print job, and the embossing's spot on. Register's perfect. But you probably want to know who did it.'

'That would help, but I couldn't see a printer's mark.'

'Did you check the seams?' Matt nodded. 'Then it's down in the bottom corner. D'you mind?' He produced a scalpel and worked it lightly over the edge where the seam that sealed the bottom of the packet met the seam that ran down the back.

'They're crimped and heat-sealed, but there's a double fold here and you can usually ... unfold it. There you go.' He looked up grinning and turned the packet Matt's way, pointing to a tiny CP inside a circle. 'Cristos Print, Peckham.'

'You're a wizard, Brian.'

'I've been called worse.'

'What would a short run of these things be?'

'That sort of quality, you'd be looking at a thousand, minimum, though your best economies would start about ten thousand plus mark. I can get the office to do you some costings if you'd like.'

'Not necessary, but thanks.'

'So what is it this time, Matt? Murder most foul? Drug smuggling? Gun running?' Laing regarded him expectantly.

'Counterfeiting. Starting with these things.'

Laing pushed the bag back at him. 'If that's a counterfeit, they're bloody good. Right down to the printer's mark? That's impressive!'

* * *

Matt returned the way he'd come, calculating the numbers in his head. If a short run was a thousand bags and each bag contained thirty-five grams of coffee, it would take thirty-five kilos of coffee beans to fill them all. There were eight different varieties in the H&V range, all apparently copied. That equalled eight separate print runs and two hundred and eighty kilos of coffee beans. Even by the short-run numbers, this was a big operation.

So why couldn't he find more of the damn stuff?

He had another cafe to check on the upper reaches of Holloway Road and sought directions from his phone. The shortest walking route was via a dogleg of streets, alleys and lanes that he'd never have found without studying a detailed A-Z, but halfway there he came across a patch of waste ground where, in a layby on the right, he spotted a police constable balling up a line of Do Not Cross tape while another waved in a waiting tow truck. There was a black and white, its lights flashing, parked on the shoulder, and another unmarked car behind it. In a ditch at the edge of the layby, half obscured by scorched scrub, lay another vehicle, on its side and completely burnt out.

As he approached, a voice called, 'There's our man, sergeant. Arrest that villain!'

'Avery! Is this your big north London case? An RTA? Who have you upset?'

'Fuck off, Healy,' Detective Inspector Colin Avery said, then introduced his DS, a young man with bad skin.

'I'm in civvy street now. You can't tell me to fuck off any more.'

'Oh Christ, an MOP. Sorry about that, sir. Would you mind moving along, please?' Then he added quietly, 'Cunt.'

'That's more like it.'

Detective Sergeant Dixon tucked the forensics toolkit he was carrying into the boot of the unmarked car and closed the lid. Matt nodded at the wreck. 'This is a bit mundane for you lot, isn't it? Or have you sorted out all the organised crime since I quit?'

He and Avery had spent eight months together working on a gangland killing, back in the days when the NCA was known as SOCA, the Serious Organised Crime Agency.

'Connections,' Avery said. 'Though there's fuck all to connect down there.'

The tow truck had a steel hawser on the wreck and was winching it from the ditch.

'The cyber boys asked us to look at a computer whiz. Smart kid, except he got knocked off his bike yesterday, so maybe not so smart after all. Died at the scene. A witness gave us that index number.' He nodded at the vehicle as it lurched upright on to blackened wheel rims. 'Stolen, of course, and sod all use to us in that state.'

'What's that got to do with Organised Crime?'

'Suspicious circumstances. The lad's gaff got turned over

shortly after the accident. All they took were SIM cards, USB sticks and hard drives. He had several PCs. All stripped bare.'

'So someone wanted to get hold of what he knew. Or who he knew. Or whatever data he had.'

'Or get rid of it.'

'Hacker, was he?'

'Didn't seem to be.'

'You said he had several machines.'

'Keen gamer, apparently. Could all be perfectly innocent. Bit hard to tell what he was up to without the drives.'

'So what's your angle?'

'Like I said, suspicious circumstances. He worked for a big backup company with a lot of government and corporate contracts. There's no hint of any data breach, but their security people are wetting themselves about what might have been on those drives.'

'They're not going to find out now.'

'That's what I told them, but ...' he rolled his eyes, '... they've got friends in high places. Whoever did the break-in picked the lock. Nice job, very pro. And none of the neighbours saw a thing.'

'No dabs?'

'What d'you think?'

'Sounds like a professional hit followed by a cover-up.'

'Thank you, Sherlock. Hear that, Dicko?' Avery called to his sergeant. 'This MOP-head here's just sorted out our case for us. Whoever said members of the public were useless twats?'

DS Dixon grinned.

The tow truck, the wreck strapped firmly to its deck, pulled away. Avery had a quick word with the uniforms before they followed it up the quiet lane.

'That's it. We'll call that in and call it a day. You got time for a swift half before the festivities begin?'

'Only a half?' Matt turned to Avery's DS. 'Your boss always was a cheap bastard.'

'Who says I'm buying?'

'The prosecution rests,' Matt said.

17

Jane's mobile rang as she reached Charing Cross Road. She didn't recognise the number but ducked into a doorway to take the call.

'Jane Child.'

'Ms Child, my name's Barton Thomas. You left a message yesterday about our missing cat. I'm sorry, I meant to call you earlier, but ... well, it's been one of those weeks.'

Jane recalled the picture she'd taken of the corner shop window and the message she'd left for its owner. 'The Selkirk Rex, wasn't it?'

'Bobby, yes.'

'Any news, Mr Thomas?'

'Yes, he's back with us safe and sound, but ... well, there is a bit of a story attached. I can't go into it now, I have a patient due shortly.'

'I'd love to hear it. And meet Bobby. Could I come to you?'

'Certainly. Sometime at the weekend, perhaps?'

'I'm free this evening.'

He gave her the address.

* * *

Andrej Bilic blinked awake at the sound of knocking. He'd been dozing, elbows on his desk, chin cupped in his hands. The monitor had gone into sleep mode after thirty minutes inactivity, but the music from his iPod dock continued in the background; Parazitii playing *Suge-o*. The detritus of a marathon hacking session lay around him. Discarded takeaway wrappers, empty Red Bull cans, a brimming ashtray and two empty cigarette packets. He pushed himself away from it all, got to his feet and staggered into the hallway, shielding eyes from the uncurtained glare.

Dmitri and Od stood on the bare concrete landing outside Andrej's flat, shuffling casually, keeping an eye on all four sets of doors. There were two flats to a side, east and west, a lift and stairwell on the southern end, and a half-height brick barrier on the northern side that gave way to a fourteenth-floor view of five identical tower blocks nearby. Not seeing so much as a curtain twitch from the other flats, Od knocked again.

Andrej opened the door but kept one foot behind it. He didn't recognise the men. One looked like a nightclub bouncer, standing to one side, his arms crossed, his face a blank slab as expressionless as stone. The other, a tall, rangy African, had his thumbs hooked in the top of his stonewashed jeans.

'Knightmare?' The African asked, giving him a friendly smile. 'With a K?'

'Who ...?' Andrej blinked, scratching his dishevelled hair. Even half-asleep he was cautious.

'It's all right, man. We ain't cops or nothing. Just need your skills to help us out.' He held up his hands and made keyboard-tapping gestures. 'Know what I mean?'

'How do you ...?'

'It's OK, man. Spree gave us your address.'

'He does not know it.' The words slipped out before he could stop himself.

The African gave him a pitying look, then said to his companion, 'Looks like we got our man, Dmitri.'

The big man reached through the door, seized Andrej by the scruff of the neck and forced his way inside. After a further check around the vacant landing, the African followed him in and quietly closed the door.

When it opened again ten minutes later, the African emerged alone, carrying a small holdall. He checked the landing and the stairwell, then summoned the lift. When it arrived, he set the bag between the doors to keep them open and gave a low whistle.

The other two emerged at a run, not that Andrej had much say in the matter. Dmitri held him in a stooped position, one hand gripping the back of his T-shirt, the other gripping the top of his trackpants. All he could see was the heavy fall of a pair of large brown boots.

Instead of turning towards the lift as Andrej expected, they headed in the opposite direction, towards the half-height wall. Dmitri gave his companion a little upward boost just before they reached it, then stopped short and let him go.

He turned back towards the lift, dusting off his hands. Od picked up the holdall and held the doors for him, a hand cupped to one ear. 'Hear that, Dim? Fucker barely even screamed.'

18

Gerrard Vine took a bus from Leicester station then walked the last mile to his aunt's house. He could have got a cab but preferred to keep his visit low-key. The Burberry and fedora were back in his holdall. He was back to playing himself again.

His pace slowed and his footsteps dragged as he neared the gate. Then he thought of the business, thought of Mel and what it would mean to her, and poor old Henry too. He steeled himself.

The house, like his aunt, was ridiculously modest. A two-storey detached place in a quiet country lane, it sat in the middle of a large plot of land with hedgerows separating it from its neighbours. The path from the front gate was crushed white gravel bordered by dianthus, marigolds and two low lines of impeccably clipped box. The lawn either side was so fresh, green and perfectly maintained that it looked more like carpet. He imagined her having a little man around twice a week to vacuum it.

Myra Vine answered the door herself, as he expected. The housekeeper, some Polish prole with an unpronounceable surname, had a half-day on Fridays and the whole weekend off. Bloody foreigners. He worked longer hours than she did and it was his country!

'Gerrard! What are you doing here?' she said, looking past him. 'Where's Melody? You two haven't broken up, have you?'

'No, no, aunty, nothing like that.' Myra Vine looked vaguely disappointed. 'I was in the neighbourhood so thought I'd pop in.'

'Where's your car? Why didn't you park in the drive?'

'Because I'm not driving. I came by train.'

'Train?'

'Yes, I had business in town and thought I'd stop by and say hello. Perhaps even stay over, if that's all right?'

'You should have telephoned. I'd have had Jadzia make up the room and leave something extra for supper. Well, you'd better come in.'

She stood aside and let him into the spacious hallway. He gave her a dutiful peck as he passed.

'Are you sure you haven't broken up?'

'No, no. Mel's got a girls' night tonight and I was up here for a meeting, like I said.' He glanced up at the stairway. Polished oak. Hard wooden treads and risers.

'Are you all right, Gerrard? You look rather pale.'

'Actually, I am feeling a bit squiffy. That's ... partly why I came. Didn't fancy the trip back.'

Myra Vine harrumphed.

'I was planning to call in anyway, honest.'

'I'm sure you were.' She regarded him with a raised eyebrow. 'Squiffy, how?'

'Pardon?'

'Call a doctor, squiffy, or just too much lunch, squiffy?'

'Oh, the latter, I think.'

'What did you have?'

Knowing his aunt's bias against of any kind of shellfish he said, 'It might have been the oysters.'

She harrumphed again. 'Could you stomach tea?'

'That would be splendid, Aunty.'

'Go and sit down. I'll see to it.'

He set down his holdall, unbuttoned his jacket and settled in a leather armchair in the lounge. He wanted to ask for biscuits or cake. He'd eaten nothing since breakfast but a crusty railway pie, but could hardly ask for nibbles after his mythical lunch. Or with his supposedly squiffy stomach.

The room was chintzy, fresh and bright, which rather summed up Myra Vine too. At eighty-six, she had more vim and vigour than many half her age; still danced and played golf regularly, thought nothing of cycling two miles to the nearest shops, and was a prime mover and shaker on more committees and neighbourhood groups than Gerrard could ever hope to recall.

The money helped, of course. Vast stacks of it, if Melody was to be believed, money bins full, though Myra Vine was far too shrewd to leave it just sitting around.

Her elder brother, Thomas, had made it in Malaya. Something to do with railways. Gerrard was hazy on the details, but Melody insisted he'd been looting the Third World. 'And why not?' she'd tell their chums. 'The locals still don't know what to do with what they've got.'

After his sudden demise – again, Gerrard was hazy on the details – though it was possibly at the hands of the lootees, Thomas's estate had been divided equally between his younger brother and sister. The brother, Gerrard's father, was inept with money – a characteristic he passed on to his son – and it was gone within a decade. From then on, Myra had kept the family financially afloat.

She was a confirmed singleton – she loathed the term spinster – and had swung her way through the Swinging Sixties and Seventies amidst rumours of involvement with at least one Beatle and a Rolling Stone. Too slight and skinny to ever be regarded as a looker, her assets were her greatest asset, and she became adept at avoiding any sign of avaricious affection.

Then, at an age where many of her contemporaries were embracing grandchildren, she became a de facto parent herself. A traffic accident claimed her brother, sister-in-law and favourite nephew, leaving her with Gerrard, eleven years old and already too much like his father to be likeable. But family was family; she stood by him and supported him, saw him through private school and on to university. Now he was established in a business of his own in London – and doing well, by all accounts – but she still paid him an allowance, partly to assuage the guilt of her refusal to support him in the business, and partly in the hope that he'd one day shake off the loathsome Melody Harper.

She brought through a tray of tea things, but no biscuits, damn it.

'How's Melody?'

'Splendid, splendid. She sends her regards.'

'I'm sure she does.'

The question had caught him off guard. He'd been preparing for a grilling about who he'd seen in town, but all she said about the matter was to add, 'And business?'

He assured her that was booming too and they sipped their tea in silence for a while.

'And you, aunty? How are you?'

'Perfectly fine,' she said. 'All this "old age" business is a lot of nonsense if you ask me. People decline because they *let* themselves decline, even *think* themselves into it. "Oh, I shouldn't be doing that at my age." What tosh! A fresh challenge is all they need, preferably something physical. You look like you could do with a challenge yourself, Gerrard.'

'Oh, this?' He patted his belly. 'Mel keeps saying I should join a gym. Can never seem to find the time.'

'Still find time for your club though, I expect.'

'The Chesapeake? Yes ... but that's ... you know ... business.'

'I'm sure it is.'

His stomach rumbled as if objecting to being disturbed. Myra Vine affected not to notice. 'You don't need a gym, you know. You could do what I do. I've taken up jogging.'

'Jogging?'

'Half a mile out and back, first thing every morning. Sets one up for the day.'

Gerrard looked appalled and had to check himself from speaking the words she loathed most: *At your age?*

'I push myself a little further each time. I've been toying with the idea of training for a marathon.'

'A marathon?' He almost choked on his tea.

'I've been reading about a chap named Fauja Singh. He ran a marathon in five hours, forty minutes at the age of ninety-two, set five world records in a single day at the age of a hundred, then three days later ran the Toronto marathon in a little over eight hours. They call him the Turbaned Tornado.'

'Indian, is he?'

'What difference does that make?'

'So you think you might—?'

'Run a marathon at a hundred? Why wait that long? A challenge, you see. That's all you need.' She set her cup in its saucer. 'Now, how long are you staying? Just overnight?' He nodded. 'You'll find toiletries and towels in the guest room, and a bathrobe in the en suite. I suppose you can sleep in that. The bed hasn't been aired, but I don't expect that will bother you.

'I shall be up at six for my run. I do my warm-ups on the landing. Don't let me disturb you. Unless, of course, if you want to join me?'

Gerrard took refuge behind his cup and regretfully declined.

* * *

The Thomas's place was semi-detached, one half of two mirror-image houses separated by a privet hedge. A photograph of them with a line drawn between could have been labelled Before and After some unspecified disaster. The house on the left was well maintained, neatly whitewashed, tidily curtained and trimly lawned. The one on the right looked like it had been hit by a dust storm. The lawn was overgrown, the windows and paintwork grimy, and even the near-new BMW X6 parked in the drive appeared to have just crossed the Sahara and been lucky to survive the trip.

Jane had an inkling of the cause of the disaster as she approached the front door, stepping over a litter of brightly coloured toys and hearing squeals and shouts from inside.

The wooden door had a lead-lighted insert. An attractive feature, except that two of the coloured glass panes were missing, replaced with pieces of cardboard.

Jane pressed the bell.

The door was answered by a small blonde girl of about four wearing a string vest and nothing else. She was chewing on something red – it was all round her mouth and chin – and for a moment Jane thought she'd stepped into a movie set of the zombie apocalypse. Other zombies ran back and forth behind the girl, shouting, shrieking, throwing things.

'You must be Jane.' A man in his mid-forties stepped into frame and bustled the mini-zombie away. He had watery eyes, a somewhat bemused expression, and was wearing a very smart suit but no tie. He held out his hand, introduced himself as Barton Thomas, the man she'd spoken to on the phone. He beckoned her in.

'Excuse the mess. I've just got in from work.'

A large friendly face appeared from the kitchen at the other end of the hallway, called hello and waved.

'My wife, Mary.'

Jane waved back.

'And these,' he spread his arms, gesturing at the mass of jumping, running, shouting children all around him, 'are the Mongol hordes, despoiling everything in their path.'

'How many?' Jane asked, trying to keep count.

'Nine. All under twelve. With one more on the way.'

'All yours?'

He nodded and led her to the front room where a small boy was balanced on the back of the sofa while another took potshots at him with a Nerf gun. He shooed them out and closed the door.

Nine kids under twelve! Jane understood his dazed look.

'We're due to move out to the country in a few weeks,' he said. 'We've got a place in Godalming all lined up with a bit more room for the kids. Which is partly why I called you back.'

Only then did she notice the cat sitting on the bookshelf, a perky, bright-eyed, multi-coloured fluff bundle that appeared to be regarding them – as he seemed to regard the rest of the household – as a source of entertainment.

'Is that Bobby?'

Barton Thomas nodded as he gestured her to a seat. 'Got him back yesterday, the day you called. Then last night we had another call about him. Which is really why I phoned you.'

Jane took out her notebook and asked him to start from the beginning.

It was a familiar story, though in Bobby's case it took them a little longer to notice his absence.

'We've had him since we were first married. He's actually a bit of a fossil. Fifteen, would you believe? But cat's don't show their age, do they? Lucky beasts.

'In many ways, we regard him as our first child. And in many ways, he acts like it. He's master of that lot out there; has a positively civilising influence on them at times, although I expect you'll find that hard to credit. So when we received the calls and the request for a reward, we were happy enough to pay it.'

'How much did they ask for?'

'A hundred pounds.'

'No problem with that?' Jane asked, thinking of the hordes outside and the bigger place in Godalming.

He shook his head. Evidently not.

'He was returned on Wednesday. I wasn't here, of course, I was at the practice. Mary will be able to tell you about that bit. But there was another call that evening, just after half-past seven. The same man as before, the same voice.

'The telephone's on the wall to the left of the front door. You might have noticed it as you came in.' Jane recalled a small creature of indeterminate sex swinging from the shelf below it. 'The voice said, "You've got the cat back, but it would be a shame if anything happened to it, wouldn't it?" I was puzzled, I said, "Such as what?" and he said, "Maybe something like this." There was a slight pause then bang! One of the leadlight panes in the front door right behind me shattered. "Or this," he said, and bang! Another one. Before I fully realised what was happening, he said, "So think on," and hung up.

'I'm not the gung-ho type, Ms Child, but that was a threat and there are children in here, for heaven's sake. I charged out that door like I was on fire, and by heavens, if I'd found anyone out there, I wouldn't have been answerable for the consequences.'

He was a slight man, but he bristled at the recollection. Man the Protector, Jane thought. She didn't doubt his words.

'What did you find?'

'Nothing at all. I went straight out – the front garden was empty – and into the street. There was no one around. No movement anywhere. I came back and checked more thoroughly – the back garden, the neighbour's, behind the fence, behind the car and even underneath it – but there was nothing at all.'

'What did you expect to find?'

'Someone with a mobile phone in one hand and a pile of stones in the other.'

'Any cars parked in the street?'

'Of course. But no people.'

'You didn't hear a door slam as you ran out? No one driving off?'

He thought back for a moment then shook his head.

'What did you do then?'

'I called the police. They sauntered round in their own good time. Broken windows don't have a very high priority, apparently. The calls weren't overtly threatening, they said, and they seemed to think the damage was coincidental.

'We'd cleaned up the broken glass by then. It wasn't stones, it was an air rifle. We found a flattened lead pellet amongst the debris. We showed it to the police, but they said it was probably youths taking potshots at the street lights. It was dark by the time they got here, but it wasn't when the shots were fired. The street lights weren't even on.

'It was all very unsatisfactory. Then last night there was another call. No shot out glass this time, and no doubt the police would consider it a coincidence too. Which is why I called you back. I thought perhaps a little publicity ...'

Jane looked up from her notepad, pen poised.

'It was someone selling pet insurance. No overt threats, but I recognised the voice immediately.'

'What exactly did he say?'

'"Good evening, Mr Thomas. I believe we've spoken before. About Bobby." Then he went on about how hard it was to insure a cat of his age, but that there were certain events that you could insure against. He said, "I'm sure you know the sort of thing I mean," which I took to be a reference to the night before. Then he said it would only cost ten pounds a month. "A small price to pay for peace of mind, wouldn't you say?"

'He said he hoped I'd think about it for Bobby's sake, confirmed my email address and said they'd send me directions on how to make payment.

'I considered calling the police back, but there was no direct threat. No demanding money with menaces or whatever they call it. And it's such a trivial amount I doubt they'd be interested.'

'You say he confirmed your email address, meaning he already had it?'

'It's no big secret.' He handed her a business card which identified him as the partner in a firm of opticians.

'And you use this address for all your communications?'

'Business and personal, yes. Have done for years.'

Jane made a note.

'After that demand for regular payment, it occurred to me that this might be some sort of racket. That we might not be the only ones being subjected to it. I certainly don't intend to pay. We're out of here in a few weeks so good luck tracking us down in the wilds of Surrey. But I'm happy for you to feature this in your newspaper. A little publicity might flush them out, or at least highlight other cases. And if there are other cases, it might spur some action from the police.'

'I can confirm there are other cases, Mr Thomas,' Jane said. 'At least two that I know about. But I have a confession to make. I'm afraid I'm here under false pretences. What I told you on the phone was untrue. I'm not actually a reporter, I'm a private detective.'

She handed him her own card.

He studied it a moment, frowned, then said, 'Why, that's absolutely perfect!'

19

Five members of KDM – Kill Death Machine they called themselves – sat in the flickering light of a campfire in the dusty vee of a narrow dry stone gully on the eastern corner of the Badlands. It had been a lucky find. Without it, the Death Winds would have swept them away the week before. Now they'd established a base here, they could safely venture out into the strange desert landscape above, fight off its Sand Snatchers and Toxic Trolls and gather hidden power-ups, ammo and more pieces of the mysterious Artefact.

'C'mon, 'mare. Where the fuck are you?' Sh4d0w, a steroid-muscled dwarf with long red hair and a long red beard, muttered.

'Nothing on IRC,' Nemesis said. 'Just tried him again.'

'Shit, man. We're already one down.'

Barcode sat tapping his Crystal Club on the ground, checking its power-ups for like the fifty-thousandth time.

'Bitch about Spree,' Archangel said at length, her gossamer wings reflecting the flickering firelight.

'Yeah. Fuckin' ass-wipe car cunts. This mission's for him. *When* the 'mare gets in.'

'You heard anything, Bitz?' Archangel asked the half-human beside her. Like Sh4d0w, he too had bulging muscles, but his hair was ragged and cropped short, and his clothing – such as it was – was ripped and torn and showed patches of his pale blue skin.

'Why the fuck should I?' he snapped.

'You are GL. Thought maybe he IM'd or something.'

'Nah,' their group leader relented. 'Like Nem said, nothing.'

The real life Bitz drummed his fingers on his desk and turned to his other monitor. A white cursor blinked against the black background, but the screen remained blank. No instant messages, and the last sign of Knightmare on Internet Relay Chat had been just after ten that morning.

Bitz knew he'd been up to something new. 'mare was always on the prowl. The East European groups were more active and more open than the local ones, but he'd never yet missed an *Artefact X* session.

Until tonight.

Still, Bitz wouldn't have given it a second thought if it hadn't been for the untimely death of Spree earlier in the week, a death the feeds were now reporting as suspicious. The burnt-out wreck of a stolen car believed to have been involved in the incident had been recovered, although the police were remaining tight-lipped.

On the positive side, none of his newsfeed triggers had been tripped, but maybe all that meant was they hadn't yet identified the body.

In the normal run of things, he wouldn't have cared who his KDM teammates were in real life, but after certain business dealings some months before, weaselling out their RL identities had become something of an obsession. Bitz had always been careful in his online dealings, and his daytime job frequently emphasised the subtle data trails left by the unwary. Even guys as good as Knightmare could get over-confident and cocky, and he'd seen too many hackers taken down by their own carelessness.

He'd learned, for example, that Archangel – despite her pixie face and lithe, voluptuous body – was actually a tubby twenty-four year old still living with his mum in Harrowgate, and that he/she'd had cybersex with the over-muscled Sh4d0w in what they laughingly imagined was a private chat room. But he'd saved his most diligent research for Spree and Knightmare, his two companions in what they privately called TBO – The Big One. He knew their names, where they lived and what they did. And if he could track them down, so could others.

Like Barcode checking the power-ups on his Crystal Club, Bitz ran through his checks and perimeter defences yet again. Drawbridges up, moats undisturbed, honeypots untouched. All was well with the world.

So where the fuck was Knightmare?

* * *

Mary Thomas was a bouncy woman of Jamaican descent with a lustrous copper-coloured skin and large, dark brown eyes that seemed perpetually amused. She and her husband exchanged places, taking turns to supervise – if that were possible – the unruly mob outside the lounge.

'How on earth do you cope with nine children under twelve?' Jane asked.

Mary smiled beatifically. 'Most of the time, I don't.' Then she laughed and added, 'But seriously, evenings are the crazy time. Especially Friday evenings when they're allowed to stay up a little later. You wait. In an hour's time, it'll be all quiet on the Western Front and Barty and I will snuggle up in front of the telly.'

Bobby climbed down from the bookcase, padded across the carpet and jumped into her lap.

'I mean Barty, Bobby and I,' she added. 'Eh, baby?'

Jane was still flushed from her new commission. She'd told Barton Thomas everything; of her employment by the Tinchcombes and subsequent dismissal. What she'd learned from Lowella Foote, her suspicions about the men involved and their method of operation, and how it had became a something of a personal crusade after her firm had had to drop the case.

'How about if Mary and I signed up as clients for a week and had you reopen the case? Would that be long enough to track these men down?'

Jane assured him it would, which was rather reckless, but with his new information and copies of the payment emails he'd already forwarded, she was confident of a result.

'Consider it done.' He offered his hand to cement the deal. 'I'll teach those buggers to take potshots at my home. No one intimidates a Thomas.' For a moment, Man the Protector returned and his watery eyes burned with a fierce passion. Then he seemed to step back from the emotion, smiled almost shyly, and called his wife.

'I understand that Mr Thomas took the phone calls, but you took delivery when Bobby was returned,' Jane said. 'Can you tell me how it came about? What you saw, heard, anything that might be relevant.'

'They said it would be sometime Wednesday morning. Turned out it was about ten-thirty. I was just sitting down for a cuppa with Wendy, the day girl who comes in three days a week, when the doorbell went. I answered it and found a man from BT.'

'British Telecom?'

'Well, that's how he was dressed. I think I surprised him. He wasn't expecting a large coloured woman. He took a step back and asked for Mrs Thomas. Must've thought I was the home help.' She laughed.

'Can you describe him?'

'Tall and rangy. Barty's build, but a head and shoulders taller.'

Jane made a note. The gas man had been stocky.

'He was wearing a baseball cap, had a grey beard and kept his head down so I never got a proper look at his face.

'He said he was here about Bobby, and did I have anything for him? I gave him the money, he took it, checked it, then opened his toolbox and Bobby jumped out.

'I was surprised and pleased – it had been almost a week – and before I could really take it all in, the man was gone.'

'Did you see where?'

Mary shrugged. 'Up the street to the right. I didn't really pay much attention. I was just pleased to get this fellow back.' She stroked Bobby under the chin. Bobby closed his eyes and purred.

'He didn't say anything after he released the cat?'

She shook her head.

'No threats?'

'Not till that evening, on the phone.'

'Bobby's a pedigree, isn't he? Do you remember where you got him?'

'Some place down on the south coast. From a breeder. Got his birth certificate and lineage somewhere. A lot more impressive than mine.' She laughed again. 'We used to show him for a while, at least until ...' She gestured over her shoulder to where a loud thumping from the hall suggested a demolition crew had started work. 'He's still registered with the FCF, but we haven't been to a meeting for years.'

'The FCF?'

'The Fancy Cat Fanciers. They sound a bit snooty, but they're a fun group. There's an annual show every year at Earls Court. The kids love it.'

Jane wondered how they managed nine kids at a cat show – especially the horde outside the door – but she made a careful note of the group's name.

'So you're still registered with the FCF? Do you have any contact details for them?'

Mary Thomas gave her a quizzical look.

'I was wondering how the catnappers found Bobby in the first place. They knew your address, your husband's email address, even Bobby's age. All that information will be in a database somewhere so I'm wondering if the FCF is the link.'

'You're quite the detective, Ms Child! I can do better than an address.' She set Bobby aside, got to her feet and rummaged through a pile of magazines on the bookcase. 'Here. There's a couple of pictures missing, Nelly needed them for her scrapbook, but that should tell you all you need.'

The booklet was titled *Purrfection!* and subtitled *The quarterly magazine of the Fancy Cat Fanciers of Great Britain.*

* * *

Bloated bodies in the Thames, a headless corpse in Hackney, a jumper in Dagenham. It was the macabre-stories time of the evening when each of the off-duty officers tried to outdo the others with gruesomeness and its effect on their junior colleagues.

'Bugger must've landed head first. Brains all over the car park,' Bill Brooks told them. 'One of the uniforms lost his lunch, and the sight of that made the other one throw. Bloody amateur hour!'

They laughed and finished their pints. It was a kind of therapy, Matt guessed. These were the only people they could share this sort of thing with and get it off their chests. How could you go home and say you'd spent the afternoon separating bits of a young man's brain from the gravel of a car park?

Avery took orders for another round and rose to do the honours. As he was going, Brooks' DS turned to his boss and said, 'That was a weird one though, wasn't it? That flat?'

'Oh yeah,' Brooks added, 'The guy was some sort of computer nut. PCs everywhere. But get this; they'd all been dismantled. Not a hard drive to be seen. No sign of forced entry, nothing else touched, but it looked like they'd all been nicked.'

Avery returned bearing a tray, surprisingly steady given his state. He set it down and received a ragged cheer for his efforts.

Matt elbowed Brooks and nodded at Avery. 'Tell him what you just told us.'

* * *

Gerrard was having a miserable evening. The only alcohol in the house was a little cooking sherry, his aunt's taste in television ran to tedious costume dramas on BBC-2, and he'd been obliged to claim little appetite at supper even though he could have wolfed down the whole of the chicken quiche on his own. But the Polish prole had made it for her that morning, along with a selection of other tasty delicacies lined up in the pantry, and he realised that helping her consume anything but the merest sliver would leave a clue to his presence since his aunt had the appetite of a bird.

Instead, he chewed on a handful of stale crackers from a forgotten biscuit barrel at the back of the pantry and nearly choked himself on the dry crumbs. He was still red-faced and a little breathless when he carried the tea tray through, but Aunt Myra was absorbed in her programme.

At nine o'clock she switched off – no allowance for him or whether he wanted to watch something else – and announced she was going to bed.

'Are you sure you won't join me for a run in the morning?' she asked wryly.

'Er ... no, thank you.' Gerrard made a grab for the newspaper.

'Then I shall see you at breakfast. Eight o'clock. Good night.'

'Good night, aunty,' he said. Adding a silent, 'And goodbye.'

He sat flicking through the newspaper, staring at the words and pictures, taking nothing in. He read a whole feature on the Middle East situation, line by line, and it all seemed to make perfect sense until he reached the end and realised he couldn't recall a single detail. It felt as if his mind was in a holding pattern, like astronauts on the launchpad; all systems primed and ready, just waiting for the countdown.

Overhead, the sounds of footsteps on floorboards and the banging of doors ceased. A long silence ensued. He let it continue for another half-hour, willing the hands his watch and those on the ticking carriage clock on the mantelpiece to move faster. Time and again he felt for the spool of fishing line in his pocket, seeking reassurance it was still there, grounding himself in the thought of what he had to do.

Finally, at ten o'clock, he took a deep breath, folded the newspaper, placed it on the coffee table angled towards his aunt's chair and stood up, looking carefully around the room.

The tea things were put away, the sofa cushions arranged the way she liked them, and the TV remote sat on the arm of her chair. Apart from his holdall, there was nothing amiss.

He picked it up and headed for the stairs, pausing to turn off the living room light. As an afterthought, he took out his handkerchief and wiped the switch. Not that it would ever come to the place being fingerprinted, of course.

He ascended the polished staircase slowly, keeping to one side to avoid the creaking treads, just as he'd done as a youth. His aunt had always been a light sleeper.

At the top, a single up-lighter illuminated the landing. She'd left it on for him. She was very power conscious – or conservation mad, depending on your perspective – and would be cross if he left it on all night. He could imagine her snapping it off with a snort in the morning, already forming the words she was going to say to him at breakfast. It would make an excellent distraction.

He moved on to the guest room, his former bedroom, now prettified with floral fabrics and Aubrey Beardsley prints, and set his holdall on the bed. The curtains hadn't been drawn. They let in a country twilight fringed with stars. He left them open, left the room lights off, unzipped the holdall and took out a head-torch and a Swiss Army knife. Between them, the up-lighter and the contents of his pocket, he had all he needed.

In the back of his mind a voice said, 'This is Mission Control. All systems go. Commencing countdown ...'

He unspooled a length of fishing line, measuring it with his arms like an angler sizing a fish. Three lengths would be plenty. He snipped it from the spool with the little scissors on the Swiss Army knife then tucked it and spool away.

Clamping the length of line in his teeth, he slipped off his jacket to free up his movements, slipped off his shoes and tiptoed to the bedroom door. The house was so quiet he could hear the ticking of the clock downstairs.

On the landing, he dropped to one knee and glanced up the

passage to his aunt's door. Shut firmly, no sign of a light.

He turned on the head-torch, kept its beam angled down, and focused on his work. After tying one end of the line around the base of the first bannister, he shuffled across to its companion opposite, drew it tight and knotted it.

That was it. Simple. He sat back to check his handiwork.

The line ran across the top of the stairs, three inches off the floor. With the head-torch off it was practically invisible, even up close. In the early morning light, distracted by the up-lighter, she'd never see it.

He sat back on his haunches and plucked at the line like a guitar string, listening to the faint ping it gave. The sound of freedom.

20

Dagenham at dawn looked only slightly more appealing than Dagenham in daylight, and Bitz didn't even get out of his car. He wasn't sure what had dragged him there. Restless frustration after three failed missions with KDM, perhaps, or the squads' continual bleating about the absence of Knightmare.

He knew he wouldn't sleep, still keyed up, still reliving their blunders and cursing their mistakes. Driving helped on nights like this. Something to do with the mechanics of it; they way it occupied the senses and engaged the body. He eschewed automatics, preferring the feel and control of a manual, and drove by the gears, not the brakes. Reading the road and traffic, changing down to slow down, focusing on smooth shifts and maintaining steady motion. He sometimes imagined a glass of water fixed to the dashboard. His job was to prevent its contents from sloshing over the side.

His early morning drives were random. London was at its best, traffic-wise, and he'd pick a route on the fly, driving for the sake of it till weariness finally overtook him. Sometimes he went for miles in a straight line, heading for Brighton or Southend or Oxford. Sometimes he'd drive in a circle, paralleling the sweep of the M25, losing himself in a maze of back streets and half-forgotten boroughs until he could find his way again or was forced to turn on the car's satnav. But this drive hadn't been so random. At least, not consciously.

Knightmare had been on his mind. Not because of his absence from the game – at least, not *just* because of his absence. Spree's accident still played on his mind.

135

Because it had to be an accident. A random, chance event. Couldn't be anything else. And actuarial tables backed him up: the chief cause of death for men aged 18-24 was road accidents. Yet some subliminal disquiet had led him here, driving to an address he shouldn't have, to check on a man he didn't know.

The tower block was one of six, a grimy beige slab identical to its neighbours. Forty years before, council sketches had shown the blocks surrounded by terraced gardens, grassy playgrounds and tall, well-established trees under which smiling, watercolour people walked hand in hand, yet somehow the only part of the artist's impression to finally emerge had been the blocks themselves. Apart from a few scratchy patches of grass, the whole of the surrounding area was tarmac, parked cars and rubbish skips.

He paused opposite the block, counting up fourteen floors, seeing lights on in the corner where Knightmare's flat must be. Typical hacker. Burning the midnight oil. He smiled in relief and was about to head home again when a couple of carousing youths appeared, laughing and tying bandannas of yellow tape around their heads bearing the legend POLICE LINE – DO NOT CROSS. They seemed to have come from the car park round the side. He put his car in gear and swung across the road.

All he found was a fragment of tape still tied to a downpipe, a couple of kicked-over traffic cones and a small posy of flowers lying on the asphalt. Their presence seemed incongruous in all this greyness, and he looked up, counting off the floors again. There were definitely lights in the fourteenth-floor flat. Still, it wouldn't hurt to double-check.

It wasn't till the lift doors opened that he realised his mistake. The fourteenth floor was actually the thirteenth – good old British superstition – so his counting had been one floor out. Flat two was where he guessed it would be, but the lights were off and the door was crisscrossed by more of that yellow tape.

Bitz stayed in the lift and punched the ground floor button till the doors closed and it began descending. The flowers on the bare ground down below, the tape across the door; it didn't take a genius to work out what had happened. He could probably confirm it online when he got home but ... Christ, should he even go home?

Knightmare and Spree both dead. His fellow hackers. One day apart. An apparent accident and an apparent suicide. Two of the three participants in the greatest data heist in history.

Shit!

He returned to his car and sat wondering if he should even be sitting in his car. They might have its registration plate and access to the roadside camera network. There might be a GPS tracker clipped under his bumper, or perhaps he'd been followed. He thought back and thought not. Perhaps they were simply watching Knightmare's building. By stopping there, by going up to his floor, he'd just flagged his own complicity.

Shit!

He fought down a moment of panic and the inclination to flee on foot. This wasn't like the hacking world where you could consider the implications of every move – for hours if necessary – and where things really only really started once you hit the Enter key. Nor was it a game like *Artefact X* where failure would see you respawned to begin again, minus a few hit points or some hard-won treasure. This was RL; real life; fluid, complex and dynamic, where you might never even see your enemy. Or see him coming.

He had to take stock, do a damage assessment. Above all, check his perimeter defences. But he'd been away from home for hours. It would be foolish to go back before he was certain it was safe. He should ditch the car too. But not now. If it wasn't being tracked, abandoning it here might implicate him, and if it was, well, they'd already know he'd come visiting. All he could do was confuse his trail and where he went to next.

* * *

Gerrard didn't think he'd sleep at all. The night was mild and he lay on top of the bed fully dressed, wishing to minimise any evidence of his presence. He'd even placed a bath towel over the pillows to catch any stray hairs or flakes of skin in case of forensics. Not, of course, that it would ever come to that.

At seven minutes past six, there was a faint cry and a surprisingly loud series of thumps from the stairs, but at seven minutes past six, Gerrard had slipped into a state he never thought he'd reach that night. He lay on his back, mouth open, jaw slack, breathing in gargling snores, and continued that way until the sun rose high enough in the uncurtained window to hit him with a handful of golden shafts.

He woke, spluttering. 'Fuck!' He stared at his watch. Twenty past seven. 'Oh fuckity, fuckity, fuck!'

Lurching to his stockinged feet, he raced out to the landing, noticing at once that the up-lighter was off and the tripwire was broken. One curling strand of it glimmered in the morning sunlight. As he reached the head of the stairs, he looked down and saw the form below.

She lay spread-eagled, face down, one arm thrown across her head, quite still, and for a moment Gerrard didn't know what to do. In spite of all his careful planning, he stood staring, almost as still as his aunt, for a full half-minute.

Finally, he drew a breath and turned away.

Using the little scissors on the Swiss Army knife, he snipped at the tied ends of the fishing line and tucked the broken strands into a trouser pocket. Back in the bedroom, he straightened the bedspread, fluffed up the pillows, rolled up the towel he'd rested his head on and stuffed it in his holdall.

As he tied his shoes, he realised his hands were shaking.

'Get a grip, old man,' he told the figure in the mirror.

He slipped on his jacket and paced around the room, making one final check to see it looked undisturbed. There were a few splashes around the sink bench in the en suite. He took out the towel again and gave a final wipe.

Tiptoeing down the stairs – really, who was he going to wake? – he stumbled partway, grabbed at the railing for support and paused, heart pounding in his chest. A pause for breath, a quick flurry with his handkerchief in case of forensics (which would never happen), and he continued down at a more measured pace.

He skirted his fallen aunt, avoiding even a glance at her, checked the kitchen and the lounge one last time, then skirted her again as he made for the back door. It had a Yale lock. The bolt closed quietly behind him.

The ivy-covered gate in the hedge at the bottom of the garden opened on to a walking track. He slipped through, closed the gate and headed towards town, blinking and squinting as he left the dappled shade of a line of elms, his eyes finally adjusting to the sunlit view ahead.

21

Matt groaned as he flushed the toilet, feeling the empty pull of the handle and realising the water was still off. Quietly cursing Jake, Avery, the Metropolitan Police and the entire National Crime Agency, he closed the lid on his misdeeds and went to wash his hands.

'Oh for fuck's sake!'

Why would the tap work if the cistern didn't?

He stared at his face in the mirror, seeing the ruins of the night before reflected back at him.

Christ, what a night.

It had been bigger than he'd planned. He'd meant to ease away about nine o'clock, using Jane as an excuse, but somehow he'd got swept up in festivities and lost track of time. There was a nightclub in there somewhere, and a night bus too, but they were only hazy recollections. What wasn't hazy was Colin Avery's case; two dead computer geeks connected by missing hard drives.

In fact, that was the only connection. One had been a respectable middle-class Computer Science graduate with a good degree and a night shift job at a large data backup company, the other was an unemployed Croatian with a council flat.

Bill Brooks DS was into computers and counted the storage media off on his fingers. 'No hard drives – internal or external – no SSDs, USB sticks or flash drives. They left his phone and camera, just took the memory cards.'

A suicide and an RTA: what was the connection? Was there one? If it hadn't been for last night's drinks no one would have even linked the deaths. But now they had, Matt was intrigued.

He realised with a pang that this was the sort of thing he missed. Real police work. Not chasing counterfeit coffee or missing cats.

Missing cats, for fuck's sake!

His reflection went to shake its head, but the real Matt only got part way before cradling it in both hands. Moving it in any direction, even fractionally, didn't seem a good idea.

Bending his knees so he wouldn't have to bend his neck and further exacerbate the pounding in his head, he went through the cabinet drawers until he found a half-empty packet of paracetamol. He popped two from the silver foil, considered the scale of the devastation, then popped two more and held them in his hand. There was bottled water in the fridge downstairs, but that might as well have been on the moon in terms of accessibility. There was, however, a bottle of cough medicine in the drawer.

Any port in a storm.

He swilled the pills and cough mixture back, swallowing with difficulty, fighting off the urge to make a second dash at the toilet. Somehow, the absence of a flush added to the imperative to keep the vile combination down, and when it stayed there, and when the world had reduced its unnatural rocking spin to something more manageable, Matt breathed a heavy sigh and staggered back to bed.

* * *

'What time do you call this?' Bernard Carpinter scowled at the figure at the door. 'It's the crack of Saturday!'

Ernest Cricklewood tried for nonchalance. 'I was in the neighbourhood so I thought I'd see if you and Uncle F fancied a spot of brunch.'

'Brunch? Bit fucking early, isn't it?'

'Breakfast then. On me,' Ernest added, knowing Bernard had a weak spot in his wallet.

'Well, you'd better come in. Francis is in the shower. Coffee?'

'No, I'm good thanks.' Ernest knew that Bernard's idea of coffee came granulated in a Tesco's jar and was best avoided.

'So, how's the computer business?' Bernard asked for the sake of something to say while busying himself in the kitchen and wishing Francis would get a move on.

'Booming.' Ernest took a seat at the breakfast bar and slumped on his elbows. He'd managed to grab a few hours sleep in his car, but its overall absence was starting to catch up with him. 'Maybe I will have a coffee after all. Make it two spoonfuls. And two sugars, please.'

Bernard arched an eyebrow. *Two* spoonfuls of coffee? Typical! If the little prick was going to spring for breakfast, he'd make sure it was somewhere flash.

'So ... how's your business? I mean, you and Uncle F's?' Ernest said.

An offer of brunch *and* civilised conversation? What the fuck was this?

'I take it you mean ...' Bernard nodded at the laptop on the breakfast bar.

'Yeah.' A noncommittal shrug. 'Mind if I ...?'

'Go ahead.' Bernard set the young man's coffee down beside him. 'You set the thing up.'

Ernest opened the laptop and within seconds his fingers were flying over the keys.

Bernard watched him, seeing him slip away. It was almost a tangible thing, the way his attention shifted into that world beyond the screen, blocking out everything else. Good job too. He wouldn't have to talk to the little prick.

'I'm just going to get dressed,' he said, but the little prick didn't respond.

* * *

The copy of *Purrfection!* lay on Jane's bedside table. She took it up and carried it through to the office, settling at her desk with a cup of tea and a bowl of breakfast cereal. Despite what she'd told Sally about the office door remaining closed on the weekends, she couldn't resist. She'd slept poorly, her mind revolving around the re-opened case and the new information she'd gleaned from the Barton and Mary Thomas. At the very least she should type it up while it was still fresh in her mind.

Bluebelle joined her, taking particular interest in the empty cereal bowl, lapping at the last traces of milk with an expression of intense concentration while Jane dashed off an email to the chairperson of the Fancy Cat Fanciers of Great Britain then sat back, drumming her fingers on the desktop, wondering what else she could do.

'Oh Bluebelle,' said mildly, seeing the cat finish up and commence cleaning its paws. 'I don't want you becoming a plate licker. That's doggy behaviour.'

Bluebelle regarded her inscrutably and blinked.

'Still, I'm hardly a role model, am I? Coming into work in my PJs.' She glanced at the clock on her desktop. 'Oh god, I'm supposed to be at Matt's at ten.' She shut off the computer, patted the cat and dived for the shower.

Half an hour later, heading for the Tube station, she saw Gordon Tinchcombe through the window of the Post Office, queuing. A Saturday morning queue. He was near the back.

On a whim, she turned back, heading in the opposite direction.

She called Matt on his mobile and left a message saying she'd be a little late.

Tibbles McVicar watched her from his window, saw her come up the path and knock at his front door.

'Who is it?'

'Jane Child,' she called back.

The door was unlocked and opened a fraction, Patricia Tinchcombe visible through the gap.

'I was going to say I was passing and just popped in,' Jane

said, 'but that's not true. I saw your husband at the Post Office and thought it might be a good time to call so we could chat, woman to woman.'

'About what? I really have nothing to—'

'I was curious about Tibbles' return. Was it a gas man or a BT engineer who brought him back?'

The woman's eyes showed a flicker of surprise. She hesitated a moment then wheeled backwards, opening the door wider. 'You'd better come in.'

Jane followed her into a front room filled with polished furniture and portraits of children and grandchildren. She noticed the spines of several copies of *Purrfection!* slotted into a bookcase as she took a wingback chair by the window. Tibbles McVicar's regarded her impassively. She rubbed his ears and he accepted the obeisance with a benign look, arched and stretched, then jumped down and padded to his food dish in the kitchen.

'He's magnificent,' Jane said. 'Very stately.'

'Don't be fooled,' Patricia Tinchcombe said. 'He can be quite an ass. We've had to put a catch on the refrigerator because he learned to paw it open, and you should see him after supper, racing around like a kitten, batting ping pong balls about and playing chase with Gordy.'

'The evening crazies, eh? Mine's the same.'

'It's not just Tibbles, it's Gordy too. The pair of them are like children.'

Jane smiled at the thought of portly Gordon Tinchcombe, racing around like a kitten and pawing at the fridge.

'You must be pleased to have him back.'

'It's a great relief. They're very loyal, British Shorthairs, and I'm sure he thinks it's *his* house and we're *his* pets. He's aware of my condition too.' She gestured at her wheelchair. 'If I go out the back when Gordy's out, he struts around me like a bodyguard. It's very amusing.'

Jane took out her notebook. 'Can you tell me about the phone calls and his return, please?'

'Gordy took most of the calls. He wouldn't tell me at first. He thought it was someone playing a prank. Then an envelope arrived addressed to me. There was nothing in it, just a piece of paper with a clipping of fur stuck to it with tape.'

'Cat fur?'

'They clipped some from his back. That bald patch by the base of his tail. There was no doubt it was him. That smoky blue colour is very distinctive.

'There was another call that evening. Gordy withdrew some money the next day, put it in an envelope by the door, and late that afternoon a gas man called, just as you said.'

Her description was the same as Lowella Foote's; blue overalls, average height, average build, sunglasses, beard and peaked cap. He delivered a similar warning too: "You'd better look after him. Nasty things can happen to cats in quiet streets."

Jane made a note and glanced out the window at the view of the cul de sac and a handful of parked cars. 'How was he delivered? Did you see a vehicle?'

Patricia Tinchcombe shook her head. 'He must have parked around the corner.'

'Have you heard from them since?'

Patricia Tinchcombe pursed her lips and looked away.

'You have, haven't you? Was it the broken lamp?'

She looked up, startled. 'How on earth did you—?'

'I saw your husband with a ladder yesterday. He said it was a blown bulb, but there were shards of glass on the path and he had a brush and pan. Bulbs just stop working, they don't explode. My guess is it had been shot out, along with its glass surround. An air rifle pellet. A warning. Tibbles likes to sit in the front window, doesn't he? If they can shatter a carriage lamp, they can certainly hit him through plate glass.'

Patricia Tinchcombe swallowed.

'How do you think they got him in the first place? Does he

stray? Would he have gone to a stranger, let them pick him up?'

'You think he was taken deliberately?'

'Yes, because he's not the only one. I know of at least two more in the area. Someone's either very patient and very good with cats, or is trapping them. Or possibly even shooting them with tranquillizer darts.'

Patricia Tinchcombe went pale. 'There was another call shortly after we heard the lamp go. They said it would cost ten pounds a month to keep him safe. Insurance. To be paid by automatic payment. He gave my husband the details. That's where he is now, setting it up.'

'You don't happen to have a copy of the account number?'

'He scribbled it on the pad by the phone and took it with him.'

Jane got up, went to the hall and checked. Gordon Tinchcombe had a heavy hand. There was a clear impression on the page beneath.

'May I ...?'

Patricia Tinchcombe nodded. Jane tore it off, folded it carefully and tucked it into her notebook.

'After you heard the lamp go, did you see anything unusual in the street? Anyone moving about? Anything suspicious?'

'I was upstairs at the time. I heard a tinkling sound and looked out.' She frowned, trying to recall. 'There was a small blue van I hadn't seen before. It drove off from outside number twelve.'

Jane went to the window. A van parked there would have a clear line of sight from its rear doors.

'You don't think ...?'

'I don't know,' Jane said, 'but it's a strong possibility that's where they were shooting from.'

22

Jane raced home in a state of high excitement, bounding upstairs to the office. Matt had told her about times like this. A breakthrough after days, weeks, sometimes months of patient work. The feeling of things falling into place, of real leads emerging, of a sudden expansion in the web of possibilities while at the same time narrowing them down as they closed in on a target.

She took the pad page from her notebook and studied the impression of Gordon Tinchcombe's handwriting. The classic way to reveal a palimpsest was to lightly graze the surface with a soft pencil lead. There were probably more reliable forensic ways to do it these days, but there was no need of them either. Simply angling it to the light was all that was required. Details of the payee's name were muddled with previous page impressions, but the account number was perfectly clear. Like he'd gone over it twice.

Jane reached for the phone. It was answered after two rings. 'Alistair, you *are* at work!'

'Where else would I be on a Saturday fucking morning?' Alistair Downley growled. 'After all, I have no fucking life, not after I sold my soul to the fucking bank.'

This was something she didn't miss. Although employment contracts spoke of thirty-seven-and-a-half hours per week, they also mentioned longer hours "as and when required". Voluntary, of course, but the pressure was there. Want to keep up? Want to get ahead? And look, all your colleagues are doing extra. You wouldn't want to let them down ...

'At least you're happy in your work.' Jane grinned.

'Have you just called to gloat?' He dropped his voice. 'At least you saved me from a fate worse than Barry.'

'You mean another fascinating discourse from Roger Roger?'

'Ten-four.'

'What?'

'Roger roger, ten-four ... It's trucker slang, darling. Didn't think you'd understand. You obviously move in more refined circles.'

'Not that refined, Alistair. I talk to you.'

'*Ka-pow!*' He laughed. 'There, you've gone cheered me up despite myself. Oh, do come back and work with us, Jane. I miss our cheeky banter and your outright bloody rudeness.'

'*Ka-pow* back.' Jane laughed.

'I take it this isn't a social call,' he said.

'Why do you say that?'

'The mere fact that you called me here first, not on my mobile.'

'You should be a detective, you know.'

'I should be anything but in this bloody job. Go on darling, hit me.'

'I've got an IBAN. I wondered if you could tell me who it belongs to.'

She read out the twenty-two digit alphanumeric code as Alistair typed it into his computer.

'It's one of ours. Douglas, on the Isle of Mann. PetSure Insurance Inc.'

'Can you tell me any more?'

'*A-hem!*' He made a show of clearing his throat. 'Whatever happened to customer confidentiality? Anyway, I couldn't even if I wanted to. IOM's on a different system. You know what the Manx are like.'

'No tails?'

'And no telling tales.'

'That's all right. Now I've got a name, I can do a company search.' She was already on her keyboard. 'Huh! Did you know they charge two quid for a copy of the COI?'

'Save your coppers,' he said quietly. 'I'm not on IOM, but I know someone who is. And he's currently on the other side of the floor, boring for England.'

There was a faint squeak, indicating he'd kicked his chair across the cubicle.

'Alistair, there's really no need—'

'Too late, darling, I'm on. Here we go ... It's a Bermuda-based holding company registered to a firm of Manx lawyers. That's all you'd get on your Certificate of Incorporation, but let's see what Amil-Catfuck has to say about it ...'

Amil-Catfuck was Alistair's colourful name for the bank's Anti-Money Laundering and Counter-Terrorist Financing system – AML-CTF for short. As an associate of the Wolfsberg Group of International Financial Institutions, Bartley's bank maintained an internal and highly confidential database of the actual names and addresses associated with all holding companies. It was something even most of their staff weren't aware of.

'Here we go ... Got a pen and paper? The actual directors are a couple of local lads from down your way.' He rattled off two names and a single address.

'Cricklewood and Carpinter?' Jane repeated. 'Why do those names sound familiar?'

'Oh-oh, the bore returneth.' There was a quick tapping of keys followed by another squeak of wheels. 'And ... back to home base now.'

'Oh my god, I'll get you fired, Alistair!'

'I should be so lucky. Anyway, if anyone checks, the info req didn't come from my machine.' He chuckled. 'I was going to say don't use that in court, but on second thoughts ...'

Jane laughed. 'You evil man!'

'Well, I saved you a couple of quid.'

'*And* a lot of pointless running around. I'd never have got their real names out of a firm of lawyers. You're priceless, Alistair.'

'I know it, you know it, so what the fuck am I doing here on a Saturday morning?' A voice sounded in the background. He added, 'Sorry, darling, I'm going to have to dash. My cube-mate needs some guidance.'

'Good luck!'

'And fuck you too,' he said, with a smile in his voice.

* * *

Jane studied the address. *Ka-pow!* all right. Another piece of the puzzle slotted into place. A large one. Suspects!

She checked the address online. Street View showed a slate grey four-storey apartment block with a gated ramp leading to an underground car park. The aerial view showed a rectangle of walk-through greenery at the back, a faux garden that serviced half a dozen similar blocks. 2B, like all the other apartments in the building, had a shoebox-sized balcony with a view of the street and the apartment blocks opposite.

Rotherhithe. A few miles away. Only a slight diversion on her way to Matt's.

She called him again and got an answer this time, although it was more of a croaky groan.

'Are you all right?'

'Self-inflicted wounds.'

'Last night?'

'Mmm.'

'I'm running a bit late.'

'Take your time. In fact, why not make it this afternoon? One o'clock? Actually, two might be better.'

'You *are* in a bad way. Can I bring you anything?'

A long pause. 'Drugs. Bring me drugs.'

* * *

High Down prison's weekend visiting hours were from two till four. Melody had booked her visit online the night before and now sat in the car park, drumming her fingers on the steering wheel. The dashboard clock showed 1:59, and of course, being a bunch of officious pigs, they wouldn't unlock the gate until the dot of two. There was already a small crowd gathered outside. Wives, friends, parents, children. All studiously avoiding each other's eyes, as if the guilt of those inside had brushed off on them.

She waited till three minutes past, till the stragglers had ambled through and she could go unobserved.

'Mel! You needn't have come.' Henry Baxter tried to push himself up in bed but gasped at the pain from his neck.

'Of course I did, Papa.' She bent and kissed his cheek, then brushed back a tangle of his thinning hair. 'Look at the state of you!'

'Oh, it's not so bad. Mainly my neck. Turning, looking up and down. But that'll come right with a bit of physio.'

She took his hand, squeezed it, then said quietly, 'Was it them again?'

He bit his lip and tried to nod.

'How much this time?'

'A lot.' She could see the fear in his eyes. 'Two hundred thou,' he whispered.

'*What?*' The word came out too loud. Others in the infirmary looked their way, Melody dropped her voice and repeated, '*Two hundred thousand pounds?*'

'Ten percent, they said. Like a tax.'

'Jesus.'

'I'm good for it, you know that, but there's no way I can access that sort of cash from here. Even afterwards, even when I'm out, I'm going to have to be careful. They'll keep a watch. It could take years yet. And there's all those regulations now too. All that anti-money laundering stuff. Move that sort of sum anywhere and you're begging to get noticed.'

'You have told them that?'

'I've tried, but it's like talking to baboons. They don't understand the subtleties.'

Melody said nothing.

'Still, look on the bright side. They're not going to kill me, are they? Not the goose that lays the golden eggs. At least they understand that much.'

'But how far are they prepared to go? Your neck, for example. What if you'd broken it? What if you were lying here now, paralysed?'

'I couldn't sign anything over to them then, could I?' He tried to chuckle but winced instead, which rather dented his attempt at levity.

'We'll sort this,' Melody told him, 'but they have to understand that this it. This is the end. They get this and no more. Ever.'

'But Mel, you can't possibly—'

'Can't I?' She smiled. 'Actually, I've got a little man working on something for me as we speak.'

23

Ernest Cricklewood disliked his name. His surname because of its inevitable association with the once-popular comedy programme *Crick & Carp*, and his Christian name because of its association with dour sincerity and solemn preachers. Then there was the old joke that had followed him from school to school: Should a married couple be frank and earnest, or should one of them be a woman? Still, its diminutives were worse. Who wanted to be called Ernie with its Sesame Street associations? Or Ern? A varsity wit had once called him Ode-on-a-Grecian, which, all things considered, was preferable to the alternatives.

'Ernie's here,' Bernard Carpinter called when his uncle finally emerged from the shower.

Everyone called him Ernest except Carpinter, probably because he knew the diminutive was an irritant. At least, everyone in RL called him Ernest.

'Ernest!' Francis Cricklewood said, emerging from a cloud of steam. 'What are you doing here? Is everything all right?'

'Yeah, fine.'

And it was too. A preliminary check of his defences showed he was still secure.

Francis gave him a searching look.

'No, really.'

'It's just that ... seeing you here so early on a Saturday morning, I thought ... well, Bernard and I are new to all this hacking business.'

Ernest smiled. Accessing a local copy of a three-month-old database hardly qualified as hacking, even if the data on it wasn't yours.

Guessing he'd have to have some excuse, he'd come prepared. 'Actually, Cathy and I broke up last night.' The real break-up had been weeks before, but there was no way his uncle would know that. 'I've been driving around, thinking about things. Couldn't sleep.'

'Oh, I am sorry.' Francis seemed genuinely sorry, but you could never really tell with actors.

'He's come to take us to brunch,' Bernard called, heading from his bedroom to the bathroom. 'I thought perhaps that new place overlooking Greenland Dock.'

'Whatever.' Ernest gestured at the laptop. 'How's the business going?'

'Good. We're establishing a nice little base. And that lawyer you recommended has been brilliant. We're now a corporation or something with an office in Bermuda.' Francis laughed.

'It's never going to make you rich, but it could provide a steady income.'

'That's what I keep telling Bernard. There's almost seven hundred names on that list. If we just sign up a hundred of them, that's a thousand quid a month plus ten grand in finders' fees.' He leaned forward confidentially. 'I know Bernard doesn't show it, but we both appreciate what you've done for us. If there's ever anything we can do in return ...'

'Actually Francis, now you mention it. Would you mind if I hung around here for the day? I'll go home this evening, but Cathy wants some time to clear her stuff out and ... well, I just want to leave her to it.'

'Certainly! No problem at all. Stay as long as you like.'

'Thanks, unc. You're a champ.' Ernest gave him a broad smile thinking that perhaps acting ran in the Cricklewood family.

* * *

Jane had time to kill before she was due at Matt's. She did her laundry, made some lunch and ate it in front of the computer while she went through the videos she'd taken the day before. Patricia Tinchcombe's description of the van she'd seen driving away after the carriage lamp had been broken wasn't much to go on, but it was a start.

A small blue van. There were three possibilities. Two, really, because one of them was a hulking great Ford Transit. Of the remainder, one had a personalised number plate and signwriting on its bonnet for a Camberwell florist – altogether too memorable for such a purpose, especially as its rear doors were probably sign-written too – but the other was perfect. A Peugeot. Small, dark blue, and anonymous.

Jane made a note of each of the plate numbers, highlighting the last, which had been parked outside a pub. If the van's plates matched up with the directors of PetSure Insurance, she was well on the way to tying up the case. But there were still gaps. If, as she suspected, they were working from the FCF database, how were they accessing it?

Targeting pedigree breeds was a smart move. Owners who forked out hundreds for a pet were more likely to pay a ransom for its return *and* a tenner a month for bogus insurance, but how were they catching the animals in the first place?

She'd suggested tranquillizer darts to Patricia Tinchcombe, but that was hardly practical. Even if you could get hold of a gun and the necessary drugs, it would require a lot of time and patience. Getting into position, waiting for your target to appear, then retrieving it, all without being seen. Because if you were seen, someone lurking with a gun would trigger a full-scale police alert.

She thought of the cage disguised as a toolbox used to return Tibbles and George. That made more sense. Baited traps, humane ones, perhaps even camouflaged or disguised.

Cats were largely creatures of the night. Curious ones too. You could easily set a dozen traps in a dozen different locations, go home for the evening, then return in the early hours and see what you'd caught. Working from a database would make it easier. You could sort it by suburb and clear out an area in a few days, which seemed to be what they were doing.

That led to another consideration: storage. Where were they keeping them while their owners worried and put up Missing Cat flyers?

They weren't likely to keep them in their flat. Shuttling back and forth with cages of cats would soon attract attention, so perhaps a garage or a lock-up. Somewhere quiet. Somewhere the mewing of unhappy cats wouldn't be noticed.

The doorbell rang. Jane raced downstairs to find a courier with two small cartons for Bluebelle Investigations. She signed for them, carried them back up and tore one open.

Advertising flyers for the business. She pulled out a bundle and flicked through them, breathing in the fresh-printed smell. They were the size of bank notes – something people could easily slip into a wallet or a pocket – and showed pictures of her and Matt looking serious and professional with a bullet-pointed outline of their services. There was a logo at the bottom, a profile of Bluebelle, just a few lines but somehow the graphic designer had caught the essence of the cat.

She took one out, checked it for spelling mistakes and typos, then held it out to show to Bluebelle. 'That's you there, and there's your name, look.'

Bluebelle sniffed at it then rubbed around Jane's hand.

'If I make you up some saddlebags, you could trot around the streets delivering them for us. What do you think of that?'

Bluebelle yawned mightily.

'It was only a suggestion.'

Actually, she could do a little marketing on her way to Matt's. Rotherhithe was part of their catchment area, and she could check out her prime suspects from the street.

24

Fesahaye Odman leaned back in his seat and watched the big Russian return to the hotel, raising an eyebrow by way of enquiry. Dmitri shook his head.

'You mean we got the weekend off?'

'I am to call back in three hours.'

Od looked past him to the public phone box across the road. 'Ain't you dudes ever heard of mobiles?'

'To ask this question means you are too stupid for the answer.'

'Whatever, man.' Od clapped his hands. 'Let's eat!'

They moved from the lobby to the dining room where a waitress directed them to a small table near the window. Seated behind it, Dmitri's bulk made him look like a child in a wendy house.

'That's all they said? Call back?'

Dmitri regarded the rangy black man coolly.

'The magic phone to the secret people?' He gestured across the road.

Od wasn't stupid. He wouldn't have been hired as local liaison if he was. But he was too gregarious for Dmitri's taste. In this business there were things one observed but didn't mention. Most things, in fact.

Dmitri signalled to the waitress and ordered the big breakfast, forcing Od to make a hasty choice of his own. 'And coffee. Large pot.'

They watched her leave.

'So, your first weekend in old London town, huh? What you wanna do, Dim?'

'Do not call me that. I am Dmitri Olegovich Podvyshenskaya.'

'Fuck, man, you got more syllables than a haiku.'

'Then you will call me Dmitri. I know the implications of the word you use.'

'What implications, man? Who cares anyway? Everybody calls me Od. I don't care.'

The waitress delivered the coffee. Dmitri poured.

'Your people hired me for a week so I'm guessin' it could take that long to find this other dude. That means you an' me got time to fill, so how you wanna fill it? Like, what d'you do on your days off, man?'

'There is hunting near London?'

'Hunting? Fuck, man, you sure like killing things.'

Dmitri stiffened and glared then glanced around the near-empty dining room.

'Relax man, I'm joshing with you! Ain't no hunting round here. No bears or shit like that. Maybe a little clay pigeon shooting.'

'Pigeon?'

'Not the flap-flap kind. They're ... I dunno ... little plates or something. They shoot 'em into the air and you shoot 'em down.'

Dmitri snorted. 'Target practice. Not needed. I am professional.'

'So ... after hunting, how d'you like to chill?'

The waitress passed their table. Dmitri let his eyes linger.

Od grinned. 'Now you're talking my language, Dim. I mean, Dmitri.'

* * *

Matt's place was four miles away. A diversion through Rotherhithe would add two more but there were no hills involved so the whole run would only take about an hour. Add another half-hour for stops and she'd be there by two. Perfect!

Jane had worked out a route via community centres, libraries, supermarkets and shopping malls – anywhere she could leave a few flyers or pin one to a noticeboard. After topping up Bluebelle's food and water bowls, she headed out.

Her runner's pack contained little more than a bundle of flyers. She had some decorating clothes at Matt's place – an old pair of slacks and blouse, worn but clean – and she'd shower and change when she got there.

The day was clear and bright and she took the first half mile at a steady pace, warming up and getting into her stride. Normally she didn't like stopping and starting on a run, but this was different. Technically it was work, but how many people got to combine their work with exercise and enjoyment? By the time she reached Rotherhithe, half her flyers had been placed.

Turning into Tempest Lane, she found a street lined with laundromats, takeaway bars, off-licenses and empty shops. The buildings had an air of neglect. Some windows were boarded up and graffitied. One neatly sprayed message read "Soon to be picturesque."

Partway along – past an area of demolition followed by another of construction – the atmosphere changed. The shops and people looked a little sharper, a little brighter, and the buildings looked considerably newer. Dirty brick gave way to concrete slab. Waste ground to mowed grass. Then the shops petered out altogether and Jane found herself in an area of medium- and low-rise apartment blocks.

Number 264 stood on a corner. Apartment 2B was on the second floor, a north-facing unit with a pocket-handkerchief balcony and French doors open to the afternoon sun. Jane glanced up as a stocky, nondescript man came out carrying a newspaper.

She paused, adjusting the straps of her pack and retied one of her shoelaces, studying him from the corner of her eye. He was joined by a taller man with a long face and dark sideboards. It was them all right, Cricklewood and Carpinter. The names had seemed familiar so she'd looked them up on the internet and found references to a BBC comedy cancelled after a poor second series. Actors. That explained the disguises and the put-on accents Lowella Foote's trained ear had detected.

She straightened, stretched and let her gaze slide over them. Target sighted! A thrill ran through her. Then she turned and ran on.

* * *

Bernard was delighted with brunch. It had been ridiculously trendy and ridiculously expensive, with a breezy view of Greenland Dock and all points east. They'd had to go in the van because the little prick had parked his car on double-yellows and had it towed. He didn't seem bothered about it. He didn't even mind squatting in the back of the van. If the idiot boy could wave off two hundred quid in fines and towing fees and another hundred for breakfast for the three of them, he had too much money to begin with, Bernard thought.

They returned, replete, swung into the underground car park and headed up to the apartment. There really was no such thing as a free lunch though; the idiot boy was with them for the day, apparently. Still, at least he didn't require much in the way of entertainment. Point him at the laptop and he'd play for hours.

'Thank you, Ernest. That was splendid,' Francis said.

'Yeah, thanks Ernie. Top nosh.' Bernard gave him a thumbs-up and retreated to the balcony carrying the *Daily Mail*.

'You're welcome, guys.'

For his part, Ernest was pleased to see his car gone. He was wary, despite the preliminary check that showed his perimeter defences were secure. None of his tripwires had been tripped or his honeypots touched but a detailed examination would take several hours, and anyone good enough to track down Spree and Knightmare might be smart enough to slip through and close the door behind them. What's more, he might have given himself away by driving to Knightmare's place and going up to his flat. That had been stupid. If the building was being watched, there was now a circumstantial link, but one that should lead nowhere. If, on the off chance, they did track his car, they'd follow it first to an illegal park miles from his real abode, then to a pound where it could sit, for weeks if necessary, until he was certain he was safe. He might even call the police and say it had been stolen.

'Oi, Francis.' Bernard's voice from the balcony. A low but penetrating whisper. 'Quick. Come here a minute.'

Francis went.

A murmur of low voices, then Bernard again. 'Twice is a coincidence. Three times ... that's something else.'

'You think she's stalking us?' A chuckle.

'I think she's spying on us. Fuck, look out! ... Did you see that? She looked right up here.'

'That little lovely can stalk me any day she likes.'

Something in Bernard's tone reached through Ernest's intense concentration. The initial urgency, the surprise, then the concern, followed by the words "spying on us". He abandoned the laptop and joined them on the balcony.

'What is it? What's going on.'

'Bernard's getting paranoid.'

'Being paranoid doesn't mean they're *not* out to fuck you over.'

Francis nodded at Jane's retreating form. 'We've seen that lovely a couple of times before.'

'A couple of times in the *last twenty-four hours*,' Bernard said. 'Taking pictures outside a pub right after we'd made a drop-off, then in the street right after Deadeye Dick here had fired a couple of warning shots. Now she's outside our gaff, checking the place out.'

'Oh, she wasn't checking—'

'But you don't know who she is or what she's up to?' Ernest

said.

'No, but—'

'Bernard's right. You need to be careful. We should check her out.'

Bernard looked round in surprise. The little prick was backing him up!

'How on earth can we—?'

'The van. Catch her up and drop me off. I'll follow her. She won't know me. Have you got an old pair of trackies or something? I can get changed in the back.'

25

The absurdity of the situation only struck Gerrard when he was on the train to Great Yarmouth. Till then he'd been so focused on making a clean getaway that he hadn't thought things through.

What the devil was he doing? Why was he sneaking around like this? What could have been more natural than a regular visit to his only living relative? She might have tripped on the stairs during such a visit. Accidents happened, and the presence or absence of visitors had no bearing on their contingency. Now, all this flitting about just added a layer of complexity – one might even say suspicion – to the whole affair.

Why the deuce hadn't he thought of this before?

In truth, he'd been overcome by the cleverness of the scheme. It had come to him in a flash on hearing of Henry Baxter's accident. Nothing like that ever happened to his aunt, he thought, then realised how easily it might.

From there on, each step in the process had seemed like a natural progression. Tying a tripwire made it a criminal act, therefore he must distance himself from it. That thought alone had swept him up, trapping him in its own momentum. The weekend in Paris alibi; paying cash for the Leicester ticket; the way he'd disposed of his mobile phone so he wasn't responsible for its movements from St Pancras station; walking to his aunt's place instead of taking a taxi ... clever, clever, clever ... and totally unnecessary. Even starving himself last night when he could have been wolfing down chicken quiche!

It was too late now. He couldn't go back. That would just add more complexity, especially after all his preparations. Best stick to the plan. But he really was an ass.

A rich ass now though.

It might take months to sort out probate, but the chain of events was as inexorable as the movement of the planets and the rising of the sun. He was a wealthy man. Would never want for anything again. He could settle Henry's problems without a second thought and treat Mel to all the things she desired and so richly deserved.

By god, he should have thought of this years ago!

And sometime in the future, when it was all done and dusted, he'd tell Mel how it had come about. Of his cleverness and guile. She'd look at him the way she used to when they first met. They'd rekindle that old spark, that old flame. And she'd never stray again.

* * *

It was awkward changing in the back of the van as it bumped over road humps and swung round corners, but Bernard was right; a little paranoia was a good thing. Even if there was no connection between the mysterious runner and his recent troubles, it was a fun way to pass a Saturday afternoon, Ernest thought. And there couldn't be a connection. The piddly database he'd given his uncle was a discard, an outsort, a joke, really. Cat owners? It was hardly in the league of the other databases they'd accumulated. Besides, as coordinator, decrypter and middleman, his alter ego Bitz was the only one who knew about it. Spree had no idea what he was copying, and Knightmare just took what Bitz passed on for sale.

This had to be something else. If it was actually anything at all.

There was a bag of clothing bumping around with him in the back. Overalls, baseball caps, cheap plastic sunglasses. Even a small make-up kit. He picked out a hat and a pair of shades.

'Lost her,' Francis said, bringing the van to a halt on a bus stop. 'She came this way but can't have got this far.'

'Over there!' Bernard pointed. 'Coming out of that supermarket.'

They watched as Jane exited, zipping her backpack, slipping it on and recommencing her run.

'She didn't buy much.'

They let her pass them on the other side of the road.

'Time to go!' Francis jammed the van in gear as a bus swung in behind them, blaring its horn.

They passed her again on Albion Street. This time Francis found a park and Bitz was ready at the rear doors.

'Hold on, she's going into the library.'

'What sort of run is this? Shopping? Books?'

Ernest climbed out and trotted back. Francis and Bernard stayed in the van.

Five minutes later, Jane re-emerged, adjusted her pack and continued on. But there was no sign of Ernest.

'He's supposed to be following her.'

'Maybe she knifed him in non-fiction or kicked him in the bibliographies.'

'It's not funny, Francis. This could be— Oh, there he is. Oi, get your skates on! She's got about two blocks on you.'

'No need.' Ernest ambled back waving a leaflet. 'I've ID'd her. Name, address, email and phone number.' He thrust the flyer through the open window.

Bernard studied it muttering, 'Oh fuck, fuck, fuck ...'

'Why, what is it?' Francis craned over to look.

'A private dick!'

'Not a dick,' Ernest said helpfully, 'but a Jane.'

26

Matt had just got up when Jane arrived. He moved slowly and gave her a world-weary greeting.

'Urgh! Have you not showered yet?' she pushed him away. 'You should. You'll feel better.'

'I can't. The water's off.'

'What? Why?'

'Jake shut it off to do the bathroom.'

'You might have warned me. I just ran here.'

'Oh.' He rubbed his stubbled chin. 'I s'pose you could have a scrub down in the laundry.'

'A scrub down?'

'I'll borrow the neighbour's hose. Fill some pots. Warm some water.'

'Later. Have you at least got enough for a cuppa?'

'Um ...'

She checked the kettle, switched it on then spied a pile of clothes in the corner. 'My things!'

'We needed some rags.'

'Rags?' She picked up a torn blouse and a pair of slacks that looked like they'd been used to mop up a water spill then wipe off grubby hands. 'These were all perfectly good.'

'You were painting in them.'

'You were painting in old clothes too. You could have used them. This was all I had here.'

He sighed, slumped at the kitchen table and pressed his fingertips to his temples by way of an answer.

'Looks like it was quite a night,' Jane said, emptying her pack.

'Anyway, I've brought you extra-strength paracetamol and some vitamin C tablets. They're supposed to be good for hangovers, but you need to dissolve them. In water.'

'There might be a bottle in the fridge.'

'Half a bottle. It'll do.'

She gave him two tablets and he swilled them down with the fizzing orange liquid.

'Honestly Matt, is it going to be like this every month?'

He looked at her. Said nothing.

'Can your police chums look up a vehicle registration and find the owner?'

'It's only supposed to be for legitimate enquiries. I wouldn't want to abuse the privilege and get them in trouble.'

'Of course.'

It didn't seem the time to mention the missing cat case had been re-opened. Instead, she told him of her visit to the Philadelphia Hotel the previous afternoon.

'Smith wasn't in so I left him my card and asked him to call me, but I don't expect to hear till Monday. Office hours and all that.'

Matt nodded.

'But I did speak to Maurice Todd and learn the name of his friend. Looks like there might have been a romantic connection. A woman by the name of Lydia.'

'Surname?'

'Todd didn't know.'

Matt grunted.

'I also discovered a connection with the Trivets. It seems that Mrs T's a real connoisseur. Writes a coffee column for one of the colour supplements. She put in a bid when the contract for the restaurant came up late last year. Wanted to separate out the cafe and specialise in posh coffees, but the hotel owners went for a package deal with JMJ Catering instead. It looks like Smith borrowed her idea, which may explain why Trivet was so keen to dob them in to Melody.'

Matt said nothing.

'Did you find any more stockists?' He shook his head. 'How did you get on with that printer friend?'

'That packet's not counterfeit at all.'

'Then what is it?'

'Stolen, most like.'

'Stolen?'

'Someone's knocked off a few, filled them and flogged them off.'

'But—'

'Either that or they copied eight separate designs, had them printed up – minimum run of a thousand of each – then just sold a couple of dozen to the Philadelphia Hotel. It doesn't make sense.'

'But I thought Melody did a stocktake.'

'I doubt she unwound every roll and counted every bag. It's an inside job. Some friend of this Lydia character. You said you checked all the staff.'

'I did.'

'You must've missed something.'

Jane went to speak then held her tongue.

'I'll check them on Monday. There'll be something you overlooked.'

The kettle boiled, filling the kitchen with steam. And kept on boiling.

Jane unplugged it. 'Doesn't anything work round here?'

'Jesus, Jane.'

'What?'

'Criticising.'

'Me? Criticising?'

Silence.

He sighed heavily. 'What's next? What other riveting cases have we got on the books? Anyone lost their keys? Maybe someone's hamster died in mysterious circumstances.'

'What's wrong, Matt? Is this about last night?'

'Yes, it's about last night. Of course it's about last night. Those blokes are out there doing real work; tracking down murderers and paedophiles and drug pushers. What are we doing? Missing cats and petty theft.'

'So what are you saying?' She set down the cups.

He didn't reply.

'Because if you want to go back to your old job, there's nothing stopping you. I've made my decision and I'm sticking with it.'

Matt stared at his cup.

'And I don't remember you being too enamoured with your old job either. You said you'd spent the last three years pushing papers and organising meetings. I even recall the term "bullshit job".'

He gave her a closed look. Looked away.

A minute ticked past. She tried changing tack. 'Anyway, what do you fancy doing this evening? I thought we could rent a DVD and get a takeaway.'

'Jesus Jane, I don't care. Do whatever you like. I'm not in the mood.'

She took a sip of tea. The taste of stale tea bags. 'No, me neither. Not now. What I'd really like to do is have a decent wash, find some clean clothes and have a civil conversation – even if it is only with the cat.'

With that, she set down her cup, picked up her pack and walked out.

27

When she got to New Cross Road, Jane spotted a number 53 bus approaching and felt her heart sink a little. Did she really expect Matt to follow her, apologise, call her back? Well, he wouldn't get a chance now. With the weekend timetable and feeling weary from her run, she'd be foolish to let it go.

And didn't.

The right decision. She saw that from the back window as she moved down the aisle. Honestly, what did she expect? Some sort of Hollywood rom-com scene with Matt running along behind, waving and shouting he was sorry?

The idea made her angry, but with herself this time.

He never actually said it, but she felt the sting of implied criticism. The suggestion she hadn't checked H&V's employees properly. She had. She knew she had. Not only that, she was the one who'd screwed Melody Bloody Harper down and got them a prime rate for the case. Plus she'd got the cat case re-opened too. Another week's work!

She hadn't said a word about him going out with his old cronies, getting blasted out of his tree and wrecking their time together. Or about not warning her the water was off. Or even using her spare clothes for rags.

She sat fuming as the bus rumbled on.

Then the phone rang in her backpack. A proper call too, not a text. She scrambled to get it out then saw an unfamiliar number redirected from the office phone.

'Bluebelle Investigations. Jane Child speaking.'

'My name is Jonathan Smith from Philadelphia Hotel,' the

voice on the other end was a crisp as a new banknote. 'You had words with one of my colleagues yesterday, I believe.'

'Yes, Mr Smith, I wanted to ask—'

'I don't know what this is all about Ms Child, and frankly, I don't care. I'm a busy man and I don't appreciate you making aspersions about my business practices to members of my staff.'

'Staff? I thought Mr Todd was your business part—'

'What you suggested is frankly libellous. I've already mentioned the matter to my lawyer.'

'I beg your—'

'The stock you asked about was legitimately acquired and properly receipted. As you'll discover in court if you continue to pursue this nonsense.'

'Mr Sm—'

'That is all I have to say on the matter. Good day!'

He hung up before she could reply.

Jane stared at the phone, stunned. Then hit the button to return the call.

'Smith speaking,' a smooth voice said.

'Now listen to me, you jumped up turd, if you're going to go around sounding off about lawyers and libel suits, you'd better get your facts right. Number one, Maurice Michael Todd isn't a member of your staff, he's your co-director. Number two, as a private investigator, I have every right to ask legitimate questions in the pursuit of stolen property and counterfeit goods. And number three, there was nothing at all libellous in my conversation yesterday. I recorded the whole thing and will happily submit it in defence of your ridiculous accusations.'

Only point number one had any truth to it, but Jane knew from long experience that the best way to respond to bullying was to come back harder and meaner. Private investigators had no particular right to ask questions or demand answers, but there was a good chance Smith didn't know that, and she could easily have used her phone to record the conversation with Maurice Todd.

There was certainly no evidence she hadn't.

The other end of the line was silent, but he didn't hang up. She fancied she heard him swallow.

'Oh, and in case you hadn't guessed, this is Jane Child from Bluebelle Investigations.'

Passengers nearby were staring, nudging each other. Jane didn't care.

'I ...' Smith cleared his throat. 'Perhaps we got off on the—'

'We certainly did get off on the wrong foot, Mr Smith. And that was down to you. I strongly suggest you don't take that attitude again.'

Another long silence.

Jane checked her watch and looked around to see where she was. Not far from home now.

'I take it you'll be at your post in an hour's time, Mr Smith?'

'Er, yes.'

'Then I shall see you there. I suggest you spare me a few minutes of your time.'

This time, Jane hung up before he could reply.

28

Matt stared at Jane's half-finished cup of tea as she closed the front door. She didn't stomp her feet and didn't slam it, which somehow made her departure even worse. It wasn't her fault he'd woken in a foul mood, not helped by the pounding in his head – which only now seemed to be easing, thanks to her.

She was right about the police too. He wasn't cut out to be an administrator and hated being kicked upstairs to act as a glorified civil servant. And while Avery and Dixon might have an intriguing case on their hands, it would be one of at least a dozen others, and the odds were stacked against it getting a proper investigation.

He should have leapt to his feet, run after her, caught her by the shoulder, apologised. Or at least called out. But his reactions weren't the best today, and by the time he'd thought it through ...

Then his phone rang. He couldn't help the smile that spread across his face as he rummaged through last night's pocket litter on the sideboard. Wallet, keys, miscellaneous receipts, Oyster card ...

Good old Jane. She's such a—.

But the number wasn't hers.

'Hello?'

'Is that Matt? Melody Harper from Harper & Vine,' a chirpy voice said. 'I know it's the weekend, but I wondered if you were free for a little powwow?'

'What? Yes, I s'pose so.'

'Great. Where abouts are you? I'm out and about in the car at the moment. I can pick you up if you like. We can go for coffee.'

'I'm not at the office,' He croaked and gave her the address.

'Let me put that in the satnav ...' There was a brief pause.

'Great, you're only twenty minutes away. See you shortly. Toodle.'

Twenty minutes? he thought, catching his reflection in the lounge mirror. '*Shit!*'

* * *

He made the best of a bad job, wondering how the hell people lived without running water. He guessed it was probably still something of a novelty when the house was built around the turn of the previous century, and he had a boyhood memory of his late grandfather talking about the coming home from school to find "the electric" had been connected. In those days there was probably still a village pump nearby. Well, there wasn't now. But there was the neighbours' hose.

They were out. Matt vaulted the fence and filled a bucket. The water was warm, the hose had been lying in the sun, and he stripped to the waist in the back yard and gave himself a lukewarm sponge bath. Primitive, but he felt better for it.

He thought about Melody calling him on a Saturday. A powwow about the case. Perhaps she had some new evidence.

Or perhaps it was something else.

He wondered.

She was an attractive woman despite that bitchy edge, but she was involved with Gerrard Vine, in business and personally. Still, Matt was a man of the world. He'd lived undercover for years on end. That meant living off your wits and trusting your instincts. If there was one conclusion he'd come to in all that time, it was that things were seldom as straightforward as they seemed. Private lives were often messy and complicated. People were duplicitous, selfish and often driven by urges they barely understood themselves. Scratch the veneer of the perfect couple and you might find a fairytale, but you'd more likely to encounter unhappiness, discord, or even a perfect firestorm.

He changed into a fresh shirt, a pair of chinos, and took his leather jacket from a hanger. It was the colour of dark chocolate. Jane loved it.

Jane.

Now there was someone who'd confounded his theories. Open, honest and – an old-fashioned word, perhaps even an old-fashioned concept – but *decent*. He'd sensed it from the outset, from the time she'd dropped a fiver in his begging bowl when he was working undercover on a private job. They'd got talking and she'd struck him as someone he could trust. The only mystery was why she hadn't already been snapped up.

After the tea, the pills, the vitamin C, a proper wash and a change of clothes, he felt better and decided to call her to apologise. As he gathered up his wallet, keys and phone, a small green sports car pulled up outside. The top was down. Melody. She tooted. He made the call as he made his way to the door, but before it even went through, his phone bleeped and died. Another legacy of last night; he'd forgotten to charge the damn thing.

* * *

Men were basically simple creatures, Melody Harper thought, though you could never tell them that. Gerrard, for example, thrived on the push-pull of affection then distance. By keeping him uncertain and off balance, she'd kept him entranced; for years. And one day he'd make her a wealthy woman.

One day.

Some men wanted sex. The notch-on-the-bedpost type. They often made lousy lovers because they were preoccupied with themselves and their own enjoyment. Others merely wanted the appearance of sex. Elderly businessmen who wanted some young, pert arm-candy. They could be strung along for months or even years simply by hinting to their friends and business associates that the intimacy was deeper than it really was.

So what about this one? A married man with six kids, Jane

said. And a vasectomy. And an ordinary house on the end of an ordinary row of terraces.

What indeed?

She smiled to herself and undid the second button on her blouse.

She hadn't found out much online. Apart from a brief biography on the Bluebelle website, there were no social media pages or blogs or anything of that sort. The legacy of a career policeman, perhaps. Or a crashing bore. The mention of undercover work was intriguing though, suggesting someone worldly wise, someone sharp enough to spot the age-old games and disciplined enough to walk away if he sensed he was being played. In short, a challenge. Perhaps even one equal to her wiles.

Of course, it may never come to that. But if it did she liked a challenge.

29

Jon Smith was expecting a ball-breaker. A tough, aggressive, hard-bitten private eye who took no nonsense. Someone in a pantsuit with a button-down collar, cropped hair, androgynous features and the build of a wrestler, most like. So Jane decided to mess with his mind. She went for the feminine, delicate and pretty. A short, crème, lightweight summer dress with a risque neckline more suited to a beach stroll in the south of France. High-heel slingbacks, a little time on her make-up and hair as she waited for the cab, and a pair of big, lightly tinted sunglasses in case he remembered her from the other day.

She asked for him at the hotel's reception desk and saw the effect the moment he walked around the corner from the restaurant. He was stiff, upright and solemn, marching like a man being led to face a firing squad, then looked about as he approached, scanning the lobby, actually overlooking her as she stood at one end of the counter pretending to study her phone. She waited, making him ask the receptionist.

'You said there was a—'

'Mr Smith?' She moved forward and held out a hand. 'Jane Child.'

The term *disconcerted* was an understatement. Pole-axed might have been more appropriate. He gaped at her, his handshake mechanical as she smiled at him sweetly.

'Nice to meet you.'

'You ... ah ... you too. Would you come this way, please?'

He led her to a pokey cupboard of a room at the back of the restaurant with a sign on the door saying *Private*. The restaurant was closed, sectioned off by a folding partition that separated it from the coffee shop, and a cleaner was at work with a Hoover. With the lights up, what by night seemed intimate and atmospheric, showed as an empty cavern somewhat frayed about the edges.

The tiny office had a narrow desk fixed to one wall. It was covered with piles of papers and an elderly laptop. There was a swivel office chair in front of it and a metal garden chair to one side. His composure restored, Smith directed her to the comfortable seat and took the plain one for himself.

Jonathan Patrick Smith was dapper and neat. Every inch an archetypal maitre d'. His head was as smooth and polished as a billiard ball, and his bristly moustache was neatly clipped. Jane noticed his hands. They seemed to have a life of their own; explaining, underlining, emphasising. Nerves, perhaps, but the nails were beautifully manicured – better than her own – and even the cuticles showed rigorous attention.

His skin, lightly tanned, had a sheen to it. Body lotions, washes and scrubs, she suspected. There was a hint of expensive cologne. Clearly a man who looked after himself and cared greatly for his appearance. The kind of man who'd check his profile as he passed a mirror.

'I should apologise for that phone call, Ms Child. This business ... A stressful afternoon ...' He let her fill in the gaps.

'Tell me about Lydia.'

'Lydia?'

Again she disconcerted him. She could see it in his eyes.

'I'm investigating counterfeit coffee, Mr Smith. She was your source, was she not?'

'Not ... not exactly. She had a friend, a contact in the trade. She detested the stuff herself. Couldn't drink it. Said it gave her migraines. But this friend ... on the wholesale side, I think ... had access to a number of exclusive brands.'

'Does this friend have a name?'

'Lydia acted as intermediary. I never met him.'

'Him?'

He saw her raised eyebrow. 'No, no, it was nothing like that. Lydia knew everyone. Moved in all sorts of social circles. The people she knew, the stories she'd tell ...' There was something in his eyes. Something wistful. Lost, even.

'You're married to the other JMJ partner, aren't you? Jennifer Joan Smith?'

The question brought him back to earth.

'Yes.' He swallowed.

Jane glanced towards the closed door. Outside, the whine of the Hoover grew louder as the cleaner approached. 'Why don't you start at the beginning, Mr Smith? With her full name, perhaps.'

'Turner. Lydia Turner.'

'Where did you meet?'

'Here. In the coffee shop. Eight weeks ago last Wednesday.'

Jane took a notebook from her bag and began writing, noting the date and Smith's particular precision.

'And when did you last see her?'

'Six weeks ago today.'

Jane looked up. 'You only knew her for a fortnight?'

'It seemed ... longer than that.'

'You said you met her in the coffee shop, yet she doesn't drink coffee.'

'She came in for a chai latte. We got talking.'

'Was she alone?'

'Yes.'

'Can you describe her?'

'About your age and build. Long auburn hair, brown eyes. Well-dressed, witty. A cultured woman. Someone who moves in the right circles. Someone who knows people.'

'Where was she from?' He shrugged. 'You must have an address, a phone number.'

'She was a very private person. There was a husband. A

jealous, powerful man. She had to be careful. She never gave me her number and I never found out where she lived.'

'But you had a fling?'

He pursed his lips, dropped his voice and glanced at the closed door. 'An *affaire de couer*, yes.'

'That ended six weeks ago today. What happened? Did you row, fall out?'

'Nothing happened. She just popped in, dropped off the coffee and said she'd call me next week.'

'And she never has?'

'No.'

'Have you tried to find her?'

'Do you know how many Turners there are in London?'

'How about the coffee? How did it arrive? How was it packed?'

'In a cardboard carton.'

'Any markings on the carton or printed labels to say where it was from?'

He rubbed his forehead. 'I ... don't remember.'

'How did she deliver it? Just breeze in carrying a carton?'

'She came in the back, through the kitchens. We'd arranged it. Jen has a break between two and three on Saturdays and Lydia arrived with one of those bags-on-wheels things. The carton was inside.'

'And afterwards, where did she go?'

'Out the back. I presume she had a car.'

'Did you see it?'

'No.'

'So no make, colour, registration?'

He shook his head.

'You weren't curious?'

'I'd just spent two thousand pounds on coffee. I was more curious about that.'

'How did you pay for it?'

'Cash. In an envelope. She took it with her. She gave me a peck on the cheek, said, "I'll call you next week" and dashed out. I never saw her again.'

His mobile buzzed as he was speaking; a series of insistent vibrations. He took it out and glanced at the screen. Jane saw the caller had withheld their number.

'Smith speaking.' The words were terse, his expression cool, then his attitude changed completely. He got to his feet so quickly he knocked over his chair and didn't bother righting it.

'Excuse me,' he muttered to Jane and hurried to the door.

She watched as he crossed the empty restaurant and stood talking, a hand clamped against his left ear to dampen out the sound of the vacuum cleaner. The call didn't last long, but when he returned, tucking the phone into an inside pocket and straightening his jacket, his manner was brusque and businesslike.

He paused at the office door, regarding Jane with a coolness bordering on suspicion. As if, in his brief absence, she'd been replaced by an imposter.

'I'm afraid that's all I can tell you, Ms Child.' He glanced at his watch. 'Now, if you'll excuse me, I have much to do before we open the restaurant.'

'Well, thank you for your time,' Jane said, getting to her feet. 'I'll leave you my card in case you think of anything else.'

'Don't bother.' He held the door for her. 'I have nothing more to add.'

<h1>30</h1>

Melody saw Matt had made an effort as he came out of the front door, tucking his phone into a jacket pocket. If he really was a jeans-and-T-shirt-for-an-afternoon-in-front-of-the-telly type, he'd smartened himself up. An encouraging sign.

'I'm not dragging you away from anything, am I?' she asked, looking past him to the quiet house as he got in the car. 'Wife, family?'

He shook his head.

'They don't mind?'

'No, because I don't have either.'

'Oh, I thought ...' Jane! What was all that talk about an old photograph on the website and him having six kids and a vasectomy? Was she trying to deflect her interest? 'I mean, I just assumed,' she added.

Were they an item, or did Jane just have hopes there? She'd soon find out. Either way, it was a clue. Jane liked men with depth which would make him the slow-to-unravel type; an outer toughness with an inner warmth. Hints of deeper streams and flashes of vulnerability played well with men like that. And the thought of thwarting or even cuckolding her old friend added a frisson of excitement to the undertaking.

'All set?' she asked with a broad smile, then spun the wheel and accelerated.

* * *

A couple of neighbours saw Matt get into the little Mazda beside

182

its attractive strawberry blonde driver. One winked and gave him a thumbs-up. He didn't return either gesture.

'There's a new bistro near the Maritime Museum,' she said. 'Have you tried it?'

'Not yet.'

'Let's take a look.'

She swung the car in a U-turn and accelerated away.

Riding with the top down was refreshing. The air was warm and it was nice to be able to look up at the trees and sky. Melody drove well and clearly enjoyed it, flicking up and down through the manual gearbox, following the satnav through a maze of back streets to avoid the traffic.

'I understand you and Jane know each other from university,' he said.

'It seems a lifetime ago. I don't think I was a very nice person in those days. She's probably told you.'

He shook his head.

'My parents split up when I was a child, a very acrimonious split, and for years I was tugged back and forth between my awful birth father and my mother's new man. My real father had money, you see, but Mum had signed a prenup and got almost nothing. Going up to Leicester, I finally escaped all that and ran a little off the rails. Drink, drugs, parties. I was pretty horrid to some pretty decent people, Jane amongst them, and I never actually finished my degree.

'Papa saved me. My mother's second husband. I owe him everything. He even got us started in H&V. Technically, he's no relation – well, stepfather – but he's been more of a real father than my biological one.'

Her candidness surprised him. 'Where is he now?' he asked.

'Surrey. He and my mother split up a couple of years ago. She lives abroad now with someone I hardly know, so Papa's all I have left.'

'No brothers and sisters?'

She shook her head. 'Or aunts and uncles. My mum was an only child too. There's a heap on my real father's side, but I haven't seen them, or him, in years.'

Someone was reversing from a park outside the bistro. Melody swung into it and clicked a remote to close the top as they stepped from the car. Matt held the door and followed her in, noting the light scent like a summer breeze, the snugly fitting short-sleeved blouse with the top buttons undone, and the flared skirt that swayed to the movement of her hips.

A waiter escorted them to a pebbled courtyard dotted with wrought-iron tables and chairs. They took a spot beside a high rear wall now almost completely covered with ivy. Only one red brick corner remained. Tendrils of green, like the fingers of an outstretched hand, reached out for it.

'I was just thinking of coffee,' Melody raised her sunglasses, perching them on top of her head as she studied the blackboard menu, 'but I skipped lunch and I'm feeling a bit peckish. Could I tempt you to a light meal and a glass of wine instead?'

Matt, who'd skipped breakfast *and* lunch, nodded his agreement.

They ordered, then she crossed her arms, leaned on the table and studied him with her dark blue eyes. 'How's the case going?'

'Making progress. The good news is the counterfeit coffee doesn't appear to be widespread – at least, not yet. In fact, the only place we've found it so far is *Le Chat Noir* at the Philadelphia Hotel.'

The waiter returned with a glass of Chablis for each of them. Melody toasted him and sipped. 'That is good news.'

'The thing is, I'm starting to suspect it's not a counterfeit operation at all.'

'What do you mean?'

'Tell me about your packaging process.'

'I'm not sure what you mean.'

'You're a small company. I imagine you use the same

packaging machine for each of your eight different types of coffee.'

She nodded.

'You did a full stocktake of the coffee and the unused bags, but how thorough was it? The bags come in rolls of a thousand. They're folded, cut and heat-sealed by the packaging machine, and I imagine there's some sort of counter on it, but it must be hard to estimate the number of bags left on a part roll. You'd be reliant on the figures recorded by the operator.'

Melody's face paled. She was a smart woman, he thought. She caught his gist immediately.

'You think the bags were stolen by one of my staff?'

'So far we're only talking about a few dozen bags found at the Philadelphia. The sort of quantity that could be written off as misfolds or test runs.'

'What about the coffee?'

'That too, possibly. Reg Trivet's wife – who's no slouch in the matter – rated the their Finca Sanssouci as perfectly acceptable.'

Melody picked up her glass and took a long sip. 'Any idea how it got to the Philadelphia?'

'We've made progress there, too. Do you know anyone called Lydia?'

'Lydia?' She blinked and shook her head.

'A friend or someone in the business. A rival, perhaps.'

'No. Why?'

'Because someone called Lydia – I don't have a surname yet – acted as a go-between for the coffee's source and one of the directors of JMJ Catering – the people who run *Le Chat Noir* at the Philadelphia.'

'Good god.'

'Our next job's to track her down. Jane's already been in touch. We're waiting for a call back.'

'Well,' Melody said, 'that's great work! I see we made the right choice hiring you two.' She toasted him again, took a sip and excused herself to go to the bathroom.

Matt watched her depart, swinging her hips, shapely and lithe. He thought of their first meeting at her office. Quite a change from the brusque businesswoman.

He took another sip of wine. Hair of the dog was supposed to be good for a hangover, but this tasted precisely like dog hair to his jaded palate. He made a face, glanced around and dumped half of it in the planter beside him.

Melody returned, closely followed by their meals; roast cod with clam and saffron broth, and a mushroom and spinach linguine. She drained her drink, encouraged him to do likewise, ordered two more, took up her cutlery and set about her food.

She'd done something with her hair, he thought. Fluffed it up. Touched up her make-up too. And had the third button on her blouse hadn't been undone when she left.

'So, Mr Detective, tell me all about yourself.'

'There's really not much to tell.'

'I don't believe that for a moment,' she said, smiling sweetly.

* * *

Gerrard Vine hadn't been to Gorelston-on-Sea since he was a boy, back when his parents and younger brother were still alive. He wandered from Lower Esplanade out on to a patch of sand. The view had hardly changed, but it almost felt like someone else's memory. Had he really eaten ice cream here, or fish and chips at that place on the corner, or taken a donkey ride over there? Or was it just something he'd seen on TV?

He felt the same emptiness about his aunt. He hadn't really done anything, had he? She could have tripped on a frayed end of carpet, a loose board, even her own feet. The surreal aspect was tying the tripwire in the first place.

And cutting it free.

He took the broken line from his pocket and studied it a

moment, then dropped it in a litter bin. The seaside seemed a natural place for it to end up.

The whole visit to his aunt had a dreamlike quality to it, like the family trip to Gorelston all those years ago. As if it wasn't really a part of him, the here-and-now Gerrard Vine. As if they'd been done by someone else. An alter ego or a double.

The bit that did seem real was the sight of his aunt's sprawled body and the way he'd been obliged to step around it. She was in running gear: track pants, T-shirt, a towelling sweatband round her head to keep her curly grey locks out of her face. He thought she looked foolish. She wouldn't have cared, but he hated the idea of her being found like that. Undignified for a woman of her age.

But that was all he did feel. There was no regret, no shame, no latent emotion bubbling to the surface. He hadn't loved her, but he hadn't loathed her either. Perhaps that was the problem. She'd just been there, always. A presence. A supervising adult. Even long after he'd grown up.

There was a pub on the way back to his boarding house. He stopped for a scotch and loosened his tie. After a second one, he took it off completely, reminding himself he was more than just a trust fund now. No more going cap in hand. No more sacrifices. No more scrimping and saving. He was a wealthy man. Captain of his own ship. Reborn, for the second time. The first came after the car crash that claimed his parents and brother, but that was an accident. This was different. This was his own doing. There was something powerful, something manly in acknowledging it.

Yes, all right, he'd killed her. He'd broken free. At last. Time to celebrate!

Three women entered the bar. Early twenties. Short skirts. Shapely. Giggling in the self-conscious fashion of the young. Gerrard regarded them for a long moment then waved to the barman for another drink as he went to see what they wanted.

* * *

'How's the cod?' Melody asked.

'Delicious. Yours?'

She picked at her linguine, nodding by way of reply, then looked into his eyes.

Matt returned to his food. 'You said you wanted a powwow.'

'Did I?'

'It sounded like you had some information for me.'

'No, I ... was just interested in progress.'

'Checking up on the workers?' He smiled.

'To be honest, I was at a loose end. Gerrard's away for the weekend and I ... didn't have anything else. The worry of this has been gnawing away at me. I suppose I just wanted some reassurance.'

'Well, you're in good hands.'

'Am I?' She looked away. 'I mean, are we?'

They ate in silence for a while, then she said: 'It's difficult being in a relationship and working together. That twenty-four/seven thing, I suppose. You need a breather sometimes. Your own space. I think that's the mistake Gerrard and I made, living in each others' pockets all the time. It sometimes feels like the business is all we have in common now.'

'How long have you known him?' he asked, although he already knew the answer.

'We met at varsity. One of those whirlwind things. Head over heels, you know? And it was good for a while. For a long while. Then he ... started to drift ...'

'Drift?'

'Other women. I'm not supposed to know about it. He thinks he's being clever,' she flashed him a look, 'but I can always tell. Do you know where he is this weekend? Paris. On *business*.' She gave the word a slight emphasis. 'He says things too, about how we should have a more open relationship. But that's not me. I'm not like that. Since Gerrard ... well, there's only ever been Gerrard.'

She sighed. 'It's the wretched business, you see. I'm bound to him by it, but it's not like he takes any interest in it these days. If I could make a break somehow, pay him off, get shot of him and find someone else. Someone decent.'

She toyed with her food then looked up, giving him a desolate smile. 'Ah well, enough about my woes. I fancy more wine.'

'Should you? You're driving.'

'Is that Matt the former policeman speaking?'

'No, it's Matt the concerned citizen speaking. I wouldn't want you to have an accident.'

She held his eyes for a long moment then said throatily, 'What if I promise to be careful?'

The third drink was definitely a mistake, but there was no dissuading her. By then she'd reached that pleasant stage of mellow relaxation where everything was right with the world and the future looked glorious. Particularly the immediate future.

She proved good company. Quick with a joke, carefree, gay. Her bright laughter filled their corner of the bistro, drawing lingering glances; questioning, approving and envious. There was something about her, about the way she held herself, spoke and gestured – a kind of conscious unselfconsciousness – that suggested she was someone you should know. A film star, TV presenter or singer, perhaps.

It was her look too. The cropped blonde hair, the blue eyes, the pale skin and slim figure. That third undone button. The tight-waisted skirt. The sway of her hips as she went to the bathroom a second time.

'I've settled the bill,' she said when she returned. 'We should go.'

The waiter returned for the last of their plates and asked if they wanted coffee.

'Coffee? God no!' Melody exclaimed, and they both found the idea unspeakably funny.

Outside, she cannoned into him and required his support.

'Where's your keys. I'll drive,' he said.

'You've had as much as me.'

'Yeah, but I'm a policeman.'

'A used-to-be policeman.' She stumbled on the words. 'Here. You'll have to drive me home.'

He helped her into the car, helped her with the seatbelt. There was some difficulty with the strap and that unbuttoned blouse. A lot of giggling and hand-slapping. He finally settled beside her in the driver's seat, turned on the ignition and punched the Home button on the satnav.

She fell against him, despite the seatbelt, one arm round his neck and whispered, 'You know, there is ... *something* ... you could do for me ...'

31

Jane's phone rang and she snatched it up eagerly, only noticing at the last moment that it wasn't Matt but Sally.

'Hi Janey. Thought I'd get in a quick call before you and Matt head out pubbing or clubbing or ...' Sally put on a croaky old granny voice, '... whatever it is you young people do these days.'

Jane smiled. 'Actually ...' She hesitated, wondering whether she should mention the argument. It was still a bit fresh, a bit raw. 'Actually, we're just staying in tonight.'

'Even worse! A romantic evening in. I can't remember when I last had one of those.' Sally raised her voice, obviously for Paul's benefit. 'I said, *I can't remember when I last had a romantic evening in.*'

In the background she heard Paul yell, 'Shut up, woman. I'm trying to watch the football.'

Jane laughed. She knew Paul hated team sports.

'I shouldn't complain,' Sally said. 'He's actually cooking dinner. Which is what gave me the idea. Why don't you and Matt come over for dinner tomorrow night?'

'I'm ... not sure we can make that.'

'Sorry, it is a bit short notice. Next weekend then?'

'Yes, all right. I'll give you a call during the week.'

'Lovely.' The granny voice again. 'Now I'll just have me cocoa and head off to me bed.'

Jane hung up, her smile fading. Next weekend seemed a long way away right now.

* * *

Bitz found it hard to concentrate because Francis and Bernard had been bickering on and off for most of the afternoon. They were like an old married couple, sniping at each other at every opportunity.

'You must've been followed,' Bernard said.

'Oh, so it's my fault because I drive the van? You're in the passenger seat, pal. You should be keeping watch.'

'You don't do the threats properly. You've got to scare the shit out of them. I bet it was one of *your* customers that blabbed.'

Francis snorted. 'More likely you got a skin full and blabbed to one of your floozies.'

'I did no such thing!'

'Look, she won't know about the lock-up, and she certainly doesn't know that we know about her.'

'How's that any bloody use? She knows about *us*, doesn't she? We'll have to ditch the van, ditch the scheme and find a new place to live.'

'Oh for fuck's sake.'

'For fuck's sake, the pair of you!' Bitz snapped, slapping down the lid of the laptop. 'Leave it to me, will you. I'll sort something out.'

'What can you possibly—?'

'I can't do it here.' Ernest gestured dismissively at the laptop. 'I'll need to work from home.'

Francis and Bernard exchanged a look.

'I thought you said Cathy was moving out and you were giving her some space.'

'Yeah, she texted me. She's all done.'

'Oh. Right. Well, can we give you a lift?'

'Yes, please.'

Ernest had done as much as he could with the limited access he had here, cycling through his perimeter defences, tripwires and honeypots at least a dozen times now without finding any hint of untoward activity. A more thorough audit would require better hardware and a faster connection, but he was reasonably happy with what he'd found so far. There was, however, still one possible flaw; the damned car that he'd stupidly driven to Knightmare's place. A check of its plates would tie him back to his apartment, the perfect place for a reception committee, and only a fool would walk into a trap like that. He certainly didn't intend to do so. Not when he had a couple of stand-in fools right here.

They took the van again, and again Ernest was happy to squat in the back.

'You might as well use my car park.' He passed Francis the tag to his building's underground garage. It would allow him to exit the van and enter the complex unobserved from the street.

As they stood waiting for the lift he said, 'I think I'm out of milk. Here, go on ahead and let yourselves in, I'll pop up the road and get some.'

He handed them his keys and was racing up the stairwell before they had time to react. He paused half a flight up, listening for the lift's arrival and the closing of its doors. After that, it was just a matter of waiting. Five full minutes should be enough.

As he sat in the silent car park, he reflected on the last twenty-four tumultuous hours and the scheme that brought him to this point.

By rights he shouldn't have known any more about his hack buddies than their handles, just as he shouldn't have known or cared about the rest of his teammates in KDM. All that counted online was your tech: technique in games, technological prowess elsewhere, but Ernest was as curious as he was cautious. His daytime job gave him access to a number of local and national databases, and putting together snippets of seemingly disparate information was as much a game as it was second-nature.

When Spree suggested a collaboration, every alarm bell he'd ever heard sounded simultaneously. The approach had all the hallmarks of a honeytrap set up by the law enforcement to entice the greedy and unwary, so he'd gone overboard in backgrounding his man.

It wasn't easy. Spree knew his network lore and how to hide online, but Ernest eventually tracked him down via an unguarded comment he'd made months before on one of the IRC boards. Someone mentioned Brighton, which Spree renamed Giant-fuckerton after cracking up his favourite road bike there in a race crash the previous summer. Tracking down the event online was a piece of cake. There was a PDF of all the participants along with their times, including a handful marked DNF – Did Not Finish. He even turned up a shaky YouTube clip of the crash showing a spindly guy in yellow Lycra going over the handlebars of his bent bike.

James Lawrence Burton. Jamie to his friends. Spree to his KDM teammates.

A little more digging in work databases turned up a twenty-four-year-old Computer Science graduate with a hefty student loan, maxed-out credit cards, and expensive tastes in bikes and computers. He was working as an admin for an off-site backup company based in a series of old World War II bunkers in northwest London. A go-nowhere role, a glorified filing clerk dealing with vast amounts of duplicate data from some of the capital's biggest corporations. It would be easy enough to dupe the dupes, Spree reckoned. The problem was, they were all encrypted.

It seemed like a marriage made in heaven – which was why Ernest was initially so cautious. By day he might be a database supremo, but by night he wasn't just Bitz, the crack game player, he was also Bitz, the crack encryption cracker.

This wasn't some Edward Snowden, for-the-good-of-all-mankind gig. This was strictly a money-making venture, and for that they'd need a broker with the right contacts.

Knightmare was the obvious choice – a hacker and cracker with contacts in Eastern Europe – but Ernest made no approach until he'd tracked down and thoroughly vetted the guy. Andrej Bilic, 28, unemployed, with a flat in a Dagenham tower block.

The deal had netted them a fortune – in bitcoins, of course.

Digital currency. Untrackable. The smorgasbord of databases they'd delivered represented one of the biggest data heists in history, yet no one knew of it except Spree, Bitz, Knightmare and the unknown buyer. Now that number had been halved. Ernest was determined it wasn't going to drop any lower.

He'd expected fallout. Whoever had invested would expect a return, most likely in the form of identity theft or stolen credit card numbers, and Ernest – ever prepared – had created a sort of insurance for himself. A bargaining chip if, by some chance, the spotlight ever did swing his way. He'd made a record of all the databases he'd copied. Not online. Not on a computer or in a file, but handwritten in a notebook. A scribble that read like amateur poetry but was, in fact, a memory aide based on the Method of Loci. Each line linked to the next location in an imaginary stroll along an imaginary street, but one that would kick off a specific recollection of the database concerned. The first page began:

Statues of Diana,
Hand-built houses,
Foreign devils amidst a jumble of numbers
with three night watchmen standing guard.

The first databases he'd cracked: an online dating site, a DIY company's customer details, a list of overseas staff for some government department, data from an accounting firm and three sets of personnel records from three separate security companies.

As the months ticked past, the notebook lay half-forgotten in a drawer. There was no sudden upswing in the usual background hum of illicit transactions, no rumours of a large-scale breach, nothing to send the authorities out on a witch hunt.

That alone was curious. He didn't know who the buyer had been, and with Knightmare's demise there was little chance he'd ever find out. Still, there might be a way to lure them from their lair ...

His mobile showed five minutes were up. He called his uncle.

'Hey, it's me. I'm at the shop. I meant to ask if there's anything I can get for you or Bernie.'

'I don't think so,' Francis replied. 'You don't even need milk. I looked in your fridge. You've got enough in there already to float a boat.'

'Oh, well I won't bother then. Thanks. See you in a bit.'

He hung up. They were both clearly still alive, hadn't been defenestrated or set upon by goons, so it was all clear. He hit the button and waited for the lift to return.

* * *

Ernest, the earnest employee of one of the City's biggest brokerage houses, was doing very nicely, Bernard thought. At twenty-nine, he was a Senior Database Administrator and, if his apartment was anything to go by, a well rewarded one. The place was large and tastefully furnished, thanks to an ex-girlfriend doing a course in interior design. In the end, she'd given up on him, unable to compete with his real passion.

Bernard said nothing, but his pursed lips gave him away. He'd struggled all his life, scrimping, saving, compromising, giving up all for his art, and here was this ... creature who treated the home comforts he'd sweated blood for with casual disdain. The gleaming appliances in the kitchen were barely used; he lived on takeaways. The fifty-inch television on the lounge wall – there was a sixty-inch one in the spare bedroom for playing fucking games! The mere fact that he could afford to have a spare bedroom in the first place – here in Docklands, in the heart of the city, with a proper balcony and a proper view.

Ernest entered, beaming, gesturing them to seats in the open-plan lounge as he took some beers from the drinks fridge. He even had a fucking drinks fridge!

'No glass?' Bernard cocked an eye at the can.

The young man's sigh was barely audible as he returned to the kitchen and came back with a pair of tall glasses. He set one in front of each of them, then pointedly ripped the tab off his own can and swilled straight from it.

Bernard poured his drink, tilting his glass at just the right angle.

Give the little shit something to put in his fucking dishwasher.

'You said you might be able to sort out something,' Francis said cautiously. 'To get that firm of private detectives off our backs.'

Ernest took another swig of beer, the pieces coming together in his mind. 'Mmm,' he said. 'Intimation.'

'Intimation of what?'

'What if I was to drop them into the middle of something that left them no time to do anything else?'

Like, go on living, for example.

Francis considered. 'You mean like a stopgap to give us time to reorganise?'

'No, this would be a long-term thing. Quite ... life changing. Believe me, you'd be long forgotten.'

'You could do that? For us? No need to change vans or move or anything?'

'No need for any of that.'

'What exactly are you proposing?' Bernard asked.

'Do you really want to know?'

Francis raised a hand and answered for his friend. 'No, we don't. It's probably all too technical anyway.'

Ernest smiled. 'Yeah, it is a bit.'

'When—?'

'How about tonight?'

'You can do it right away?'

'It'll take a few hours, and maybe a day or two to kick in fully, but no time like the present, eh?' He drained his beer and crushed the can in his hand. 'Fancy another before you go?'

32

Jane woke from an uncanny dream of a world without Matt. Not a world where they'd rowed or broken up, but a world where he'd never existed in the first place. Everything else was as it was now; the business, her life, her new career. It was simply Matt-less. Like someone she'd made up. An imaginary friend.

A storm had broken in the early hours of the morning. She could hear it battering the roof tiles. A muffled pounding like static on a mistuned radio, coming in wind-blown surges as if an unseen listener was trying to tune in to an elusive station. She lay on her back staring at the ceiling, disquieted by the dream and almost ready to believe it in the half-light of this static-filled world.

She reached out her left hand, letting it crawl between the sheets, sensing another presence in the bed, proof that it was a dream and nothing more. The form, the shape she could feel, wasn't in the bed but on it, lying where he should have been.

'Bluebelle,' she whispered to the rain.

The cat arched and stretched, and for a moment Jane was seized with panic. She leapt from the bed, hurried across the landing to the spare room and snapped on the light.

The curtains weren't drawn. Steel bolts could be glimpsed in the overspill of light outside the window, but all else was still and silent and not quite like her dream. Two desks, not one. Two cups on the credenza. Two different hands in the lettering on the whiteboard.

She sighed, switched off the light and stood in the darkened doorway, letting this new reality sweep the dream away.

Then she snapped it on again. Just for a second. Just to

double-check.

* * *

Matt woke from troubled dreams and a rumble of thunder, wondering if this was it; the beginning of the end. Something inside was already bowing to the inevitable. He'd known, or at least suspected, this would be a short-run thing. All his relationships were. Inevitable, considering the life he'd led. But this been had nice. No, this had been spectacular. The best ever. Jane was something ... special. A fresh breeze through the cluttered corridors of his mind.

Once again the old feeling returned; that there was something fundamentally different about him. Something that set him apart from others. That he was wired wrongly. Faulty. Damaged goods. Matt Healy, the defective detective. Had he become an undercover cop, living lives filled with lies, simply to escape his own?

He didn't know any more. He didn't know anything. The older he got, the more the wisdom of advancing age seemed to elude him. Four years short of forty – a time when his contemporaries had settled for modest careers, modest wives, a couple of kids and a modest house in the commuter belt – he looked forward and back and saw only a wasteland on either side of now.

The analytical, scientific part of his brain assured him it was just the old curse; the innate restlessness that drove mankind onwards. Evolutionary companions had been happy with their lot, remaining in the forests and woodlands where they were born, but not homo sapiens, a tormented species, driven by the desire to try new things, to see what lay beyond the next range of hills, to question everything.

But that was too grand. Claiming an evolutionary imperative for a personal malaise was a cop out. After all, others managed. Others beat it and went on to live happy, productive lives.

Or did they? How did one judge these things? How could you

ever know how others really felt deep down?

He remembered a fellow recruit at police college; cheerful, happy, always quick with a salacious joke or a ribald comment, always the first to suggest the pub or a party. Three months into training, they'd found him in his car with the windows down; a locked garage and the engine running. He'd been there all night, but the tank was still three-quarters full. His last public act had been to top it up. Matt still wondered about that final service station visit. What had he been thinking as he closed the filler cap? As he paid the cashier? As he drove home and closed the garage door one final time?

There was no perfect solution, no happy-ever-after. In his later years undercover, he'd longed for the steady security of a nine-to-five desk job, and when he finally landed one, he longed to be out on the streets again. When an opportunity to reprise his undercover activities had come up, he hadn't hesitated, relishing it more than any holiday he'd had in years. And there, of course, he'd met Jane.

Funny how everything came back to Jane.

* * *

Lazy sunlight was the next thing that woke her, followed by Bluebelle. It was breakfast time, at least on the cat clock, and she delivered this reminder by licking Jane's brow with a tongue that felt like a damp emery board.

Jane groaned and pushed her away, but Bluebelle knew this routine and simply change position.

'Don't you have a snooze function?' Jane pulled the sheet over her head.

Bluebelle gave up licking and settled against it, pressing her back into the hollow between Jane's arm and face, apparently deciding to smother her mistress instead.

Five minutes later, the bedside phone rang and she fumbled for it with her free hand.

'Hello?'

'Hey.' Matt's voice. 'Sorry, I didn't wake you, did I?'

'Nah, Bluebelle beat you to it.'

Silence. But a comfortable silence. Then he said, 'I'm an arse, Jane. A complete fuckup.'

'Yeah.' She smiled. 'I know.'

33

He might have a pounding jungle drum of a headache and eyes that felt like they'd been rolled in salt, but Ernest 'Bitz' Cricklewood reckoned he was feeling a lot better than his late hack buddies. At least he was feeling *something*. And after a long night's work, he should continue doing so for some time to come.

Pushing himself away from the desk, he stretched and yawned amidst a litter of pizza boxes, energy drink cans, stale coffee cups and chocolate bar wrappers. It was done. The tricky business of salting his trail with suggestive hints and misdirection. A fine balance. Too much, and his pursuers might suspect they were being played. Too little, and they might miss it entirely.

He'd gone for a scattergun approach. Fragments here and there, tempting hints but nothing conclusive. Suitably backdated and suitably placed, someone like himself – an analyst trying to connect the dots in a plethora of data dumps – would register them almost subconsciously. Then the motherlode. A simple error that drew the strands together forming a subtle but traceable link between Spree, Knightmare and Bluebelle Investigations.

* * *

Matt knocked. He had a key but he still knocked, and when Jane opened the door he stood on the step looking contrite and holding out a bunch of flowers.

'They're not service station jobs either. They're proper ones.'

'Proper ones,' she repeated. 'Thank you.'

'Pinched 'em off a proper grave and all.'

She smiled. 'You are an arse, Matt Healy.'

'No disputing that.'

'Well, are you going to stand out there all morning like Bluebelle beside her cat door, or are you going to come in?'

A moment later, he was in her arms.

Many long moments later, he eased away again. 'I really am sorry, Jane. It won't happen again.'

'Don't say that because it probably will.'

He shook his head. 'That was an aberration. I haven't had a night like that in years. And after the way I felt yesterday, I remember why.'

'Well, having no water wouldn't have helped.'

'I've put Jake on notice about that. He's rigging up something temporary today.'

'A plumber on a Sunday? Who are you, God?'

'Not only that ...' He held her at arm's length and gestured to the Plover's Plumbing van parked in the street. 'I've got his wheels too. Not as flash as Melody Harper's, but I left them with her when I drove her home last night.

'What?'

'She came round after you left. Took me out for a meal and I ended up taking her home.' Jane's pulse skipped a beat. 'We went to some place near the Maritime Museum. *The Cheating Heart*. Do you know it?'

He was trying to be casual, conversational, but she saw from a twinkle in his eye that he was teasing her too.

'I think I do, actually. I've been there. Several times.'

'Have you now?'

'But not yesterday. I had a date with Jon Smith at *Le Chat Noir*.'

Now he looked surprised.

Jane pushed him away and strode off to the kitchen. 'Fancy a coffee?'

'Er ... sure.' He followed her through, closing the front door behind him.

'It won't be up to Melody's standards, but you said yourself you don't mind the difference.'

He watched her fill the kettle and set out the cups. 'Did you catch up with Gerrard too?'

'No, he's away. How's our Mr Smith?'

'He's quite a ladies man, actually.'

'Is he?'

They regarded each other for a moment. The remains of Jane's breakfast lay on the benchtop. Toast crumbs. Breadboard. She cast an eye over it saying, 'They reckon the way to a man's heart is through his stomach. I think they're wrong. Much quicker to go through his chest with a bread knife.'

Matt grinned.

She launched herself at him, seizing him by the shirt. 'Tell me what you were doing with Melody Bloody Harper, you bastard, or I'll put it to the test!'

He wrapped his arms around her. 'Only if you tell me what you were doing with Jon Bloody Smith!'

'*I* didn't drive him home.'

'Fair point.'

'And it's your turn first anyway. You started it.'

'But you cracked first.'

'We'll call it draw then.' She let him go. 'But I want to know *every* detail.'

'So do I.'

'Right then. Sit.' She pointed to a stool beside the breakfast bar as the kettle came to the boil. 'And start talking!'

* * *

'She called shortly after you left. Said she wanted a powwow. I was feeling a bit chirpier by then, thanks to your ministrations, and it sounded like she had some fresh information about the case –

which she did in a way, just not the way she intended.

'She picked me up from home, we went to a restaurant and had a drink. Only, I wasn't really drinking. I was still feeling a bit delicate and couldn't face the taste of it, so I fed most of it to the pot plant beside the table.

'I told her how the case was going – how it looked like the packaging had been stolen from H&V and how you were aiming to grill Jon Patrick Smith at *Le Chat Noir* about his source – and she started coming on to me. At first I thought I'd imagined it, but when she came back from the loo, I noticed she'd undone an extra button on her blouse and kept leaning across the table to me. The icing on the cake was some story about Gerrard being away and playing around, how they had nothing in common these days but the business, and how she was looking to shake him off and find a decent man.'

Jane scowled.

'I'm a professional, Jane. I did this sort of thing for years. When you're undercover, your whole identity depends on remaining alert, so when someone comes on to you like that – especially a client, out of the blue – it may be that she really does just fancy a roll in the hay, but it's far more likely that she's after something.

'So I played along, pretending to get merry alongside her while surreptitiously watering the pot plant. She seemed more pissed than she should have been. Three glasses will make anyone merry, but not staggering and almost falling-over drunk. Except for when she paid the bill. By credit card. Her fingers didn't miss a beat on the keypad.

'Out at the car, I took her keys and helped her into the passenger seat. She made it very clear she'd welcome further attention – and no doubt blame it on the booze tomorrow – and when I got in, she asked me to do something for her.'

He paused and sipped his coffee. Jane waited.

'Could I get a report of our findings to her first thing on

Monday morning? And backdate it? Make it look like we've been working on it for weeks instead of a few days? I played along, and there was more. If I could state that H&V were the victim of a high-quality counterfeit campaign of unknown origin – most likely foreign – she'd be very, *very* grateful.'

'She was prepared to sleep with you to speed up her report?'

'Not just speed it up, dictate its contents. Think about it. What would your average PI do? He's been paid for a week – very generously – and only done a few days work so far. She wants a report saying XYZ? She's got it. Case closed. Move on.'

'So why the come-on?'

'Because she's smart enough to see that's not how we operate. If she'd asked for it straight out, I'd have told her she could have a report of our findings to date. That's it. No suppositions, no speculations, just the facts. If, however, she could win me over ...'

'She'll get it by the end of next week anyway. Why the rush?'

'I'm guessing something's changed. She needs it urgently.'

'But who for? It's clearly going to someone else.'

'*That* is the sixty-four thousand dollar question.'

'So what did you tell her?'

'That I'd get to work on the case as soon as I'd dropped her home. Which is exactly what I did.

'I started by asking myself who Harper and Vine really are. I checked with their registration at Companies House and it's a fifty-fifty split; Gerrard and Melody. No third parties, no other interests.

'Then, thinking about things, I realised I'd made a critical omission. Remember that list of employees I gave you to check? I missed out a couple of people; Gerrard and Melody themselves. I'm an idiot. It's basic police procedure. Rule number one is trust no one.

'So I checked up on them. Melody Ann Harper's as clean as a whistle, while all Gerrard Sidney Vine has against him is an ancient charge, subsequently dropped.'

'What for?'

'Unlawful sexual connection. The girl was fifteen, he was twenty. She went to the police, he was interviewed, then a few days later all charges were dropped. The subtext reads like a cover-up. I suspect money changed hands.'

'So *that's* why he was sent down from Oxford,' Jane said. 'I always wondered how he ended up at Leicester. But how does any of that help us?'

'It doesn't. At all. So I started looking into the criminal connections side. You know, family, friends and associates.

'Apart from being a blue-blooded member of the upper-class mafia, old Three-R's pretty clean, but Ms Melody Ann Harper has an interesting skeleton in her closet.'

'You mean her real father? The one she calls Dagenham Daddy? The used car dealer?'

'Not him. Magnus Harper's a straight shooter. Always has been. Pays his VAT and taxes – no offshore trusts or any of that nonsense. He makes a point of advertising the fact. He's big on charitable donations too, and between you and me, he's been a good friend to the police over the years. Lots of useful tip-offs about shady deals and dealers.

'No, it's the other one. The one her mum took up with she was a kid. Henry Morton Baxter.'

'Islington Papa?'

'High Down Dad might be more appropriate.'

'Why?'

'Because he's currently serving five years for embezzling two million quid.' Matt took a printout from his pocket and handed it to her.

Henry Morton Baxter had joined the Greater London Council shortly after completing an accountancy degree in the early 80s. He survived the GLC's dissolution in 1986, moving from borough to borough as the work required, and was well-placed and well-credentialed for a senior role when the Greater London Authority was established fourteen years later.

Presiding over a mini fiefdom from his eighth-floor office in City Hall, Baxter was known for his long hours, diligent work and careful attention to detail. Little wonder when some of those details involved non-existent contractors dating back to his borough days. More than twenty, the prosecution alleged, all carefully structured and managed to draw tiny sums from the GLA's eleven billion pound annual budget. Nothing greedy, nothing dramatic. On-going maintenance type sums that wouldn't get more than a second glance from the internal audit team.

Baxter maintained an outwardly modest lifestyle quite in keeping with his salary and position, and the ruse might have continued till the day he retired if it hadn't been for a bank processing error while he was on one of his rare holidays. An over-zealous clerk checked up on a transaction, setting in motion a chain of events that led to his downfall.

A few tens or hundreds here and there each week didn't amount to much – until you added the numbers up and multiplied them by almost two decades. Two million was considered a conservative estimate, and there was little to show where it had gone. Baxter was as careful with its disposition as he had been with its acquisition.

'Five years for two million quid?' Jane put down the printout. 'I hope they got it back.'

Matt shook his head. 'Almost none of it.'

'What did he do with it then? Wild women, gambling, drugs?'

'Not Baxter. Not the sort – at least as far as anyone can tell. There's rumours of offshore trusts and secret bank accounts, but no one knows for certain. And Baxter's not telling.'

'That's like four hundred thou a year – while the taxpayer's paying for his board and lodgings!'

'Actually, it's worse than that. He'll probably be out in three with good behaviour.'

'Bastard! But what's that got to do with Melody?'

'Nothing directly, but it adds a new dimension, don't you

think?'

She sipped her coffee. 'He was always her favourite, always showering her with gifts. He bought her a sports car for her birthday once, while she was still at university.'

'Maybe *he* didn't. Maybe it was London's ratepayers.'

'Bastard!' she said again. 'But it does take out the money angle, doesn't it?'

'Not necessarily. It's probably not money he can readily get his hands on, especially in the nick.'

'But Gerrard's rolling in it anyway. Got a rich aunty or something.'

'He's in Paris this weekend, ostensibly on business, but Melody thinks it's another woman.'

'Could that be it? They're breaking up and your report's to leverage the value of the business down so she can buy him out cheaply?'

'You might be right.'

'So what are you going to do?'

'The only thing I can do. We were employed for a week by Harper *and* Vine to investigate the counterfeiting of *their* coffee. There's still two days left on the contract, and at the end of it, copies of my findings will go to *both* partners.'

Jane smiled. 'You're so ethical.'

'And sensible. If this is going to turn into a matrimonial property spat, I don't want to end up in the middle of it.'

'Not even as co-respondent?' she asked.

'*Especially* not as co-respondent,' he said emphatically.

'You weren't tempted then? She is quite a looker.'

Matt glanced at the bread knife. 'Are you going to use that? Because it'd be a waste of time if you do. You're already in my heart, Jane. Forever.'

A moment later, she was in his arms.

34

Gerrard didn't recall Gorelston-on-Sea as ever having been this much fun as a boy. Then again, his boyhood definition of fun was somewhat different.

The pub girls had turned out to be very accommodating of a stranger who was happy to buy them drinks all evening. He'd pretended he was a talent scout for a London recording studio, and they'd pretended to believe him. The latter parts of the night were hazy. There'd been a trip to an off-license, a visit to the beach, a bit of snogging and groping behind a beach hut. Then Betty, (or was it Betsy?), mentioned she was having a trouble keeping up with her rent. Gerrard kindly offered to help, but by that stage he was almost out of cash so they'd gone off in search of an ATM.

She cuddled him from behind and slipped a hand down his trousers to show her gratitude as he withdrew however much it was, and he'd almost had her right there in the main street, up against the front doors of the bank. She'd giggled and pushed him away, saying she wanted to enjoy him properly and that they should go back to her place, but he lost her somehow in the hunt for a mini cab. She'd spotted one down the end of darkened lane and hurried off, telling him to wait there, that she'd bring it round to meet him, but she was as squiffy as he was and must've got lost herself.

Ah, well. The prospect of a bit of Norfolk nooky hadn't eventuated after all, but it was still only the first night of his liberation.

Who said money wasn't everything?

* * *

'Tell me about your hot date,' Matt said.

It was much later in the morning and they lay tangled in a sheet on her bed, the curtains drawn against the intrusive daylight and the door closed against the intrusive cat.

She told him about the threatening phone call on the bus and her immediate reply. 'I was still mad at you I guess and gave him both barrels.'

He chuckled and stroked her hair.

A thought suddenly occurred to her. 'You told Melody I was tracking him down, didn't you?'

'Yup.'

'What time was that, do you remember?'

'Want me to get my notebook.'

'*You made notes?*'

'It was a client meeting. Of course I made notes.'

'Right there, while she was coming on to you?'

'Of course not, but afterwards.' He tapped his head. 'I make mental notes and scribble them down when I get a chance. It's an undercover thing.'

'So you brought her up to date on the case, then she went off to the loo. Interesting ...'

'Why?'

'When I talked to Smith in person, I found out his contact's full name: Lydia Turner. Long auburn hair, brown eyes, approximately my age and build. A cultured woman with a lot of contacts. She didn't supply the coffee herself. It came through a friend of a friend.

'He last saw her when the coffee was delivered and hadn't heard from her since. That was six weeks ago. He didn't have her number, and all attempts to track her down failed. Then, at approximately 4:28 yesterday afternoon, he got a call from someone by the name of Number Withheld. He was snarky at first at the interruption, but his attitude changed dramatically the moment he heard who it was. He hurried out the office to take the call so I didn't hear what he said, but when he returned, he couldn't get rid of me fast enough.

'I had the strong impression the call had come from her.'

Matt said nothing, simply retrieved his notebook from the pocket of his chinos and pointed out the entries:

16:05 (approx) arrive at CH bistro with MH.
Progress report deliv.
16:27 loo break (MH).

'She was gone about two minutes. I wrote that up while I was waiting.'

'Interesting coincidence, isn't it?'

'You think that Lydia Turner is really Melody Harper? That she called Smith and warned him off us? But the hair, eyes—'

'A wig and coloured contacts. Simple.'

Matt blew out his cheeks. 'It does make a kind of weird sense. That so-called counterfeit coffee does appear to be genuine. And Melody has full access to everything. She could easily fiddle a stocktake. It even adds a nuance to her little seduction game yesterday. But there's still the question of motive. What the hell is she up to?'

'Let's confirm it's her first,' Jane said.

Later, after they'd showered, he found her in the box room leafing through an old photograph album. The album was one of her mum's treasured possessions, and now one of the few traces left of Elsie Child's life. She'd loved her albums almost as much as she loved her children, adding carefully selected cuttings and photos to mark each of their milestones. She'd kept one for each of them – Jane, Tom and George – and Jane's was complete, from the yellowing birth notice to a picture of her first steps and first day at school. A curled lock of blonde hair in a cellophane bag. A note saying "Love you, Mum" written in childish blocky letters. A postcard from Europe detailing her travels with the only other man she'd ever really loved. Jane looked at the date. A month before his death. A year before her mum's.

'My god, is that you?' Matt said, peering over her shoulder at a page containing a photograph of Jane, her mum, and her brothers standing round a cake decorated with eighteen candles and a big chunky 18 in pink icing. 'What was with the hair?'

'I was going through a David Bowie phase.'

'Sorry, a total failure. At least the androgynous look. *Phwoar!*'

Jane smiled despite the melancholy mood the old album brought with it.

'The university pictures should be near the back,' she said, flicking through a quarter-inch of empty black pages. Somehow they seemed most poignant of all. They should have been filled, continued right on to the present day. Her mum would have been so proud ...

Jane had meant to keep the album up to date. But people didn't do that sort of thing any more. It was all digital, instant, beamed around the world, shared, commented on and then forgotten. No one seemed to have time for memories these days. They were too busy with the here and now.

'You OK?' She felt Matt's hand on her shoulder.

'Fine,' she sniffed. 'Just remembering.'

He refused to remove the photograph and insisted on scanning it in-situ, an awkward process on their office combo printer-scanner-fax machine, but he said it didn't seem right to disturb something so lovingly arranged.

The comment made Jane weepy all over again. If she hadn't already been head over heels about him, she'd have fallen in love with him right then.

The picture showed Jane and two girlfriends at a university party. Melody Harper had photo-bombed it and could be seen on one side, her arms wide, her mouth open, her face bright and full of mischief. Elsie Child had written "Les Girls" and the date in white chalk pencil underneath it.

'How's that?' Matt asked as the scanner's glow faded.

Jane checked her computer screen. 'That's it. Sharp as a tack.'

He removed the album, closed it carefully and set it to one side while she cropped the picture down to Melody's face and enlarged the image. Then she transferred it to her phone. It was a little grainy, but Melody's hair was longer back then and her distance from the flash made it look darker too.

Still abashed at her crying jag, Jane said, 'Sorry for being such a girl just now.'

'Don't ever apologise for something like that. It's like saying you're sorry for being a human being. For having feelings.'

She bit her lip and focused on the screen. God, she loved that man!

35

Od didn't even need to ask. He could see it in Dmitri's walk as he headed back from the pay phones across the road from the hotel. He got to his feet and summoned the lift as the big Russian re-entered the lobby. The down button. For the basement level car park.

'We on?'

'We are on.'

* * *

A whiteboard in the lobby of the Philadelphia Hotel welcomed members of a Chinese tour party whose coach blocked half the narrow street outside and whose luggage choked half the entrance. While porters and counter staff fought to clear the backlog, the group themselves were lunching in *Le Chat Noir*. Every table was full, the waiting staff scuttled about like demented hens, and the room reverberated with the sound of raised voices and happy laughter.

Jane spotted John Patrick Smith to one side, ingratiating himself to a table of well-dressed businessmen and their over-dressed wives, every one of whom seemed to be clutching a gaudy designer handbag in gold and black. A waiter stood nearby with a question. Smith answered curtly before returning, bowing, to his guests. Then he caught sight of Jane. He stiffened, his former affable expression turning to one of furious disdain.

'I told you, I have nothing more to say to you,' he said, coming quickly to her side and steering her back towards the luggage-choked lobby.

'I have one more question for you, Mr Smith, and the answer will only take a second.' Jane held up her phone. 'Is this Lydia Turner?'

'I—' He froze. 'Where did you get that?'

'I take it that's a yes?'

He looked stricken for a moment then glanced around to see where his wife was. Jennifer Joan Smith was busy at a table near the back. He nodded and swallowed.

'That's all. Thank you.'

The Plover's Plumbing van was double-parked outside behind the coach. Matt leaned across and opened the door as Jane approached.

'It's her, all right,' she told him.

'So she's hawking her own coffee, but why? For a few extra quid? And why did she hire us?'

'Because she *thought* she was employing a couple of patsies. A new startup desperate for any work they could get. Desperate to make a name for themselves. So much so they'd let her write their report.'

'Still begs the question why?'

It would have been quicker to walk to Covent Garden – if they could have found a car park – and they were forced to employ the same strategy there, Matt minding the car and moving it on at the first glimpse of a parking warden while Jane made enquiries.

The Fancy Cat Fanciers Association ran a charity shop amidst the gaily painted frontages in one of the alleys leading to Neal's Yard. Amidst signs for holistic healing, natural remedies and Shiatsu, the FCF's front window featured a banner advertising their upcoming annual show and a number of the unusual breeds visitors would find there. Four roomy cages were arranged side by side with cards identifying their occupants. Jane recognised a young British Shorthair like Tibbles McVicar, a fully-grown Foldex whose clipped ears and wide eyes made it look like a permanently amazed kitten, and a stolid Havana Brown, curled up and ostensibly asleep, though its twitching ears suggested otherwise. The one she didn't recognise – and the one attracting most attention, not all of it complimentary – was a Sphynx. It stared back, equally curious, with a triangular face, enormous ears, yellow eyes and fur so short and light that it appeared to be wearing skin-tight suede. The deep lines and folds in the skin around its cheeks and brow made it look more alien than feline.

'They're wonderfully affectionate,' a volunteer told Jane as she entered, still staring at the cat and being stared back at in return. 'They like nothing better than cuddling up next to you on cold nights.'

'I think I can understand why,' Jane said as the cat kept pace with her to the end of its cage. 'I'm looking for Dr McKellar. He said he'd be here for a couple of hours this afternoon.'

'Yes, just though the back there.'

Jane was directed past cluttered shelves and closely spaced display cabinets featuring everything from paperbacks to porcelain, Toby jugs to toys and games. A beaded curtain behind the cash register revealed a broom-cupboard-sized space occupied by a middle-aged man in cords and a T-shirt that emphasised his ponderous belly. He was perched on a stool at a narrow bench, stuffing envelopes with the latest issue of *Purrfection!*.

'Dr McKellar? Jane Child. We spoke on the phone.'

'Ah, yes,' he rose and shook her hand. 'You wanted to talk about cat fanciers in your area, I believe.'

'Not quite,' she said, handing him her card. 'I'm a private detective investigating the disappearance of several pedigree animals, all belonging to members of your group. The cats were effectively held to ransom and only returned after a cash payment. Now their owners are being extorted to buy insurance to ensure their on-going safety.'

'What? Good heavens. I had no idea!'

'It seems they were deliberately targeted. The three cases I'm looking at all occurred within a week, all in the same area. And all are members of the FCF.'

'I see. And you, naturally, thought of our database?' His eyes were bright and alert.

'Specifically, who has copies of it and who has access to it?'

'Specifically no one, Ms Child, apart from my wife and myself. Clarisa is chair of the group and I am its secretary, and I'm an old hand at this sort of thing – database security, I mean.

'You've probably gathered that FCF members are generally more well-heeled than regular cat owners. They spend considerably more on their pets in the first place and tend to have more discretionary income. That makes them a target for all sorts of marketing. We have eighteen hundred members in Greater London alone, and I could sell our database a dozen times a year. But I don't because I respect our members' privacy. Besides, we can channel that interest into advertising in our magazine.' He gestured at the copies of *Purrfection!* on the bench beside him and the closed-up laptop beside it.

'There's only one copy of the database, on that machine there. The hard drive is encrypted, the machine is password protected, and the database likewise. There are backups, of course. One kept on a flash drive, updated weekly and stored in the safe at home, and one held off-site and updated monthly via a secure connection.'

'What about address labels, things like that?'

'Print them off myself or send out a print-ready file. Clarisa and I manage all the admin ourselves. Updates and all that. Occasionally a committee member will ask for an extract or an individual's details, but we keep a weather eye on things. I'm happy to provide the information to trusted personnel, but they rarely ever get more than a subset of the data we hold.

'One thing though. Our magazines go out in distinctive envelopes.' He held one up, branded with the FCF logo. 'You might be looking for a postman.'

'I think it's a little more organised than that.'

'Well, whatever information these people are using, it's not coming from here.' He tapped a fingernail on the laptop and crossed his arms. 'I know about these things, Ms Child. I worked in the computer industry for more than thirty years, ten of them as Chief Security Officer for a number of large corporations. I know all about data security; hackers and crackers and the like. And I still keep up to date. It may sound boastful, but our little organisation's data is as secure as GCHQ's.'

Jane texted Matt and met him outside the Crown on Monmouth Street.

'No luck?'

She shook her head as she climbed into the van. 'That's *it* for work-related stuff. It's the weekend, damn it!'

'Allow me to whisk you away from all this.'

'Please do!'

But with the Sunday traffic, there wasn't much whisking.

* * *

'Gotta admire your people, man,' Od told Dmitri. 'Working on a Sunday.'

'What do you know of my people?'

'Nothin', man. 'cept they's hard working. Gotta admire that.'

Dmitri glanced at his companion. He didn't like that kind of talk. Any kind of talk, really. About him or who he worked for. Speculation was dangerous. It led to doubts. Questions. Don't talk, just do. And once it was done, put it behind you and don't look back. That was how he'd been trained and that was how he lived. But this guy was a gasbag. A liability. Still, the mission was almost over. Once it was, he'd been ordered to remove any footprints. He knew what that meant.

'No, no, don't slow down, man. Keep going.'

'But that is address,' Dmitri gestured as they cruised past.

'Yeah, but it's a residential street, man. And it's Sunday. People home. Kids out. Dudes washin' cars. Grannies gardening.' Mommy 'n' daddy's pushing prams, see? They gonna notice a blackfella and a big Russian dude.'

'I thought you say the place is office?'

'It is, but it looks like a home office, like they got a desk in the living room or something. And there's two targets this time, so it's going to be harder to set up.'

They turned left at the next intersection and pulled over. Dmitri took an A-Z from the pocket in the driver's door. Od would have offered him his phone, but the big man seemed to have an aversion to anything electronic.

'Gotta take 'em both, but it'll be the dude, man. It's always the dude. Chicks is too smart for that shit.'

'One is woman?'

'Pretty one too, 'cordin' to the website. Why, didn't you get lucky last night?'

'Of course, but is like hunting. Always room for more trophies.'

Od laughed. 'Ain't you the man! So how d'you want to do it?'

'Murder-suicide. Easy. Stabbing one. Cut wrist other. Quiet also. Like you say, residential street. Do not disturb the neighbour.'

'We're gonna have to come back anyways cos no one's home right now.' He held the cellphone away from his ear where Jane's voice could be heard asking the caller to leave their name and number after the beep.

Dmitri studied the street map. 'They both live in office?'

'I dunno, man. The house is in the chick's name.'

'We come back later, after dark. If both together, finish job. If not, we keep her and wait till morning. Till man arrive. Time of death must be the same.'

'And we can *entertain* her in the meantime. I like your thinking, man.'

Three boys went past, one of them bouncing a football. Dmitri wound down his window. 'How much you want for ball?'

'Huh?' The bouncer squinted at him.

'Football? How much?'

After a canny glance at his friends the kid said, 'A tenner.'

'Pay,' Dmitri told Od.

'What? That thing's kicked to shit. You could get a new one for two quid. It's only plastic.'

'Pay.'

Muttering his disapproval, Od pulled out his wallet and took out a ten-pound note. Dmitri handed it to the boy. He held it up to the light to check the watermark before handing over the ball. Then the three of them ran off, laughing.

'What the hell you want that for, man?'

'Football. National sport. What else would grown men do in school playground?'

'Playground? What you talkin' about?'

Dmitri tapped the street map. 'There is school behind the office house. Playground. We go that way tonight. Now, we go there for reconnaissance. Maybe accidental kick will take ball over fence and we must retrieve, yes?'

Od grinned. 'You the man. Good thinking, Dim.'

The big Russian glared.

'I mean, Dmitri.'

36

'I promised my girl sand and seagulls,' Matt gestured expansively from the driver's seat, 'and sand and seagulls she shall have.'

'I certainly can't fault you there,' Jane said, peering into the limpid blue sky at the birds circling a tidal shore of the Thames, at the sunlight glinting off the expanse of water, 'but what's that smell?'

'Oh god, don't do that,' he cried as she wound down her window, letting in a fine, gritty dust, the roar of bulldozers and the stench of refuse.

Jane sniffed. 'Something seems to be a little off out there. I think the ocean's gone bad.'

'All right, all right, you've made your point. Can we have that window up again? Please!'

Jane complied, but somehow the van retained an aftertaste, like the opposite of a fine wine.

'I heard Gerrard Vine takes *his* dates to Paris.' Jane said.

'That place? It's full of foreigners. I mean, what could compare with that view? What could be more English than a common gull or a JCB digger?'

'Or a brown rat?'

'Precisely.'

'I can see you're a wild romantic at heart, but it is still a tip.'

'No, it's a *Reuse and Recycling Centre*. Didn't you see the sign?'

'So can we reuse, recycle and retreat, please?'

They stopped in the unloading lane outside a cavernous secondhand facility the size of a disused aircraft hangar. The old vanity unit from his bathroom was in the back. One of the staff helped Matt unload it while Jane went inside to browse aisles, racks and stacks of recyclables. He found her out the back, pedalling round in circles on an ancient Raleigh Twenty.

'I knew I'd get you re-*cycling*,' he said.

Jane groaned and braked in front of him. 'I think I've found the answer to our company transport problem.'

'I wasn't aware we had one.'

'We can't keep Jake's van forever. And it's only a fiver.' He regarded the bike dubiously. 'The brakes are fine – as you've just seen – and two of the three speeds work too. It just needs a little TLC.'

'I like the paint job. Blue and rust are my favourite colours.'

'Can we have it, Daddy? Please, please, please?' Jane said, circling him.

'All right, all right.' Matt laughed. 'I'll pay the man. You throw it in the van. I suppose I should be grateful it's not a pony.'

They left the seagulls, sand and stink behind and headed on into the more rarefied airs of the Kent countryside. They took in a village pub, lingered on a village green, explored B roads off the beaten track and found a secluded layby beside a rushing stream. But they never quite made it to the seaside.

There was no sign of Jake, but the water was back on at Matt's place. He'd even jury-rigged a shower curtain round the bath. Jane showered and changed into some of the fresh clothes she'd brought with her. Downstairs, the house was filling with the smell of the roast he was preparing.

'Mmm,' she said, towelling her hair as she stepped into the kitchen. 'That's better than your *eau de recycling centre*. I'm so hungry I could eat a horse.'

'Damn it, now you tell me. I'm doing pork.'

'Oh well, it'll have to do.'

'The crackling's better on pork anyway. And my crackling's sensational.'

'Is that a euphemism, Mr Healy?'

'Get your hands off me, woman, I'm preparing dinner. Never interrupt a culinary *artiste*!'

'Even to give them a taster?' She kissed him long and hard.

He eased back a minute later, smacking his lips like a connoisseur. 'Hmm, yes, very moreish. I'll have a double helping of that later. But I need a shower first. And it's still not a patch on my crackling, you know.'

She smacked him on the bottom and sent him on his way.

Dinner was all he claimed and more. The meat was mouth-watering, the crackling crunchy and delicious, and the Yorkshire puddings were so light and airy they seemed to hover half-an-inch above the surface of the plate.

'I proclaim you King of the Roast,' she said, pushing back from the table and knighting him with a napkin.

He bowed, accepting the honour. 'It's not a skill I get to practice often. My dad taught me after Mum died, but you don't bother much when you live alone.'

He was right, Jane thought. There was a lot you didn't bother with when you lived alone. A couple of months ago, Sunday evening might have meant time with Sally and Paul or, more likely, getting a head start on Monday morning. Going over her work schedule for the week, maybe even doing a little prep. At the very least she'd be ironing blouses and sorting out her wardrobe before crashing into bed, her mind spinning with the things she'd have to remember, the people she'd have to see, the things she'd have to do ...

True, she had spent half her weekend working or thinking about Bluebelle Investigations stuff, but it was different somehow, something she'd *wanted* to do. And this evening, all she had to look forward to was Matt's sway-backed sofa, putting her feet up, watching a movie and probably falling asleep in his arms before being carried up to bed. A thought almost as delicious as the meal itself. She was glad she'd put Sally's dinner invitation off for a week. She'd give her a call tomorrow and confirm it.

Matt gathered up the dishes and put them to one side. 'Now for dessert ...'

'Oh god, really? I couldn't eat another thing.'

'Well, I'm having some.' His face took on a demonic look and he rubbed his hands.

Why? What is it?'

'Didn't I tell you?' He waggled his fingers and made chomping sounds. 'It's you, my dear. I've fattened you up, now welcome to the cannibal feast. Bwa-ha-ha-hah!'

Jane gave a little shriek and he chased her into the lounge.

* * *

Melody met Gerrard on the concourse of St Pancras station. He came bounding out with a spring in his step, but she greeted him with a sombre glare.

'Where have you been? I've been trying to call you?'

'My phone ...' he said. 'Something ... I'm not sure. I think it was stolen.'

'Oh for goodness sake, Gerrard. I do wish you'd look after things.'

He gave her a warm hug. She returned a dutiful one. He wanted to hold on longer, spin her around like they did in movies and tell her all his news, but she was in one of her businesslike moods – like so often lately.

'How was Paris?'

'Fine, fine.'

'And Harvey Harry? Did he come through with this investor consortium?'

'It's ... all ... still ...'

'Seriously, Gerrard?'

'No, no I don't think he can.'

'I told you it was a waste of time, didn't I? Come on, I'm

parked out the front. Have you reported your phone?'

'Not yet, I—'

'When did it go missing?'

'I'm not sure, I—'

'I'm not the only one who's been trying to contact you, you know. The police even called at the flat.'

'The *police?*' The word came louder than he intended. That was quick. He didn't expect anyone to find her till tomorrow. 'What ... er ... what did they want?'

'They wouldn't say, but you're to call them as soon as possible. I've got the number. Here, use mine.'

Gerrard stood on the footpath and made the call while Melody retrieved her car. She swung up to the kerb and he got in.

'Well?' she asked as he handed back her phone.

'It's Aunt Myra. She's had a fall.'

'Nothing trivial, I hope,' she said, immediately regretting her levity when she saw the stricken look on Gerrard's face.

'She's ... unconscious. In hospital. In. Hospital,' he repeated as if he couldn't quite believe it.

37

Traffic was still relatively light when Matt dropped Jane off at her place. He had to get the van back to Jake and wanted to pick up a new vanity unit while he still had it. He unloaded the old bike, gave her a farewell peck and said, 'I'll be in about ten.'

'You treat this business like you own it.'

He grinned. 'I'll bring morning tea.'

Jane wheeled the bike in, closed the gate behind her and rummaged for her key. She didn't notice the twitch of the lounge curtain.

Bluebelle sat watching from the step.

'Oh no, you haven't been out here all night, have you? I put out extra food and everything. Why on earth won't you use this? Look, it's really, really easy.' She knelt and demonstrated the cat door for the umpteenth time, hoping that if Bluebelle had been out all night, the smell of her food dish might provide a final incentive.

'Look, I'll even hold it up for you. See?'

Bluebelle looked, edged forward, sniffed, then backed away sharply.

'What on earth is it? Anyone would think there was a ...' Jane looked through the opening and saw a pair of brown leather boots standing in the hallway behind the in-swing of the front door. A pair of boots that neither she nor Matt owned.

'... bogeyman in there ...' she continued, her voice trailing off as she let the cat flap go.

She straightened.

'OK then, let me just get my key,' she added unconvincingly, then scooped Bluebelle up in her arms and ran for the gate.

The door was snatched open behind her. A figure darted out and grabbed her by the shoulder as she fumbled for the gate latch. One-handed, armed only with a cat, she did the only thing she could think off. She spun and hurled Bluebelle at him, trusting to the animal's natural instincts to defend them both.

Bluebelle didn't let her down.

Suddenly airborne, launched at an unknown object, the cat did what any self-respecting cat would do and extended her landing gear: eighteen razor-sharp claws, five on the front paws, four on the back. Her rear paws snagged on the lapels of the man's jacket, giving her excellent purchase, while her front ones raked the sides of his fleshy face, tearing long scratches before sinking deep.

The big man bellowed. '*Pizda!*' He released Jane's shoulder and clawed at the cat.

Bluebelle, meanwhile, was doing more clawing of her own. She didn't like where she'd landed and struggled to get off, tearing threads in one shoulder of the man's jacket and raking the side of his neck with a rear paw as she leapt on to the front fence and raced away.

With both hands free, Jane tore open the gate, slipped through, slammed it behind her and sprinted up the road at such a pace that she probably set a new personal best. There were shouts behind her, but she didn't turn, and the sound of car doors slamming spurred her on.

Get off the street! You're a sitting duck!

The car roared into life and accelerated, but she was now only yards from a cycle path, a shortcut to the shops. It was too narrow for a car and had concrete bollards at either end. There, she slowed and glanced back to see if they would stop, perhaps follow her on foot. But the car raced straight past without slowing.

* * *

Matt came at once, the moment he got her call, executing an illegal

U-turn, forcing his way into a packed line of traffic, even cutting across the footpath at an intersection to avoid the red light on a left turn. Pedestrians leapt for their lives and motorists blared their horns and yelled abuse as he crashed down the other kerb and back on to the road. Matt was glad it wasn't his van and his suspension. Or his signwriting on the side. He just hoped Jake was well insured.

Nine words: 'I've been attacked. Someone was waiting in the house.' He sprang into action even while he was still taking the call, driving one-handed and cursing the lack of a siren and blue and reds on the roof.

She was all right, she insisted, but he didn't slow. Threw the phone on to the passenger seat and floored the accelerator. She'd told him where she was – a coffee shop in the shopping precinct – and he brought the van to a skidding halt on a pair of double-yellow lines opposite.

She looked fine. She was calm, steady, rational. He was in a worse state than she was. The call had shaken him. He'd forgotten how smart and self-reliant she was. When he burst through the door, she stood up, staring at his ashen, anguished face and put her arms around him. 'Are you all right?'

For a moment he couldn't speak. Just held her. Eventually he managed, 'Jesus Jane, I should be asking *you* that.'

She signalled the waitress for another coffee, sat him down and told him what had happened.

'Brown leather boots?' he repeated.

She consulted her notebook.

What a pro!

'Clean. Well cared for. A bit like cowboy boots. Size: enormous. There was someone else too. A shadow of movement down by the kitchen. And when they came after me, there were voices, two sets of footsteps, and I heard two car doors slam.

'I didn't get the make and model. It raced past the entrance to the walkway. All I can tell you is that it was a silver coloured sedan of some kind. Four-door.'

'And the one that came after you said *Pizda*?'

'It's Russian. The C-word. I looked it up.' She tapped her phone.

Matt shook his head. 'You're bloody remarkable, Jane. Look at you. An experience like that and you're as solid as a rock!'

'I've been there before, remember?'

He bit his lip and nodded.

'I'm worried about Bluebelle though. I think she got away all right, but I didn't stick around to check.'

'I hope she got the bastard's eye. Have you called the police?'

'Why would I do that when I have my very own personal policeman?'

'*Ex*-policeman,' he reminded her. 'They'll have resources I can't access. Like the ability to check all A&E departments for big Russians with clawed eyes. Give me a moment.' He took out his phone.

Jane sipped her coffee, reviewing the notes she'd made.

'He'll meet us outside in forty minutes.' Matt said, putting his phone away and sighing. 'Gives us time for another cuppa.'

'And for you to shift that van,' Jane gestured to the parking warden opposite, her ticket book already out.

'Oh shit!' Matt said and bounded from the cafe.

38

Detective Inspector Colin Avery looked every inch a policeman. It wasn't just the off-the-peg suit and scrappy tie – poorly tied and slightly misaligned – or the summer-weight trench coat that hung limply from his broad shoulders, it was something in his bearing, his manner, the proprietorial way in which he looked up and down Jane's street: as if he owned it. His measured confidence was instantly reassuring. Here was a man who took charge, who could be relied on. He could also, as Matt knew to his cost, drink like a fish.

He was as tall as Matt, a little more solidly built though about the same age, but his close-cropped hair and the telltale signs of male-pattern baldness – heightened temples and thinning at the vertex of the scalp – made him look older.

There were no sirens, no lights, no drama, just a dun-coloured Ford Fiesta parked up on the kerb opposite. He strode across, nodded to Jane then said quietly, 'What've you fucked up now, Healy?'

'I thought you and Dock Green could do with a break from traffic patrol and RTAs,' Matt replied, nodding across to DS Dixon who was extracting a forensics toolkit from the Fiesta's boot. 'You know, a little *real* police work.'

'I take it this is your gaff, Jane?' Avery said. 'It's a bit more upmarket than Healy's Greenwich squat.'

Jane smiled. Despite what she'd been through and the invasion of her house – her *home* – there was something affirming and reassuring in this banter.

DS Dixon came across lugging a grey plastic toolbox. Avery

introduced Jane, then the four of them stood surveying her house from the footpath as Dixon handed out latex gloves.

Avery lifted the gate latch with a pencil, pushed it wide and paused. He pointed to a couple of spots of fresh blood on the path and Dixon got to work. Stepping round them, they approached the front door, which stood ajar. A brief flurry of movement made them pause a moment, then Bluebelle pushed her way out the cat door and settled on the step, regarding them calmly as she licked the side of one paw.

'Bluebelle!' Jane exclaimed, relieved to see the cat unharmed. 'You used your cat door! Good girl.'

'While the real one's standing open.' Matt shook his head.

'Is that the assault weapon?' Healy asked.

'Used purely in self-defence,' Jane said.

'Still, we might have to take her in for questioning, especially if she keeps destroying possible evidence like that.' Bluebelle was now chewing at her claws.

Standard procedure meant Matt and Jane had to wait outside while Avery and Dixon checked the house. They stood on the step, Matt with one arm around her, Jane cradling the cat. Now Bluebelle was safe, she was dreading their report. Things stolen, the place smashed up, her small treasures ruined ...

'All clear, nothing touched as far as I can see,' Avery reported, coming back downstairs and joining his colleague in the hall.

'No sign of forced entry either,' Dixon added.

Jane stepped inside, still holding Bluebelle, feeling like a stranger in her own home. She peered into the lounge, the kitchen, the laundry. It was just as they'd said. Nothing stolen, nothing touched. The only anomaly was two mugs on the bench beside the kettle, cold tea in the bottom of both. She pointed to them. 'That wasn't me. I hardly ever use those cups.' Dixon went to work, bagging each one carefully.

Jane and Matt checked upstairs together. In the wardrobes and under the bed too, just for their own reassurance, but all was as she'd left it the day before.

The red light on the answerphone was blinking. Two missed calls, one timed at 00:32, the other at 00:47, but no messages left. Matt checked the log. The caller's ID had been withheld.

'Someone was checking to see if you were home,' he said. 'The first time when they were en route, the second time when they were standing outside.'

Jane felt icy fingers run down her spine. 'But I didn't get in till almost eight. You mean they were waiting for me?'

'Or us.'

Back downstairs, Avery asked her to walk through what had happened, positioning Dixon behind the door and stepping out with her.

Jane came through the gate as she'd done earlier, mimed tending to the cat then kneeling to demonstrate the cat flap.

'I didn't notice them at first,' she said, 'just a movement down the hall. Like a shadow darting into the kitchen. That's what made me look again. That's when I saw the boots. Boots, not shoes. And they were bigger than that.' Inside, Dixon shuffled forward. 'A bit more ... Yeah, they came out to about there.'

'So you legged it to the gate and they came after you. You threw the cat – ah!' He pointed to some more spots of blood on the wall and some wispy fibres caught on a rough edge of brick. 'Then headed east, down to the cycle lane.'

'I don't think they actually came after me. I think they just ran for their car and drove off.'

'That suggests whatever they were after wasn't that important.'

'It was important enough for them to break in at one o'clock in the morning then sit around for seven hours waiting for me to come home!'

'*If* those calls came from them.'

'They were there long enough to make a cuppa.'

Back inside, they found Dixon measuring the approximate

shoe size Jane had seen from the cat flap. 'Big plates. Thirteens at least, I'd say.'

'Which ties in with your description of the bloke that came after you,' Avery said to Jane. 'Also, a big guy, clawed and bleeding, would block your narrow gate, preventing his mate from coming after you. I don't s'pose you got any sort of look at number two?'

'I was somewhat distracted.'

Matt made tea and the three of them settled round the kitchen table while Dixon studied the locks on the back door and the sliding door through an otoscope. 'No scratches on the tumblers,' he observed. 'If they did pick a lock, they were good.'

'Sounds professional.' Avery turned to Matt and Jane. 'If that's the case, who have you two been pissing off?'

'We've only been in business five minutes,' Matt said. 'We've only had two cases and both are still open. Counterfeit coffee and missing cats.'

'Missing cats?' Avery repeated, raising an eyebrow at Matt.

'Hey chief, got something here,' Dixon called from the back fence. 'I reckon they came in this way. There's a partial print on this railing. Some sort of boot. A big 'un.'

He returned for his tape measure and camera.

Avery said, 'We'll run the forensics and see if they turn up anyone we know about, but apart from that all I can suggest is you change your locks.'

'That's it?' Jane said. 'Someone breaks into my home, makes tea, sits around waiting for me to come back, attacks me when I try to get away, and ... you're just going to leave it to forensics?'

Avery turned to Matt, guessing the explanation might come better from him.

'It's a question of priorities, Jane. The police get thousands of calls a day, just in London alone. Murders, muggings, rapes, robberies with violence, child abuse ... Yes, there was an illegal entry here, and yes, someone came after you, but ...'

'But he didn't stab me or beat me half to death,' she said.

Matt sighed. 'If I hadn't called in Avery, we wouldn't have got this level of attention. We'd still be waiting for a panda car. They'd turn up around lunchtime, have a quick shifty, fill out a form and tell you to change the locks.'

'Which is about all that's happened anyway!'

* * *

Getting Dmitri back into his hotel without drawing attention to his clawed face had been tricky. Od had surrendered his baseball cap to pull it down over the temple wound – which bled profusely – and Dmitri had kept his head down as they'd hustled in the back way, through the busy kitchens. Now, in his room, perched on the side of the wash basin with a collection of hastily bought supplies, Od inspected his handiwork.

'You clean up all right, man. That's the best I can do, but you should really see a doc.'

Dmitri inspected his plastered cheeks in the mirror and studied the long plaster strip running from his forehead down to the side of his right eye. 'Fucking animal. I gut and kill it. Bitch whore too.'

'Some of them scratches are deep. You might need stitches, man. And you definitely need antibiotics. I hear cat claws got all sorts o' shit in 'em on account of them having hollow points or somethin'.'

'I give her hollow-point, right between the eyes. Fucking bitch.'

'I'm serious, man.'

Dmitri slammed a fist down on the sink bench, making the First Aid kit and the scattered supplies jump into the air. 'You think I am not? Bitch almost take my eye out. That alone she die for. And this time, I make it slow. No building jump or bike crash. In the end, she will beg me to finish her.'

39

Jane fumed, but did so quietly. Avery and Matt were right in a sense – she was OK, no harm had been done and nothing was missing – but they were also terribly wrong. Someone – two someones – had broken into her home in the dead of night. Experts, apparently, picking locks and letting themselves in. Then, finding no one home, they'd settled down to wait for her return.

What if she'd been there when they broke in? What if she'd walked through the front door unaware of their presence? Would this now be a murder scene?

Avery suggested her early arrival had disturbed them, but what sort of burglars were so twitchy about being disturbed that they settled down for a cuppa? What sort of burglars, on being disturbed, rushed after and tried to detain the homeowner? Any regular villain would *block* the door and leg it out the back.

'You've worked on nothing else?' Avery said to Matt. 'Just those two cases?'

'As I said, we've only been going a few weeks.'

'If it's neither of those, then what about someone from your past? You've put away more than a few villains over the years. Anyone you know been sprung lately? Anyone with a grudge?'

'Not that I know of. Anyway, if they were after me, why come here? Why Jane's place? Why not mine?'

Her phone rang. Jane was relieved at the distraction.

'Ah, Ms Child. Duncan McKellar here from the Fancy Cat Fanciers. We spoke yesterday about the database.'

'Yes, Dr McKellar.' She got up and went out on to the patio, into the cooler air and the slanting morning sunlight. DS Dixon was fussing round the footprint on the back fence.

'I spoke to my wife after your visit and she recalled a spot of bother with a couple of our Bermondsey members a month or so ago.'

'A spot of bother?'

'Missing cats, one of them a particularly valuable breeding animal. Now, we don't keep a register of missing pets – they were both enquiries to see if we did – and both have now been happily resolved, but the thing that stuck in Clarisa's mind was the coincidence. Two enquiries on the same day, both from members living in the same area.'

'Would you mind if I spoke to them? See if this has anything to do with what we're working on?'

'I can't see it would do any harm. Let me give you their numbers.'

Jane took out her notebook and scribbled them down. 'And you still don't think this could have anything to do with your database?'

'I've double-checked out systems and I don't see how it can be. These two live a couple of streets away from each other. They probably go to the same vet.'

Jane thanked him and hung up, staring thoughtfully at the garden where DS Dixon was flicking through pages on a tablet, comparing illustrations with the dusty print on the fence railing.

He looked up excitedly, suddenly seeming very young. He had reddish-coloured curls a girl would die for, and bad skin accentuated by the slanting sunlight. 'I've found a match!'

He showed her the tablet with its illustration of a sole pattern, then held it beside the print on the railing. Though it was only the left side of the right boot, the match was perfect.

'That's a Spetsnaz combat boot. Russian Special Forces. You said you thought he was Russian.'

Jane stared at the print. *Russian Special Forces?*

Back inside, Matt looked at her expectantly and she realised she was still holding her phone. 'Just the database guy from the FCF,' she told him. 'A possible lead.'

Avery perked up. 'Database guy?'

'Pedigree cats. Why?'

Avery made a dismissive gesture.

'I saw that look,' Matt told him. 'Why the interest?'

'Something and nothing. You know how it is; random words making random connections. That burnt-out car the other day. The one up Islington way.'

'The one you thought might've been used for a professional hit?'

'The victim was a computer whiz. A database guy. See?'

'Plus ...?'

'Plus what?'

'It's more than that. Come on, Colin, you said *connections*, plural. I know how a copper's brain works. It's not as random as all that.'

'There's another one. Small, tenuous. Almost nothing.'

'Go on.'

'The witness who gave us the index number of the vehicle involved said she saw two men at the scene. They checked the victim before driving off. One was black and athletic looking, the other built like a brick shithouse. "Plates on him like an elephant," were her exact words. Plates of meat: feet,' he added for Jane's benefit, although she already knew the expression.

'And you think there might be a connection with Bigfoot out there?'

'Yeah, right. A cat database.'

Matt said nothing.

'I told you it was tenuous. You said yourself you know how a copper's brain works, especially when you hit a dead-end. But I'll take your database guy's number if you don't mind,' he said to Jane. 'Give him a call.'

DS Dixon gathered his samples and swabs and repacked the

forensics toolkit. They saw the two policemen to the door.

'I'll let you know if forensics turn up anything, and in the meantime I'll get the locals to put you on their patrol list, keep an eye on the place.

'Sorry Jane, that's the best I can do. As Matt said, it's a question of priorities.'

Matt closed the door behind them. 'You know that business agreement of ours, about keeping our work and private lives separate? It's in the bin, as of now. At least until we find out who these characters are.'

'But what about the office? The business?'

'We'll take what we need, forward the landline to one of our mobiles, and set up at my place.'

Jane bit her lip.

'Don't tell me you're happy staying on here? With those two on the loose?'

'I was wondering about Bluebelle.'

'Bring her along. It's about time she had a proper garden to play in.'

40

That was it: end game. Ernest Cricklewood stared at the screen. If it wasn't over already, it soon would be. How would they do it this time? he wondered. A gas leak? A car crash? An overdose? He'd keep an eye on the news feeds. A purely professional interest, of course.

The important thing was that he was out of the woods. The honeypot he'd set up – a tiny data trap of immense subtlety – had been triggered only hours after he'd laid it. Whoever was tracing the hackers was good. Very good indeed. But Ernest had stayed one step ahead.

The tripped bit was like the tug of a fisherman's line. It showed him the bait had been taken. The third and final party involved in possibly the largest hack in history was being dealt with. An innocent party in this case, but that didn't bother Ernest. If Spree and Knightmare had been the canaries in the coal mine, the principals of Bluebelle Investigations were decoys, flapping off in another direction, drawing the guns away.

Bang, bang ...

He grinned, shut down the computer and snatched up his keys. Mustn't be late for work.

* * *

Bluebelle glared from a cage on the occasional table as Matt carried in the last of their office equipment and set it on the lounge floor. 'Are you sure you know how to connect all this stuff back up again?' he called.

The wall between the lounge and dining room had been knocked through to combine the functions of both, but there was a smaller room in front with a view of the street. Matt's mum's *best room*; a second lounge kept for visitors. It was a quaint, old-fashioned custom, but Jane's Aunt Daisy maintained something similar to this day. It was currently home to a range of redecorating supplies, which Jane was transferring to the hall in order to make room for their second office.

'No problem,' she replied, 'but I'm going to need more power points.'

He appeared in the doorway, holding an extension lead with three outlets. 'That do?'

'Perfect. If you bring the printer through, I'll set it up on that trestle.'

Matt's mobile rang, a cheerful tune with a jungle drumbeat. He glanced at the screen and muttered. 'Shit! Melody Bloody Harper. I'd forgotten about her.'

'You're in trouble!' Jane called.

He held up a silencing hand. 'Melody, good morning. How's things? ... Yes, fine thanks.'

Jane waved two fingers.

'Jane says to say hello ... Yes, the report, I was just going to call you about that. We had a bit of an interruption this morning ... Oh, I'm sorry to hear that ... No, that's fine, really. You have paid a week's retainer, after all ... Yeah, sure ... I will. Take care.'

He hung up and made a face.

'Well?'

'She said to say hi back.' He held up his middle finger.

Jane punched him. 'What was the rest of that about? Come on, spill the beans.'

'I've got a reprieve. Gerrard's aunt's in hospital and they're on their way to Leicester. No urgency for the report. Close of business tomorrow will be fine.'

'You jammy sod!'

'Double-jammy, actually,' he said thoughtfully. 'I think a proper look round Harper and Vine. Talk to some of the staff. With the cat and cat-ess away, it'll be interesting to hear what the mice have to say.'

'Like what?'

He raised a hand. 'Rule number one: go in with preconceived ideas and you'll come back with a preconceived result.'

'I thought rule number one was trust no one?'

'This is the other rule number one. Want to come?'

Jane looked around at the chaos. 'I should really sort this place out first. And get Bluebelle settled. Plus, I want to call those Bermondsey people about their catnapped cats. See if there's any connection with our lot. You go. It's your case.'

'You sure?' He took her by the shoulders and studied her face.

'Positive. I'm fine, Matt. Really. And by the way, it's not cat and cat-ess, it's tom and queen.'

'Queen Melody?' he mused. 'I bet she'd like that.'

* * *

Matt had called in all manner of favours in order to hold on to Jake's van, and by the time they'd finished with Avery and Dixon, the issue was moot. Jake had been called out to an emergency and forced to take his wife's car. Cheryl wouldn't be happy, but Matt was confident he could charm her with flowers and chocolates. Besides, he was relieved not to have to deliver the van back right away because it had developed an alarming tendency to edge left when steered straight, probably the result of his kerb-jumping activities. Heading to Catford, he spotted a wheel alignment franchise on the opposite side of the road and resolved to get it sorted on his way back into town.

He pulled over just before he reached the industrial park and slipped on a spare pair of Jake's overalls. They were a little grubby, too big in the body and too short in the sleeves, but they'd do.

Then he continued on and swung into one of the empty parks at the rear of Harper and Vine.

The steel-shuttered door was partly open and just inside a couple of men in pressed blue smocks stood on the loading dock. One of them was smoking.

'Wotcha,' Matt called in his best Jake impression. 'All right if I park over there?'

'Take your chances,' non-smoker said, nodding at sign warning that unauthorised vehicles would be towed away.

'Reckon I will. Guvnors are away, aren't they? I'll only be half an hour.' If the van, overalls and clipboard he was carrying lent him any of credibility, his knowledge of Melody and Gerrard's absence underlined it. 'I'm here to check your sprinklers. Routine stuff. Health and Safety. You know the score.'

Smoker rolled his eyes. He knew the score, all right.

Matt looked up, tracing a line of red-painted pipes across the ceiling and made a note on his clipboard. 'What's that pong?'

'Roasting coffee.'

'Smells like you burned it.'

Smoker laughed wheezily. 'That's what I tell him.'

'Yeah, but you have the palate of an ox,' Non-smoker said. '*That* is the gentle aroma of wild Jacu Bird beans being toasted to perfection.'

'Still smells burnt to me,' Matt said.

'You want to taste it. It's shit.' Smoker chuckled.

'Coffee, eh?' Matt said. 'Business all right then.'

'Why, you in the market?'

'Why, you selling?'

'Not our call, mate. You want to talk to them upstairs.'

'I don't believe it's on the market any more,' Non-smoker said. 'I think they were just testing the waters, seeing what it was worth.'

Matt checked his clipboard. 'Where's your riser then? Out the front?'

'Yeah, through them doors. Combination's 5566 if you want to get back in.'

'Cheers. I'll check it out and do upstairs. See you shortly.'

There was a bathroom on the landing. Matt had come prepared. He pulled off the overalls, did up the collar of his shirt and took a tie from his pocket before stuffing the clipboard and his former clothing in the rubbish bin and covering them with crumpled paper towels.

The reception desk was vacant when he approached. The big-boned receptionist was leaning in the door of one of the offices further down, talking to someone, and started when she saw him.

'Cynthia, isn't it?' He said as she approached and held out a hand. 'We met a few days ago.'

She looked flustered and a little confused but took it anyway.

'The chaps downstairs let me in.'

'Oh.'

'Matthew,' he added. 'I came and saw Melody and Gerrard last Thursday.' He saw the light of recognition in her eyes. 'I know they're away today, but Melody said to come in and look around if I was in the area. We haven't started due diligence yet, but I thought I'd take a quick look at the plant and machinery and meet the staff.'

'Oh,' she said again, fingering her necklace, a silver chain with *Cynthia* written on it, no doubt wondering how he knew her name.

'I'm a bit of an idiot, I'm afraid. I've come out without my paperwork. I wonder if I could get another copy?'

'You mean ... the sales details? I didn't think it was still on the market.'

'Not officially.' He gave her a wink. 'And I'm not officially interested, but between you and me, it's looking pretty good.'

She settled at her desk and worked her computer, then turned the screen his way. 'Is this the one she gave you the other day?'

'That's it.'

'There's also the latest financials, but I'm not sure if they're part—'

'No, she gave me them too. If you wouldn't mind.'

'Sure.'

He stood with his hands resting on the counter, looking round proprietorially as Cynthia printed off the documents for him.

41

Jane carried the cage through to what she was already thinking of as their Greenwich office, set it on a shelf beside the trestle table and opened it up. Bluebelle stepped out warily, sniffing and studying this strange new environment as Jane arranged food and water nearby.

'How's my little lifesaver?' she said, stroking the cat's head.

Bluebelle veered away. She wasn't in the mood for distractions right now. This new world demanded her attention.

Jane sat back, watching as the cat jumped down and explored the room; the stacked boxes, the quietly humming computer, the tray of kitty litter. They'd keep her in here today, let her establish a base before allowing her to venture out into the rest of the house.

She'd told Matt she was fine, and she was, really. The office move had been good therapy. Plenty to do, plenty of distractions, no time to dwell on things. But she was finished now. Now she could dwell on things. Think things through.

The attack didn't fit with a few sachets of counterfeit coffee or catnappings by a pair of out-of-work actors. Neither were Great Train Robbery stuff. That left the most disturbing possibility; that it was random and opportunistic. They'd spied an empty house, broken in, been disturbed and panicked ...

While making tea?

That didn't fit at all.

Still, the thought lingered: what if she hadn't spotted those brown leather boots through the cat flap? What if she'd walked in unwittingly? Where would she be now?

Baseless speculation. That way lay madness. Or at the very

least, numbing inaction. If she dwelt on thoughts like that she'd never go anywhere alone again.

So what *were* they doing there, in her house? Two thugs? There *had* to be a connection.

Counterfeit coffee and cats. Cats on a database. Avery said something about a dead database guy and someone with big feet. It was all a bit random, but at least she could find out who he was.

An online search of local papers turned up a short piece about the death of James Lawrence Burton, age 24, a database analyst at Mercury Backup Systems. He'd been returning home from a night shift when the accident happened. A later item spoke of "suspicious circumstances", showed a picture of the burnt-out vehicle believed to have been responsible, and spoke of a hunt for the driver of the stolen vehicle.

Nothing useful there.

In distraction, she searched for the other database guy, the FCF's Duncan McKellar, and quickly found a beaming picture of him and his wife below the caption "Couple Breathe New Life Into Cat Group". The item was five years old and described him as having taken early retirement after a distinguished career in information technology.

Our data's as secure as GCHQ's.

There'd been a degree of hubris accompanying the remark, and Jane found herself wondering about it.

Early retirement was sometimes a euphemism for getting the boot. She searched further.

Not in this case.

Dr Duncan Anthony McKellar, PhD (Oxon), had had an illustrious career and was something of a rarity in IT; a specialist consultant with a broad span of general business knowledge. He'd worked for government agencies, banks and energy companies in a wide variety of roles, more latterly specialising in data security. He was correct when he told her he still kept up to date. The links and commentaries on his personal website showed that, and he remained something of a go-to guy for the media on the subject of hacking. There were links to newspaper stories and radio and television interviews, some of them quite recent. But one item from his impressive list of roles and responsibilities leapt out at Jane as she scrolled down. For a time he'd served as Chief Security Officer at Mercury Backup Systems.

* * *

Despite the van's wandering wheels, it was only another forty minutes from Catford to Banstead in Surrey, and Matt, armed with what he'd learned from his visit to Harper and Vine, decided it might be a worthwhile diversion.

Her Majesty's Prison, High Down was built on the site of a former mental hospital. Opened in 1992, with additions in 2009, it was what the Prison Service called a Local prison: a place where people were detained before trial or directly after conviction. It housed more than 1,100 Category B prisoners – those who didn't require maximum security, but whose escape could pose a risk to the community.

Visitors weren't permitted on Mondays or Fridays, which meant the visitors' car park was almost empty when he swung into it. He'd called ahead and one of the custodial managers met him at the gatehouse.

'Hello, Kate.'

'DI Healy. Except it's not DI any more, is it?' Kate Blumer had always been sharper than the average CM.

'Is that what I said on the phone? Sorry. Force of habit. I've only been back on civvy street a few weeks.'

'In which case, I shall see you tomorrow.' She gestured at the visiting hours sign riveted to the steel entrance door.

'You can't make a tiny exception for old time's sake? It is important, Kate.'

'Who's it concerning?'

'A fiddler. Cash, not kiddies. Henry Baxter.'

'Oh, I know Baxter. He's in the infirmary. Slipped on the stairs, apparently.'

'Apparently?'

'That's what he insists. A little too forcefully for my liking.'

'Has he had any other *accidents*?'

She looked at him archly. 'Who's asking?'

He handed her his card.

'From DI to PI, eh?'

'I'm working for his family.'

'I didn't know he had any.'

'Well, stepdaughter. Melody Harper.'

'Ah.'

'You know her then?'

'She's a regular.'

'Does he get many visitors?'

Blumer shook her head. 'Only her.'

'You couldn't tell me when she last visited?' Matt gestured at the PC on the desk beside her. All visits had to be booked in advance.

'I can, and I don't need that thing to tell me. Saturday. Right after his fall.'

'You open at two, don't you?' He glanced at the sign. Blumer nodded. The timing worked out. A visit to her stepdad then on to his place.

'So did he fall or was he pushed?'

'Is that why you're here?'

'Baxter was convicted of embezzling two million quid, most of which hasn't been recovered. That's got to make him an attractive target. He was sent down three months ago, which means he's been here a while. My guess is you were waiting for a suitable slot in a Cat D nick. After all, he's an accountant with no previous, not a blagger with a string of convictions. He's not going to run from an open prison.

'Finally, a slot opens up, but he misses it due to a fall down the stairs.'

'It's not the first time either,' Blumer said.

'Really?'

'Rather accident-prone, our Baxter.'

'But you don't believe that.'

'What can I say? I have to take him at his word. Do you really think he's going to tell *you* what's going on?'

Matt shrugged. 'He might. It's worth a shot. A third party with no connection to HMP or the other lags? And who knows? There's still two million quid missing. I reckon your governor would be chuffed if one of her staff helped facilitate its recovery.'

'You've always been a silver-tongued bastard, Healy.'

'You mean it's not just my charm and boyish good looks?'

She laughed. 'You wish. Go on then. Sign your life away.' She pushed the register across to him.

There was a buzz and clunk and the steel door swung open.

* * *

Fesahaye Odman sauntered back up the street to the car. 'No one home, man.'

'You are sure?' Od nodded. 'We wait. They'll be back.'

'Yeah, but when? Listen to this.' He pulled out his mobile, punched in a number and flipped on the speaker. It went to Jane's voicemail.

'Cat Bitch. *Dead* Cat Bitch.' Dmitri muttered.

No, man, not the voice, the message. It's different from last night. Last night it was all *You've reached Bluebelle Investigations* shit. Business, you know? This one's personal: *Hi, Jane Child from Bluebelle*. See?'

'So?'

'So I called that number when no one answered the door. Ain't no phone ringing in there, man. The office phone's been switched through to a mobile.'

'Maybe out doing business. We wait.'

'Or maybe they've flown the coop. Maybe we scared them off.'

'Why you smile?'

'Because the phone has been diverted, man. *To a mobile*.'

'Explain.'

'If the birds have flown the coop, where'd they go? Could be anywhere. Could be hard to track down. 'cept they fucked up. Diverted the landline to one of their mobiles.'

Dmitri frowned.

'You can track a mobile, man. Triangulation. cellphone towers and all that shit. It's how they work. They can pinpoint a user's location down to fifty metres. Place like London, maybe down to twenty, even ten.'

'You can do this?'

'No, but I know a man who can. It's what you're paying me for, ain't it? Local liaison? Lemme give him a call.'

Od tapped some keys on his phone. Dmitri looked over at the number that came up and memorised it. He'd have to give that number a call himself when all this was over. A follow-up followed by a personal visit. He'd been told to leave no loose ends and Dmitri Olegovich Podvyshenskaya was a professional.

42

'Dr McKellar? Jane Child again from Bluebelle Investigations. Thanks for your call this morning. Sorry if I sounded a little distracted earlier. We'd just had a break-in and were dealing with the police.'

'I'm sorry to hear that, Ms Child. I hope everything's all right.'

'The interesting thing is, there's a possibility it was related to this case.'

'The missing cats?'

'Yes. Or more specifically, to your database.'

'Surely you're not talking about the coincidence of those two Bermondsey enquiries?'

'I called the numbers you gave me and spoke to the members concerned. Both confirmed the circumstances of their pet's disappearance and return, and both are almost identical to the three cases I'm currently dealing with.

'My suspicion is this gang have worked through that district and moved on to another. Which strongly suggests they have a database of some sort, wouldn't you say?'

'It's ... possible ... they have a copy of the old typewritten list. The FCF was in a bit of a muddle when my wife and I took it over.'

'That was five years ago, wasn't it? One of the stolen animals was three years old, another only two.'

'I've reviewed all my procedures here. There are no other copies.'

'Tell me about the backups, Dr McKellar.'

'Backups?'

'The off-site ones in particular. They wouldn't be held to your old employer, would they, Mercury Backup Systems?'

'How do you know that?'

'Who else do MBS hold backups for? I see their website mentions corporations, major banks, government agencies and departments, but there are no specifics.'

'Of course not. Security, Ms Child. You don't advertise your client base.'

'Would the Government Communications Headquarters be one of those departments?'

The phone was silent a moment. 'Why would you ask that?'

'Yesterday you said your backups were as secure as GCHQ's. It struck me as an odd thing to say. *As safe as houses* or *As secure as the Bank of England*, perhaps. But as safe as the country's intelligence gathering unit ...?'

'I can assure you that MBS do *not* hold any data of that sort, backup or otherwise.'

'But ...?'

'But ... there may be ... related government departments ...'

'Such as the Secretary of State for Foreign and Commonwealth Affairs?'

'I really couldn't comment.'

'But that's who GCHQ report to, isn't it?'

'I believe so.'

'And ...?'

'I really can't comment any further. I'm still subject to non-disclosure agreements, you know. Some very high-level ones at that.'

'Tell me about the backup process. You said you encrypt the database, store one copy locally and the other off site. I imagine the one that goes to MBS gets sent over a secure encrypted connection?'

'A VPN, yes.'

'And there it's archived.'

'Yes, but only after anonymising the database's name and source. Not even the staff know whose data they're dealing with.'

'I imagine those staff are thoroughly vetted.'

'Absolutely.'

'What would happen if one of them died in suspicious circumstances? Would there'd be an investigation?'

'Of course.' A pause. 'Why? Has that happened?'

He was no slouch. Jane could hear the tap of a keyboard in the background.

'You're probably looking at James Lawrence Burton. Died in a traffic accident on Thursday morning. You'll see later stories mention a stolen car, burnt-out and abandoned after the accident. There's an on-going police investigation.'

'So I see.'

'Did you know him?'

'No, but MBS employ more than three hundred staff.'

'You see, my thinking, Dr McKellar – and please correct me if I'm wrong – is that there's an inevitable weakness in the backup process. Everything's encrypted, fine, but the end point is still an actual physical copy of the database held in a silo somewhere. That data could, at least theoretically, be duplicated by someone with access to that silo.'

'You mean a backup of the backups?'

'Yes.'

'In theory. But are you suggesting someone's copied the backup of the Fancy Cat Fancier's data? Why on earth would anyone go to that much trouble?'

'I'm not suggesting they did. Not deliberately. Not for the FCF data. You said yourself, not even the staff know who the data belongs to. What I *am* suggesting is that that database was incidental to a bigger haul. An unwanted castoff that somehow found its way into the hands of a couple of petty criminals.

'If James Lawrence Burton was the man responsible for

copying that data, if it was a grand sweep that scooped up everything – including tiddlers like the FCF – and if some of that information related to the Foreign Office or Foreign Affairs or the GCHQ, then Burton's untimely death conveniently removes the source of that leak.'

A long silence followed. 'That's an interesting speculation, Ms Child. Have you put it to the police?'

'Not yet, because that's all it is right now: pure speculation. I'll need a bit more evidence first, and I may be barking up the wrong tree entirely, but I thought I'd put the idea to you. With your background and experience, is that even remotely possible?'

Another long pause. So long Jane wondered if he'd hung up.

'I ... would say it's a possibility. Not a likely one. MBS is very, very security conscious. But I've been in this game long enough to never say never.'

Jane thanked him for his help and hung up. Her phone beeped almost immediately. Two missed calls from the office phone while she'd been talking. No message left, the caller's number blocked.

Them again? Her visitors?

Stop it, she told herself. Don't dwell on that. There's work to do.

* * *

The top end of Henry Baxter's infirmary bed had been mechanically elevated and he was lying back against it with a book resting on his knees. He was wearing a neck support with his left arm crossed against his chest in a sling, but the book must have been amusing because when he looked up he was smiling.

'A visitor, Baxter,' CM Blumer told him.

The smile vanished. 'It's not a visiting day.'

'A special one.' She stepped aside and let Matt introduce himself.

'I'm a private detective working for your stepdaughter.' Matt offered his hand. Baxter shook it. Cautiously. 'Been in the wars, I see.'

Baxter shrugged, attempting nonchalance. 'I missed a step. Fell.' He glanced at Kate Blumer by the door.

'Five minutes,' she told Matt, closing it behind her.

'That's not what I've heard,' Matt said.

'What?' Baxter closed his book.

'That's not what Melody told me.'

'She didn't ...? She shouldn't have ...' A long sigh. 'Are you her little man then? The one that's going to sort it out?'

'Let's start at the beginning, shall we? When did the threats start?'

Baxter glanced at the closed door. 'When I was on remand. But they were just ... half-joking, you know? It wasn't till after I was convicted. A couple of thousand, that was all. Then ... twenty.'

'Twenty thousand pounds? And you paid?'

'Melody and Gerrard sorted it out, on my behalf. But now they want two hundred thousand. That's ridiculous. Who has that sort of money lying around?'

'Who indeed? Although I've no doubt you could raise it. If you weren't in here.'

'What's that supposed to mean?'

Matt took a sheaf of papers from the pocket of his jacket and unfolded them. 'Your stepdaughter's business is a little shaky, you know. It seems an angel investor has been propping it up for some time now. At least, until recently. The payments stopped about nine months ago. How long were you on remand, Mr Baxter?'

Baxter said nothing.

'CM Blumer tells me it was about five months. Plus three in here since you were convicted ...'

'Harper and Vine is a good solid business.'

'It might be one day, and if this royal appointment comes about ... who knows. But until then, they need support.'

'Nonsense. Gerrard Vine is wealthy in his own right.'

'On paper, perhaps. But I hear his aunt keeps him on a tight reign. His quarterly allowance has been going straight into keeping H&V afloat, so much so that it's left him short in other areas. Like paying his annual subs to the Chesapeake Club, for example.'

Baxter said nothing.

'My theory is that you were the mysterious angel investor in Harper and Vine, through fronts and shadow companies and all the rest. Perhaps that was even why you kept the embezzlement going long after you really needed to, long after Melody's mum had fled to pastures new.

'Perhaps it was a long-term loan or even an investment to be paid off once Gerrard comes into his inheritance. If so, it was a great ruse. The Serious Fraud Office wouldn't look too deeply into the affairs of a stepdaughter hooked up to the likes of Gerrard Vine and all that family money.'

'Who did you say you were working for?' Baxter snapped.

'Your stepdaughter. And I'm trying to prevent her from making a serious mistake.'

'What do you mean?'

'Trying to stop her from ending up where you are. Not High Down, of course, it's men only. But Bronzefield perhaps. Or Downview. That would be convenient, wouldn't it? Just across the way.'

'I don't know what you're talking about.'

Matt studied what seemed like genuine puzzlement. 'No, I don't believe you do. Well, I'll tell you.

'They tried to sell the business a few months back. I don't know if they were genuine or just wanted a market evaluation, but either way, without the propping up, it's not really a going concern yet.'

Matt tapped the sheaf of papers. 'Shortly after that, your stepdaughter took out some expensive insurance. Not fire or theft or on the lives of the principals, but counterfeit insurance. She then sold some of her perfectly legitimate coffee, under the counter, to someone H&V wouldn't normally supply. I think she had more sales planned, to more unlikely outlets, to boost her claim of widespread damage, but unfortunately the very first people she sold to tripped an alarm with their biggest legitimate customer; their buyer at the Chesapeake. Naturally, he alerted them to the situation. And naturally, they had to be seen to be taking action – especially with the prospect of a royal appointment in the offing. So she employed a startup private detective to do some superfluous investigations and write a report largely dictated by her. A report she no doubt intends to send to the insurance company, along with a hefty claim.

'I think initially the idea was to take some of the strain off Gerrard and fill in the financial gaps, at least until your release or dear old aunty dies. Now, I suspect she has another motive; to pay off the men hounding you.'

Matt handed him the papers. 'You mentioned the sum of twenty thousand pounds a few minutes ago. Would that have been a month ago? Because according to those, just that sum was withdrawn in cash for the purchase and signwriting of a company van. Yet it seems to be missing. Not only that, but the storeman tells me all deliveries and despatches are handled by couriers.

'That's an accounting irregularity. It pales into insignificance compared to fraud. Insurance companies, in particular, don't take kindly to that sort of behaviour.'

Baxter's face hardened. 'So what's your angle, Healy? Are you in on it too? The money train? You want your share?'

'Not at all. I'm old-fashioned ex-copper. I just want justice.'

Baxter's eyes narrowed.

'My guess is that you're in a Catch-22 situation. You wouldn't be in this difficulty if you weren't in here. If you had all the access you had before your arrest – unmonitored phone calls, internet, post office boxes, personal contacts and so on – you could easily make another investment in Harper and Vine *and* pay off your tormentors. But you can't do that from here. Even in an open prison, even after you're released, the authorities are going to keep an eye on you for years to come. You might have salted the money away where they can't find it, but hard to find implies it's hard to get at too – at least quickly.

'As far as I can see, you have two choices. Tough it out, suffer more intimidation and watch your stepdaughter go to prison for attempted fraud, or make it all go away. If the authorities recover what you stole, your value vanishes. You're just another sad old lag doing time.'

Baxter's lips compressed.

'Think about it,' Matt handed him his card, 'and give me ring. That report is due to be delivered to your stepdaughter tomorrow afternoon. I don't believe she'll hesitate filing a claim. Over to you, Mr Baxter.'

43

Melody drove. Gerrard wasn't in a fit state. He'd been up half the night pacing the floor and Melody was surprised at how badly he'd taken the news of his aunt's accident. Between the pair of them, Aunt Myra had always been a figure of fun and an object of derision. He'd never shown her any great affection, even on the obligatory quarterly trudge up to visit the old bat, but Gerrard had never been a man to show much outward affection. Melody supposed that, as his last surviving relative, this intimation of mortality had brought back memories of the family he'd lost as a boy.

For his part, Gerrard was in shock and filled with a sort of sick dread. How could he have been so stupid, so remiss? He was certain she was dead, but hadn't actually checked. How had she been discovered so quickly? Had she dragged herself to a phone? Had someone found her? Seen him, perhaps? What if Aunt Myra woke up and regained even a fraction of her former formidable senses?

He made several calls to the hospital overnight to check on her condition. It remained unchanged, and now, as they swung into the hospital car park, he all but convinced himself that she would slip away without regaining consciousness.

They checked in at Intensive Care and were directed to a small serviceable room lined with morning sunlight from partly drawn blinds. Aunt Myra lay inclined a little from the horizontal, a crisp white sheet and a light blue blanket covering her to her armpits. Her arms lay outside them, one in plaster from wrist to elbow. There was a shunt in the other wrist and a trail of wires connected her to a couple of monitors. But that was all. No wheezing respirator, no tracheotomy. There was, however, a very human attachment.

The young woman holding Myra's hand relinquished it and rose when they entered, her face drawn, her eyes sunken with fatigue. 'You are nephew? They say you are come. My name is Jadzia Sobczak.'

'Gerrard Vine.' He took her hand. 'My partner, Melody.'

'Pleased to meet.'

She was pale with dark, wanton eyes and lush hair drawn back in a ponytail. Jeans, T-shirt, no bra, Gerrard observed. Definitely foreign. A touch of the gypo about her. A padded jacket hung over the back of her seat.

He looked away to the reclining figure. Myra seemed to be taking a nap, or meditating. Her breathing was normal, her pulse – reflected in one of the monitors beside the bed – seemed strong and steady. Even in the depths of a coma she didn't look her age. She might have passed for someone twenty years younger.

'I'm sorry, who are you?' Melody asked the young woman.

'Jadzia. Housekeeper to *Bab*— I ... I mean, to Miss Vine.'

Melody's eyes narrowed. 'What did you call her?'

The young woman coloured. '*Babcia*. It mean grandmother. She ... let me call her this because ... she is like the grandmother I have no more. She is like my friend also.'

'She pays you, doesn't she?'

'Of course.'

'Then you're just an employee.'

Jadzia's colour deepened, her dark eyes flashed, but she held her tongue and turned to Gerrard. 'I find her. Yesterday. In the morning. On floor at foot of stair. She is dressed for run. Fall, I think. I call for ambulance. It come quick.'

Gerrard cleared his throat. 'What ... what were you doing there? I thought you only worked weekdays?'

'I visit often. We are friend.' She gave her head an upward tilt, showing a hint of pride, avoiding Melody's glare, then looked down and took Myra's hand again. 'Doctor say lucky visit. If I do not find, maybe she would not be with us.'

'Did she ... did she say anything when you found her?'

'Was not awake. Breathe only, very slow. Bad head.' She tapped her own. 'But doctors say all look OK. Strong woman. Soon she will wake.'

'Any ... other ... injuries?'

'You would think, yes? Woman her age? But only break the wrist and arm. Also dislocate the shoulder. Think, maybe, she catch herself. There are many bruise, however. Maybe also tissue hurt. But they say she is tough old bird.' Jadzia gave a little laugh and wiped the corner of her eye. 'Fall like the stuntman in the movie. Good, yes?'

Gerrard stared at the old woman. He hadn't really known what to expect, but the words "in a coma" suggested a more parlous state than this ... repose.

'Excuse. I should leave so you are alone. Doctor say to speak with her normal. Help sometimes. Also sing is good. I sing her Polish folk songs.' Jadzia bent and kissed the comatose woman, touching her cheek with her fingertips before hurrying from the room.

'Who the fuck ...?' Melody muttered. 'Sing? What planet is she from?'

Gerrard snorted. 'Polish proles. Coming over here, stealing the jobs of hard-working English—'

Myra Vine's hand stirred and she gave a faint sigh. The monitor showing the steady pulse continued, but the beats were stronger and their frequency increased.

Gerrard glanced at Melody, alarmed. By the time he looked back, Myra's eyes were open.

She'd always been a sound sleeper and a fast waker. What was a coma but a particularly sound, particularly deep sleep?

She looked around without moving her head, slowly taking in

her surroundings before her eyes fixed on Melody and Gerrard.

She raised the plastered arm, palm out. 'No! Get him away from me!'

Her voice was like a rusty hinge, but her actions were decisive. Her other hand scrambled round the bed, searching for and finding the emergency call button on a lead plugged into the console behind her. Before Gerrard could say a word, she jammed her thumb down, pressing it again and again, summoning two nurses who arrived at as close to a run as hospital regulations permitted.

* * *

If databases really were the key to all this, Jane thought, then she had something the police didn't have: the address of the catnappers. But if Cricklewood and Carpinter *did* have a copy of the FCF data, it seemed unlikely that a couple of out-of-work actors would be involved in hacking an extremely well-secured site. (If there really had been a hack – which she was starting to doubt.) The truth was almost certainly more mundane. Momentary carelessness on the part of McKellar or his wife, perhaps. A forgotten copy given to a fellow committee member. A lost USB stick ... The permutations were endless. Besides, there really couldn't be any connection between that and the break-in of her house this morning. No one was going to call out a couple of professional thugs to protect a ten-pound-a-month extortion scheme.

The bleep of her phone interrupted her pacing. A text from Matt: he wouldn't be back till late afternoon now. Jane sighed, regretting not going with him. She was starting to feel a little stir crazy.

Fresh air and exercise, that's what she needed to clear her head. She was suddenly grateful they'd brought the old Raleigh Twenty with them. The bike was parked in the hall. She wheeled it out, inspecting its faded paintwork. 'Bluebelle, Blue Bike. BB for short. There, you have a name.' She patted the saddle and went back inside to get ready.

It was like being a schoolgirl again. Faster than walking, more fun and more scenic than driving, although the busier roads were unnerving. She meandered, losing herself in the quieter streets of an unfamiliar area, taking access lanes and pedestrian paths at random, stopping to buy sandwiches and a bottle of fruit juice then seeking out somewhere to enjoy her late lunch.

She found a small park which, she realised, was just up the road from Cricklewood and Carpinter's apartment. She had a clear view of the back of the building, and when a blue van emerged from its underground car park and headed towards her, she almost choked on her juice.

A van like the one Patricia Tinchcombe had described. The same registration number as the one she'd photographed outside the pub near Lowella Foote's place.

She capped the bottle, stashed her lunch leftovers in her backpack and grabbed the bike as the van turned off and headed down a side street. Jane pedalled after it.

It paused at an intersection, giving way to a couple of cars, then moved on.

She kept her distance. It wouldn't do to show too much interest, but keeping it in sight wasn't difficult. Traffic lights, give way signs, other vehicles; the general stop-start-slow of city driving. Then it ran an orange light. She was too far behind to follow it through so rapidly dismounted, scooted up on to the footpath, crossed with the pedestrian lights, then continued her pursuit on the other side.

It turned off into an old industrial area where the footpaths were broken, the verges knotted with weeds, and rundown warehouses lined each side of the street. She mounted the footpath to give them more distance, then slipped behind a parked truck as the van drew up opposite the rise of a long railway bridge that spanned a broad area of marshy wasteland. There were five lock-ups built into the arches at the start of the bridge, closed off by five dark green doors, all padlocked shut.

The van turned, reversing hard up against the one on the end. The passenger got out, unlocked the door and the van's back doors, and disappeared inside.

The angle was wrong, Jane couldn't see what he was doing, but the driver didn't budge and in less than a minute the passenger reappeared, closing and locking up again. Bernard Carpinter. She recognised him now.

Jane slipped around the other side of the parked truck as the van passed her, but she made no attempt to follow it this time. She'd found their lock-up. The place where they kept the cats while they tormented their owners. A good spot. Out of the way. No one nearby to hear the plaintive mewing or observe their comings and goings.

She rode over, studied the door and the stout padlock, then pressed her ear to it.

Nothing except the growing vibration of an approaching train. No way in either. Perhaps around the other side ...

The road met a gravely end just beyond where the bridge began to span the swampy ground. She glimpsed a broken tow-path littered with rubble and shattered glass running beside a dank canal. The underpass was deep in shadow, heavily graffitied and smelled of piss, but there was no one about. The train thundered overhead as she made her way through.

The other side of the bridge faced southeast. Back in daylight, she propped her bike against a fencepost and continued on foot.

The backs of the lock-ups were bricked up except for small arched windows near the top of each one. The first two had been boarded up from inside. The third was cracked and broken, but the glass still hung together, reinforced with fine steel mesh. The fourth and fifth were grimy but intact.

They were eight feet off the ground, steel-framed, set almost flush with the brickwork. At full stretch, Jane had a reach of about seven feet. She looked around for something to stand on.

An old pallet lay amongst the weeds. A couple of the boards were rotten but it seemed solid enough. She dragged it over and propped it against the wall.

Balanced on top, she was only tall enough to see through the bottom edge of the window, so she hooked her hands over the narrow ledge and raised herself to peer inside. The mortar on the ledge was weathered and mossy; hard to grip. Then her phone rang. She jumped clear, landing on the balls of her feet and pulled it out to check, thinking it might be Matt, but the caller ID was blocked so she let it ring through till her voicemail kicked in. There was no message.

'Well, thanks for your call,' she muttered as she scoured the waste ground, finding a couple bricks on which to wedge the pallet.

The extra inches made all the difference. This time, at full toe-stretch, she managed to prop her her left arm on the ledge and rub away some of the window grime with her right hand. Shielding her eyes, she peered inside.

A little light filtered in, illuminating a patch of brickwork and the inside of the wooden door, but the rest of the interior was dark. She reached around and took out her phone again.

One of the apps illuminated the camera's LED flash lamp, turning it into a torch. She activated it, wedged the phone against the glass behind her left arm then peered inside again.

The light glanced off the edge of a metal rack and a line of cages before reflecting back at her from a pair of unblinking eyes that seemed as bright as the headlamps of an approaching car.

Feline eyes.

Jane stared and almost lost her footing. She was right!

* * *

'This is right?' Dmitri asked, accelerating towards an area of rundown warehouses.

'It's what the signal says, man.' Od had his phone in one hand and was balancing the tablet he'd borrowed from his friend on his knees. 'Turn here.'

The car swung right.

'Then right again.' Od zoomed the map out then checked the view from the front window. 'What the hell's she doin' down here, man? Middle of nowhere?'

Dmitri smiled. 'Good place to meet with her, I think.'

44

Matt pulled up under a sign promising wheel balancing and wheel alignment *While-U-Wait!* Jake's van was still tracking badly and getting it fixed was the least he could do.

He settled on one of the plastic chairs in the breeze block waiting room attached to the garage. It was decorated in the red, yellow and black of the franchise and had a drinks dispenser in one corner. A hand-lettered sign on it said *Limit, one per customer. Thank u!!* The place seemed to have a shortage of Ys and Os and a surfeit of exclamation marks.

Two other customers were *while-u-waiting*, browsing dog-eared motoring magazines from a rack on the wall. Matt took out his notebook and scribbled down a few observations about his visit to Henry Baxter. He'd been careful not to mention that *he* was writing the report for Melody. Letting Baxter think it was coming from a third party would crank up the pressure.

He turned to a blank page and considered what he would actually write.

There was no question of not detailing everything he'd learned, along with his suspicions. She may not like it, but that wasn't the point. She'd paid them to investigate and they'd done so. If they'd been more thorough than she imagined they would, that wasn't his problem. Besides, there was no way he'd let Bluebelle Investigations be associated with fraudulent insurance claims, even indirectly.

The question was, would Baxter cooperate?

Melody's fraud attempt was clumsy and inelegant; a rushed job. Baxter would see that. He was obviously a man of care and finesse since his own scam had run successfully for almost two decades. He wouldn't decide right away, of course. He'd call Melody first and check on Matt's bona fides. But he wouldn't say too much. Not on a prison phone. It was unlikely he'd reveal he knew about her scam.

Then what?

Baxter wasn't stupid. He'd know that being moved to an open prison – even being released – wouldn't make the intimidation go away. Not now. Not after parting with two, then twenty thousand quid. Matt could have used up a handful of the franchise's exclamation points right there: *Idiot!!!* Hadn't he realised that doing so would simply whet their appetites? That they were like piranhas. Accommodating them in any way was like dripping fresh blood into their pool.

Apart from the report – and regardless of what Baxter decided – the H&V case was done and dusted, which meant tomorrow he'd be looking for missing cats. A dull case turned interesting – the complete reverse of his own – and all down to Jane's – dare he mention it? – *dogged* persistence.

Oh yes, he must. He wondered how she was doing.

* * *

Jane dropped to the ground and flexed the arm that had been supporting her on the window ledge. She had them! The evidence was right there in the lock-up. Poor cats, kept in the dark with thundering trains passing overhead day and night. She'd like to lock those two bastards in there for a few weeks and see how they liked it. No company. No kind words. Just fed and watered once a day.

The question was, what now? The police? Search warrants? A raid of some sort? Or perhaps a stakeout. Wait till they returned and catch them red-handed. What could a private detective do in this sort of situation? She had no idea. Matt would know.

And the database connection? They hardly looked like hackers. She doubted they could manage a remote control between them. But once cornered, once confronted with the evidence she'd accumulated, they'd surely talk.

She retrieved her bike, eager to get home and tell Matt all about her lucky break, but not before she took some photographs of the place, back and front. Location shots too to give a feel of the surrounding area. She finished quickly and tucked her phone away at the sound of an approaching car, mounted her bike and pedalled back the way she'd come.

* * *

'Fuck it, man, that was her! Back there, on the bike!'

'Cat Bitch!' Dmitri stabbed the brakes, bringing the rental car to a grinding stop.

'Easy, man. Easy. Don't tip her off.'

'I tip her off all right. *Pizda!* Grind her bones under my tyre.'

He executed a U-turn, thumping the front wheels up and down the opposite kerb, and was about to accelerate after her when Od grabbed his arm.

'No, whoa. Hold up, man, I been thinking.'

'What?'

'Where's the dude? He'll be the hacker, man. It's always the dude.'

'Who care?'

'Office phone's goin' to *her* phone, man. We take her out, we lose our lead.'

Dmitri slowed. 'So what we do? Cannot follow bicycle in car.'

'No, man, I got a better idea. We make the dude come to us. Take her out, but do it gentle. Just a love pat, yeah? And hurry, man. This is the perfect spot.'

45

Jane heard the car approach but thought nothing of it till it gently tapped the back of her bike and made her wobble.

'You idiot!' she muttered, correcting the wobble, regaining control then glancing over her shoulder in time to see it coming in again, harder and faster.

This time, instead of nudging, the car swung left and clipped the rear wheel, knocking it sideways. There was nothing she could do. The bike skewed right and she fell. If the driver hadn't anticipated the result, she'd have gone under the front wheels or over the bonnet, but the car braked hard and stopped short as she hit the tarmac.

The bike slid from under her, under the nose of the car, and Jane reflexively kicked away, rolling to avoid the approaching wheels, not yet aware the car had already stopped. She took the impact on her left shoulder, but it was partly cushioned by the backpack. She cracked her head too, but that was nothing. The helmet took the blow. Fuelled by anger and adrenaline, she scrambled to her feet, fists bunched, ready to upbraid the driver.

The passenger door opened and a tall African leapt out. He was wearing cotton pants and a brightly patterned striped shirt. 'Whoa, man, you all right?'

Jane glanced at him, her breathing hard and fast. Striped shirt. Something registered. The figure in the passenger seat of the car as it raced away from her house that morning. All she'd seen was a silhouette and the shoulder of a brightly patterned shirt. A blink-of-an-eye impression, but not a silhouette at all. A black man.

In a silver car.

Like the one that had just hit her.

'I said are you OK?'

The man was approaching, one arm outstretched, a concerned look on his face.

Jane glanced at the driver. She couldn't make him out clearly through the windscreen but he was big, she could tell that much, and there were what looked like white stripes on his face and neck. Wound dressings.

The driver's door popped. He was moving, perhaps coming to assist. The black man's hand closed around her forearm. Not a reassuring or a steadying touch. A grab. Jane pulled back. The grip tightened as the second figure emerged. The top of a massive head rising up between the widening angle of the opening door.

The black man seized her right forearm with his other hand. He was grinning now, a nasty look, saying something, but all Jane registered was white, white teeth. She drove her head at them, hard, feeling the impact through the rim of her cycle helmet, and his grip slackened. As she pulled away, he staggered back, gurgling, spitting blood and broken teeth.

She didn't hesitate. She turned and ran.

Od staggered back, hands to his mouth, blood running between his fingers. He moaned, stumbled over Jane's fallen bike, fell backwards and landed unceremoniously sitting in the road still cradling his jaw.

Dmitri was halfway out the car when Cat Bitch turned and ran. He dived back in, jammed it into gear and accelerated, hard, grinding the fallen bike beneath his wheels, along with the right leg of his fallen companion.

Od shrieked, surprisingly high-pitched, the pain from his smashed teeth now wildly overridden. Dmitri ignored his cries – they soon faded anyway – aiming the car squarely at the fleeing figure.

Jane ran.

She heard the shrieks mingled with the accelerating engine

and guessed what had happened. If anything, if she needed any more incentive to get away, the howls of pain provided it.

'Get off the road! Get off the road!' she told herself as she ran, bounding up on to the weedy footpath. Behind her, the thump of car-on-kerb told her it had done the same.

She was racing along the front of an abandoned warehouse. There were no turns, no alleys, no way out. *Wrong side of the road, damn it!* There were gaps between the buildings on the other side.

The accelerating car drew nearer. Jane risked a glance, judged the timing, then darted right, angling across the footpath and back on to the road. The car followed immediately, too focused on pursuit to take account of the lamppost she darted round, and she heard a grinding graunch as it glanced the concrete pole. It slowed, but only briefly, then came on.

Jane sprinted across the street, picking a weedy alley between two buildings. It was shadowy and dark, and only when she ran into it did she spot the high metal gate partway down. Too late to change her mind now. At least the car couldn't follow her down there.

Dmitri cursed when he saw where she was heading. The car thundered up the kerb and he slammed on the brakes, but the locked wheels skidded on loose gravel, causing it to plough into the buildings either side of a gap too narrow for it.

There was a loud hiss as the airbags inflated, slamming him back into his seat. It took him several seconds to fight his way out through the rapidly deflating rubber cushions. The graunched door was stuck. He forced it open and leapt out.

The gate was locked and bolted, a heavy steel thing more like a door, too high to climb. Not that its featureless face had any toe- or hand-holds. Behind her, the big man was scrambling over the crumpled bonnet of his car. Jane made a snap decision, retraced her steps and headed back towards him.

He paused, seeing her approach, and braced himself, evidently thinking she had some sort of weapon. Then she turned again and sprinted away, back towards the gate.

She had no idea if it would work. It was a stunt she'd seen in martial arts movies but had long suspected the actors were on wires. There was one precedent. As a small child she'd frightened her mother by scaling the insides of doors. With one bare foot against one jamb and the other foot against the other, she'd been able to work her way right to the top by rocking to and fro. Similar principle here. All she needed was the momentum of a running start.

She hoped.

Six feet from the gate, she aimed her left foot at the left wall, kicked back when she felt it connect, and aimed her right foot at the right wall. It worked! Springing back and forth, she rapidly gained height while her forward momentum moved her towards the gate. She stopped when she was over it, dropped on to the top, and sprang down lightly on the other side.

A second later, Dmitri slammed into it like a charging rhino. He was too big for such an acrobatic feat. His gangly companion with the smashed jaw and smashed leg would have been a better candidate, but he wouldn't be going anywhere for a while. Instead, Dmitri tried brute force, slamming into it time and time again, bellowing in fury with each charge.

The gate held, at least for now, and Jane didn't fancy waiting round to test its long-term prospects.

The alley led to a lane behind the buildings, a lane that ran parallel to the main road at the front. She looked left and right. Both ways led to side streets going back to the main road. If the gate gave, he'd come after her on foot. She could almost certainly outrun him. But if it held, if he went back to the car, he'd circle round and mow her down.

Going left would take her out of the estate. The instinctive direction. The direction he'd anticipate. Jane went right, racing back the way she'd come.

As she reached the intersection of the side street, she heard the whirr of a starter motor and paused, peeking back down the main road. The gate had held. He'd returned to the car and was having trouble getting it restarted. Then it roared into life, he backed out and headed away, going in the direction she guessed he'd go, trying to cut her off before she could escape the estate. As he turned down the side street that led to the lane behind the buildings, she sprinted across the road and up the steep embankment leading to the railway bridge. It was overgrown and scrubby, a dead-end against the railway fence above it, but it was high ground and good cover and he was just one man. Even if he spotted her, he'd have to pursue on foot, and whichever way he came, she was confident she could avoid him.

From her vantage point, she saw him cruise around again, moving slowly, still searching. Then he appeared to give up and drove back towards his fallen companion.

Shit! She'd forgotten about him. Had he seen her sprint across the road?

It didn't seem likely. He was facing the wrong way, back towards the railway bridge, and he had both hands clamped tightly around the top of his right thigh. He was rocking backwards and forwards, gasping and moaning, his lower leg and foot oddly angled, the flesh torn back by skidding wheels.

The battered silver car stopped. The big man got out and looked down at him. Brown boots. Jane saw them for the first time. The same brown boots she'd seen through the cat flap.

The black man reached out an arm for assistance. The big man said something then reached down and took him by the scruff of the neck, dragging him to his feet one-handed. She saw the flash of a flick-knife in the afternoon sun. Saw its blade driven into the black man's stomach and ripped upwards. Saw the rush of blood and entrails. Saw it pulled out and stabbed into his neck as the arm holding up the mutilated body thrust it away, tearing a gaping wound like a second bloody mouth.

The body fell face down in the gravel amidst the pooling

blood.

The big man knelt and wiped the knife on the back of the dead man's brightly patterned shirt, closed the blade and slipped it into his jacket pocket. Then he stood up and looked around carefully, searchingly. Looking for witnesses.

46

Gerrard hurried from the hospital room. Melody followed. His aunt's cries finally faded as the door banged shut behind them. Even the presence of a nurse and the return of the housekeeper hadn't been enough to silence Myra's outraged cries: 'Get him out! Get him out! Get him away from me!'

'What the hell was that about? Sounds like the old bag's finally lost it,' Melody said then checked herself, recalling Gerrard's upset at hearing of his aunt's fall. 'Sorry, I didn't mean ...' but Gerrard wasn't listening.

She hurried up the corridor after him and caught him by the elbow. 'Shouldn't we stick around? Wait for a doctor? She just needs a sedative or—' The words died on her lips as she saw his face. Grey and bloodless. Like he'd seen a ghost.

'What is it? What's the matter?'

'N ... nothing,' he stammered. 'Hospitals ... I ... don't like them.'

For one reckless moment he thought of telling her everything. The words bubbled up in the back of his mind. The relief of confession. The blessing of a trouble shared. But what would she think of him? She might approve. Then again, she mightn't. After all, it was a dirty, rotten, low-life trick. Like ... he struggled for a synonym ... like bowling underarm at cricket. Would she ever trust him again if she knew he was capable of doing something like that?

Besides, she was part of his alibi. Her and Harvey Harry.

Not that he would ever need one.

Aunt Myra was concussed, confused. What could she possibly

know – airborne one moment, unconscious the next? The fall had triggered some sort of brain fart, perhaps even the long-dreaded dementia.

He slowed, regaining control as they reached the end of the corridor, his initial panic now back in its box.

'Sorry. Sorry, it's ... it's this place and ... seeing her like that. Everything comes crowding back. Memories. You know ... Mummy and Daddy ...'

Melody touched his shoulder. 'Of course. I understand. And you didn't sleep much either, did you? Tossing and turning all night. Come on, let's get out of here. We'll find somewhere nice for lunch and come back later once they've got her settled.'

Come back later. The words filtered in slowly. He had no choice. They'd have to.

* * *

The big man in the brown boots turned slowly, taking in the scene, a full three hundred and sixty degrees, his keen eyes studying every nook and crevice, searching out witnesses. Searching out Jane. Finally, he walked back to his car. Both headlights were broken, both front wings crumpled from the impact with the buildings either side of the alley Jane had run down. The driver's door creaked ominously and had to be slammed shut, but drove away as casually as if he were driving to the shops. Jane could see from his hunched shoulders and the way he peered left and right that he was still looking out for her.

She stayed where she was, phoned Matt, gave him her location and said, 'There's been a murder. I'm calling Avery.' She rang off, surprised at herself. The clearness of her instructions. The steadiness of her voice. She found Avery's card, told him what she'd told Matt, and settled down to wait, remaining in the patch of low scrub where she'd taken shelter, her eyes fixed on the road they'd have to come down, the body of the black man shielded by a low branch.

Her first inclination after Brown Boots had left was to go to his assistance. Perhaps there was something she could do ... But when she looked again at the huge pool of blood still expanding on the dry ground, at the gashed throat and ripped belly, at the puddle of viscera already attracting flies, she knew it was hopeless. She gave a small whimper and sank back into her hiding place.

She'd seen death before, but not murder. Her mother, passing away in a hospital bed, serene and peaceful, the ravages of the cancer that claimed her finally at bay. But this? This was something else entirely. It had been brutal, savage, yet mind-numbingly casual too. Like someone filleting a chicken carcass or carving a roast.

The analogy made her shudder.

The way Brown Boots had walked off, driven off afterwards. No hint of flight or panic. The sheer – there was only one word for it – *professionalism* of it ...

That man had been waiting for her. In her house. Behind her front door.

The scene below was still. Even the sound of traffic seemed muted. The sun kept shining and somewhere she heard the song of birds.

She checked her watch.

Where the hell were they?

A siren sounded in the distance.

More importantly, where the hell was she?

This coolness, this quiet, this analytical thinking after all she'd been through, all she'd seen, was something new. An almost out-of-body experience. Part of her wanted to scream, shout, wail at the horror and injustice of it all, but another stronger part coolly asked what good that would do? The world was full of horror and injustice. Pick up a newspaper. Turn on the television. The most useful thing she could do was remain calm and bear witness.

She took out her notebook and started writing; dates, times, locations. What she'd done. What she'd seen. The sequence of events. There was something calming, almost ritualistic, in the process, and she thought of generations of policemen doing just what she was doing now after a traumatic event. Perhaps that's what it was really for. Making careful notes helped distance you from what had occurred.

The siren's wail grew louder but Matt arrived first, the Plover's Plumbing van practically taking the corner on two wheels. It braked hard at the sight of Jane's mangled bike and the dead man nearby, and he leapt from the van looking wild and distressed – a bit like Jane imagined she must look. She raised a hand as she got to her feet and started down the slope. He raced towards her, meeting her halfway, threw out his arms and seized fiercely, the grip of a drowning man grasping floating timber. For several seconds she found herself consoling him.

'It's OK. I'm all right.'

They held each other for a long minute as the siren's wail grew. Neither spoke. Both were lost in the single realisation that right here, right now, together like this, they had all they'd ever wanted.

The siren's wail grew louder then died as Avery's dun-coloured Fiesta swung into the street below and came to a halt. Its concealed red-and-blues continued flashing as the two policemen took in the scene. Avery checked the body while DS Dixon reversed, angling the car to block the road before popping the boot.

Avery strode up to meet them. 'He won't be walking away from that.'

Below, they watched Dixon place traffic cones and unfurl a spool of black and yellow tape. Avery's radio crackled with traffic. He issued a few curt instructions and then turned it down. He said to Jane, 'You said you saw it happen?'

She nodded.

'And you think it's related to the events at your house this morning?'

'Definitely.'

'Reason?'

'Brown boots. The same ones I saw through the cat flap.'

Avery glanced back at the body.

'Not his. The murderer's.'

'Anything else you can tell me?'

Jane held up her notebook. 'Anything on that index number I gave you?'

'Jesus, you got his registration as well?' Matt was impressed.

Avery shook his head. 'All we've got for now is it's a rental, but he won't get far. That your bike down there?'

'It was. They tried to run me down.' She paused, 'No, that's not right. They knocked me off it.'

'There's a difference?'

'If they wanted me dead, they'd have driven straight into me. They didn't care what happened to the car. But it was a tap. A gentle nudge. Just enough to push me off.' She held up the side of one grazed hand.

Avery glanced back at the mangled bike.

'That happened afterwards,' Jane added, guessing his thoughts. 'After they knocked me off. The black guy got out, asking if I was all right. He helped me up, then grabbed me. I struggled. Head-butted him. Hit him in the mouth with my helmet. He fell back as the big guy – Brown Boots – got out to assist. But by then I was free and running. So he got back in the car and came after me. Must've run over his mate in the process.'

'Then, once you'd escaped, he came back and finished him off?'

Jane nodded.

'Some mate.'

'I'll take you down and walk you through how I got away if you like,' Jane said. 'He came after me on foot at one point. Might have left some clues.'

'I'm going to need a statement too, but away from the circus.'

Avery nodded down the slope as two marked cars drew up followed by a police van.

Matt studied Jane as they moved off, thrown a little by her cool professionalism. She smiled and gave his elbow a reassuring squeeze.

Trailing them down the slope he said, 'I have two questions. I think I know the answer to the first one, but I'd be interested in your opinions: Why did Brown Boots kill his mate?'

Avery glanced at Jane. Jane said, 'Because he wasn't really a mate, just someone to be used. Hired muscle, perhaps. Now, injured, he was out of the game. Like a racehorse with a broken leg. No use to anyone. He'd need treatment, hospital, ambulance. That made him a liability.'

Avery lifted the yellow tape so they could move beyond the murder scene. Jane kept her eyes away from the body and her thoughts on Matt's question.

'Which implies that this – whatever it's all about and whoever Brown Boots is working for – is serious. They're playing for keeps. No loose ends. No leaks.'

They walked on. Jane pointed out the alley where the big man had tried to batter down the gate. Avery whistled DS Dixon and a couple of the forensics team over, then he said, 'What was your second question, Matt?'

Matt hesitated and looked at Jane, unwilling to voice it.

'I can guess,' she told him, 'and I've been wondering that myself: Why did they want to kidnap me?'

47

The questions continued long after they'd left the grey-green walls and the antiseptic smell of the police station's interview room. Matt, who'd sat at her side saying nothing while Jane delivered a full and comprehensive statement, was a little in awe of her, and a little wary. This wasn't the woman he knew. This was someone else entirely.

The collapse came after the second glass of wine while he was frying chicken pieces for one of his specialities: sticky chicken with ouzo, olives and charred lemons. Jane was sitting at the kitchen table, freshly showered, her hair curly-damp, wearing a white T-shirt and slacks. She'd been drinking steadily. Not gulping, just sipping, but sips punctuated with crisps from the bowl in front of her. Heavily salted ones. Perhaps that was it.

Arranging the pieces in a casserole dish, he glanced over and noticed a fat tear running down her face. She seemed unaware of it, then looked up and caught his eye.

'Shit,' she muttered, lowering the glass. He saw her hand was trembling.

He didn't move. Watched her. Nodded. 'Let it come.'

It came.

There was nothing he could say, nothing he could do but sit beside her, one arm resting on her bowed shoulders as she sobbed, the fright, fear, anger and relief leaching out with her tears.

After five long minutes, they lessened and she took a breath. 'That poor, poor man! He gutted him. Like ... I was going to say a carcass ... but he was still alive!'

'The man who grabbed you? Tried to kidnap you?' he said

283

gently.

'I know but ... Why would anyone do *that*?'

'A calling card. A signature.'

'*What?*'

'Mafia. Typically Russian or Sicilian. From your description and what you heard at the house, I think we can eliminate the latter.'

Jane reached for her glass and drained the dregs. Matt opened another bottle and topped it up. His own glass too. He read the label as he set it down and turned it away from her: a Nero d'Avola from southern Sicily; a deep, arterial red.

'Thanks for the heads-up,' she said, something of the old Jane returning.

'You're tough. You can take it.'

'The sympathy too.'

She looked at him with a tear-stained face then raised her glass. He clinked it. 'Welcome to my world,' he said. 'My old world, at least.'

'You think that's what it is? Something from your past?'

'What else could it be?'

Jane sipped her wine. Matt went back to his preparations, charring the lemon wedges and garlic before adding them to the chicken. He sliced and fried some onions, adding oregano, fennel seeds, sea salt and a dash of ouzo, stepping back as it bubbled up, filling the kitchen with the smell of anise.

'So they came after me to get at you,' she said at last. 'Why not you directly?'

'Maybe they think I have something or can do something for them, but need to be pressured into it. Or maybe they just want to torment me. Play cat and mouse.'

Jane didn't like the sound of that, but she put a brave face on it. 'Just how many Russian Mafioso have you pissed off, Matt Healy?'

'Honestly, I can't think of any. But Avery's going through my old cases.'

She watched him transfer the contents of the frying pan to the casserole dish and set it in the oven. The smells were tantalising. She hadn't eaten much today, and wine and crisps simply didn't cut it.

'I think you're wrong. I don't think they are just after you.' Jane moistened a fingertip and dabbed at the crisp crumbs. 'The phone number for this place might still be under your dad's name in the white pages, but you're not *that* hard to find.'

'They were at your place this morning.'

'Which doubles as *our* office, remember? And Avery said all the calls on the dead man's phone were all to our office number.'

The phone had been a "burner", bought months before at a discount warehouse but only activated the previous week.

'That's how they tracked me,' Jane continued. 'Then they realised they only had half the team. That with the office number switched through to my phone, they'd have no way of tracing you. But if they used me as a hostage, you'd come running.'

'Nice theory, but flawed.'

'You mean you *wouldn't* come running?'

'Of course I would. But they can't be after both of us, Jane. We haven't been in business long enough to piss anyone off. We're still on our first cases.'

'There's always the Trotter family,' she said, referring to the case that had brought them together in the first place. The case that had been instrumental in them founding Bluebelle Investigations.

'I mentioned them to Avery, but it doesn't seem likely. They wouldn't risk all that Old Boy stuff and the cover story we agreed to. Besides, it's not the way the gentry work. They might black ball you at the club, but they don't usually stick a knife in you. Or hire someone to do it.'

'So that leaves only one conclusion. It has to be one of our current cases.'

'You think Melody's expressing disappointment with our

work?'

'Not that one.'

He stared at her, would have laughed openly if it hadn't been for the look on her face. 'You can't mean the missing moggies?'

'Indirectly, yes. I've cracked that one anyway, but it still needs a final resolution.' She nodded at the stove. 'What are you doing after what promises to be a spectacularly tasty dinner?'

'I was thinking of a little candlelight and a lot more wine.'

'With a professional hit man on the loose?'

'You really know how to kill a mood.'

'Better a mood than us.'

'What do you have in mind?'

'Fancy an old-style police raid on a flat in Rotherhithe?'

'A raid?'

'Don't you always say it's a good idea to keep the perps off balance?'

'I do, yeah, but—'

'In fact, I'm pretty sure you told me it's rule Number One.'

* * *

It was almost six o'clock by the time they got back to London. Traffic on the northbound lanes of the M1 grew consistently more snarled as they approached the capital, but apart from the latter stages when they plunged into the rush-hour snarl themselves, they'd had a clean run. Gerrard had driven the whole way with rare concentration, declining their traditional stop and swap at Junction Nine, and even now, two miles from their flat, wedged in bumper-to-bumper traffic, he kept both hands on the wheel and both eyes fixed on the road ahead.

The second visit to Aunt Myra had gone even less well than the first. She'd been moved, at her own insistence, to a private clinic on the other side of Leicester. It had taken a while to track her down.

The place reminded Melody of High Down prison. A functional, two-storey brick building set in leafy grounds, it was almost as well guarded too. The staff were firm but professionally pleasant: Ms Vine was still settling in at the moment, would they care to wait? Another enquiry forty minutes later yielded the news that Ms Vine was consulting with her specialist. Would they care for tea or coffee? After another half-hour, they were asked for their names again. A clipboard was consulted and they were informed that she'd asked for no more visitors.

'He's her next of kin,' Melody exclaimed.

The woman at the reception said she was sorry, but the client had insisted. They'd have to go.

Her hand moved to the side of the desk and her fingers reached beneath it. A second later, a security guard in a crisp brown uniform appeared. He said nothing, just stood to their right with his thumbs hooked in his leather belt as the woman repeated her suggestion that they leave and try tomorrow. Perhaps they might telephone ahead first ...?

'Client. She's a fucking patient!' Gerrard muttered as they left.

'Not if she's paying the bills,' Melody said.

As they reached the car they saw the Polish housekeeper, Jadzia Sobczak, arrive. The clipboard was consulted and she passed unchallenged through the glassed-in reception area. Gerrard said nothing. But when a police car swung into a car park near the entrance, he seemed keen to get away.

48

It was after nine when Jane and Matt pulled up outside the Rotherhithe apartment block. Light was fading in the iridescent sky and the street was Monday-quiet. A warm glow from the first-floor apartment's windows showed there was someone home.

Access to the building was controlled by an electronic tag issued only to residents. Beside the reader was a numbered list of the block's inhabitants alongside individual call buttons. Many labels were handwritten but some, including their target, had been clipped from a printed list, which suggested they were of similar vintage and were more likely to know each other. Jane found another printed name and pressed their target's call button.

After a couple of seconds, there was a scratchy crackle from the speaker and a voice said, 'Yes?'

'Oh, hi. It's Marcie James from 1D,' Jane said, giving her voice a slightly tipsy edge and standing close to the microphone so her voice would be distorted. 'Sorry to bother you, but I've lost my keys and—'

The speaker gave an exasperated sigh. There was a hum and a click and the door unlatched.

They took the stairs to the first floor and found themselves in a beige corridor with a terracotta floor. Apartments B to F let off left and right. 1A stood at the end.

There was a bell but Matt used his knuckles, rapping hard and loud. A trick of the trade. A sharp knock was more attention-getting and intimidating than a simple *ding-dong*, and more likely to arouse the interest of the neighbours. That meant you were less likely to end up discussing matters on the doorstep – or in this case the corridor. People liked their privacy.

The door opened a fraction – along with the doors of 1B and 1C – and Matt said in a loud voice, 'Francis Cricklewood? I have a warrant for your arrest.'

'*What?*' The door opened wider.

Matt took out his wallet and held it up for the neighbours' benefit. It contained his driver's licence, credit cards and a picture of Jane, but 1B and 1C couldn't see that, and Cricklewood, in his surprise and confusion, barely took it in.

Matt's attitude, his tone, the expectation he wouldn't be challenged. Years of similar scenes in TV dramas had accustomed people to the procedure.

'Shall we do this out here, sir?' he said, keeping up the pressure.

Cricklewood glanced past him, saw the neighbour's interest and beckoned them in.

'Who are y—?' Only then did he take in Jane.

It was an odd sensation, being recognised by someone you didn't know. Jane stared back. She recognised him all right from the photographs and video clips she'd seen online, but how did he know her?

'You're not police!'

'I never said we were.'

'You said you had a warrant.'

'Call it *déjà vu*. The real police will certainly have one with all the information we can provide.'

Bernard Carpinter appeared from his bedroom wearing a baggy sweatshirt and track pants. He froze in the doorway when he saw Jane. Another flash of recognition.

'Bernard Carpinter,' Matt said. 'I remember you from the telly.'

'Who the hell are you?'

'I think you already know that,' Jane said. 'Or me, at least.'

Cricklewood and Carpinter exchanged a glance.

'You ... resemble someone we used to work with.'

'Really? You've never heard of Bluebelle Investigations then?' Head shakes. 'We're private detectives.'

'Well whoever you are, you don't have the right to barge in on people under false pretences,' Francis Cricklewood said, regaining his composure and adding a dash of outrage. 'I demand you leave immediately or I shall call the police. The *real* police.'

Jane ignored him. 'We know all about your activities. The catnappings, the demands for money, the drip-feed extortion, the offshore bank account. We even know where you keep the animals.' She held up her phone to display one of the pictures she'd taken that afternoon.

Matt added, 'Do you know the penalty for extortion? Fourteen years. You'd probably only get seven. With good behaviour, you might be out in four or five. But there's another consideration in your case, a sort of long-term punishment. You'll never tread the boards again. The stigma of this will follow you everywhere. After all, you know how the British public feel about their pets.'

'Fuck!' Carpinter muttered. 'I've got an audition next week.'

Cricklewood kept his composure. '*You* can't arrest anyone.'

'It would only take a call to pass on our information.' Jane waggled her phone.

'And the police will be speaking to you anyway,' Matt added. 'Did you know there was a murder this afternoon not far from your lock-up.?'

Jane flipped pictures to one she'd taken from the embankment slope while waiting for Matt and the police. It showed the black man face down in the road; the body in the foreground, the lock-ups on the curving approach to the railway bridge visible on one side.

Cricklewood glanced at Carpinter. 'That's nothing to do with us.'

'That's where you're wrong,' Jane said. 'We think it has everything to do with you, at least indirectly. And that's what we'd like to talk to you about.'

Cricklewood's mouth tightened.

'Or we could hand over all we've got to the police and leak it to the press. Trial by media, how does that sound? Lot's of widows and kids out there with heart-breaking stories of stolen cats. You'll be centre-stage for weeks.'

Neither man spoke.

'As you wish.' Jane put away her phone. Matt turned back towards the door.

'Wait ...' Carpinter said, turning to his friend. 'At least we can hear them out.'

Cricklewood glared. Carpinter jerked his head towards the lounge. 'Come through.'

The room was the same beige as the corridor outside. A sliding glass door leading to a balcony occupied one end and a wooden unit faced them, its segmented shelves filled with books and knick-knacks and a widescreen television. The picture on the screen was frozen. Someone in army uniform caught mid-bellow. The remaining walls were covered with posters and photographs, some framed and hung squarely, others pinned or Blu-Tacked at random angles.

'Can I get you something?' Carpinter asked.

'For fuck's sake, Bernard. You'd buy your executioner a beer!'

'Just being civil, Francis. Sorry, I didn't catch your names.'

Matt and Jane introduced themselves but declined his offer of refreshment.

Cricklewood shut off the television. 'Well? What do you want?'

'We're interested in the source of your information,' Jane said. 'About the cats. Is it on there?' She gestured at a closed laptop propped against one of the armchairs.

'That's none of your damn—'

'Yes,' Carpinter said.

'A database? From the Fancy Cat Fanciers group?'

'Yes.'

Cricklewood scowled at Carpinter.

'She already knows, for Christ's sake.'

'Tell me about it,' Jane said. 'Everything.'

'Not really my department.' Carpinter looked at his scowling companion. 'Francis handles that side of the operation.'

Francis pursed his lips and said nothing.

'I should tell you that the man who was murdered this afternoon was involved in attempting to recover that database.'

'*What?*'

'It appears he was staking out your lock-up, awaiting your return. Fortunately for you two, someone else found him first. A rival gang, we think. Unfortunately, that means there are two groups after you.'

'*Jesus H Christ!*'

Cricklewood remained impassive as Jane continued her bluff.

'It's only a matter of time till they follow the same leads that led us here. They might even be on their way now. As you can see,' she zoomed in on the photo of the fallen man and held it up again, 'their methods are a little more direct than ours.'

'For fuck's sake, Francis.! You said Ern—'

'I don't believe you.' Cricklewood cut him off. 'A cat owners' database? No one kills for that sort of thing. Are you seriously suggesting a couple of criminal gangs are duking it out for the knowledge of who owns a Burmese or an American Bobtail?'

'It's not the database itself, it's where it came from. What you've got there is a throwaway. Something for petty criminals. But that was part of a much bigger haul. Serious corporate data. Financial, industrial, governmental and god knows what else. *That's* what they're interested in: the source. *That's* what they're killing for.'

'Holy fuck,' Carpinter muttered. 'You don't think—'

'Shut up, Bernard!' Despite his attitude, her words clearly disconcerted Cricklewood. He added, 'I don't see how that can possibly—'

Jane thrust the phone in his face. 'Look closely, Mr Cricklewood. That man was disembowelled before he died.'

Cricklewood jerked his head away but stayed mum.

'His nephew,' Carpinter said. 'He put us on to it. We're actors ... It's hand-to-mouth a lot of the time. You have to do other things to survive. Part-time jobs, shit work, minimum wage. We just ... wanted a steady income. What's a tenner a month to someone who can afford a thousand for a fucking cat ...'

'Does this nephew have a name?'

'Ernest. Ernest Cricklewood. He's some sort of IT whiz in the City.'

Francis stared at the floor, shaking his head as if disassociating himself from the betrayal.

'You have an address?'

'I can take you. Sod hanging round here if there are gangs after us!'

* * *

Dmitri Podvyshenskaya took the rebuke stoically. No operation ever went perfectly. Setbacks were expected, but the news that they had not yet eliminated the final links in the chain – indeed, that "they" had now been reduced to "he" – was not received well. Did he imagine that fake IDs grew on trees? That the supply of vehicles and equipment was limitless? Did he appreciate the consequences of every day's delay?

He did, of course. He understood the urgency.

He glanced back at the burning car, the flames of which were towering into the night sky, licking at the undersides of overhanging branches.

He was directed to a bench in Hyde Park in one hour's time. He would find the key to a luggage locker taped beneath it. In the locker he would find new papers, keys to another vehicle, and a phone preloaded with directions to a new address. A residential address in Greenwich. The time for subtlety was over. 'End this now!'

49

'What the hell is this?' Ernest Cricklewood said as four figures, led by Bernard Carpinter, trooped into his apartment. His uncle, trailing, gave him a helpless shrug.

'These,' Bernard announced, 'are the people you said you'd dealt with: Bluebelle Investigations.'

'*What?* What the hell did you bring them here for? No, no, no. Out, out, all of you. You two especially!'

'Dealt with?' Matt mouthed at Jane.

She was wondering the same thing.

Ernest was pushing now, wild-eyed, trying to shove them by the shoulders.

'Get out! Get out! Go away!'

'We just want to talk to you about—' Matt said.

'I don't know anything. Whatever these idiots told you, it's nothing to do with me. Go, go. Go on!'

Jane grabbed him by the sweatshirt and slammed him against the wall. He was a head and shoulders taller than she was, but lanky and unfit, and Jane had fury on her side. 'Listen, you piece of shit. I saw a man murdered this afternoon. Butchered like an animal while he still lived and breathed. You want to know how it was done?' She jabbed three fingers in his gut. 'Ripped open here first.' She mimed the action then jabbed them his throat. 'Then here. You want to give me one good reason why I shouldn't tell the man who did it where you live?'

Ernest made an inarticulate noise and Jane let him go.

The others looked on, stunned by her outburst – Jane had even surprised herself – and for a moment something like an embarrassed silence settled on them all.

'She's got pictures,' Carpinter said.

Jane pulled out her phone.

'No, no, no. Don't turn that on!'

'Really?' Jane said, another piece of the puzzle slotting into place. 'Why's that?

'I ... I don't want to see.'

'But my phone's already on, look.' She held it out.

'Oh Jesus!'

'But I haven't had any calls. At least not in the last few hours.'

Ernest let out a sigh.

Matt, only half a step behind her reasoning, slipped out his own phone and hit speed dial.

Ernest jumped as the phone in Jane's open palm lit up and played a cheery tune.

'Well look at that. Talk about coincidence. Redirected from our office too,' she lied.

'Don't answer! Don't answer it!' He snatched the phone from her hand, tore off the back, clawed out the battery, then dropped it to the floor as he slid down the wall, holding a hand to his head and muttering, 'Oh Jesus, Jesus, Jesus ...'

'What's the problem?' Matt held up his phone. 'It was only me.'

Ernest looked up ashen-faced.

'Do you have something to tell us?' Jane asked.

* * *

Ernest sat on the sofa, his eyes fixed on the carpet as he talked, downplaying his role and underscoring his innocence. It had all been Spree's idea. He was just the middleman – the password cracker and database organiser. Then the data had gone to Knightmare who'd handled the sale.

'Sale? Singular?'

'One buyer took the lot.'

'Who?'

He shrugged. 'Didn't ask.'

'You were paid, of course. How much?'

'Ten K.' The words were mumbled.

'Each, or in total?'

'That's what I got.'

'You little shit!' Till then Bernard Carpinter had seemed gleeful at the young man's comeuppance, serving them all tea and coffee from his kitchen, helping himself to a hefty measure of scotch from his liquor cabinet. 'You charged us five hundred for the fucking cats?'

Jane glared at him. He fell silent.

'How were you paid?'

'Bitcoins.'

'Digital currency,' Jane translated for the others. 'Decentralised. Untraceable. Untaxable too.'

'Who are Spree and Knightmare in real life?'

'Dunno.'

'You never met?'

'No.' He finally looked up and Jane suspected this answer was honest. Possibly the only honest one he'd given her so far.

'But you must know their real names.'

He looked down again and shook his head.

'Why then was it necessary to *deal with us*?'

'What?'

'The way we were introduced: *These are the people you said you'd dealt with.* Remember? Why did we need dealing with?'

He looked up again, this time to glare at Cricklewood and Carpinter. 'Because those two said you were on to them. They saw you outside a pub taking pictures. Then outside their apartment. We followed you. Saw you putting out flyers for your business. Identified you from that.'

'And how did you plan to deal with us?'

Ernest's eyes went back to the carpet.

'I'll tell you, shall I? My theory? You may not have met in person, but you knew exactly who Spree and Knightmare really were. You'd been keeping a discreet eye on them because you were worried about the deal. After all, you're the only one who knew the full value of all the information you stole. Spree copied encrypted databases, Knightmare sold them, probably from an inventory you created, but *you're* the only one who knows what they contained in any detail.

'So you kept a watching brief. If anything unusual happened to the other two, that might jeopardise you. And last Thursday something did happen. Didn't it, Matt?'

Matt took over. 'Last Thursday, an employee of Mercury Backup Systems was knocked from his bike and killed on his way home from a night shift. Two men attended the scene. One was very big, one was black. The stolen vehicle involved was later found burnt out.

'The death was widely reported: James Lawrence Burton. What wasn't reported was that Burton's apartment had been carefully searched. It was an expert job. No signs of forced entry, nothing of value taken, except for one curious thing. What sort of burglar dismantles a computer and steals its hard drives? When the police noticed this, they realised that Burton was a computer whiz who didn't own so much as a USB stick. Not even a home-burned DVD. Curious, wouldn't you say?

'The following day, a young man in Dagenham named Andrej Bilic went out for a walk – off the fourteenth floor of his tower block. There was nothing to connect him with Burton except that he too didn't own so much as a floppy disk – despite being a computer whiz with a history of hacking.'

Jane watched Ernest. Though his eyes were still on the carpet, she saw them widen.

'You heard about one or both of those and thought *someone's on to us,*' she resumed, 'at about the same time the comedy duo here told you *we* were on to *them*. So you decided on a two-for-one. Redirect any interest in yourself and point it our way. Perhaps even plant some false clues.'

'You little shit,' Bernard Carpinter said again, but quietly this time.

Ernest said nothing.

'Why else would you be so nervous about my phone? Especially calls rerouted from our office?'

He bit his lip.

'They broke in last night, you know? They were waiting for us this morning. Have you been checking the news feeds for word of us?'

Ernest said nothing, but she saw her words strike home.

'We got away, but they tracked me down this afternoon, courtesy of a forwarded phone. Forwarded to this one.' She picked up the battery and began reassembling it. 'Geolocation, right? It's pretty accurate in a place like London. Down to a few square metres with the right access and the right gear.'

Ernest glanced at her and glanced away.

'That guy lying dead in the road? That was very nearly me. Obviously, they're not happy I got away. Obviously, they're keener than ever to find me. So do you know what I'm going to do?

'My friend here is going to tie you up and I'm going to turn this on and slip it in your pocket.' She pointed at the breast pocket of his Hermes shirt. 'Then we're going to leave you. Because that will solve *our* problem. Won't it, Matt?'

Ernest stared back, speechless, a look of horror on his face.

'You have precisely ten seconds to tell us the truth.'

He looked to Matt who, by way of reply, picked up a table lamp, studied the lead, pulled the plug from the wall, tore it from the base and tested it as a hangman might test the rope for a noose.

'*Ten!*' Jane said.

'So,' Matt asked, doubling and flexing the lead, 'is this Spree character really James Burton?'

Ernest hesitated.

'*Nine!*'

'I ... Yes, it was him.'

'And you knew he'd been killed?'

'*Eight!*'

'Yes, yes, I saw it on a news feed.'

'And who was Knightmare?'

'I don't know anyth—'

'*Seven!*'

'It was the guy from Dagenham. We never met either, but ... but I knew ... I mean, I heard that something had happened to him ...'

'*Six!*'

'And who really organised this data grab?'

Silence now. A telling silence.

'*Five!*'

Jane switched on her mobile phone.

'All right, all right, it was me! It was Spree's idea but I set it up. I found Knightmare, set it running.'

'*Four!*'

The phone beeped and played its start up tune.

'For a mere ten K?'

'It was fifty K each, all right?'

A murmured but explosive, 'You little fuck!' from Bernard Carpinter.

'And the buyer?'

'*Three!*'

'I don't know. I really, really don't.'

Jane slipped the phone into Ernest's pocket and stepped back.

'*Two!*'

'Honestly! I don't know! I don't know! I don't know!'

'But you're going to tell us all you *do* know, right?'

'*One!*'

'Yes, yes, I will. Just turn that damn thing off. *Please!*'

His hands hadn't yet been bound, but he glared down at the phone as if was radioactive or a horrendous growth bubbling from his chest.

Jane plucked it out again and switched it off. Once they'd realised that was how she'd been tracked, she'd made one last call to the office phone and, using her PIN number, remotely switched off its redirection. But there was no need to tell Ernest that.

Matt had his own phone out now and selected the digital recorder app. 'Monday evening.' He gave the date and time. 'Ernest Cricklewood in conversation with Jane Child and Matthew Healy, witnessed by Bernard Carpinter and Francis Cricklewood.' He set the phone down and added, 'Away you go.'

* * *

Like all great ideas, this one had emerged fully formed. A re-arrangement of the cubicle spaces at Mercury Backup Systems had left a spare network port behind James Burton's desk. Like any curious computer geek, he'd tested it and found it was still live, but it was months before he realised its potential.

Vast quantities of data flowed through MBS's systems every night, rivers the equivalent of the Nile or the Amazon, while Burton and his colleagues stood on the shore, managing and directing the flow. It was routine, repetitive work. The biggest excitements involved rebooting crashed servers or restarting sluggish connections.

A chance remark to a teammate playing *Artefact X* had led Burton – whose online handle was Spree – to send a private message to the character known as Bitz. Bitz didn't reply for almost a week, and when he did it was via an even more discreet private messaging service. By then, Bitz knew precisely who he was dealing with.

They conducted a trial run, a trio of 10GB databases transmitted via a third-party server. It worked, but the size of the motherlode and the volume Bitz demanded made that delivery method impractical. So they settled on a series of Cold War-style dead drops instead.

For days running, Spree carried a 2TB disc drive into work with him, connected it to the port behind his desk and left it gathering passing traffic while he worked his shift. Ernest collected the drives from railway station luggage lockers, lost property offices and once from a shopping bag left beside a bin in Regent's Park. The hard drives – tucked inside sneakers, hidden inside gift-wrapped books, in the pockets of backpacks or wrapped in old clothing – were encrypted in case an outsider chanced on them. Once he'd collected a drive, Ernest would place a pre-arranged message on a particular Reddit board, and some time later a one-time link to the drive's encryption key would appear by way of reply.

The hard work, as Bitz had emphasised from the outset, was decrypting the encrypted databases, but it actually wasn't too hard at all. Ernest had built a cluster of linked Linux machines in his apartment, a sort of mini supercomputer, and simply left them grinding away in a brute-force attack, trying every letter, number and character combination in sequence until, with tinny fanfare, the machine announced its success. A six-character password would take milliseconds, eight digits a few minutes, ten or twelve digits a day or so. It was unusual to find any that used longer passwords.

One of the toughest ones to crack, and one he'd thought the most promising, turned out to contain nothing more than the names and addresses of the owners of pedigree cats. His machine spent almost a week on it, but it was useless to on-sell. Time wasters like that deserved to suffer, and he quickly figured out a way to make them do so – at least indirectly – by giving it to his uncle.

Once he'd catalogued and collated the data, he recruited Knightmare – Andrej Bilic – to dispose of the haul. All Ernest knew of that end of the operation was that the data had gone to a shadowy East European group, bought as a job lot and probably on-sold from there. Bilic took twenty percent of the seventy-five thousand bitcoin sale price. Bitz paid Spree ten thousand for his trouble and kept the remaining fifty thousand for himself.

As middleman, Bitz was the most secure of the trio. Salesman Knightmare, the most exposed. If the databases had been split up, Spree too would have been relatively secure, but their purchase by a single entity meant it wasn't difficult to pinpoint a likely common source for such a disparate collection. Narrowing it down to a particular individual would have been trickier, but Spree/Burton had already shown his gregariousness in suggesting the scheme in the first place. Perhaps he'd done so to others.

What the unknown buyer couldn't intuit was the connection between Spree and Knightmare. And Ernest/Bitz had been very happy about that.

Until now.

50

Two women were waiting for the lift when it arrived at the third-floor lobby. They stepped aside to let Melody and Gerrard out, then one of them said, 'Mr Vine? Gerrard Vine?'

'Yes.'

'I'm Detective Inspector Achebe. This is DS Wardle. I wonder if we could have a word with you, please.'

As they produced their warrant cards, Melody saw the look on Gerrard's face. An unguarded moment. The look of a rabbit caught the headlights of a rapidly approaching car.

'What's this about?' she asked, unlocking the front door of the apartment and ushering them in. Whatever it was, she didn't want it conducted within earshot of their nosy neighbours.

'Your aunt, Ms Myra Vine, had a nasty fall early on Saturday morning,' Achebe said.

'We know.' Melody answered testily. 'We've just got back from the hospital.'

'We're trying to account for peoples' movements over the weekend.'

'Why? What's the old b—. What's she been saying?'

'I was away,' Gerrard put in. 'Paris. Business. Didn't get back till last night.'

'Yes, Leicester police tried calling you, but it seems your mobile phone was out of action.'

'It was stolen,' Gerrard said. 'Or I lost it somewhere.'

'Did you lose anything else, Mr Vine? Wallet, credit cards, ATM card ...?'

'No.' Gerrard patted his pockets. 'Just the phone.'

'You're sure about that?'

'Absolutely.'

'What is this about?' Melody repeated. 'We've had a long day, a long drive and Gerrard hardly slept last night after hearing about his aunt. Now we'd just like to sit down and have five minutes peace and quiet.'

'Of course. We won't keep you long.' Achebe turned back to Gerrard. 'When did you leave for Paris?'

'I took the 4:30 on Friday.'

'You were there on business, you said?'

'Yes. A friend met me at the station. We went on to his club for dinner.'

'May I have the name of this friend?'

'Harvey Harry. It's actually Harrison but we all call him ... It's an old school thing.'

'Do you have his contact details?'

'They were on my phone.'

'I do.' Melody found them on hers and held it out so the DS could copy them in her notebook.

'And you returned Sunday night?

'Well, evening.'

'I collected him from St Pancras myself,' Melody said.

'And that was the first you'd heard of your aunt's ... accident?'

'Yes.'

Melody, noticing the DI's slight hesitation, said, 'Is Myra saying it wasn't an accident?' When no one answered, she added, 'Oh for god's sake, she was unconscious half the weekend. She tripped on the bloody stairs. She's about nine hundred years old. She should have been in a nursing home years ago, all those crazy ideas of hers.'

'She did trip on the stairs,' Achebe said, 'and gave a very lucid account of the circumstances. That she'd had an unexpected visit from her nephew the day before, for example.'

'Oh and I suppose Gerrard hid round a corner and stuck his

foot out as she passed or something?'

'No, that someone set a tripwire. Possibly a piece of nylon line.'

'What? But Gerrard wasn't even there.'

'Not according to Ms Vine. According to her, he stayed overnight. The last time she recalls seeing him was early on Saturday morning, although she herself admits that sighting wasn't definite. All she actually saw was a pair of brown Oxford's standing over her at the foot of the stairs. Do you own a pair of brown Oxford's, Mr Vine?' Achebe glanced down at the evidence still on Gerrard's feet.

'This is preposterous!' Melody said. 'She was in a coma. She dreamed it all.'

'I'd have said the same, except for two things. She has a fresh horizontal cut about three inches up her right ankle conducive to having tripped on something fine and strong. And when our people in Leicester took a closer look at the bannisters at the head of the stairs, they found identical marks either side, fine bruises in the wood which, allowing for the running shoes she was wearing, exactly match the height of the ankle cut.'

Melody said nothing, thinking how typical it was for Myra to get such service from the Leicester constabulary. Any other old duck would have been dismissed out of hand, but not bloody Myra, darling benefactor of god knows how many local charities. She probably had the Chief Constable to tea every Sunday.

Only belatedly did she glance at Gerrard and see his ashen face.

'So you were in Paris at the weekend?' Achebe continued.

'Um ... yes. I ... I still have the ticket stubs somewhere, I think.'

'You lost your mobile phone, but nothing else? Nothing from your wallet?'

'No. Nothing else. I told you. I checked.'

'So how do you explain your ATM card being used at

Gorelston-on-Sea at 12:22 am on Sunday morning?'

'What?' Such little colour as Gerrard still possessed drained from his face.

That bloody girl! He'd offered to help her out. He realised now she'd robbed him.

And destroyed his life.

'The bank has faxed us the pictures from the ATM, Mr Vine, and we're currently going through footage of passengers boarding and departing the Eurostar on the dates and times you mentioned. We've also requisitioned video footage from Leicester and Great Yarmouth railway stations, but it'll take a while to go through. Unless you fancy helping us out there?'

Gerrard swallowed lumpily, his eyes wide.

'No rush,' Achebe said. 'Something to think about while you accompany us to the station.'

* * *

There was a policeman at Ernest's apartment door, another at the door of his building. Others were loading an unmarked van with computer equipment from his flat.

Avery had arrived with a search warrant half an hour after Ernest finished his story. Matt and Jane had been obliged to sit around and wait, and the young man seemed relieved at the prospect of being taken in for further questioning and the idea of protective custody. Francis and Bernard were introduced as supporting relatives. Their details were taken and they'd been sent on their way, but Jane checked them by the door and delivered a quiet ultimatum.

'At twelve o'clock tomorrow, I'm going to visit your lock-up. I expect to find the door open, the place empty and all the cats returned unharmed. Do you understand?'

Francis Cricklewood pursed his lips but said nothing.

'I'll give you a little longer to return all the rewards and insurance money you've stolen. Let's say two full days. On Thursday morning, all FCF members will receive an email detailing your little scam and asking if anyone has not yet received a full refund. If I get one single complaint ...'

A burly policeman brushed past them carrying more computer equipment. Bernard and Francis's eyed followed him warily.

'... I'll go to the police *and* the newspapers. CRICK & CARP: CATNAPPERS. Make a great headline, wouldn't it? Problem is, with faces as familiar as yours, you'll never work again. Even flipping burgers.'

Francis Cricklewood snorted and stormed away. Bernard Carpinter touched her elbow and gave a faint nod of acquiescence. Funnily enough, she believed him.

Matt sent Avery a copy of Ernest's confession from his phone.

'Any news of Brown Boots?' Jane asked.

'The car he used has been found. burnt-out, like the first one, but damage consistent with what you told us. The rental company's video shows it was hired by the black guy using a false ID. He drove it out of the lot too. No sign of the big bloke.'

'Have you identified the deceased?' Matt asked.

Avery nodded. 'Gentleman by the name of Fesahaye Odman. Minor previous, but word is that these days he was specialising in local liaison.'

'Local liaison?' Matt seemed surprised. 'You mean a fixer?'

'What does that mean?' Jane asked.

'Think of it as a concierge service for visiting criminals. Anyone we know?'

A closed look came over Avery's face and he dropped his voice. 'I can't really say, but as of early this afternoon, that dead database guy – James Burton – got his case kicked on to the front burner. You two have stirred up something because when I called this in, the Super practically wet himself with excitement.'

'You still working for McCauley?'

Avery nodded.

Superintendent McCauley was an old adversary of Matt's. A career administrator with little on-the-ground experience. But he had the right school tie and a very brown nose.

'It must be big if that prick's taking an interest,' Matt added.

'I've heard a whisper of KPG involvement.'

'You're joking?'

'It fits with the Spetsnaz boots and the Russian swearing.'

Matt blew out his cheeks.

Avery gestured at Ernest's apartment. 'Seems like this chap and his chums might have picked up more than a few million credit card numbers.'

'And that's why they're picking them off,' Matt said. 'To eliminate the source.'

'We've got an all-points out for Brown Boots. He won't get far. But until then, you two be careful, eh?'

51

'Mind giving me a translation,' Jane said as they made their way back to Jake's van. 'Who's the KPG?'

'Didn't you get the reference? The Russian Embassy's on Bayswater Road. It overlooks Kensington Palace Gardens.'

'You think they're involved?'

'It's got to be something like that. Hackers don't usually get bumped off for doing what they do. Someone's got hold of some very useful information and is trying to protect it by eliminating its source. Hiring a local liaison would fit with someone brought in from overseas, but the question is, what could be so important?'

Jane thought as they walked. 'I have an idea, and I think I know why the James Burton case got prioritised this afternoon.' She told him about her conversation with Dr McKellar of the FCF and the theory she'd put to him. 'He was Chief Security Officer for MBS for several years. Probably still has his old contacts. He was the one who used that line about their backups being as safe as GCHQ. When I put that to him, he said categorically there wasn't any of that sort of data at MBS, but he went all non-disclosure agreement on me when I mentioned the Secretary of State for Foreign and Commonwealth Affairs.'

'The people who manage the Cheltenham spy base? If that's the case, then whatever those guys nabbed could be of national significance.' He stopped and unlocked the van. 'Listen, I don't think we should go home. If they lucked out at your place, it won't take them long to move on to mine. We should find a hotel till all this is over.'

'You're forgetting something: Bluebelle.'

'You can't be serious?'

'She's there on her own in a strange house, locked in a room with hardly any food and only some torn-up newspaper for a litter tray. She likes company. She'll be worried. And I'll be worried about her. Besides, we should pick up some things if we're going to a hotel. And you've got to return the van anyway, so what's the difference?'

'The difference is, Brown Boots could be waiting for us. And you can't take a cat to a hotel.'

'You can if you smuggle it in.' He laughed, then saw she was serious. 'She saved my life this morning, Matt. She probably saved yours too. Now hers might be in danger. Do you think someone who disembowels a work mate is going to have any sympathy for a cat? Especially after what she did to his face.'

'So we put both our lives in danger to rescue her?'

'You heard what Avery said. The police are after him. He's probably gone to ground by now.'

'What if he hasn't, Jane?'

'What if they never catch him? How long do *we* stay on the run? And do we just leave her there to starve?'

He blew out his cheeks and switched on the ignition. 'If we're going to do this, we should assume the worst. We'll need a plan to get her out.'

'Yes, I've been thinking about that too ...'

* * *

Number twenty-six had no front garden. The fence had been bowled and the old bricks used as the fill for a couple of off-street car parks. Matt swung the van in beside Jake's wife's Toyota, then went through the keys till he found one that looked like it would fit the front door.

The front room, hallway and dining room of the house had been knocked through to make a large open-plan interior space, which meant Matt walked in on Jake and Cheryl having a snog on the sofa. The lights were off and the TV muted. He thought they'd gone to bed. Had planned to leave the keys on the sideboard.

'What the fuck ...?' Jake leapt to his feet, straightening his clothes.

The TV was playing highlights of one of Saturday's matches.

'Chelsea were rubbish, weren't they?' Matt kept his eyes on the telly. 'That striker ... There you go, mate.' He held out the keys. 'Sorry I've had it so long. Been quite a day, what with one thing and another. Remind me to tell you about it some time. Evening, Cheryl. Mind if I go out the back way?'

He was already halfway there before Jake could respond.

'What's out the back?'

'Gardens.' Matt gave him a wink. 'Oh, and I also borrowed this.' He held up a short length of galvanised pipe. The end had been threaded and screwed into an even thicker right-angle coupler. 'I'll let you have it back tomorrow.'

'What the hell's going on, Matt?'

'Might have a visitor at my place. Thought I'd surprise him.' He slapped the pipe into the palm of his hand.

'You want some help?'

Matt hesitated. 'You be up for another half-hour?'

'I can be.'

Matt checked his watch. 'If you haven't heard back from me by eleven, call this number.' He felt around in his pocket and handed him a card.

'Detective Inspector Avery?'

'An old mate. He knows the score.'

'You sure you don't want a hand?'

'I'm good, but thanks.' Matt stepped out into the garden, shielding his eyes from the porch light which came on automatically. 'Should have a straight run to my place from here.'

'Only if you're good at the high-jump. And watch out for Collet's dog.'

Matt gave him a thumbs-up and headed down the garden.

* * *

Jane drummed her fingers on the steering wheel of Sally's car, anxious to get moving. She was parked half a mile from Matt's house at the edge of a service station forecourt, sitting in the shadow of its towering sign, lights off, doors locked, waiting for his call.

She'd also borrowed Sally's phone, fearing to use her own now after seeing Ernest's reaction to her simply powering it on.

Sally wanted explanations. Jane said they had an urgent surveillance situation and had to move fast but promised to tell her all about it in the morning. Then she'd driven off, feeling bad about the lie, and – despite herself – hoping she'd still be around in the morning to deliver the explanation.

* * *

Collet's dog came out at full tilt, yapping its head off as Matt climbed the neighbour's fence and dropped into their garden. It yapped at everything, from the postman to sparrows farting according to Bernie Collet, but it soon recognised Matt and turned its alarm into an enthusiastic greeting, rushing round his ankles and rolling on its back. It was part Yorkshire Terrier, part fucking loony – at least according to Bernie Collet – but a great favourite in the street for its sheer energy and endearing manners.

'Hello Ripper,' Matt whispered. 'Yes, yes, it's good to see you too.'

The dog's name was really Mr Ripley – Liz Collet was a fan of Patricia Highsmith – but Bernie Collet shortened it, largely because it amused him to have a dog the size of a shoe box with such an aggressive name.

Matt still had two gardens and three fences to go, but seeing

Ripper gave him an idea, and he scooped the dog up under one arm and pressed on. For his part, Ripper was delighted with this unexpected adventure and wagged so enthusiastically that it was like trying to hold on to a manic metronome.

Five minutes later, Matt reached the fence to his own garden, leaned over and lowered Ripper into it. The dog raced off, scurrying and snuffling in an ecstasy of exploration.

The bottom of the garden was overgrown, more like a jungle. A perfect hiding place for a would-be assailant. But Ripper's excited scamperings – along with his continued silence – suggested the coast was clear.

Matt vaulted the fence and dropped into the undergrowth. Ripper bounded up in greeting then raced away again as he made his way to the back door. Gesturing silently to the excited dog, he opened it and bundled him inside, listening to the clack of nails on the kitchen lino and the snuffling at all the strange new scents. At the very least the dog might provide a distraction.

Kitchen's clear, he thought.

There was no guarantee there was anyone here at all. Brown Boots was more likely watching Jane's house since they'd already had contact there, but there was no point taking chances.

Ripper gave a single bark then snuffled and scratched at the door of the room they were using for an office; the room containing Bluebelle. Which suggested he'd found nothing else of interest in the open areas downstairs.

Matt dragged the dog away and directed him to the upper storey. Ripper's short legs struggled with the stairs but he was propelled up by unbounded enthusiasm and skittered around up there too.

Matt took a breath, kept low, gripped the length of pipe firmly and threw open the office door.

* * *

Dmitri Podvyshenskaya listened to the radio as he ate the last of the pre-packaged sandwiches he'd brought with him. He threw the container into the footwell of the front passenger seat thinking how he both missed and didn't miss the gangly black man's company. Od had been restless, not a watcher, and had appalling taste in music. The tinny tribal tunes would leak from his earbuds, and his twitching to the beat was infuriating, but at times like this, Dmitri could have sent him off in search of food – Od had a sort of radar for tasty ethnic takeaways – and he'd have returned with plastic containers filled with jerk chicken, curried goat or salt fish and ackee. They'd have sat steaming up the interior of the car and belching in contentment. All Dmitri could think of now was the radio jingle for a pizza franchise that promised delivery within thirty minutes *or your pizza for free!* They seemed to play it every five minutes.

He picked up the mobile phone they'd provided to replace Od, dialled the number, and made his selection, giving the target's name and address for delivery. Providing the target didn't arrive home in the next thirty minutes, he could whistle the delivery guy over and say he'd been called out.

Dmitri checked his watch. Matthew Healy was probably in one of those awful English pubs which served warm beer at ludicrous prices. What was it with the English? A good shot of vodka would produce a similar effect to three pints of brown ale, in less time and without all the extra fluid. Which reminded him, he needed to piss.

Surveillance really was a two-man operation.

Still, it was a quiet street. Not one of those locations where you had to keep on constant alert, tracking the ebb and flow of passers-by in order to spot your target. All that had happened in the last twenty minutes was the return of the neighbour – a plumber – parking his van up a drive half a block away.

Plumber: *vodoprovodchik.* With luck, one more night's work and he could return to civilisation.

Lights! Front room, lounge. A few seconds later, upstairs too. There *was* someone home after all. He'd checked earlier, banged on the door, but no one answered. He'd walked around the side too, checking for another entrance. Were they asleep? Perhaps wearing earbuds filled with tribal music, like Od.

He watched and waited, seeing shadowed signs of movement in the room upstairs. There had been a little extra in the luggage locker; a Glock pistol with a threaded barrel, a silencer and a dozen rounds of subsonic ammunition. A clear indication his masters were serious when they demanded an immediate resolution.

Dmitri checked the gun, made ungainly by the added length of the silencer, then gingerly touched the side of his face where the cat's claws had sunk in deepest. It was hot and swollen and he could feel it pulsing in time to the beat of his heart. Fucking animal! It was as dead as its owner. Despite his brief, if there was any chance of making them both suffer long and loud before they died, he'd take it.

He checked his other weapons. The knife he carried in a sheath on his belt and the thin, needle-like one tucked into his left boot, imagining their dance in living flesh.

Lost in reverie, he snapped to attention as a pair of headlights swung into the street behind him. His pizza, already?

Dropping low in his seat, he watched the rear view mirror as the vehicle drew level with the line of cars parked at the side of the road and reversed smoothly into a vacant spot. The lights went off. Someone got out. A woman.

Cat Bitch!

Angling the mirror, Dmitri watched her cross the street, go straight to the door of the target's house, unlock it and let herself inside.

'Time to play,' he muttered, and had just popped his door when another set of headlights swung into the street. A pizza delivery van.

He closed the door again and checked his watch: twenty-two

minutes. No free pizza tonight.

The van double-parked right outside the target's house and flicked on its hazard lights. A tubby guy in a red and black uniform got out, consulted a clipboard and took a thermal zip bag from the rear before heading up the path. Perfect cover for the perfect entrance.

Dmitri slipped out and followed him.

52

After Gerrard's arrest and an interview at which his lawyer advised him to say nothing, he got to spend a few quiet minutes with Melody.

'Well?' she said.

Gerrard studied the hands clasped in his lap.

'You're an ass, Gerrard. Why the hell didn't you tell me?'

'Who says I actually—'

'Oh, come on! You haven't got an original bone in your body. It was right after you heard about Papa's fall, wasn't it?'

He said nothing.

'For god's sake, these things take planning. *Careful* planning. If you'd told me, we could have worked something out together.'

'You were my alibi,' he said weakly.

'A fat lot of good that's going to do now. They've only to look at video footage from St Pancras and Gare du Nord to see you didn't arrive or depart at the times you claimed. And how long do think Harvey Harry's going to stand up to questioning? They've only to hold out a glass of whisky and he'll confess to the Great Train Robbery.'

'I was going to tell you. Later. When it was all over.'

'Well, it's all bloody over now. You'll be lucky if Myra leaves you a penny. You can kiss your allowance goodbye. And the family money. It'll probably all go to Polish refugees now.'

Gerrard groaned.

'Christ, what a bloody mess! And I had it all under control too.'

'What do you mean?'

'I said I'd sort something out, didn't I? Why don't you listen? Why don't you trust me?'

'That was month's ago, Mel. You've said nothing since. Last week, after Papa's *accident*, I thought I'd better do something ...'

She closed her eyes and shook her head. 'It was in progress, Gerrard. There were a few hiccups but I've got them sorted now. At least we'll come out of this with *something*.'

'Why? What have you done?'

She lowered her voice further. 'The counterfeits. I took out insurance through that old chum of yours.'

'Fucky Findlayson?'

'He let me backdate the policy a couple of years so it doesn't look suspicious.'

There was no need to go into the details of why he'd done so, except that the repulsive little man had lived up to his nickname. It was one of the reasons she'd never mentioned it to Gerrard.

'So that chap that came in last week, the detective ...?' he said.

'That was to cover over the hiccup. Can you believe Reg Trivet got wind of the very first place I sold the fake stuff too? I had to make it look like we were doing something, so I hired a couple of Keystone Cops.'

'But ... it wasn't fake. Was it?'

'Near enough. A few floor sweepings and some out-of-date beans. But that's the point. It still has to taste pretty good. We are an exclusive brand, after all.

'Anyway, I've got a report coming that'll go straight to the insurance company. The payout will ensure we survive in the short term *and* look after Papa till he gets out. All we've got to do now is work out a way to get you back into aunty's good books.'

Gerrard looked at her hopelessly.

'What about stress? Some sort of breakdown or a blow on the head? Disease, maybe. A tumour. Something that makes you act out of character from time to time. Something really expensive to cure ...' She was away now, brainstorming, and he knew better than to interrupt her.

At length she said, 'Don't worry. With that insurance money, we'll get you a top-class legal team. I'm sure they'll come up with something. Just hold tight and keep mum.'

* * *

Jane received the all clear on Sally's phone but still proceeded cautiously. She checked the street before leaving her car, and as far as she could make out there was no one sitting in the lines parked along either side. But one of the street lamps was broken further up, leaving a pool of darkness beneath it. She moved steadily, trying to keep her steps unhurried and her demeanour casual. If Brown Boots was watching, it wouldn't do to tip him off about her suspicions. Still, she didn't let out her breath until Matt's front door was closed and locked behind her.

The first greeting she got came from Ripper, now confined to the back yard and awaiting return to his own. Two short barks. She looked up as Matt came down carrying a couple of overnight bags.

'I've got biscuits, bowl and tray for Bluebelle. We'll stop at an all-nighter for some kitty litter. We can hide her carry-box in one of these bags if necessary.'

'Got anything for me in there?' Jane gestured.

'Everything you brought over the other day.' It would have to do. 'We'll stop and get you some kitty litter too, if you like. But we really shouldn't linger.'

'I'll get the cat.'

Jane froze as she moved towards the front room, hearing a car stop right outside, seeing its headlights and the wink of orange hazard lights through the frosted glass panel in the door. She ducked into the lounge and peeked through the curtains as a tubby guy trotted up the front path.

'You didn't order pizza, did you?'

The doorbell chimed.

'Pizza?' Matt repeated. 'Not me.'

He went to the door.

'Double meat lover's with garlic and olives,' the pizza guy said, holding up the insulated pouch while glancing at his clipboard which, along with the delivery docket, contained a mobile EFT-POS unit. 'That'll be eight ninety-nine, please.'

'Sorry, I think you've got the wrong addr—'

* * *

Dmitri's timing was a fraction out. He reached the delivery van as the front door opened and was forced to use its roof to steady his aim. Not as close as he'd wanted to be, but no point spooking the target.

A head shot would be best. Quick and clean. But the beefy delivery guy blocked off most of his view. He'd seen plenty of odd head wound deflections in Afghanistan caused by the thick bone and the shape of the skull to risk going through two heads – especially with subsonics – so he went for body mass instead. Three quick rounds through the delivery guy's right side, starting at waist height and letting the pistol's kick bring the barrel up. One or two rounds should make it through the blubber and at least shock and incapacitate his real target long enough for him to get in a fatal shot.

Three silenced rounds. The two figures crumpled.

53

Jane was partway back from the lounge window when a small piece of plaster hit her in the chest. She didn't realise its significance, or the significance of the three thumps – like the sound of a hammer striking a watermelon – until she saw Matt stagger back in the doorway and fall to the floor, the larger form of the pizza delivery guy falling with him. Even then she might have assumed some sort of comical accident except for three things: her heightened state of awareness given all that had happened, the exploding plaster shard which came from a small, steeply angled hole in the wall, and the stillness of the two figures on the floor.

Four things: Blood.

There was suddenly a large quantity of it pooling in the doorway beneath the heads and shoulders of the fallen figures.

As she reached the hallway, she heard the sound of heavy boots on the footpath outside, moving swiftly. The street lamps showed a figure dodging round the delivery van and heading her way. A large figure. For an instant, she glimpsed the exaggerated length of the silenced pistol in his right hand.

Her first inclination was to slam the door on him, gain a little time, but the feet of the fallen figures blocked it. And one of them was Matt, she thought desperately.

She hesitated.

Dmitri fired as he ran. A fair shot from a moving man, it slammed into the door jamb an inch above the fingers of her left hand, leaving a neat circular hole but evidently tumbling in its passage through the timber because it burst through the other side tearing out a nasty splintered gash.

Jane moved. Pushed herself away. Headed for the kitchen and the back door, but her feet slipped in the pooling blood and she staggered, lurching wildly before righting herself. A bit of luck because another watermelon thump sounded behind her as the wall-mounted telephone to her right exploded into shards of plastic.

She slammed the kitchen door behind her, raced across and snatched at the back door. Locked! Matt must've relocked it in preparation for their departure, forgetting Collet's dog was still in the back yard. As she fumbled with the key, she saw the length of pipe he'd borrowed from Jake's van. She snatched it up in her free hand, tore open the door and ran, almost breaking her neck falling over the excited dog that wound around her feet.

Dmitri slowed as he entered the house. The front door was partly blocked by two bodies, one atop the other. There was a faint grunt as he stepped on the back of the pizza guy. Maybe not a living grunt, just the expulsion of air from a compressed chest. Going by the rapidly expanding pool of blood, at least one of his shots had nicked a main artery.

Inside, his years of training kicked in. It wasn't just natural caution that made him pause and swing his gun, first up the stairway, then into the lounge. A fleeing figure was a classic decoy. With the blood up, the natural tendency was to race after it, making you a perfect target for an ambush, crossfire or a planted bomb. Even though he knew there were only two targets – and one of them was down – he couldn't help himself. It was instinct. He was professional. And a survivor.

The lounge was clear, the stairway too. He swung back to put a finishing bullet in the head of the main target when he heard a door slam behind him. He spun, dropped, covered and advanced, moving rapidly, kicking open the entrance to the kitchen and hearing a startled small-dog-yelp from the garden beyond.

'Cat Bitch!'

He had her now. He knew there was no rear exit, no side gate, just high walls around the perimeter and the back. He threw open the door and studied the scene.

Light spilled from the kitchen and the windows upstairs, but it only illuminated a small part of the long, narrow garden. It would silhouette him neatly and wreck his night vision, so he ducked back into the house, threw open the switchboard in the hall and shut the power off at the mains.

Ripper was enjoying this new game and this new player, even if she had almost stepped on him. Being stepped on was a hazard when you were part Yorkshire Terrier and part "fucking loony", but it had never bothered him in the past and he wasn't about to let it bother him now. He raced after the fleeing figure, yapping happily, and when she dived into a dense patch of undergrowth, he bounded back and forth around the perimeter, pointing out he knew exactly where she was.

'Get off! Go away!' Jane hissed at the yapping dog, scrambling around to find a stone in the hope of dissuading it.

The house lights went off. All at once. Upstairs and downstairs. Brown Boots must've thrown the mains.

Though the light didn't reach her hiding place, the sudden darkness was disconcerting, distracting even Ripper. Then a new sound came across the yard. Movement and a closing door. Soft, unhurried, and Jane had a strong sense of someone standing in the darkness, watching.

Ripper raced off to investigate the new arrival. For a moment, Jane missed the little dog's attention and suddenly felt desperately alone.

* * *

Dmitri slipped out the back door and squatted on his haunches, his back against the back door, waiting for the rods or cones or whatever it was in his eyes to reactivate and reach their maximum night-time sensitivity. Even now, with the deep shadow of the brick walls contrasting with street lights and the starry sky beyond, he'd be able to spot a climbing figure and could easily get a round or two into it. Then something charged at him from the undergrowth. Something small, fast-moving, yapping. He swung the pistol sideways with both hands, hard and fast, and felt a connecting crack from the extended barrel. A lucky blow. The movement and the yapping stopped.

A silencer in more ways than one, he thought.

The yard was quiet. Nothing stirred now. The only sound was the murmur of distant traffic. Already he could pick out darker shapes in the shadows; the outline of a tree, some sort of trestle, a garden shed.

The problem was a simple logistical one, but time wasn't on his side. With the lights off, the bodies piled in the front door wouldn't be obvious, but there was still a delivery van double-parked outside, its hazard lights flashing. Even though it was late on a Monday night, someone would eventually get curious.

He could have done with Od now. A second pair of hands to move the van and move the bodies. Someone to climb the side fence and flush the bitch his way. Failing that, a pair of night vision goggles. Or even just a torch. The garden was wild and unkempt. She could be anywhere.

Dmitri considered his options. He could patrol and try to flush her out, but there were risks in that. She might slip past in the darkness like a wily mujahideen, or even attack him with a garden implement like one of their shrewish wives. Better, then, to sit and wait; let her make the first move. Most people couldn't abide stillness and silence, not for long. Most creatures too. And under the comforting blanket of darkness they'd eventually give themselves away.

Dmitri the hunter made himself comfortable. If it hadn't been for that damn pizza van, he could've waited all night if necessary. Still, he doubted it would take that long.

* * *

There was an old Hollywood myth about being shot; that a bullet's impact would send you reeling backwards. It may well do so once you *realised* you'd been hit – the shock, the pain, the blood – but there was no way the actual impact would have that effect. Basic physics spoke against it. A hard metal object weighing eight grams and travelling at over a thousand kilometres an hour striking a soft squishy object weighing eighty-five kilos was simply going to pass straight through it. Even three such objects fired in quick succession. Even those passing through a larger, squishier object first. So Matt didn't even realise he'd been shot until the pizza guy stumbled forward on the step, threw out his arms in a gasp at the severance of his iliac artery, and collapsed against him, carrying him to the hall floor.

Three piercing shots plus the impact of that weight – somewhat more than his own modest eighty-five kilograms – stunned and winded him at first. He may have even clipped his head in the backward fall and been briefly knocked unconscious. But only when he blinked his eyes open in unexpected darkness did he realise that the intense pain in his chest didn't come from the fall alone. That he too must have been hit.

He tried to push at the obstruction pinning him down. His right hand and part of his right side were free, but the angle was wrong, the pain too strong and he couldn't get any real purchase. It was like trying to move an immense water-filled balloon. Besides, he became aware that he was lying in a large quantity of blood. How much of it was his own? He had no idea. But perhaps the weight – now dead weight – on top of him was actually holding him together.

54

The stillness was unnerving. What had happened to the little dog? If it hadn't been for its sudden silence, Jane might have believed she was alone in the garden, that she'd been mistaken about the sound at the back door, that the deep shadow around the rear of the house was just that; an empty shadow.

But what about the dog? She hadn't been mistaken about the that.

And what about Matt? Christ, he'd been shot! She had to get help. Had to get an ambulance. Time was of the essence.

Brown Boots had a gun, but it was useless if he couldn't see her. There was just him too. For now, at least. Perhaps he was waiting for backup. Perhaps someone would soon join him. Several someones. Coming over the walls and through the back with torches and knives. She recalled what he'd done to his injured companion; gutted like a fish on a filthy footpath. If that's what fate had in store for her, she wasn't going to meet it cowering under a bush and begging for mercy.

In some ways, the whole thing seemed absurd. There was an air of unreality about it. This was a quiet suburban garden, for heaven's sake! Three doors up along the line of terraced houses, she could see a bedroom light on and imagined someone sitting up in bed, gripped by the climax of the latest thriller. Things like state-sanctioned killings didn't happen in places like this.

Did they?

She recalled the "traffic accident" and the "suicide" and gripped the length of galvanised pipe she was holding more tightly. She still had Sally's cellphone in her pocket, but a call on that would be a call for death. Its LCD screen would light up the darkness like a Christmas tree. Still, it was a comfort to have. As she checked it was secure, she realised she was still holding the stone she'd planned to throw at Ripper.

If Brown Boots was summoning reinforcements, perhaps she could do the same.

She felt around, found three more stones, set the pipe down and carefully eased out from the patch of scrub where she'd been crouching. It felt reckless and exposed to stand upright in the face of someone with a gun – like stepping in front of the target on a shooting range – but it was the only way she could get the necessary swing. Besides, she reminded herself, she was still cloaked in darkness.

She took her time, aimed as best she could, and flung the stone hard. It soared in silence then clattered briefly on the neighbour's slate roof before rolling down to the guttering where it stopped with a faint clunk.

Too high. The range was about right, but it needed to be lower.

She tried again and this time was rewarded with the snick of stone on brick. That was it, but in the darkness it was hard to tell exactly where she'd hit. She was aiming for a window, a bedroom window, preferably to break it and wake the buggers up. Have them investigate. Call the police. Scare Brown Boots away.

Even a light on at that end of the garden would help.

She tried again and this time got a reaction, but not one she was hoping for.

Three shots, neatly spaced. Three quiet thumps, like muffled door knocks. She glimpsed the muzzle flash and heard the ping of ricochets off the high wall at the back of the garden. He was good. They'd come close. One either side of her current position. He must have heard the movement. The swing of her arm. The swish of her clothing.

Shit!

And she had no idea where the last stone had gone, except that it still hadn't provoked a reaction from the neighbours.

So he had good hearing, she thought. Perhaps she could use that ...

She dropped to her knees and let out a faint gasp as if she'd been hit. Followed it with two short cries, stifling them with her fist as though desperate to keep silent, then lay flat, found the length of pipe, reached out as far as she could with it and disturbed the lower branches of a nearby bush.

Let him think she was hit, that she was scrambling for the cover of the garden shed. He wouldn't know how badly she was injured. A flesh wound or a fatal shot? He'd *have* to come and investigate. And this time *she'd* be waiting. The hunter hunted.

* * *

Dmitri heard the whisper of movement followed by the sharp clack of the first stone and realised she was trying to attract attention from the sleeping house next door.

Smart move, but dumb execution.

Throwing a grenade at the enemy then staying in position was simply inviting a mortar round. The rule was throw then move, throw then move.

He cupped both ears and focused on the garden's darkness, trying to home in on the source of the sound. A second throw. He picked up the gun, aiming roughly. A third. From the same spot again. He had it.

Three quick shots, spaced perhaps a metre apart, then listen for the reaction.

Someone hit the dirt. No surprise there. Then a gasp and a stifled groan.

A hit!

By god, he was good.

He came up out of his crouch. Now was the time to move. Now, while the shock of the wound filled the victim's mind. A faint rustle to the left showed she was panicking, heading for the shelter of the garden shed. Which was where she would die.

* * *

Jane heard movement near the house. He was coming.

She took out Sally's cellphone, slipped off the jacket she was wearing and rolled it into a tight ball with the phone at its centre. Only the side was exposed. The side with the power switch. She reached in and switched it on. As she'd hoped, the tight folds masked the screen's glow. She gripped the balled-up jacket and hurled it behind the garden shed where it landed, unfurled slightly and spilled a muted bluish glow of light.

He was fast. He was there in seconds and fired two rounds into the space surrounding the phone, but Jane was fast too, swinging the metal pipe horizontally, aiming for the side of his head. It was hard to judge distance in darkness lit only by the glow of a cellphone and she was a fraction too close. Instead of connecting with the weighty end and its heavy right-angle coupler, she hit him with the pipe just above his right ear. A stunning blow, but not a knockout one.

He staggered, spun towards her and aimed the gun as she lurched back and brought the pipe straight down. This time the weighted end connected, making the gun sing briefly as it went spinning from his hand.

He lunged, his other arm outstretched, and caught her by the scruff of the neck, pitching her over backwards, throwing them both towards the ground.

Words echoed in her skull, complete with the Scottish accent of her self-defence instructor: 'Go for the squishy bits!' As she fell, Jane cocked one leg, bringing up her knee.

The impact plus his added weight winded her, but he slammed his own testicles into her bent leg and let out an explosive howl. She made a fist, raised a knuckle, ('Dinnae wanna wreck yer nails!') and punched at his left eye-socket.

Contact! Another howl. He pushed away, flailing to protect himself, half-blinded, doubled-up, as Jane struck with her left hand. Not such a useful blow, but equally effective. Her fist struck the swollen side of his face, the infected side, the side Bluebelle had sunk her claws in deepest, and he roared now, furious with the pain as she wormed herself free from under him and scrambled about, trying to find the length of pipe she'd dropped.

He rolled away, scrambling for his gun, and found it first. Brought it up, aimed it at her chest and fired from a distance of less than ten feet.

The world seemed to slip into a slow-motion replay. As his finger squeezed the trigger, Jane registered two things: the odd angle of the extended barrel and a picture she'd once seen of a hunting rifle after someone had tried to shoot fish with it. Dipping the end in the pond before pulling the trigger might seem a clever thing to do, but bullets were propelled by an explosive charge of gas. If the gas couldn't vent smoothly behind the projectile, the energy went back into the gun.

The blow to the gun had clipped the silencer, bending the threaded joint where it connected to the barrel, adding a twenty-degree downward kink to it. In his haste, and with only one good eye, Dmitri didn't notice till he fired. With no smooth exit even for the bullet, the compression wave blew the gun apart.

There was a sharp, unsilenced *crack* and a tiny fireball flash of light through which she glimpsed a snarling face intent on murder, not yet registering what had happened to his weapon. Or his hand. Superimposed on the flash were the silhouettes of fingers in positions fingers were never designed to go.

The slo-mo replay ended. Real-time resumed, and Jane continued searching for her own weapon. She'd dropped it when he grabbed her. It must be here somewhere ...

She glanced back as she felt about the grass.

The guy was a machine! Mangled hand, half-blinded, still

staggering from a knee in the goolies, he came at her again, drawing a knife with his good hand. She saw the glint of its polished blade, recognised the weapon in an instant and sprung to her feet in a low, defensive crouch.

He parried, feinted, snarling like an enraged bear. She ducked and weaved. She was lighter, more nimble, and managed to stay clear of the slashing blade, but all too late she realised he'd boxed her into the corner behind the garden shed.

Arms outstretched, mangled hand on one side, angled blade on the other, he came at her in a final rush.

* * *

In his five long years of life, Ripper had been joked about, made fun of, yelled at, even threatened once or twice, but he'd never, ever been hit before. And such a blow! Unwarranted. Unprovoked. His head was still ringing and he was unsteady on his feet, but fury filled his mind.

There was no doubt of the culprit. Stinky humans left stinky trails everywhere, and this one was fresh and easy to follow. He raced down the garden, his mind set on one thing; revenge.

* * *

'Cat Bitch!' Dmitri snarled, a sneer of victory on his face. The knife came in low, aimed at her belly with enough driving force behind it to carry it through to her spine.

Jane couldn't dodge. His outstretched hand, mangled and bloody, would restrain her long enough for the knife, so she focused instead on the thrusting arm. Twisting, throwing out both arms, she caught his knife hand by the wrist, managing to divert the blade a fraction, feeling it slash the front of her T-shirt and graze her skin.

The knife stuck fast in the timber the shed, but he had her now,

332

boxed in, the forearm of his mangled hand pressed against her throat. He'd only to withdraw the knife ...

It was wedged deep. His whole weight had been behind the thrust and he was obliged to step back to use some of that weight to help free it. As he did so, an angry set of jaws snapped at his ankle and he stumbled.

The movement left just enough room for Jane to free herself. She dropped, ducked under the restraining arm and dived for the patch of ground where she guessed the length of pipe must be. She found it, rolled and spun around on her knees, swinging it in both hands like a mace as he charged after her, freed knife in hand.

The blow was low, deliberately so, and smashed into the knee of his outstretched leg a moment before it connected with the ground. He howled again as the shattered joint, unable to take his weight, collapsed under him and sent him pitching down face-first, sprawling right in front her. By some instinct of self-preservation, he still gripped the knife in his good hand. Jane saw it, leapt at it and slammed her foot down. Spetsnaz boots would have been better, but even in running shoes she heard and felt the crack of breaking bones. Like stomping on the carcass of a roast chicken. Then the metal bar. A golf swing to the side of his head, the heavy coupler connecting solidly at last.

She staggered back and dropped the pipe, gasping as the little dog came trotting up to, wagging furiously, clearly delighted at what they had done.

55

'Matt!' Jane raced back into the house, surprised to see a set of red and blue flashing lights draw up behind the pizza van and DI Avery and DS Dixon emerge. They came racing up the path as an anxious looking Jake Plover hovered by the gate.

'Jane,' Matt croaked, rolling his eyes her way.

She dropped to her knees, heedless of the pooling blood and placed a hand against his cheek. His skin was pale, cold. The free arm beneath the fallen figure that almost enveloped him moved weakly.

'*Ambulance!*' she screamed at Avery, but he was already on his radio.

'What ... about ...?'

'Ssshh,' she told him. 'Don't talk. It's over. Help's coming.'

'You're ... OK ...' he sighed, smiling weakly as consciousness slipped away.

* * *

'I'm here to see Melody,' Jane told the receptionist, holding up a hand before she could ask about an appointment and added, 'Don't worry, I know the way.'

As she passed the desk, she saw a newspaper on a nearby credenza. It was folded in half, the headline upside down, but she knew what it said. It must've been a slow news day. Gerrard had made the front page.

Melody was on the phone, staring out across the parkland and the river when Jane entered. 'I understand that, of course, Mr

Trivet, but can't we—?' There was an angry crackle from the other end followed by a click.

'Well fuck you too!'

Jane cleared her throat. 'Morning.'

Melody turned. She looked twenty years older for a moment and struggled to regain something of her usual composure. 'Jane! I didn't hear you come in. Is that my report?'

'Two copies,' Jane said sweetly. 'One for you, one for Gerrard.'

Melody's face clouded, but she forced a smile. 'Thanks. I'll see he gets it.'

'Sorry about the delay. You heard about Matt?'

'Yes, he called me. Something about an infection.'

'The vasectomy, apparently.'

Melody made a face and flicked through one of the bound reports. 'There's rather more to this than I expected.'

'That's because we found out rather more than we expected. But it's all there. Everything.'

Melody glanced up at that last word, but Jane didn't elaborate.

'There's an executive summary at the front. You might like to read that first. As far as the account's concerned, we're all paid up. I sent you a VAT receipt last week, so all that remains is for me to thank you for choosing Bluebelle Investigations.' She offered her hand and, after a slight hesitation, Melody took it.

'Goodbye Mel,' she said. 'I'll see myself out.'

* * *

'I wish I could have seen her face,' Matt said.

'I didn't stick around till she actually read it, but I can imagine steam blowing out of her ears when she did. It's not going to be much use for an insurance claim, plus I think they've lost the Chesapeake Club account.'

'And that Royal Appointment, I imagine.' He nodded at the

newspaper on the tray beside his bed with its banner headline: COFFEE TOFF PLOTS AUNTY'S KILLING.

'Do you think they read that rag?'

'Reg Trivet clearly does.'

She held up some cards. 'You've got mail. The nurse handed them to me when I came in. There's one from Jake and Cheryl, one from Bernie and Liz Collet – with a *woof* from Ripper – and who's Kate Blumer?'

'Kate? She's custodial manager at High Down Prison. What does she say?'

'*To Matt ("Old Silver Tongue") Healy. I don't know what you said to our mutual friend, but shortly after your visit he started singing like the proverbial. All the best for a speedy recovery, Kate.*'

He grunted. 'Sounds like Henry Baxter spilled the beans on what he did with the loot he embezzled. But I don't think that's all down to me. I suspect it might be more to do with his son-in-law joining him down there while on remand.'

'I hope they have good coffee.'

'I doubt it. Not like this place.' He looked around at the pale blue walls, the gleaming medical equipment and the other fittings in his private room. The widescreen TV behind the folding doors in the mahogany unit opposite, the Bang and Olufsen headphones draped casually beside his bed. There were vases of flowers on a sideboard and behind it, a view of the Thames with its lazy river traffic. 'Seriously, Jane, we can't afford this.'

'We can now I've mortgaged your house, gone on the game and sold Bluebelle to a fur coat maker.'

'The first, maybe. The second? Well, you'd make a fortune. But I *know* you'd never sell Bluebelle.'

Jane was about to explain when the door opened and Colin Avery appeared, scowling, holding out a huge bunch of flowers as if they were surrounded by a swarm of bees.

'All right then, don't get up you lazy sod,' he said by way of greeting as Jane relieved him of his burden. 'How are you?'

'The drugs are great. I'm having all sorts of fantasies. A private room in London Bridge Hospital. You, bringing me flowers ...'

'They're from a Superintendent McCauley,' Jane said, reading the card, '*And all at the NCA.*'

'I am tripping. McCauley sending *me* flowers? I don't even work for him any more. And when I did, he hated my guts.'

'Yeah, well, they're not *actually* from him.'

'You mean ...? Aw, you sweetie.' He blew Avery a kiss.

'Piss off!'

Matt gave a throaty laugh, then winced. The drugs weren't *that* good.

'You know what he's like,' Avery said. 'He was following orders.'

'Orders?'

'Seems you have a grateful admirer.' Avery glanced around the room and looked out at the view. 'Who do you think's paying for all this?'

'I haven't got a clue.'

'That gentleman we took in the other night, shortly before you got yourself shot up.'

'Ernest Cricklewood? The hacker who put Jane and me in the frame?'

'Turns out he's not only unusually skilled at what he does, but he also proved a fount of information about the data he and his late chums acquired. Made notes, apparently. Written ones disguised as poetry that only he understands. Faced with the prospect of a lengthy prison term or a well-paying job with certain government agencies, he made the sensible choice and gave us all the details.

'Seems there was something highly sensitive in there and our friends at Foreign and Commonwealth Affairs are extremely grateful to have its loss pointed out to them. Hence ...' He gestured at the room.

'The flowers too?'

'They can't be too overt about this sort of thing. Officially, McCauley's department is picking up the tab in recognition of your efforts in tracking down and apprehending a dangerous killer.'

'The big Russian?'

'Not a Russian.' Avery held up a cautionary finger. '*A suspected member of an Eastern European criminal gang.* According to our friends in Kensington Palace Gardens, he was nothing to do with them.'

'Yeah, right!'

'An independent operator. They've disavowed him completely.'

'As they would, of course.'

'We're all to go along with it, Matt,' Avery said seriously. 'Orders from above. It seems the FCA don't want the Russians knowing that they know their data's been compromised. You know how spooks work. So the hit-and-run's been filed as a road accident, the suicide as a suicide, and big fella's been charged with the murder of a fellow hood and gunning down an innocent pizza delivery man. You and Jane aren't even officially involved.'

'Jane and I must still on the Russians' radar though.'

'Not any longer. That hacker chappy salted a few more records to make it look exactly like what it was: the framing of an innocent party in order to disguise someone else's identity. It's all smoke and bloody mirrors, isn't it? He's going to do well at Cheltenham.'

Matt sighed. There was a lot to be grateful for, not least his own life. The pizza delivery guy's metal clipboard had deflected one of the bullets intended for him and greatly reduced the impact energy of another, but it had cost the man his life. Others had died too. And now, it seemed, favours were owed.

'Where does that leave us?' he asked.

'With friends in high places who like the way you two operate. They may call on you again. Although,' Avery tapped his nose, 'you never heard that from me, all right?'

He straightened and checked his watch, suddenly looking every inch a copper. 'Right, enough of this bedside banter. Some of us have got work to do. Look after him, Jane. Oh, and if you need anything, Matt ... call a bloody nurse, will you? Leave me out of it!' He winked and left them to it.

Jane perched on the side of the bed and took his hand. 'Friends in high places, eh?'

'I don't like the sound of that.'

'What about this sound?' She gave him a smack on the lips.

'Now that, I do like.'

'Well get yourself mended and you can have a lot more of it.' She gave him another kiss then got up again.

'Where are you going?'

'Visiting hours are almost up and I've got a lock-up full of cats to get back to their rightful owners. On top of that, you'll be out of here in a few days and I've got a party to organise.'

'Oh Jane, you know I don't like a fuss.'

'It's all you, you, you, isn't it? The world doesn't revolve around you alone, Matt Healy. *We* have something to celebrate.'

He looked at her quizzically.

'Our first two cases, solved simultaneously. Bluebelle Investigations is up and running!'

Matt's Sticky Chicken with Ouzo, Olives & Charred Lemons

(Chapter 47)

Ingredients
- 4 chicken thighs, bone in, skin on
- Sea salt flakes
- Freshly ground black pepper
- 1 tablespoon olive oil
- 4 lemon wedges (half a lemon)
- 1 garlic bulb, cloves separated and peeled
- 2 white onions, sliced
- 1½ teaspoons dried oregano
- ½ teaspoon fennel seeds
- 1½ tablespoons ouzo
- 75g pitted green Greek olives
- Juice of 1 lemon

Method
- Pat the chicken dry with paper towel. Season with sea salt and black pepper.
- Heat the olive oil in an ovenproof frying pan over medium heat.
- Add the chicken, skin side down. Sear until golden (about 5 minutes).
- Flip and cook for a couple more minutes on the other side.
- Transfer to a plate with a slotted spoon.
- Pour all the oil out of the pan and then pour ½ tablespoon back in. Keep the rest for later.
- Add the lemon wedges and garlic. Fry until the lemon wedges are charred on both sides.
- Transfer the lemon and garlic to the plate with the chicken.
- Add the onions, oregano, fennel seeds and a pinch of sea salt to the frying pan, and stir to coat in the oil.
- Gently fry over medium-low heat, stirring frequently, for 10 minutes or until the onions are soft, sweet and golden. Add more oil if they start sticking to the pan or colour too quickly.

- Pour in the alcohol and stir with a wooden spoon as it bubbles up to scrape up all the delicious bits stuck to the pan. Cook until the smell of the alcohol subsides.

Preheat the oven to 180C / 350F / Gas Mark 4.

- Arrange the chicken in the pan in a single layer, skin side up, then nestle the olives, lemon wedges and garlic in between. Pour the lemon juice over the top and add a little more salt and pepper.
- Roast for 45 minutes or until the chicken skin is crisp and golden, and the flesh is very tender.
- Serve with rice and the pan juices spooned over the top.

Serves 2.

About the Author

Geoff Palmer is an award-winning novelist and technical writer based in Wellington, New Zealand.

You'll find him online at
www.geoffpalmer.co.nz

and on Facebook at
www.facebook.com/geoffpalmerNZ

*If you enjoyed this book, please
consider leaving an online review.
They really help authors!*